# Baking Cakes in Kigali

Gaile Parkin was born in Zambia and lives in Africa. *Baking Cakes in Kigali* is her first novel.

# Baking Cakes in Kigali

## Gaile Parkin

Atlantic Books
LONDON

First published in hardback and export & airside trade
paperback in Great Britain in 2009
by Atlantic Books, an imprint of Grove Atlantic Ltd.

1 3 5 7 9 10 8 6 4 2

A CIP catalogue record for this book is available
from the British Library.

978 1 84354 985 7  (Hardback)
978 1 84354 746 4  (Export/Airside Trade Paperback)

Designed and typeset in Mrs Eaves by Lindsay Nash
Printed in Great Britain by MPG Books Ltd, Bodmin, Cornwall

Atlantic Books
An imprint of Grove Atlantic Ltd.
Ormond House
26–27 Boswell Street
London WC1N 3JZ

www.atlantic-books.com

# 1. An Anniversary

IN THE SAME WAY THAT A BUCKET OF WATER reduces a cooking fire to ashes — a few splutters of shocked disbelief, a hiss of anger, and then a chill all the more penetrating for having so abruptly supplanted intense heat — in just that way, the photograph that she now surveyed extinguished all her excitement.

'Exactly like this?' she asked her guest, trying to keep any hint of regret or condemnation out of her voice.

'*Exactly* like that,' came the reply, and the damp chill of disappointment seeped into her heart.

Angel had dressed smartly for the occasion, in a state of great anticipation of the benefits that it might bring. Completing her ensemble by pushing a pair of small, gold hoops through her earlobes, she had stepped out of her bedroom and into the lounge, scanning the room again to check that it was ready for her special guest. The children's clutter had all been put away in their bedroom, and the tiled floor had been scrubbed to a shine. The wooden frames of the three-seater sofa and its two matching chairs had been polished, and each of their cushions — encased in a sturdy fabric patterned in brown and orange — had been plumped to the full extent capable of a square of foam rubber. On the coffee table she had placed a gleaming white plate of chocolate cupcakes, each iced in one of four colours: blue, green, black and yellow.

Then the shout had come through the open doorway that led off the lounge on to the small balcony: the signal that she had been waiting for from her neighbour, Amina, who had been standing on the balcony immediately above her own, on the look-out for the expensive vehicle making its way up the hill towards their compound.

With a renewed surge of excitement, she had slipped back into the bedroom, and, concealing herself behind the curtain to the left of the window, she had watched through the ill-fitting louvres as the smart black Range Rover with its tinted windows had turned right on to the dirt road and pulled up outside the first of the building's two entrances. A smartly uniformed chauffeur had stepped out from behind the wheel, and holding the passenger door open, had called to the two security guards lounging beneath a shady mimosa tree on the other side of the road. The taller of the two had shouted a reply and had stood up slowly, dusting the red earth from his trousers.

Mrs Margaret Wanyika had emerged from the vehicle looking every inch the wife of an ambassador: elegant and well-groomed, her tall, thin body sporting a Western-style navy-blue suit with a knee-length skirt and a silky white blouse, her straightened hair caressing the back of her head in a perfect chignon. As she had stood beside the vehicle talking into her cell-phone, her eyes had swept over the building in front of her.

Angel had ducked away from the window and moved back into the lounge, imagining, as she did so, the view that her visitor was taking in. The block of apartments, on the corner of a tarred road and a dirt road in one of the city's more affluent areas, was something of a landmark, its four storeys dominating the neighbourhood of large houses and high-walled gardens, where drivers hooted outside fortified gates for servants to open up and admit their expensive vehicles. People knew that it was a brand-new building only because it had not been there at all a year before: it had been constructed in the fashionable style that suggests — without any need of time or wear — the verge of decay and collapse.

With mounting excitement, Angel had awaited the security guard's familiar knock at the door of her apartment, and when it had come, she had opened the door, beaming with delight and effusively declaring it a very great honour indeed to welcome such an important guest into her home.

But now, sitting in her lounge and staring at the photograph that she held in her hand, all of her excitement fizzled suddenly, and died.

'As you know, Angel,' the ambassador's wife was saying, 'it's traditional to celebrate a silver wedding anniversary with a cake just like the original wedding cake. Amos and I feel it's so important to follow our traditions, especially when we're away from home.'

'That is true, Mrs Ambassador,' agreed Angel, who was herself away from home. But as she examined the photograph, she was doubtful of the couple's claim to the traditions that they had embraced when choosing this cake twenty-five years ago. It was not like any traditional wedding cake she had seen in her home town of Bukoba in the west of Tanzania or in Dar es Salaam in the east. No, this cake was traditional to *Wazungu*, white people. It was completely white: white with white patterns decorating the white. Small white flowers with white leaves encircled the outer edges of the upper surface, and three white pillars on top of the cake held aloft another white cake that was a smaller replica of the one below. It was, quite simply, the most unattractive cake that she had ever seen. Of course, Mr and Mrs Wanyika had married at a time when the style of *Wazungu* was still thought to be fashionable – prestigious, even. But by now, in the year 2000, surely everybody had come to recognize that *Wazungu* were not the authorities on style and taste that they were once thought to be? Perhaps if she showed Mrs Wanyika the pictures of the wedding cakes that she had made for other people, she would be able to convince her of the beauty that colours could bring to a cake.

Setting down the photograph, she removed her spectacles and, delving into the neckline of her smart blouse to retrieve one of the tissues that she kept tucked into her brassiere, began to give the lenses a good polish. It was something that she found herself doing without thinking whenever she felt that someone could benefit from looking at things a little more clearly.

'Mrs Ambassador, no words can describe the beauty of this cake...' she began.

'Yes, indeed!' declared the ambassador's wife, leaving no space for what Angel was going to say next. 'And at the party, right next to our anniversary cake, we're going to have a big photo of me and Amos cutting our wedding cake twenty-five years ago. So it's very important for the two cakes to be *exactly* identical.'

Angel put her glasses back on. There was clearly nothing to be gained from helping Mrs Wanyika to see that her wedding cake had been ugly and plain.

'Don't worry, Mrs Ambassador, I'll make your anniversary cake exactly the same,' she said, smiling widely to disguise the sigh of regret that she could not entirely prevent from escaping. 'It will be just as beautiful as your wedding cake.'

Mrs Wanyika clapped her meticulously manicured hands together in glee. 'I knew I could depend on a fellow Tanzanian, Angel! People in Kigali speak very highly of your baking.'

'Thank you, Mrs Ambassador. Now, perhaps I could ask you to start filling in an order form while I put milk on the stove for another cup of tea?'

She handed her guest a sheet headed 'Cake Order Form' that her friend Sophie had designed on her computer, and Angel's husband Pius had photocopied at the university. It asked for details of how to contact the client, the date and time that the cake would be needed, and whether Angel was to deliver it or the client would collect it. There was a large space to write in everything that had been agreed about the design of the cake, and a box for the total price and the deposit. At the bottom of the form was a dotted line where the client was to sign to agree that the balance of the price was to be paid on delivery or collection, and that the deposit was not going to be refunded if the order was cancelled. Angel was very proud that her Cake Order Form spoke four languages – Swahili, English, French and Kinyarwanda – though less proud that, of these, she herself spoke only the first two with any degree of competence.

Their business concluded, the two women sat back to enjoy their tea, made the Tanzanian way with boiled milk and plenty of sugar and cardamom.

'So how is life for you here compared to at home?' asked Mrs Wanyika, sipping delicately from one of Angel's best cups, and continuing to speak English – their country's *second* official language – in defiance of Angel's initial attempts to steer the conversation in Swahili.

'Oh, it's not too different, Mrs Ambassador, but of course it's not home. As you know, some of the customs here in Central Africa are a little different from our East African customs, even though Rwanda and Tanzania are neighbours. And of course French is difficult, but at least many people here also know Swahili. And we're lucky that here in this compound most people know English. *Eh*, but you're too thin, Mrs Ambassador, please have another one.'

Angel pushed the plate of cupcakes towards her

guest, who had failed to comment on the colours — which were the colours of the Tanzanian flag — and had so far eaten only one: one of those iced in the yellow that, on the flag, represented Tanzania's mineral wealth.

'No, thank you, Angel. They're delicious, really, but I'm trying to reduce. Youssou has made a dress for me for the anniversary party and it's a little bit tight.'

'*Eh*, that Youssou!' commiserated Angel, shaking her head. She had had a couple of unfortunate experiences of her own with the acclaimed Senegalese tailor of La Couture Universelle d'Afrique in Nyamirambo, the Muslim quarter. 'He can copy any dress from any picture in a magazine and his embroidery is very fine, but *eh!* I think the women back in Senegal must all be thin like a pencil. It doesn't matter how many times Youssou measures your body, the dress that he makes will always be for a thinner somebody.'

This was a rather sore point for Angel, who used to be a thinner somebody herself. She had never been thin like a pencil, not even as a girl, but in the last couple of years she had begun to expand steadily — particularly in the region of her buttocks and thighs — so that more and more of her clothes felt like they had been fashioned by the miscalculating Youssou. Dr Rejoice had told her that gaining weight was only to be expected in a woman who was experiencing the Change, but this had not made her feel any better about it. Still, running her business in her own home meant that she was able to spend most of her time wearing a loose T-shirt over a skirt fashioned from a *kanga* tied around her waist — an ensemble that could accommodate any size comfortably.

'And how is life in this compound?' asked the ambassador's wife.

'We're secure here,' said Angel. 'And even though all of us in the compound are from outside Rwanda, we're a good community. *Eh!* We're from all over the world! Somalia, England, America, Egypt, Japan—'

'Are they all working at KIST?' Mrs Wanyika interrupted Angel before she could complete the entire atlas of expatriates. The Kigali Institute of Science and Technology — a new university that had recently been established in the capital — was attracting a great number of expatriate academics.

'No, it's only my husband who is there. KIST doesn't accommodate the ordinary staff, but Pius is a Special Consultant, so his contract says they must give him accommodation. The others here are mostly from aid agencies and non-governmental organizations. You know how it is when a war is over, Mrs Ambassador: dollars begin to fall like rain from the sky and everybody from outside rushes in to collect them.' Angel paused for a moment before adding, 'And to help with reconstruction, of course.'

'Of course,' agreed the ambassador's wife, shifting rather uncomfortably on the orange and brown cushions of the wooden sofa.

Angel knew that Ambassador Wanyika's salary would have been boosted dramatically by an additional bonus to compensate him for the dangers and hardships of being stationed in a country so recently torn apart by conflict. She observed Mrs Wanyika casting about for a change of subject, and saw discomfort giving way to relief when her guest's eyes found the four framed photographs hanging high up on the wall next to the sofa.

'Who are these, Angel?' She stood up to get a better look.

Angel put down her cup and stood to join her. 'This is Grace,' she said, indicating the first photograph. 'She's the eldest, from our son Joseph. She has eleven years now. Then these two here are Benedict and Moses, also from Joseph. Moses is the youngest, with just six years.' She moved on to the third photograph while Mrs Wanyika produced well-rehearsed exclamations of admiration. 'These are Faith and Daniel. They're both from our daughter Vinas.' Then Angel touched the fourth and final photograph. 'These are Joseph and Vinas,' she said. 'Joseph has been late for nearly three years now, and we lost Vinas last year.' She sat down again rather heavily, the wood beneath the cushions of her chair creaking perilously, and knotted her hands in her lap.

'*Eh*, Angel!' said Mrs Wanyika softly, sitting down and reaching across the coffee table to put a comforting, well-moisturized hand on Angel's knee. 'It's a terrible thing to bury your own children.'

Angel's sigh was deep. 'Terrible, Mrs Ambassador. And such a shock to lose both. Joseph was shot by robbers at his home in Mwanza...'

'Uh-uh-uh!' Mrs Wanyika shut her eyes and shook her head, giving Angel's knee a squeeze.

'And Vinas...' Angel put her hand on top of her guest's where it rested on her knee. 'Vinas worked herself too hard after her husband left her. It stressed her to the extent that her blood pressure took her.'

'Ooh, that can happen, Angel.' Releasing her grip on Angel's knee, Mrs Wanyika turned her hand over to meet Angel's hand palm to palm, and held it tightly. 'My own uncle, after he lost his wife, he devoted himself to his business to such an extent that a heart attack took him. *Eh!* Stress? Uh-uh.' Shaking her head, she clicked her tongue against the back of her neat upper row of glistening teeth.

'Uh-uh,' agreed Angel. 'But Pius and I are not alone in such a situation, Mrs Ambassador. It's how it is for so many grandparents these days. Our children are taken and we're made parents all over again to our grandchildren.' Angel gave a small shrug. 'It can be a bullet. It can be blood pressure. But in most cases it's the virus.'

Mrs Wanyika let go of Angel's hand and reached for her tea. 'But of course, as Tanzanians,' she said, her tone suddenly official, drained of compassion, 'that is a problem that we don't have.'

Angel's eyebrows rushed to consult with each other across the bridge of her nose. 'I'm sorry, Mrs Ambassador, but you're confusing me. It sounds to me like you're saying that we don't have the virus at home in Tanzania. But everybody knows—'

'Angel!' Mrs Wanyika's voice, now a stern whisper, interrupted. 'Let us not let people believe that we have that problem in our country. Please!'

Angel stared hard at her guest. Then she removed her glasses and began to polish the lenses with her tissue. 'Mrs Ambassador,' she began, 'do you think that the virus is in Uganda?'

'In Uganda? Well, yes, of course. Even the government of Uganda has said that it's there.'

'And in Kenya?' continued Angel. 'Do you think that it's in Kenya?'

'Well, yes, I've heard that it's there.'

'And in Zambia? Malawi? Mozambique?' Angel put her glasses and her tissue down on the coffee table and began counting the countries off on her fingers.

'Yes,' admitted Mrs Wanyika, 'it's in those countries, too.'

'And what about the Democratic Republic of Congo?'

'Oh, it's very well known that it's in DRC.'

'And surely you've heard that it's in Burundi, and here in Rwanda?'

'Well, yes...'

'Then, Mrs Ambassador, if you know that the virus is in every country that is our neighbour, then there are others who already know that too; it cannot be a secret. And if people know that all of Tanzania's neighbours have it, why will they think that Tanzania *doesn't* have it? Will they think that there's something special about our borders, that our borders don't let it in?' Angel stopped, anxious that she had gone too far and that she might have offended her important guest. She put her glasses back on and looked at her. To her relief, Mrs Wanyika appeared more contrite than angry.

'No, you're right, Angel. It's only that Amos is always very careful not to admit that we have the problem of that disease in Tanzania. It's his job.'

'That's easy to understand,' assured Angel, 'and, of course, as the ambassador's wife you must do the same, especially when you're talking to people from outside our country. But we're both from there, and we both know that it can come to any family there and take away somebody close.'

'Yes, of course. Although... not *every* family,' Mrs Wanyika countered. 'Not ours. And not yours, Angel, I'm sure.'

But the ambassador's wife was wrong. Had the robbers' bullet not found Joseph's head when he returned home that night from visiting his wife as she lay dying in Bugando Hospital, Angel would be telling a very different story about his death. Though perhaps not yet: he had been keeping himself fit and healthy, continuing to jog every evening and to play football every weekend; he could still – possibly – have been alive today. But Angel recognized that it was best not to say any of this to her guest, who would not be comfortable with the idea and might even feel moved to tear up her Cake Order Form. She decided to move away from the subject.

'You know, Pius and I were careful to have just two children so that we could afford to educate them well. Back in those days, family planning was still very modern. We were pioneers. Our lives should be growing more peaceful now. Pius should be relaxing more as he works the last few years to his retirement, but instead he has to work even harder. Our children should be preparing themselves to take care of us now, but instead we find ourselves taking care of their five children. *Five!* Grace and Faith are good girls, they're serious. But the boys? Uh-uh.' Angel shook her head.

'Ooh! Boys? Uh-uh,' agreed Mrs Wanyika, who — Angel knew — had herself raised three sons, and she also shook her head.

'Uh-uh,' said Angel again.

'Ooh, uh-uh-uh. Boys?' Mrs Wanyika concurred.

Both women were silent for a while as they contemplated the problems of boys.

Then Mrs Wanyika said, 'God has indeed given you a cross to bear, Angel. But has He not also given you a blessing? Is a child's laughter not the roof of a house?'

'Oh, yes!' Angel agreed quickly. 'It's only that we won't be able to provide for these children as well as we did for our first children. But we must try by all means to give them a good life. That's why we decided to leave Tanzania and come here to Rwanda. There's aid money for the university and they're paying Pius so much more as a Special Consultant than he was getting at the university in Dar. Okay, Rwanda has suffered a terrible thing. Terrible, Mrs Ambassador; bad, bad, bad. Many of the hearts here are filled with pain. Many of the eyes here have seen terrible things. Terrible! But many of those same hearts are now brave enough to hope, and many of those same eyes have begun to look towards the future instead of the past. Life is going on, every day. And for us the pluses of coming here are many more than the minuses. And my cake business is doing well because there are almost no shops here that sell cakes. A cake business doesn't do well in a place where people have nothing to celebrate.'

'Oh, everybody talks about your cakes! You can go to any function and the cake is from Angel. Or if the cake is not from Angel, somebody there will be talking about another function where the cake *was* from Angel.'

Angel smiled, patting her hair in a modestly proud gesture. One of the few luxuries that she allowed herself was regular trips to the hair salon to have her hair relaxed and kept trim in a style appropriate for her age.

'Well, being so busy with my cake business keeps me young, Mrs Ambassador. And I must keep young for the children. You know, many people here don't even know that I'm already a grandmother. Everybody just calls me Mama-Grace, as if Grace is my firstborn, not my grandchild.'

'But you are Grace's mother now, Angel. Who is Mama-Grace if it is not you? Who is Baba-Grace if it is not your husband?'

Angel was about to agree when the front door opened and a short, plump young woman with the humble demeanour of a servant walked quietly into the room.

'Ah, Titi,' said Angel, speaking to her in Swahili. 'Are the girls not with you?'

'No, Auntie,' Titi replied. 'We met Auntie Sophie at the entrance to the compound. She invited us up to her apartment. She's given me money to go and buy Fantas from Leocadie, but she said first I must come and tell Auntie that the girls are with her.'

'*Sawa*. Okay,' said Angel. 'Titi, greet the wife of our ambassador from Tanzania, Mrs Wanyika.'

Titi approached Mrs Wanyika and, with a small curtsy, shook her hand, respectfully not looking her in the eye. '*Shikamoo.*'

'*Marahaba*, Titi,' said Mrs Wanyika, graciously acknowledging Titi's respectful greeting, and submitting to the pressure to reply in her country's *first* official language. '*Habari?* How are you?'

'*Nzuri, Bibi*. I'm fine,' replied Titi, still not looking at Mrs Wanyika.

'*Sawa*, Titi, go and buy the Fantas now for Auntie Sophie,' instructed Angel. 'Greet Leocadie for me. Tell her I'll come to buy eggs tomorrow.'

'*Sawa*, Auntie,' said Titi, making for the door.

'And leave the door open, Titi. Let us get some air in here.' Angel was suddenly feeling very hot. She fanned her face with the Cake Order Form that Mrs Wanyika had completed. 'We brought Titi with us from home,' she explained, switching back to English in deference to her guest's choice. 'It was our son Joseph who first employed her, then when... when the children came to us, Titi came with them. She's not an educated somebody, but she cleans and cooks well, and she's very good with the children.'

'I'm glad you have someone to help you, Angel,' said Mrs Wanyika, 'but do you all manage to fit into this apartment?'

'We fit, Mrs Ambassador! The children and Titi have the main bedroom. It's big. A carpentry professor at KIST made three double bunks for them, and still there's room in there for a cupboard. Pius and I are fine in the smaller bedroom. And the children aren't always inside; the compound has a yard for them to play in when they're not at school.'

'And how is the school here?' asked Mrs Wanyika.

'It's a good school, but quite expensive for five children! *Eh*, but what can we do? The children don't know French, so they have to go to an English school. But the school sends a minibus to fetch all the children from this neighbourhood, so we don't have to worry about transport. The boys are visiting some friends from school who live down the road, otherwise you could meet them. Titi took the girls to the post office to post letters to their friends back in Dar, but now they've gone to visit Sophie. It's a pity. I wish you could meet them, Mrs Ambassador.'

'I'll meet them one day, Angel,' said Mrs Wanyika. 'Who is this Sophie that they're visiting?'

'A neighbour upstairs in the compound. She's a good friend to our family. She shares her apartment with another lady called Catherine. Both of them are volunteers.'

'Volunteers?' queried Mrs Wanyika, raising a carefully pencilled eyebrow.

'Yes. There are some few people here who have come to help Rwanda without demanding many dollars.' Angel gave a slightly embarrassed smile, knowing that neither her husband nor her guest's husband fell into that category.

Again Mrs Wanyika shifted uncomfortably on the sofa. 'And what do these volunteers do?'

[16]

'They're both teachers. Catherine's a trainer for the Ministry for Gender and Women, and Sophie teaches English at that secondary school that's for girls only.'

'I see,' said Mrs Wanyika. 'So these two volunteers are helping women and girls. That is very good.'

'Yes,' agreed Angel. 'Actually, they told me that they're both feminists.'

'Feminists?' queried Mrs Wanyika, and her other eyebrow shot up to join the one that had still not quite recovered from the idea of volunteers. '*Feminists?*' she repeated.

Angel was confused by her guest's reaction. 'Mrs Ambassador, is there something wrong with a feminist?'

'Angel, are you not afraid that they'll convert your daughters?'

'*Convert?* Mrs Ambassador, you're speaking of feminists as if they're some kind of... of *missionaries.*'

'Angel, do you not know what feminists *are*? They don't like men. They... er...' Here Mrs Wanyika dropped her voice to a conspiratorial whisper and leaned closer to Angel. 'They do sex with other ladies!'

Angel removed her glasses and began to polish the lenses with her tissue. She took a deep breath before speaking. 'Oh, Mrs Ambassador, I can see that somebody has confused you on this matter, and, indeed, it is very easy to become confused, because, of course, it is a very confusing matter. I believe that a lady who does sex with other ladies is not called a feminist. I believe she is called a lesbian.'

'Oh,' said Mrs Wanyika, registering both relief and

embarrassment at the same time. 'Right. Yes, I've heard of a lesbian.'

'It's very easy for us to get confused because these ideas are so modern for us in Africa,' said Angel, mindful of her guest's embarrassment and anxious to smooth over her mistake.

'Indeed,' agreed Mrs Wanyika. 'These ideas are too modern here. Amos has always been stationed in Africa, except for when we were in Malaysia. But such ideas are also too modern for Malaysia.'

'I only know about these ideas myself because I spent some time in Germany with my husband when he was there for his studies,' confided Angel. 'The women in Europe have many modern ideas.'

'I believe so. And is it not true that too many ideas drive wisdom away? Angel, I'm relieved that no harm will be done to your girls! I was confused to think that your neighbours are lesbians. They're simply volunteers.'

It was clear to Angel that Mrs Wanyika found the idea of volunteers — disconcerting to her as that was — less alarming than the idea of feminists. She looked for a fresh direction for their conversation, and, glancing at the coffee table between them, cried, '*Eh!* What am I thinking, Mrs Ambassador! Your cup is empty and cold! Let me make some more tea!'

Mrs Wanyika began to protest as Angel collected up their cups and saucers. But just as she did so, somebody called from the open doorway.

'*Hodi!* May we come in?'

'*Karibuni!* Welcome!' greeted Angel as a young woman

and a girl entered the apartment. The woman's beautiful bright *kanga*, patterned in orange, deep yellow and turquoise, swathed her entire body, including her head, so that only her face, hands and feet were visible. The girl, lighter skinned than the woman, wore a red and yellow short-sleeved dress that ended half-way down her calves, while a bright orange scarf swirled over her head and throat. Angel had always thought that both mother and daughter were thin enough to make a pencil look overweight. She introduced her guests to one another in Swahili.

'Mrs Ambassador, these are my friends from the apartment above. Amina and Safiya, this is Mrs Wanyika, wife of the Tanzanian ambassador here.'

All the guests shook hands and exchanged greetings. Then Mrs Wanyika said, 'Amina, you're speaking Swahili, but I don't think you're from any country that I know. Where is your home?'

Amina's smile was beautiful, a flash of bright white against the darkness of her skin. 'I'm Somali, *Bibi*, from Mogadishu.'

'Ah, Mogadishu!' declared Mrs Wanyika. 'That's where those American helicopters were shot down, isn't it? How many Americans died, Amina? Eighteen?'

'Something like that, *Bibi*. And a thousand Somalis were killed, too. But I don't tell many people here that I'm from there. There are people who say that the Americans refused to come here to help Rwanda because of what had happened to them in Mogadishu. It could happen that Rwandans could blame me for the Americans not coming here, or it could happen that

[19]

Americans could hate me for their soldiers dying in my country.'

'These things are very complicated,' said Mrs Wanyika, and the way that she said it – without seeming to give it any thought or inviting any further discussion – made Angel suspect that it was her standard diplomatic response in conversations concerning political matters.

Amina smiled. 'Yes, *Bibi*. But in fact I have two nationalities. My husband has Italian citizenship because his father was Italian. So I'm Somali and Italian. I like to tell *Wazungu* that I'm an Italian. They don't know how to arrange their faces when I tell them that!'

The three women laughed, and Safiya smiled shyly at the adults' laughter.

'Let me guess. Is your husband here with the Italians who are building the roads?'

'Yes, *Bibi*, he's in charge.'

'And Safiya goes to the same school as the children,' said Angel.

Safiya's smile was as bright as her mother's. 'Grace and Faith are my best friends,' she declared.

'*Eh*, but why are we just standing here? Let me make tea for us all!'

'Oh, Angel, I'm sorry, we cannot stay for tea,' said Amina. 'We're on our way to Electrogaz to buy power. We just came here to tell you that when we looked at our meter downstairs, we saw that your power is almost finished also. Shall we buy some more for you while we're there?'

'Thank you, Amina, that's very kind! But Baba-Grace has already planned to buy power after he's finished at KIST this afternoon.'

'*Sawa*, Angel. Mrs Wanyika, I've enjoyed meeting you.'

'Amina, I'm leaving now myself,' said Mrs Wanyika. 'Unfortunately I can't stay for more tea, Angel. Amos and I have been invited for cocktails at the Swedish embassy this evening, and I must go and get myself ready. My driver is waiting outside. Can we give you two a lift to Electrogaz?'

Amina clapped her hands together. 'Thank you, *Bibi*.'

'Angel, I'll send my driver for the cake next Friday afternoon. I've enjoyed my tea with you so much. Thank you.'

'It's a pleasure, Mrs Ambassador. Please come to see me any time. In my house it's teatime all the time.'

'Thank you, Angel. And once or twice a year we have parties for Tanzanians and friends of Tanzania at the embassy. I'll make sure that you get an invitation.'

'Thank you, Mrs Ambassador. I'll look forward to that.'

Alone in the apartment, Angel discarded her tight, smart outfit in favour of a comfortable T-shirt and *kanga* before gathering up her good china from the coffee table and taking it through to the kitchen. She filled the sink with warm soapy water, thinking as she did so about the deeply disappointing cake that she would have to bake for the ambassador's wife. It was not going to be a cake that would inspire people to come

[21]

and order their own cakes from her – unless, of course, there were some *Wazungu* at Mrs Wanyika's party who did not know any better. No, it was going to be a cake that would try to hide its face in shame. The best that she could hope for was that nobody would ask who had made it. Or, if they did feel inspired to ask, perhaps they would see from the Wanyikas' wedding photo – the one of the couple cutting their wedding cake – that Angel had been obliged simply to copy the original cake, no matter how unsightly that had been.

Having washed the cups and saucers, she set about scrubbing the milk saucepan, finding it rather satisfying to take her disappointment out on it. Pius had warned her that morning that she was expecting way too much from the visit, but she had assured him that he was wrong: Mrs Wanyika might not be a big person in the way that Ambassador Wanyika was, but she was a woman who entertained; and, as a woman who entertained, she had the power to tuck a great deal of money into Angel's brassiere. The afternoon could have gone quite differently: Mrs Wanyika could have ordered a beautiful cake with an intricate design or an original shape and lots of colours; it would have taken centre stage at the ambassador's party, and nobody there – surely almost all of them big people – would have left without knowing that Angel Tungaraza was the only person in Kigali to go to for a cake for a special occasion.

She set the pot on the draining board to dry and looked at her watch. Pius would be home from work before too long, and it would soon be time to start preparing the family's evening meal. In a short while she would go upstairs to fetch the girls from Sophie's apartment, and she would send Titi to fetch the boys from their friends' house down the road. But before all of that, she had some time alone to enjoy one of her greatest pleasures, something that would surely go a long way to undoing the terrible disappointment that the afternoon had brought.

Drying her hands on a tea towel, she went into her bedroom and took from a shelf in the wardrobe a white plastic bag, inside which lay a bundle tightly encased in bubble-wrap. Back in the kitchen, she placed the bundle on the counter, and her fingers began to search for, and unpeel, the strips of sticky-tape that bound it. She did this slowly, prolonging the pleasure, building the anticipation.

The parcel had come to her all the way from Washington DC, via a neighbour in the compound who returned there regularly to see his wife and children. Ken Akimoto was happy to act as a courier for Angel, and his wife never seemed to object to being sent to the shops on Angel's behalf. In fact, she regularly enclosed a card for Angel, usually to thank her for being a friend to Ken or for baking such beautiful cakes for him. And here was one of those cards now.

Snatching it quickly from inside the bundle, she spun around and leaned back against the counter to read it. She had managed to take it without yet seeing what was in the bundle: her pleasure would be all the greater for the delay. This time, June was writing to express her admiration for the cake that Angel had made for Ken's fiftieth birthday party, a party that had been especially loud, Angel remembered, on account of its disco theme. What a great idea it had been — June wrote, having seen Ken's photos — to make, for a man who so loved karaoke, a cake in the shape of a microphone. Angel remembered the cake with pride. It had not been one of her most colourful cakes, of course, although a cake for a disco party should really have had swirls of many different bright colours; after all, nobody had been afraid of colours back in the era of disco, not even *Wazungu*. But more than just a disco party, it had been a party to celebrate Ken's birthday — and it was difficult for anybody who knew Ken to think of him without a microphone in his hand, occasionally singing into it himself, but mostly pressing it on one or other of his guests. So Angel had made the cake in the shape of a microphone lying on the cake-board, in black and grey with a small box positioned on it to make it look like it belonged to a particular TV station, like those microphones that were always being pushed towards the faces of big people at important events. The box on this microphone — red on one side, green on the other, blue on top — carried on all three sides the name *KEN* in white above a large number 50, also in white. Ken had reported afterwards that everybody at the party had praised it; and now here was praise from Washington, too.

After reading June's card twice, Angel knew that the moment had come for her to turn around and savour — slowly — the contents of the bundle. Ken had delivered it to her earlier that afternoon, on his way home from the airport, and she had resisted opening it immediately, because Mrs Wanyika would be arriving soon. As she had put it away in her cupboard, she had thought that perhaps she would delay opening it until the following day, because – surely – the commission of a beautiful cake from the wife of her country's ambassador to Rwanda was going to provide more than enough pleasure for one day. But now she was very grateful that she had the bundle to lift her mood this afternoon.

She turned around. Gently, carefully, lest any of the contents should fall from the counter and spill over the kitchen floor, she peeled back the folds of bubble-wrap. What treasures lay inside! Yes, here were the colours that she had asked for: red, pink, yellow, blue, green, black – all in powder form, of course, not like the one or two bottles of liquid food colour that were available at the Lebanese supermarket in town; those were not at all modern – some big blocks of marzipan, and, as always, June had included some new things for Angel to try. This time there were three tubes that looked rather like thick pens. She picked one up and examined it: written along its length were the words *Gateau Graffito*, and underneath, written in upper-case letters, was the word *red*. Reaching for the other two pens – one marked *green* and the other, *black* – she saw a small printed sheet lying at the bottom of the bubble-wrap nest. It explained that these pens were filled with food colour, and offered a picture showing how they could be used to write fine lines or thick lines, depending on how you held them. It also guaranteed that the contents were kosher. *Eh*, now her cakes were going to be more beautiful than ever!

This conviction made her feel emotional, and tears began to well in her eyes. Pulling at the neck of her T-shirt with her left hand, she reached with her right hand for the tissue that was tucked inside her brassiere — next to the deposit for Mrs Wanyika's cake — and dabbed at her eyes. Then she became aware that her face was beginning to feel extremely hot, and she extended the dabbing to her forehead and cheeks before picking up the card from June and using it as a fan.

Really, this Change business was not dignified at all.

## 2. A Christening

THE BUILDING IN WHICH THE TUNGARAZA family lived clung to the side of the hill over whose crest the city centre sprawled, so that the apartments that were on the ground floor at the front of the building — as was the Tungarazas' — were one storey up at the back as the hill sloped steeply away at the rear. Angel's work table stood in the corner of her lounge, which was at the back of the apartment, in front of a large window which afforded a good view out over the wall encircling the compound. From there she could watch, as she worked, the busy comings and goings of people and vehicles up and down the hill, while simultaneously keeping an eye on the children as they played down in the compound's yard.

Today the boys were kicking their football around noisily, while Faith and Safiya were quietly and patiently braiding Grace's hair into neat cornrows. Titi had gone down to the yard to bring their washing in off the line, and was chatting there with Eugenia, who cleaned for the Egyptian upstairs.

The cake on Angel's work table today was for Ken Akimoto's dinner party that would take place that night. Ken was by far her best customer, ordering cakes from her two or three times a month. He loved to entertain, and it was well known that he was very good at preparing dishes from his native Japan, even though he had lived most of his life in the United States.

Angel enjoyed baking cakes for him because he allowed her the freedom to decorate them exactly as she pleased. There was only one time when he had ordered a specific design: when he was entertaining some visitors from the Japanese government who had come to Kigali to see if they might want to sponsor something at KIST. On that occasion, he had commissioned Angel to make a cake that looked like the Japanese flag, which was a very boring flag indeed: white with a big, red circle in the middle. Angel had thought at the time that the cake was extremely ugly – though now she recognized that it was not quite as ugly as the Wanyikas' wedding cake – but Ken's guests had apparently found it beautiful enough to photograph from many angles.

Today, though, Angel had free rein. She had baked a simple round vanilla sponge cake in two layers with crimson icing between the layers. Then she had coated the cake with a vibrant turquoise blue icing. Across the top she had created a loose, open, basket-weave design in bright yellow bordered with piped yellow stars alternating with crimson stars, and she was now finishing off by piping scrolls of crimson around the base of the sides. It would be a handsome cake: beautiful, but at the same time masculine. As she re-filled her plastic icing syringe with the last of the crimson, she heard a knock at the front door and a man's voice calling, '*Hodi!*'

'*Karibu!*' she answered, looking up from the table as the door opened and Bosco, the gangly young man who worked as Ken Akimoto's driver, came into the lounge. She wiped her hands on a cloth and greeted him with a handshake, in the traditional Rwandan way.

'You are welcome, Bosco,' she said, speaking in Swahili. 'But I hope you haven't come to collect Mr Akimoto's cake. As you can see, it isn't quite finished yet.'

'Ooh, Auntie!' exclaimed Bosco, his lean, youthful face breaking into a wide smile. 'That is a very, very fine cake! The colours are very, very good. Mr Akimoto will be very, very happy. *Eh!* But Auntie, what is that?' Bosco's eyes had slid away from Ken's cake and his expression was registering distaste.

Angel saw that he had noticed the cake which sat at the back corner of her work table, waiting to be collected that afternoon by Mrs Wanyika's driver.

'That's an anniversary cake for some big people,' said Angel, adding — quickly — in her defence, 'That's exactly how they want it to look.'

' *Wazungu?*' asked Bosco.

'*Wazungu* taste. *Wazungu* thinking.' She did not want to say more; it was not professional to gossip about her customers, and as a businesswoman she was obliged to remain professional at all times. 'But I'm happy that you like Mr Akimoto's cake, Bosco.'

'He'll come for it later himself, Auntie. I'm not here

for Mr Akimoto; I've come to you about a personal matter. Well... two personal matters, Auntie.'

'*Sawa*, Bosco,' said Angel. 'Why don't you go into the kitchen and make tea for us while I finish decorating Mr Akimoto's cake? Then we'll sit and drink tea while you tell me your personal matters.'

Bosco glanced with admiration at the finished cake as he and Angel settled into their chairs with their cups of sweet, milky tea.

'Auntie, it is about a cake that I've come to see you,' he began.

'You've come to see the right person, Bosco. Are you perhaps bringing me news of your marriage?'

Since returning from Uganda, where his family had fled many years ago, Bosco had been pursuing — at first rather vaguely and now with greater single-mindedness — the idea of settling down and raising a family of his own. But despite his having identified a small succession of women to propose to, he had not yet had any success in securing a wife.

'No, Auntie,' said Bosco, lowering his eyes and giving an embarrassed laugh. 'Not yet. No, Auntie, it's my sister Florence. She has delivered her firstborn.'

'Congratulations! A boy or a girl?'

'She's a girl, Auntie. She'll go for her baptism next weekend, and Florence would like a cake for the christening party. I told her that you are the one to make the best cake.'

'Thank you, Bosco. I'll be very happy to make the cake for your sister. I'll give her a good price.'

'Oh, no, Auntie,' said Bosco quickly, 'you can charge *Mzungu* price. Mr Akimoto will pay for the cake. He says it will be his gift.'

'*Eh!* Your boss is a very generous somebody!' declared Angel.

This was true. Ken frequently made his driver and Pajero available to friends — although, strictly speaking, both the vehicle and the driver belonged not to Ken himself, but to his employer, the United Nations. Angel herself had benefited from this generosity a number of times when she had needed to deliver cakes to customers who lived on roads where no ordinary *taxi-voiture* was able to travel. And, of course, Ken also helped her by buying supplies for her business whenever he went home to America, where his job gave him a week's leave every two months. Her supplies came into the country in his unsearched luggage along with his own big bottles of soy sauce, tubes of wasabi paste and sheets of processed seaweed — and he would never accept any payment for them from Angel. But despite his constant generosity towards her, she felt no guilt in charging him an exorbitant rate for every cake. When Sophie had found out exactly how high Ken's salary was, she had come to Angel in a state of high emotion, ricocheting between rage and exasperation. Angel had made tea for her and had tried to calm her down, suggesting that perhaps these big organizations needed to pay big salaries if they wanted to attract the right kind of people; but Sophie had said that they were the wrong kind of people if they would not do the work for less. Ultimately they had concluded that the desire to make the world a better place was not something that belonged in a person's pocket. No, it belonged in a person's heart.

Angel rose to fetch her photo album from her work table, and brought it over to her guest. 'Let me show you other christening cakes that I've made, Bosco. Perhaps they'll help you to decide exactly how you want your cake to look.'

Bosco looked carefully at each photograph. '*Eh*, Auntie, these are all very, very fine! How will I be able to choose one?'

Angel laughed. 'You don't have to choose one; you can design a different one. I'm only showing you these for some ideas. But always for a christening, the name of the baby must be written across the top of the cake.'

Angel thought of her new Gateau Graffito pens. It would surely be easier to write a name on a cake with one of those than with her bulky icing syringe — although, of course, the colours of the three pens that she had were not suitable for a baby's cake.

'Goodenough,' said Bosco.

'Good enough?' queried Angel. 'What is good enough?'

'The baby's name, Auntie. She's called Goodenough.'

'Goodenough? *Goodenough?* What kind of name is Goodenough?'

'It's because they wanted a boy very, very much, but the baby is a girl. She's not what they wanted, but she's good enough.'

Angel removed her glasses and began to polish the lenses with the corner of her *kanga*. 'Do you think that is a good name for a girl to have, Bosco?'

'It is not a bad name, Auntie.'

Angel was silent for a while as she polished her glasses vigorously. Then she said, 'Do you know what, Bosco? I think perhaps it is not you who should choose the cake for Goodenough. You are only the uncle. Really, it's the baby's mother who should choose the cake for the baby's christening. Do you think it will be possible for you to take me with my photo album to meet Mama-Goodenough?'

Bosco's face lit up. 'Oh, Auntie, that is a very, very good idea! I wouldn't like to choose the wrong cake. I'll ask Mr Akimoto if I can drive you there on Monday. We can't go now; I have to fetch him soon from the office and bring him home to prepare for his party tonight. You know he likes me to help him by carrying the TV from the bedroom to the lounge and connecting up all the wires for the speakers and the microphone for the singing machine.'

'*Eh*, we will have another night of noise, then!' said Angel, putting her glasses back on. The whole compound knew when Ken Akimoto's parties included karaoke. As the night wore on and alcohol increasingly loosened inhibitions, even those guests who should never be allowed to sing into a microphone would be persuaded to do just that. But nobody ever complained. Neighbours were often guests themselves, and those who were not invited had usually received some favour or another from Ken.

Angel picked up her diary and a pen from the coffee table. 'On Monday we'll decide about the cake with Florence. But now I must write the day and time of the christening party in my diary so that it cannot be forgotten.'

She made the entry in her diary as Bosco gave her the details. She was careful to record all her orders in her diary so that she could keep track of them. That was the professional thing to do — and besides, Dr Rejoice had warned her that sometimes the Change could make a woman forget things. Angel knew that forgetting to make somebody's cake would be a shame from which she would never recover.

'Now, Bosco,' she said, replacing the diary and the pen on the coffee table, 'your sister's cake is one personal matter. You said that you were coming to me with two.'

'Yes, Auntie,' said Bosco. Then he said a loud *eh!* and looked away disconsolately.

'Bosco?'

'*Eh!*'

'What is in your heart, Bosco?'

He sighed deeply. 'It's Linda, Auntie.'

'Ah, Linda,' said Angel, immediately picturing the young British human rights monitor who lived in the compound. Men tended to regard her as very beautiful, but Angel wondered how they had formed that opinion. As far as she understood it, the beauty of a woman rested in her face, but Angel had never seen a man look at Linda's face; there were always other parts of her body that were asking more urgently to be observed. Really, that was not a polite way to dress in a country where women were modest. Even Jeanne d'Arc — the sex worker who occasionally came to see customers in the compound — did not advertise her body like that.

Bosco looked embarrassed and remained silent. Angel did her best to move the conversation on. 'Bosco, I know that you used to like Linda. But that time when you drove me with a cake to that house far on the other side of the golf course, you told me then that you had stopped liking her.'

'Yes, Auntie,' said Bosco. Then he was silent again.

'You told me then that you could see that there was a problem with Linda and drink.'

'Yes, Auntie.'

Silence.

'So what is it now, Bosco? I hope you're not going to tell me that you've decided to like her again.'

Bosco remained silent.

Taking off her glasses and beginning to give them another good clean, Angel continued. 'Have you forgotten the stories that you told me about her? I haven't forgotten the story of the time you saw her outside Cadillac night club and you greeted her, but all the drink in her made you a stranger and she said something to you that was not polite. I haven't forgotten the story of the morning when you went to Mr Akimoto's house to help him clean up after a party and you found Linda asleep on the carpet and she had vomited there, and she simply got up and left you to clean up her vomit. Bosco, please tell me that you have not forgotten those stories yourself.'

Bosco rose from his chair and moved towards the window, from where he could see the children in the yard below. Then he turned to Angel and, shifting his weight from one leg to the other, he spoke at last.

'Auntie, I haven't forgotten those stories.' He began to pace. 'But now I have another story to tell Auntie. It is a story that gives me pain in my heart, even though it is many weeks since I decided not to like Linda.'

'*Eh!* Bosco! It's making my head feel confused to watch you walking up and down, up and down. But I can see that you don't want to sit. Come into the kitchen and we'll make more tea together.'

Putting her glasses back on, she led Bosco into the kitchen. It was a small room, made smaller by the presence of two ovens: the electric one that belonged to the apartment, and the gas one that the Tungarazas had brought with them from Tanzania. Kigali's unstable electricity supply meant that Angel would have lost a lot of business had it not been for her gas oven.

Bosco washed the mugs from which they had drunk their tea, and measured two mugs of water into a saucepan. Angel spooned in some Nido milk powder and a great deal of sugar and added a few cardamom seeds.

'Now, Bosco, I am going to watch this milk, and before it has boiled you are going to tell me your new story. You're going to tell me about this new pain in your heart before it eats you up like a worm inside a mango.'

'Eh, Auntie!' said Bosco, and his story came tumbling out. 'I've just seen Linda. Mr Akimoto sent me to Umubano Hotel to pay his tennis fees. After I paid, I saw Linda in the car park, but she didn't see me. She was with a man, and they were kissing. Kissing like in a film, Auntie. They were leaning against her vehicle, and he was touching her body. *Eh!* I got into Mr

Akimoto's Pajero and I watched them. At first I didn't recognize the man because I only saw his back, but after they finished kissing he put Linda in her vehicle and then he went to his own vehicle and I saw who it was. *Eh!*'

Angel stopped looking at the milk and looked up at Bosco. 'Who was it?'

'Auntie, it was the CIA.'

'*Eh?* The CIA?'

Bosco nodded.

'The CIA from here in this compound?'

Bosco nodded again.

'Ooh, that is bad.'

'It is very, very bad, Auntie. The CIA!'

'Uh-uh,' said Angel, shaking her head.

'Uh-uh,' agreed Bosco.

'He's married and he's living right next door to Linda with his wife!' said Angel. Rob and Jenna lived on the same floor as Linda. Officially Rob worked for an American aid organization, but it was well known that he really worked for the CIA.

'She could be with me,' said Bosco, looking wretched. 'I'm a young man and I have a very, very good job. It's four years now that I've been a driver for people at the UN. But instead she's with a man who is old like her father.'

'A man who is married, Bosco,' said Angel. 'Surely what matters is not that he's older than her, but that he's married.'

'Auntie, many men come here without their wives, and they get girlfriends. There's one who works with Mr Akimoto. That one has even built a house for his girlfriend and they live together and they have a child, and for holidays he goes home to his wife in Europe. Mr Akimoto says that man's wife doesn't know about his girlfriend and his child. She'll never visit him here because he's told her that Rwanda is too dangerous.'

'I've heard of that man,' said Angel. 'And there's the Egyptian upstairs. He came here on his own, without his wife, and he had many girlfriends. But when his wife came to visit, somebody told her, and now she's divorcing him.'

'You cannot have a secret in Kigali, Auntie. Eyes have no curtains here. Somebody will tell the CIA's wife, and then the CIA's wife will take the CIA's gun and shoot Linda.'

Angel was shocked. 'The CIA has a gun?'

'Auntie, can you be a CIA and not have a gun? *Eh!* The milk!' Bosco lunged towards the oven and rescued the milk as it was about to boil over.

They were busy filling their mugs when Titi came in with the basket of dry washing from the lines in the yard and wanted to make a start on the ironing. Angel and Bosco moved into the lounge and switched to speaking English, which Titi could not understand well. They both wanted to talk more about this story, but it was a story that could become dangerous if it was overheard.

They could not talk much more about it, however, because very soon Mrs Wanyika's driver brought a thick envelope of Rwandan francs to Angel and took away the ugly white cake, and very soon after that Bosco looked at his watch, said *eh!* several times and rushed off to bring Mr Akimoto home to prepare for his dinner party.

*

That night, long after the children and Titi had gone to sleep, long after Angel and Pius had retired to bed themselves and Pius had slipped into sleep beside her, Angel remained awake. Most nights, now, she battled to get to sleep, and often she awoke early, hot and perspiring.

Tonight the air was filled with distant sounds of music and singing followed by loud cheering and applause. Fortunately the Tungarazas' apartment was at the opposite end of the building from Ken's, and the two other ground-floor apartments between them afforded some degree of sound-proofing – although occasional snatches of discernible lyrics still found their way into the bedroom where Angel half lay, half sat in her wakefulness. She knew that Patrice and Kalisa, the compound's night security guards, would, as usual, be hosting a party of their own for neighbouring guards in the street outside Ken's apartment, each of them seeking to outdo the others with their dance moves, all of them humming along when they recognized particular songs.

A fragment of song – *every step you take, every move you make* – partly sung, partly shouted by a voice that could have been the CIA's now drifted across the night.

Angel's thoughts turned to Pius, breathing ponderously at her side. Would he ever treat her like the CIA was treating his wife? Would he ever take a girlfriend from right in their very compound? She did not think so. There had been times in the past when she had had her suspicions about other women – particularly when

Pius had been away studying in Germany — but it had never amounted to anything serious. And now some grey was starting to appear in his hair, and his belly was increasingly rounding out above his trousers. For him, their bed had become a place only for sleep, except very occasionally on a Saturday night after he had drunk Primus beer and watched football with his friends.

But *eh!* these young Rwandan girls were very beautiful! And many were looking for sugar-daddies — especially sugar-daddies who could take them away to better lives in other countries. There were, of course, many beautiful girls where Pius worked. Almost a quarter of the students were girls, and it was well known everywhere that beautiful young students could be a troubling source of temptation to their professors. Their own daughter, Vinas, had caught the eye of Dr Winston Moshi while he was training her to be a teacher, and she had eventually married him. But Pius did not have the direct contact with students that the teaching staff did.

Only a handful of the professors were women, all of them attractive enough. But she was sure that Pius could never be tempted by one of them, because he had confessed to being afraid of them.

'*Eh!*' he had declared, returning home after a meeting one day and shaking his head. 'Those lady professors are *tough!* They all stand together, and they refuse to be ignored or to have their opinions disregarded. I'm telling you, Angel: not all who have claws are lions.'

That left the secretaries and the female administrative assistants who had offices in the same building as her husband. Would one of these tempt him? On the whole, she thought not. All of the ones she had met had been focused on their families — and on bettering themselves through attending evening classes every night of the week. Angel considered carefully. Pius had always been a serious somebody, and now he carried the responsibility of being a father to five grand-children. *Five!* Surely he would not do anything silly or embarrassing?

And besides, he still loved her dearly, she knew that. Okay, they seemed to have communicated a lot less since losing their daughter, Vinas. But that was to be expected: in addition to Joseph's three children, she now had Vinas's two to keep her busy at home and, really, Pius had no choice but to keep himself busy at the university. Under the circumstances, it was only natural that they failed to find the time to sit together and talk things through in the way that they always used to.

A loud chorus of voices from Ken's apartment — *get your money for nothing* — interrupted this line of thought, and she became aware that her face was beginning to radiate heat. Her body — defended by two blankets against the cold night-time air of Kigali's high altitude — maintained a comfortable temperature, while her head and neck, propped up on a pillow against the bedroom wall, were now beginning to perspire. From a small pile on the floor next to the bed, she picked up one of the *Hello!* magazines that Sophie had lent her, and began to fan her face with it. The people who

appeared in *Hello!* were well known in England —
according to Sophie, although Angel recognized hardly
any of them — and the magazine had in most cases paid
them money to be photographed and to tell their
stories; in some cases the people in the magazine had
apparently received a great deal of money if they agreed
to tell their story exclusively to *Hello!* According to
Sophie, there were even local versions of *Hello!* in other
countries around the world.

As she fanned the perspiration on her face, Angel
considered a Rwandan version of the magazine. It
would be called *Muraho!*, of course, but who would
feature in it? There was the current Miss France, who
had been born in Kigali to a Rwandan mother and a
French father; she would look good on the cover. And
then there was Cecile Kayirebwa, the singer who was
famous throughout the world. But neither of those
Rwandans lived in the country. Perhaps the magazine
would focus on the big people who lived here — Angel
had never seen anybody who looked ordinary or poor in
*Hello!* — people like ministers and ambassadors. Mrs
Wanyika would surely accept a high fee to give *Muraho!*
exclusive access to her silver wedding anniversary party.

Angel's hand froze suddenly in its fanning action
and she gave an involuntary shudder. The story about
the Wanyikas' party would surely have to include a photograph of the cake, and Mrs Wanyika would definitely
not miss the opportunity to point out that it had been
made by a fellow Tanzanian. Angel's name would be
linked — nationally! — with poor taste. Her business
would be ruined!

Several high-pitched voices — *night fever, night fever* — slipped into the bedroom through the louvred windows, and Angel re-commenced her fanning, now soothing not just the heat of her face but also the turmoil in her head. *Eh!* A professional somebody must be very, very careful of bad publicity, especially in a place where a story that you were telling somebody could be repeated on the other side of town even before you had finished telling it.

After a few moments of frenzied fanning, her hand slowed a little as a new idea came to her. Perhaps — one day — there would be a special article about Angel Tungaraza in *Muraho!* magazine. There would be photographs from her album of some of her very best cakes. The whole family would be shown in their best outfits, grouped artistically in the lounge and giving their widest smiles for the professional photographer that would be sent by the magazine. There would also be pictures of Angel at work in her kitchen, beating eggs into a bowl, and at her work table with her icing syringe and her Gateau Graffito pens.

Sleep eventually tucked itself around her as she settled — still smiling — into the comforting possibilities offered by this new idea.

# 3. A Scholarship

WEDGED UNDERNEATH THE BACK OF THE Tungarazas' apartment, where the hill sloped away beneath the building, was the office of Prosper, whose job it was to manage such matters as supervising the compound's security guards, collecting rents and overseeing the general upkeep of the building – roles that he filled, it had to be said, with only token commitment. It therefore came as no surprise to Angel when, having descended the stairs into the compound's yard and knocked on the door to Prosper's office loudly enough to wake the heaviest of sleepers, she received no reply.

She went back up the stairs to the ground floor of the building and left through the front entrance. On the street corner outside, she found Modeste and Gaspard, the day security guards. They had just bought a pineapple from a woman who was now hoisting her basket of pineapples, bananas and avocados back on to her head and moving on down the hill.

Angel greeted the guards and then, ignoring Gaspard — who spoke only French and Kinyarwanda — addressed Modeste in Swahili.

'Modeste, where is Prosper?'

'He is not here, Madame.'

'Yes, he is not here. Will you bring him here for me?'

'Yes, Madame.'

'Thank you, Modeste. Tell him I'm waiting at his office.'

Modeste set off up the hill, his tall, skinny frame breaking into a slow trot. Angel knew where he was going. On most days Prosper could be found two streets up, at a small roadside bar furnished with two plastic tables and a few plastic chairs. If ever Angel went past there and she and Prosper acknowledged each other with a wave, she knew that he would come to her apartment later to assure her that his sole purpose in going to that bar had been to warn its patrons about the evil of drink. He would insist on showing her the very verse in his Bible that he had been reading to the patrons at the very moment that Angel had waved to him. But his hands would shake, and his eyes would be red, and his words would smell of Primus.

Angel went back down the stairs and waited in the yard outside Prosper's office. It was not a beautiful yard. The last of the builders' rubble still lay in one corner, in a pile partially concealed behind the trailer that had carried Angel's gas oven behind the family's red Microbus on its journey from Dar es Salaam to Kigali. The red soil of the yard was bare. Sophie and Catherine had once suggested that the compound's residents should get together and try to make the yard more beautiful by planting grass and flowers there; but, really, those girls from England did not understand the most important feature of a yard on this continent: a yard without plants was a yard without snakes. Angel had not yet seen a snake in Kigali, but she knew that not seeing something with her own eyes was no proof that it was not in fact there. The yard was a safe place for the children to play, and that was surely the most important consideration.

Wedged under the ground floor of the building, alongside Prosper's office, were four more rooms. One of these accommodated the Electrogaz cash-power meters for each apartment, nestled in an alarmingly haphazard tangle of wires and cables that Angel feared could kill a person more quickly than the venom of any snake. Bizarrely — for their apartment was on the ground floor — the meter controlling the Tungarazas' electricity supply was one of the highest on the wall, and reaching it to key in the numbers on the receipt from the Electrogaz office required the use of the ladder that was kept in the room for that purpose. Under no circumstances would Angel allow Pius to rest the metal ladder across the tangle of wires and climb it to replenish their electricity supply, a task that would have been difficult enough without the potential of death by electrocution, requiring as it did three hands: one to hold the slip bearing the numbers; one to key those numbers in; and one to hold a torch — for the room had no lighting and the ink on the slip was never bold and clear. Angel did not know how Modeste managed to achieve this task at all — let alone complete it with his life intact — but he was happy enough to attempt it for the reward of a few francs.

Another of the rooms under the building housed the water meters that had been installed just one month earlier, and that now made it possible for the compound's owner to present a bill for water to each of the apartments. The next room was nothing more than an empty space defined by three walls and open across the front. This would apparently house the diesel-powered generator for the compound that had been promised but had not yet materialized. Finally, tucked underneath Ken Akimoto's flat at the far end of the building was a room housing toilet facilities for Prosper and the guards.

Angel heard her name being called from above where she stood. Looking up, she saw Amina leaning over the small balcony of the apartment just above her own.

'Angel! What are you doing there?'

'Hello, Amina. I'm waiting for Prosper.'

'Prosper? Have you sent Modeste for him?'

'Yes. He should be here soon.'

'Safiya's waiting for the girls to come and do home-work.'

'They'll be there soon, Amina. While I'm here they're at home with Benedict. He's still sick with malaria. Titi has taken Moses and Daniel to play with their friends down the road, so the girls must stay with Benedict until I've finished with Prosper.'

'Oh, okay. Come and look at TV with me if you can this evening. Vincenzo has a late meeting.'

'Thanks, Amina. I'll come if I can. *Eh*, here is Prosper now!'

Prosper was making his way unsteadily down the stairs into the yard.

'Madame Tungaraza!' he declared, extending his hand and shaking Angel's hand enthusiastically. 'I'm sorry to have delayed you. There was some urgent business outside the compound that I had to attend to.'

'*Eh*, Prosper! You are always a very busy somebody,' said Angel with a smile. 'But I can see that you don't have your Bible with you today, so it wasn't God's business that you were attending to.'

Prosper glanced at Angel uncertainly as he unlocked the door to his office. 'Madame! You should not have waited for me in the yard! I could have come to your apartment. But come in, come in.'

'Thank you, Prosper,' said Angel, following him into the gloomy little room that accommodated a table and one wooden chair, 'but in my apartment the business is cakes. Your office is the place for compound business. No, no, Prosper, that chair is yours. I'm happy to stand. I must be quick because I have a sick child at home.'

Prosper seated himself behind the table and attempted to convey an air of efficiency by rearranging the file, the notebook, the ballpoint pen and the Bible that lay upon it.

'Now, Prosper,' said Angel, taking two pieces of paper from where her *kanga* was tied at her waist, unfolding them, and placing them on the table for Prosper to look at. 'I've come about these.'

Prosper glanced at the pages. 'Yes, Madame, these are bills for water. It is a new thing. I myself put a letter under every door one month ago to say that bills for water were going to start coming.'

'Mm-hmm. But what I want to ask is how are you calculating these water bills?'

'There are meters, Madame. The meters tell us how much water an apartment has used. They are new.'

'Yes, I know about these new meters, Prosper. And I also know the story about Mr Akimoto's meter. I heard the story from his own mouth. I know that he came to you yesterday, and he asked you to show him his meter in the room down here that is always locked. And I know that when you showed him his meter, the needle was busy going round and round, even though nobody was in Mr Akimoto's apartment, and nobody was using his apartment's water then.'

Prosper's eyes did not meet Angel's. 'That was a mistake, Madame. We were looking at the wrong meter.'

Angel persisted. 'But that meter had the same number as Mr Akimoto's apartment. How can we know that there has not been the same kind of mistake with our bills?'

'Madame, I assure you,' said Prosper, trying now to assert his authority by meeting Angel's eyes, 'after we found that mistake yesterday, I myself checked every bill and every meter. There are no more mistakes.'

'Then, Prosper, please look at these two bills and help me to understand.' Angel moved around the desk and stood over Prosper so that she was not blocking the light from the doorway — for the office had neither electric lighting nor a window – and so that he could not look up directly into her eyes. The smell of Primus threatened to overwhelm her. 'First, this is the bill for my family. See here, Prosper, it says 15,000 francs.'

'Yes, I see that; it is clear. I myself wrote that number there.' said Prosper.

'And now this one. This is the bill for Sophie and Catherine. It says here 30,000 francs.'

'Yes,' said Prosper. 'It is all very clear. What is it that you need me to explain, Madame?'

'I am confused, Prosper,' said Angel, laying the two bills side by side on the table. 'In my apartment we are eight. *Eight!* We all wash, we all use the toilet, we cook for eight people, we wash clothes and sheets and towels for eight people. But in that other apartment they are two. *Two!* How can it be right that two people use twice as much water as eight people? How can it be right that two people must pay twice as much as eight people?'

Prosper shifted his chair sideways, and by twisting his body around, managed to look up at Angel. The expression on his face implied that she was a foolish woman who understood nothing. 'Madame, of course they must pay more!'

Angel held his gaze. 'Because why?'

He sighed and shook his head. 'Because, Madame, they are *Wazungu.*'

'*Eh!*' cried Angel, looking at Prosper as if he had shocked her to the core. 'Those girls are not *Wazungu*, Prosper!'

'Madame?' It was Prosper's turn to register shock and confusion. 'They are not *Wazungu*?'

'No, Prosper. They are *volunteers!*'

'*Volunteers?*'

'Yes, volunteers. A volunteer is not a *Mzungu*. A volunteer does not earn a *Mzungu*'s salary. A volunteer cannot pay what a *Mzungu* can pay. Those girls can look like *Wazungu*, Prosper, but they are not.'

'*Eh!*' said Prosper, picking up the bill for Sophie and Catherine's apartment and examining it carefully. Then he looked up at Angel, who was still towering above him. 'They are not *Wazungu*?'

Angel shook her head.

Prosper thought for a while, and then he asked, 'How much does Madame think volunteers can pay?'

'I think they can pay 5,000 francs,' suggested Angel, having agreed the sum with Sophie and Catherine the previous evening.

'Okay,' said Prosper, and he took his pen and altered the amount on the bill. 'I did not know, Madame. I thought they were *Wazungu*.'

'Thank you, Prosper.' Angel reached inside her brassiere and removed several banknotes. 'Here's the money for my bill. I'll give this other bill to Sophie and Catherine. I think they can pay 5,000 francs each and every month. Please explain that to the meter.'

'Yes, Madame. See, I myself have signed here on your bill to say that you have paid.'

Her business with Prosper concluded, Angel went back up the stairs and out through the building's entrance into the street. Modeste and Gaspard had now finished eating their pineapple and were sitting on the ground on the other side of the road with their backs up against the trunk of a mimosa tree. They acknowledged her wave as she turned down the dirt road and headed towards Leocadie's shop, which was housed in a container at the side of the road about a hundred metres from the compound.

On the way to the shop, she passed another kind of container, longer and lower, dark green in colour with a flatter shape and four hinged lids across its top. This was the skip to which the neighbourhood brought its household rubbish in the expectation — sometimes unmet for extended periods of time — that a truck would eventually come and take it away and bring it back empty.

Angel found Leocadie sitting in the dim interior of her shop, breast-feeding her baby. Short and solid, with small eyes set deep in a rather hard face, she was not an attractive girl until she smiled — at which point she would light up as if her cash-power meter had just been replenished, and she was suddenly quite beautiful. She looked up now as Angel's frame blocked the natural light from the doorway, and beamed when she saw who it was.

'Mama-Grace! *Karibu!* How are you?'

'I am well, thank you, Leocadie. How is little Beckham?' The baby had been named long before his birth for his incessant kicking at his mother's belly.

'He's fine, Mama-Grace. But he's always hungry!'

'*Eh!* There are babies who are like that. And how is Modeste?' Modeste was Beckham's father. Angel knew very well how Modeste was, because she had just seen him. But that was not what she was asking.

'*Eh!*' said Leocadie, as she transferred Beckham from her left breast to her right. 'That other woman's baby will come in one month. Modeste says if it is a girl he will choose me. He says a man must be with his son. But if it is a boy then we don't know. He'll try to decide.'

Angel shook her head. 'I hope that he'll take the matter to his family. A family can always help a person to make the right decision.'

'*Eh*, Mama-Grace, there is no family to help him to decide. Everybody died. It is only Modeste now. He must decide alone.'

'That is very difficult,' said Angel. She meant that it was very difficult to lose your whole family, and that it was very difficult to make alone a decision that a family should make, and that it was very difficult to wait for a man to decide between you and another woman. 'Let us hope and pray, Leocadie.'

'That is all we can do, Mama-Grace.'

'But I cannot stay and chat. Benedict still has malaria and I must go home and be with him. I have only come to buy sugar.'

Stepping into the container, Angel helped herself to a small bag of sugar from the sparsely stacked shelves lining its walls. It was more expensive to buy from Leocadie than from the market or one of the small supermarkets in town, but the shop was very convenient for things that had been forgotten on the family's weekly shopping trip, or for things that had run out sooner than expected. The shop stocked essentials only: goods such as sugar, powdered milk, tea, eggs, tins of tomato paste, salt, soap, washing powder, toilet paper. A wire wound surreptitiously up the trunk of the jacaranda tree next to the container to join an overhead electrical cable; this powered the small fridge inside the container that kept bottles of Primus and soda cool.

As Leocadie was trying to count out Angel's change without disturbing Beckham, Faith appeared breathlessly in the shop's doorway to report that a lady had come about a cake, and that Angel must come home at once.

Angel found the lady seated in her lounge, encouraging Grace as the child struggled with her few words of school French. The visitor rose to shake Angel's hand.

'*Bonjour, Madame. Comment ça va?*'

'*Bien, merci,*' replied Angel.

'*Vous êtes Madame Angel?*'

'*Oui, je suis Angel.* But Madame, we have now used up all the French that I know! *Unasema Kiswahili?* Do you speak Swahili?'

'*Ndiyo.* Yes.'

'Good. Then let us speak Swahili and we will understand each other. Please sit down, Madame. Girls, Safiya is waiting for you upstairs. Take your homework.'

The girls had their homework books ready. They bid *au revoir* to their guest and hurried out of the apartment as Angel perched on the edge of the sofa and smiled at the woman who smiled back at her from across the coffee table. She was of medium build with long, delicate braids falling loosely around her pretty face, which was adorned with a pair of gold-rimmed glasses. Angel guessed that she could not be more than thirty years old.

The woman introduced herself. 'Madame Angel, my name is Odile. I am a friend of Dr Rejoice. She is the one who sent me here to you.'

'I'm happy to meet you, Odile. If you're a friend of Dr Rejoice you're my friend too, so let's not be formal with each other. Please call me just Angel; let's forget about Madame.'

'Okay, Angel,' said Odile, smiling widely.

Angel stood up from the sofa. 'Odile, you are very welcome in my home. But could I ask you to excuse me for just one minute? I have a child here with malaria, and I need to check on him.'

'*Eh!*' Odile rose to her feet, her face registering concern. 'It's lucky that I came to you when you have a sick child, Angel, because I'm a nurse.'

'*Eh!* A nurse? Come with me then, Odile, we'll check on him together. But really, I think the fever is almost over now.'

Angel led Odile into the children's bedroom, where Benedict lay asleep in one of the lower bunks. Quietly they took turns to place a hand on his damp forehead and, feeling that the fever had at last broken, they smiled at each other with relief.

'He's going to be fine,' whispered Odile.

'Yes,' agreed Angel, as they made their way out of the room, pulling the door almost shut behind them. 'Definitely after this weekend he'll be back at school.'

They took up the same seats as before, on opposite sides of the coffee table.

'Obviously you've been keeping his fluids up?'

'Yes, and fortunately he's been thirsty, so I haven't

had to force him.' Angel clapped her hands together. '*Eh!* I feel blessed that a nurse has come to me today to help me to check on him!'

Odile smiled. 'Actually, I didn't come to you as a nurse, Angel. I came to you as a person who is wanting to order a cake.'

'Then I'm blessed twice today! But before we begin to talk business, let me make some tea for us to drink. While I'm doing that, you can look through my photo album and see some cakes that I've already made, and there is also one on the table over there that's waiting to be collected.'

When Angel emerged from the kitchen with two steaming mugs of milky tea, apologizing for not having a slice of cake to offer her guest, Odile was at the work table looking admiringly at the cake that waited there. Angel put the mugs down on the coffee table and went to join her.

'That cake is for a christening,' she explained. 'The baby is the daughter of the sister of a neighbour's driver.'

'It is truly perfect!' declared Odile. The oblong, one-layer cake was coated in powder-pink frosting. Around the sides of the cake the pink was decorated with white frills resembling lace. Both the top left corner and the bottom right corner of the upper surface were adorned with lilac roses and white rose-buds tipped with strawberry pink. And across the centre of the cake, starting at the bottom corner on the left and sloping up towards the top corner on the right was the baby's name in lilac cursive script: *Perfect*.

'That is a wonderful name for a girl,' said Odile.

'Indeed,' beamed Angel. 'I helped the mother to choose it. But come and sit, Odile. You know, I thought of becoming a nurse myself, but then I became a mother instead. But the world is different now. Now a woman can become a nurse *and* a mother.'

The two women sat and took a sip of their tea.

'Are you perhaps a nurse *and* a mother, Odile?'

'Oh, no, no.' Odile shook her head, putting her mug down on the table. 'No, Angel, I'm just a nurse.' Her voice had become quieter, and a little sad. Angel watched as Odile's eyes stared through and beyond her mug of tea, and saw a vertical furrow beginning to deepen just above where the young woman's glasses met across her nose. It was clear that thinking about not being a nurse *and* a mother was making her guest feel uncomfortable.

'And tell me, Odile,' she said, her voice as cheerful as she could make it, 'where is it that you are a nurse?'

To Angel's relief, Odile's smile returned. 'I work at the *Centre Médico-Social* in Biryogo. Do you know it?'

'No, I don't know that place. But my husband and I have driven through Biryogo. *Eh!* The people in that part of town are too poor!' The tiny makeshift dwellings of wood, corrugated iron, cardboard and plastic sheeting that the people of Biryogo called home were not a new sight to Angel. Such places clung to the outskirts of most cities on the continent, providing shelter for those with nothing who had come to the city in the hope of something, only to find themselves contending instead with a different kind of nothing.

'It's not a beautiful place to work,' agreed Odile. 'But it's where God needs me. The centre is for people who are infected. We do testing and counselling, and we educate people, especially women. For example, we're training sex workers to do sewing, then they can earn money from sewing instead of from sex.'

'*Eh!* That is very good work,' said Angel, and her thoughts went to Jeanne d'Arc, the sex worker who did occasional business in the compound. She was a nice enough girl, but really, that was not a good job to have.

'This disease is a very bad thing,' said Odile.

'*Eh!* Uh-uh,' agreed Angel, shaking her head.

'Uh-uh,' echoed Odile, and she shook her head too.

'One of the girls you met here today, Odile, the one you were talking with in French. Grace. She has two brothers who are also with me here. The disease you are talking about took their mother, and it would have taken their father, too. It's only that robbers shot him instead.'

'*Eh!* Grace mentioned her *frères*, she showed me the family photos,' Odile indicated the four framed pictures mounted on the wall, 'but I thought they were all your children. I didn't know that you had adopted orphans.'

'In fact they're my grandchildren. It's my son who got shot.'

'Oh, I'm very sorry, Angel, I didn't know.'

'Thank you, Odile. In fact there are five grand-children who are now my children. *Five!* Because my daughter is late, too.'

'Oh, that is very sad.' Odile shook her head. 'May I

ask… forgive me, Angel, as a nurse I'm curious about the late. May I ask about what took your daughter?'

'Of course you can ask, Odile, and to tell the truth I don't mind at all to talk about such a thing with somebody who is a nurse. It was stress that took her.'

'Stress?'

'Blood pressure. She drove herself too hard after her husband left her. Worked herself to death. Everybody knows that such a thing is possible.'

Odile hesitated for a moment before saying, 'It's certainly not impossible, Angel. Was it her heart?'

'No, no. Her head.' Angel pressed the palm of her right hand to her temple.

'Her head?' Odile mirrored the gesture. 'Something like a stroke?'

'A very bad headache. That's how her friend explained it to us. And really, Odile, that was not unexpected, because even as a child Vinas would get headaches sometimes, especially at the time of school exams and so on. Her friend said she'd been having a lot of headaches from working too hard, and also from her blood pressure.'

'I see…' said Odile.

'And of course everybody knows that stress and blood pressure go together with headaches.'

'Yes. What exactly did the doctor say, Angel?'

'Well, no, we didn't speak to a doctor. By the time Pius and I got to Mount Meru Hospital, Vinas was already late.'

'Mount Meru? In Arusha?'

'Yes. Vinas fell in love with Winston in Dar es Salaam

while she was studying to be a teacher, then when she qualified she went to live in Arusha with him because his family was there. *Eh!* She loved him so much, Odile! When he left her, we begged her to come back to us in Dar, but by then she was deputy to the *Mwalimu Mkuu* at her school, next in line to be Head herself, and she preferred to stay there. But she pushed herself too hard. *Eh!*' Angel closed her eyes and shook her head. 'I wasn't by her side, Odile. I didn't see what she was doing to herself.'

'That is very sad.'

'I failed to recognize the signs of stress. The last few times I saw her I noticed that she was reducing nicely,' Angel patted the sides of her ample thighs, 'but I didn't know it was dangerous to be so stressed. I just hoped for myself that one day my business could grow big and keep me so busy that I could reduce like that.'

Odile mirrored Angel's sad smile, and they sipped their tea in silence for a while before Odile spoke again. 'Angel, may I ask you another question? As a nurse?'

'Yes, of course.'

'I'm wondering... bearing in mind... are all of your grandchildren well?'

Angel knew at once what she meant and nodded her head. 'When my son and his wife found out that they were positive, their doctor in Mwanza said the children should be tested, just to be sure. We were worried about Benedict,' she gestured towards the door of the children's room where the boy lay, 'because he sometimes doesn't seem as strong as other boys, but all three are negative.'

'That's good. I'm sure that five grandchildren make a heavy enough load, even when they're well.'

'Actually, there could have been six. *Six!* My daughter had a third baby, but he never thrived and he was late within just a few months. There are babies like that, Odile.'

'There are.'

Angel forced a smile. '*Eh*, but five keep me busy enough! The two girls that you met are the oldest, and I must confess to you as a nurse, that recently I've started to become afraid for them. They'll start to become young women soon and boys will start to notice them. I think my heart will stop beating if the virus gets to one of them.'

'Angel, that's not going to happen,' assured Odile. 'Obviously you've spoken to them about it?'

'*Eh!* It's difficult for somebody who is my age, Odile. We are the ones who did not talk to our own children about sex. That is how our own parents raised us. Now, how can we talk to our grandchildren about sex?'

Odile was quiet for a while as she drank the last of her tea. Then she said, 'Perhaps I can help you, Angel. At the centre we have a small restaurant. It provides jobs for women who are positive. They're not sick, but they cannot find other jobs because some employers discriminate when they know that a person is positive. So they cook and serve in our restaurant, and that teaches the community that the food cooked by a positive somebody is safe to eat. It also brings in a little bit of money for the centre. Now, I'm thinking this: perhaps the girls can come and have lunch with me at our restaurant one day. I can tell them about the work of the centre and even show them the things that we do there. We can talk about the disease and about sex, and I can answer their questions. Do you think that is perhaps a good idea?'

Angel's eyes began to fill with tears, and she reached into her brassiere for a tissue. Odile's idea was a very good one indeed. 'Would it be okay with your boss?'

'Yes, of course. It would be during my lunch break, so it wouldn't take me from my duties. You can just tell me what day you'll bring them. I've been on leave this week, but I'll be back there from Monday.'

'I'm very grateful, Odile! You're lifting a big burden from my shoulders. But how can I repay you?'

Odile smiled. 'You can give me a good price for my cake.'

'*Eh!* Nobody will get a better price than you! But forgive me, Odile, you came to me simply to order a cake, meanwhile I've bothered you as a nurse. That is not a professional way for me to behave towards a customer!'

'Oh, no, Angel, there's nothing to forgive. In any case, I'm not simply your customer, am I? You've already said that you and I are friends because we're both friends of Dr Rejoice.'

'That is true.' Angel slipped her tissue back into her brassiere, smiling at Odile. 'So tell me about this cake that I'm going to make for my friend.'

'Actually, the cake is for a celebration party for my brother. The Belgian embassy has awarded him a schol- arship for further studies in Belgium.' Odile was radiant with pride.

'*Eh!* Congratulations! What will he study there?'

'Thank you, Angel. He'll study for a Masters in Public Health. He qualified as a doctor at the National University in Butare.'

'*Eh!* He is a very clever somebody!'

'Yes, but he will deny that. He says it's only hard work and the help of God that have taken him so far.'

'And you, Odile? Are you not also a clever somebody to be a nurse?'

'Oh, no, Angel! For me also it was hard work and the help of God.' Then Odile was quiet for a moment before she said, 'Actually, my brother and I are both survivors.'

Angel knew what that meant: unlike the many Rwandans who had grown up outside the country and had come back home after the recent genocide was over, Odile and her brother had lived through it. They might have lost loved ones, they might have witnessed terrible things, they might have experienced terrible things themselves. But they had survived.

'I'm sorry, Odile,' said Angel, knowing that this was not enough to say but also not knowing the words that could say enough. She shifted uncomfortably on the sofa, not knowing quite what to say next. Perhaps the best — the most professional — thing for her to do was to bring the conversation back to the much easier topic of the cake.

But before Angel could say anything, Odile spoke again.

'I feel I can tell you about it, Angel, because you've already told me something of your own pain and loss, and because we're already friends through Dr Rejoice.' Angel gave her a small nod of confirmation. 'Actually, we were lucky. They killed me, Angel, but I did not die. My brother saved me, even though he wasn't yet fully qualified. And when they saw that he could be useful to them as a doctor they spared him and he protected me.' Odile was quiet for a few seconds before she continued. 'After..., Afterwards, I got a job with Médecins Sans Frontières, translating for them between Kinyarwanda and French. They saw that I worked well with patients. They encouraged me to train as a nurse, and they even found sponsorship for me.'

Angel shook her head and clicked her tongue against the back of her teeth. 'You are strong, Odile. And your brother is strong, too.'

'It's God who made us strong, Angel.' Odile gave a big smile. 'And my brother will be even stronger when he gets his Master's degree. Really, I'm too, too proud of him! But as for his cake, I should tell you that I need it on Sunday. Is it possible for you to make it by then?'

'No problem. We can even deliver it to your house on Sunday morning on our way to church.'

'That will be very fine. Thank you.'

'Is there already a picture of this cake in your mind?'

'Actually, I've seen it in your photo album,' said Odile, picking up the album and turning a few pages. 'Perhaps something simple, like this. We'll not be many: maybe five or six friends, and of course my brother and his wife and their two small children. Can you write "Félicitations, Emmanuel" on it?'

'No problem,' said Angel, making notes on a Cake

Order Form. 'Will Emmanuel's wife and children go with him to Belgium?'

'Unfortunately, the scholarship isn't enough for that, so they'll stay here. Actually, I live at their house, so while Emmanuel is away his wife isn't going to be alone with the children.'

'You are not married yourself?'

'Not yet.' Odile gave a small, shy smile. 'But perhaps one day soon, God will give me a husband.'

'Has He given you a fiancé at least?'

'Actually, not even a boyfriend! I like a man at my church, but it seems he doesn't like me.'

'He's a very foolish somebody not to like you!' declared Angel. Really, Odile was very pretty and she had such a good heart.

The front door flew open suddenly, and Daniel and Moses, the two youngest boys, clattered noisily into the apartment, followed by Titi. Angel made introductions, during which Benedict appeared in the doorway of the children's room with the thin and drawn look of a child who has at last stopped sweating and shivering in turn and will very soon — and very suddenly — demand a great deal of food.

Angel and Odile finished their business quickly and walked out into the street together to wait for a passing *pikipiki* to take Odile home. The motorbike-taxis were a relatively cheap form of public transport; bicycle-taxis were cheaper, of course, but this particular slope of the hill was too steep for the riders to climb and too nerve-wracking for them to descend with their unreliable brakes.

As they waited, Ken Akimoto's Pajero turned off the tarred road on to the dirt road and pulled up outside the compound: Bosco had come to fetch his sister's christening cake. Angel introduced him to Odile, and amidst much shaking of hands, he insisted on driving her home himself.

That evening, as Grace and Faith helped Titi to prepare the evening meal and the boys sat on the sofa watching a video, Angel sat upstairs watching *Oprah* with Amina while Safiya read in her bedroom. Angel and Pius could receive only the national station on their own TV. Satellite was too expensive, and in any case the enormous dish would have occupied the entire balcony of their apartment when space was already a problem. There was no dish on Amina's balcony — but there was one on the Egyptian's balcony immediately above hers. Amina's husband Vincenzo liked to do the right thing, but his younger brother Kalif was more flexible. Once when Kalif had come to visit, Amina had persuaded him to wire their TV up to the Egyptian's satellite dish. The operation had demanded a great deal of subterfuge, the ladder from the cash-power room downstairs, nerves of steel, and — unfortunately — a level of expertise that Kalif simply did not possess. The result was a clear picture — with no sound.

'What do you think?' asked Angel, relaxing in a chair identical to those in her apartment downstairs, and fanning her face with Safiya's French workbook from school.

'I think that lady is maybe taking drugs,' suggested Amina.

'No, it can't be drugs,' asserted Angel. 'Look, now she's drinking from that bottle that she hid earlier. I think she's an alcoholic.'

'Can a lady be an alcoholic?'

'In America a lady can be whatever she wants,' said Angel, who sometimes used to watch *Oprah* in Dar es Salaam. 'And also in Europe. We both know Linda upstairs here.'

'*Eh*, that Linda can drink! You're right, look, she's drinking from a glass now — and trying to hide it from her children.'

'And now she's in the studio with Oprah. *Eh*, she's crying a lot! She's a very unhappy somebody.'

'Do you think that man is her husband or a doctor?' asked Amina.

'If he's the husband he doesn't love her,' declared Angel. 'Look how he's sitting. He doesn't want to be near her.'

'Maybe he's her brother,' suggested Amina. 'Maybe she's brought shame to the family.'

'Or maybe he's the *ex*-husband. Maybe he left her because she drinks.'

'Then why is he sitting there with her now? No, after a man has gone, he's gone. I like Oprah's shoes today.'

'Mm, they're nice.'

A short while later, a sudden change of channel to CNN signalled that the Egyptian had arrived home upstairs. It was fortunate for Amina that his cleaner, Eugenia, preferred more interesting channels during the day. But in any case it was time for Angel to go home.

As she descended the stairs, she was aware of an unfamiliar lightness about her; not about her body, of course — that would have been too much to hope for — but about her spirit. She did not begin to understand it until later that night, when she looked at Grace and Faith asleep in their double bunk. It was then that she recognized that part of her new lightness was the relief that Odile had brought her in providing a solution to one of her biggest worries: these girls were going to learn about the virus and how to keep themselves safe from it.

But it was only as she sat on the sofa watching the late news with Pius, and when she glanced up from the TV — as she had come to do very often — at the photo of their late children, that she fully understood what the rest of the lightness was about. In Odile she had witnessed proof that it was possible to endure a great deal of pain and still manage to survive and go on. They had killed her, Odile had said, but she had not died.

Angel was beginning to feel that she was going to be alright. Reaching for her husband's hand, she rested her head on his shoulder.

# 4. A Birthday

D R YOOSUF BINAISA FOLLOWED PIUS TUNGARAZA
out of the university's minibus, then turned back
to address Angel, who remained resolutely seated in the
rear of the vehicle.

'Mama-Grace, are you sure you won't join us?'

'Very sure, thank you, Dr Binaisa. Why would I want
to go inside a school and look at dead bodies?'

'There may not be dead bodies,' said Dr Binaisa.
'There may be just bones. I've been to the memorial
site at the church in Nyamata; there are only bones
there.'

'Why do you want me to look at bones?' asked Angel.

'Do you not want to understand what happened here,
Mama-Grace? That is why Gasana brought us on this
detour: so that we can understand his country better.
Your country and mine are both neighbours of this
place; we slept peacefully and safely in our homes for
those hundred days while violence was tearing this

country to pieces like a chicken on a plate. Do you not think we need to look now at what we did not see then?'

'Dr Binaisa, I'm not going in there,' said Angel, shaking her head. 'I don't need to look at bones or bodies to know that people died here; that is something I can see in the eyes of the living. Look, Pius and Gasana are waiting for you.'

With a shrug of his shoulders, Dr Binaisa turned and went to join his colleagues, leaving Angel alone in the minibus which the driver had parked in the shade of some trees for her. The driver himself stood chatting to a man a short distance away.

Leaning forward, Angel flipped up and to the side the seat by the open sliding door of the vehicle, and stepped out into the fresh — but unusually quiet — air of the hilltop. To her right, the hill sloped away steeply down towards the small town of Gikongoro, where people worked at their desks, haggled in the market or bustled in the streets, choosing either to gaze at the hazy, blue-green hilltops further away or to look up at this one, in whose shadow they lived and on whose crest Angel now stood. To her left stood the classrooms of the technical school where, Gasana had told them, 60,000 people had been lured by the promise of protection, only to find themselves surrounded and systematically slaughtered.

Angel's body shuddered involuntarily; the past was not a safe place to visit in this country. It would be more comfortable to think ahead to this evening — though not as far ahead as tomorrow, when a rather difficult task awaited her — for this evening she would catch her first glimpse of Lake Kivu. They would stay at the Hôtel du Lac, situated at the water's edge right at the point where the Rusizi River begins to emerge from the southernmost tip of the lake, in the town of Cyangugu.

Pius and Dr Binaisa had a meeting scheduled for the next day at the large prison in the town, where the university was assisting in a project; Gasana's role would be to translate between English, French and Kinyarwanda for the meeting. Pius had explained the project to the children — somewhat inappropriately, Angel had thought — over dinner the previous evening.

'There are too many people in the prison,' he had said. 'It was built to hold 600 prisoners, and now it has 6,000. How many times more is that, children?'

'A hundred times, Baba?' Faith had suggested, taking the rare opportunity to prove herself while Grace — to whom arithmetic came much more easily — hurried to swallow a mouthful of rice and beans.

Pius had looked at Faith sternly. 'A hundred? Are you sure?'

'Ten!' declared Grace, her mouth no longer full.

'Ten!' agreed Pius with a smile. 'Well done, Grace. Yes, so now there are ten times as many prisoners as there should be. What do you think that means?'

'Not enough space,' Faith suggested quickly, eager to redeem herself.

'They need bunk-beds, otherwise they can't all fit in the bedrooms,' offered Moses.

'Are there enough toilets for 6,000 people, Uncle?'

'Titi!' cried Pius. 'You're a very clever somebody!' Titi's surprise — and her pride — illuminated her

[71]

sudden smile. 'Yes, Titi, the toilets are a very big problem, and that means that conditions inside the prison have become dangerously unhygienic. And not just in the prison itself. Human waste—'

'Pius!' declared Angel. 'We are eating food! Is this a good time to be talking of such things?'

'Human waste is as natural as eating food,' he countered. 'The two are not unconnected. So, as I was saying, human waste is overflowing from the prison and running down the hill on to the surrounding fields. That is dangerous and unhygienic for the prison's neighbours.'

'Are you going to fix the toilets, Baba?'

'Don't be silly, Daniel,' said Grace. 'Baba is not a plumber.'

'No, I'm not a plumber; my job is to help the university to find ways of earning money so that one day it will be able to support itself. People won't give this country aid for ever.'

'But, Baba, how do the broken toilets at the prison in Cyangugu earn money for KIST?'

'That's a very good question, Faith. Actually, there's a big international organization that's helping the prison, and that organization is paying KIST a consultancy fee. Dr Binaisa — you know, Baba-Zahara — well, he teaches Sanitation Engineering at KIST, and he's advising them on a project that will make the prison's toilets safe. The project will contain all the human waste and stop it running down the hill, then the waste will be destroyed by tiny things called microbes. That process will produce two things. Number one, it will produce a gas that's safe to use for cooking in the prison's kitchens...'

'Like the gas for Auntie's cake oven?'

'Exactly, Titi. And number two, it will produce a liquid that's safe to use as fertilizer on the prison's fields.'

'That is a good project, Baba,' declared Benedict, who had listened to Pius's explanation far more attentively than the other children.

'Is Auntie going to the prison to show them how to cook with gas?'

'No, Titi,' said Angel. 'That project has nothing to do with me. I'm going because a friend has asked me to deliver a message for her.'

'Can Baba not deliver it?' asked Faith. 'Does Mama really need to go?'

'Of course I don't really need to go,' replied Angel. 'But I want to help my friend, because we must always help our friends whenever we can. And I want to go and look at Lake Kivu, because there are people who say that Lake Kivu is the most beautiful of all the Great Lakes here in Africa. I want to see if it is truly more beautiful than Lake Victoria in our country. But you know we'll be gone only one night. You'll be fine here with Titi; and remember that Mama-Safiya will be checking that your homework is done.'

They had not originally intended to visit this memorial site on their way to Cyangugu, but when Gasana had suggested it, the others had agreed readily enough. Now Angel could see them emerging from one of the classrooms and being led into another by a woman who was acting as some kind of guide. A few minutes later they emerged from that classroom and went into another, and then another. Angel turned away and settled herself back in the minibus to wait for them.

When at last they returned to the vehicle, they brought with them a deep and impenetrable silence. They seated themselves without a word, Pius and Dr Binaisa in the row of seats in front of Angel, Gasana up front next to the driver; and the silence sat there with them all the way back down the hill to Gikongoro and a considerable distance along the road towards Cyangu- gu. But it got out with them when they stopped to buy bananas and peanuts from some women at the side of the road just before entering the Nyungwe Forest, and when they set off again, they found – to their great relief – that they had left it behind at the side of the road.

'*Eh!*' declared Gasana. 'That was a difficult thing to see!'

'Perhaps we shouldn't have gone there,' suggested Dr Binaisa.

'But we did go there, Binaisa,' said Pius. 'Let us not debate if we were right or wrong to go. No conclusion we reach will help us to unsee.'

'What is it that you saw?' asked Angel. 'What is it that Dr Binaisa wanted me to see that he now wishes he could unsee?'

'Forgive me, Mama-Grace,' said Dr Binaisa. 'You were right not to go in. *Eh!* No bones, Mama-Grace, but many, many bodies.'

'White!' declared Pius. 'Gasana, why were they white?'

'They're preserved with lime, Dr T,' explained Gasana. 'Those bodies were exhumed from one of the mass graves there some time back. The lime is supposed to prevent them from decomposing further.'

'*Eh!*' said Angel.

'And now they're lying there in the classrooms,' Gasana continued, 'so that people can go and look and be reminded of what happened here.'

'Do people need to see those bodies to be reminded?' asked Angel. 'Are they not reminded every time they turn to talk to their loved ones and they find that their loved ones are not there?'

'I'm sure that's true, Mrs T. But our children who are too young to remember will need that place to remind them, and our children's children that follow them. And many visitors from other countries have already been there to see what happened. There were many *Wazungu* who had written in the visitors' book.'

'By the way, Tungaraza,' said Dr Binaisa, 'why did you not want to write in that book?'

'*Eh!*' Pius shook his head. 'My thoughts were still lying dead with the people in those classrooms. I could not rouse them to form a sentence.'

'I know what you mean,' said Dr Binaisa. 'While Gasana was writing, I looked over his shoulder and I saw that I was going to have to write my name and my country of origin. It was a struggle for me to remember that I am Dr Yoosuf Binaisa from Uganda. *Eh*, Gasana, what did you write? It looked like you were writing an entire essay on the history of Rwanda!'

Gasana laughed. 'Do you think I even know what I wrote, Dr B? All the feelings inside me flooded out on to the page. They went straight from my heart to the pen without passing through my head. I think if you showed me my own words tomorrow, I would not recognize them.'

'And what about you, Binaisa?' asked Pius. 'What did you manage to write?'

'You won't believe me, Tungaraza, but I wrote only two words, the same two words that many of the *Wazungu* had already written. I'm embarrassed to say what they were.'

'*Never again?*' suggested Gasana. 'I saw those words written over and over again in the book.'

'That is what they said when they closed the death camps in Europe,' said Angel. 'Remember, Pius? There was a lot about *never again* at that museum we went to in Germany.'

'And if those words had meant anything then, there would not be places like the one we've just been to today, with books where people can write *never again* all over again,' said Pius.

'You're right, Tungaraza, and those words that I wrote today mean as little as they did all those years ago. No doubt sometime in the future there'll be some other slaughter somewhere, and afterwards somebody will write in a book *never again* — and again those words will mean nothing. *Eh*, but at least I wrote *something*, Tungaraza. That is better than the nothing that you wrote.'

'That is true, Binaisa.'

'*Eh*, Gasana, when will we arrive in Cyangugu? Mama-Grace, are you not ready to see this lake that is alleged to be more beautiful than the glorious Lake Victoria that our two countries share? Are you not ready to sit together beside the lake and share a nice bowl of *ugali*?'

'I'm ready for a cup of tea,' said Angel, who was dabbing at her hot face with a tissue and longing for the cooling breeze of lakeside air.

The next morning she enjoyed just such a breeze as she ate breakfast with Pius and Dr Binaisa. They were seated on the hotel's veranda, a wide concrete patio extending from the building right to the edge of the river, which it overlooked from the waist-high metal railing next to their table. The opposite bank, just metres from them, towered above both the river and the veranda, a steep incline dressed roughly in wild grass and rock. Between the breakfasters in Rwanda and the Democratic Republic of Congo's bank, a lone fisherman punted his hollowed-out *pirogue* along the river towards the lake's open waters, where the two countries shook hands across a bridge. By unspoken agreement — and in the interests of national pride — the three breakfasters had not raised again the issue of the relative beauty of Lake Kivu and Lake Victoria.

Angel had spent a restless night, rising a number of times to open the window to let in some air and then rising as many times again to close it when she could no longer tolerate the whine of the mosquitoes that were coming in. And, as her wakefulness had continued, her anxiety about the task that she had agreed to perform today had grown. It would have been unnerving enough for anybody, but for Angel it was rendered even more uncomfortable by the fact that it obliged her to dwell on the silence that had come between her and her late daughter.

She felt that she had planted the seeds of that silence herself, sowing a row of them and covering them with soil when she failed to voice her disapproval of her daughter's choice of husband. She had thought that Vinas could do so much better than Winston. Okay, he was an educated man, with a senior post at the college where Vinas was training. But Angel had heard rumours that he made a habit of taking his students as girlfriends. That was the kind of habit that made a man unreliable as a husband. Yet Vinas was in love, and happy, so Angel had said nothing – although Vinas must have felt her mother's disapproval, even if she had not heard it.

Unlike Angel, Pius had considered Winston a good match for Vinas: he was a man of letters, a man capable of discussing intelligently many important topics. Most significantly, he was a man devoted to preparing students for a career in teaching, the very career that Pius himself had followed all those years ago before further studies in Germany had become a possibility for him.

They had married in Arusha for the sake of Winston's widowed mother, whose poor health would not have permitted the journey to Dar es Salaam, and Winston's sister, Queen, had insisted on arranging everything, including the cake.

Closing her eyes with a small shudder, lying awake in the bedroom of the Hôtel du Lac, Angel could still see that cake. She supposed that it had been meant to match the colours of the bride's dress — which Queen had got just right, stitching it for Vinas herself from bright white fabric scattered with a pattern of large blue and purple flowers — but the neighbour who had produced the cake was simply not a professional. The flowers patterned across it had been inexpertly made, and some of the purple ones were a noticeably different shade from the others, indicating that she had not mixed enough of the colour at first and had then been unable to mix exactly the same colour again. That was a common mistake amongst amateurs. Most upsetting of all, the icing on which the inferior blue and purple flowers had been arranged was not the background white of Vinas's dress but the pale yellow of margarine: either the neighbour had not known to use egg-whites, or the price she had charged had not been sufficient to cover the cost of that many eggs. Had Angel's tears, as she had stood before that cake, watered the row of seeds that she had planted?

Okay, perhaps she was exaggerating. Perhaps, as Pius had told her — often — it was normal for a girl to become less close to her parents when she married and had a family of her own. And perhaps it was normal for a girl to communicate less with her parents when she had a career to keep her busy, and when she was ambitious about getting ahead in her career. But perhaps the silence, the distance, between Angel and Vinas had *not* been normal, and perhaps it had been Angel's fault.

That possibility whined at her like the mosquitoes of Lake Kivu.

Pius had had no better a night, turning over and over again in his sleep and, at one point, suddenly sitting bolt upright, his eyes wide and fearful and his pyjamas damp with sweat. Alarmed, Angel had asked him what was wrong, but he was not in fact awake – or at least not awake enough to hear or see his wife – and he had fallen back on to the pillows and resumed his restless shifting.

At the appointed hour that morning, the driver arrived at the hotel with Gasana – both having spent the night with relatives in the town – and they made their way around the potholes of Cyangugu's roads and up to the top of the hill on which the prison squatted. While Pius, Gasana and Dr Binaisa went to their meeting, Angel co-opted the driver – who knew Swahili – to act as her translator. A guard at the prison gates sent someone to locate the prisoner she was looking for.

A great deal of time passed, during which Angel's anxiety mounted further. She was uncertain about how she would feel when she came face to face with someone who stood accused as a *génocidaire* – although, in truth, she was probably looking at thousands of them right now. Large numbers of inmates milled about the crowded courtyard, some being marshalled from the chaos into lines that the guards marched down the hill to perform manual labour somewhere in the town. Their prison uniforms – Angel could not help noticing – were almost the exact shade of powder pink of the icing on Perfect's christening cake.

At last a thin, undernourished young man in pink appeared at the guard's elbow and said something to him in Kinyarwanda.

'The one you are looking for is here, Madame,' said the guard. 'This man has brought the prisoner you want.'

The thin young man pushed forward another prisoner, as undernourished as he was, and with something familiar about the eyes — small and set deep in a face that was hard — although the eyes looked right through and past Angel without acknowledging her presence.

Angel cleared her throat before speaking. 'Are you Hagengimana Bernadette, the mother of Leocadie?'

The woman gave no answer; in fact she appeared not even to register that she had been addressed. The guard said something to her, which she ignored, and then the prisoner who had found her tried speaking to her, but got no response. He said something to the guard, who shook his head and spoke to the driver, who translated for Angel.

'This man says he knows that this woman is Hagengimana Bernadette; he is sure of that because he knew her before. He says that she has not been right since being brought here to this prison. She is here but she is not here.'

Angel felt sure that this was indeed Leocadie's mother, even though she struggled to imagine the face before her breaking into a smile that would light it up in the way that Leocadie's did. The eyes were most definitely empty replicas of the ones set deep in Leocadie's face. Through the driver, she asked the guard if someone might read to her — for Leocadie had told her that her mother was unable to read — the letter that she had brought from her daughter in Kigali.

'I'll read it to her myself, Madame,' said the guard, and he took the envelope from Angel and tore it open. The envelope itself was nothing special — lightweight and white, edged with red and blue bands and bearing the words *par avion* — but the single sheet of lilac-coloured paper that the guard withdrew was thick and expensive, a testament to Leocadie's affection for her mother. Angel knew what the letter said: that Leocadie was well, that she had given birth to a baby boy called Beckham, and that she hoped one day her mother could meet, and hold, this grandchild. A friend had written it exactly as Leocadie had dictated it.

Bernadette betrayed no reaction to her daughter's words as the guard read them out; nor did she show any sign of having heard. The guard folded the letter, re-inserted it into the torn envelope, and tried to persuade the woman to take it. She made no move to do so. Eventually the guard had to take her hand, place the envelope in it and close her fingers around it. The prisoner who had brought her led her away again. She had not walked more than three metres back into the throng of prisoners before the envelope drifted unnoticed to the ground and was trampled into the red earth.

While she waited with the driver for the others to finish their meeting, Angel thought about Leocadie's mother, who had been charged — Leocadie had not specified the exact nature of the charges — but had not yet been tried. Guilty or not, something had driven her away from herself and she had not come back. Perhaps, Angel considered, it was easier — or safer — not to. But what would she tell Leocadie? The truth — that her mother had not listened to her words and had discarded her letter — would not be comfortable. But perhaps Leocadie was not expecting comfortable news of a woman allegedly complicit in mass killings.

Angel tried to think of more cheerful things. It would not do to display her unease to the others; they would press her for details and she did not want to be disloyal to Leocadie by telling them about the encounter. But in the event, they returned to the vehicle in such a buoyant mood that Angel felt they might not have noticed had they found her actually weeping. Their meeting had gone extremely well, and as their minibus weaved its way through the busy streets of Cyangugu and on to the main road back towards Kigali, they joked about whether they could attribute this success to Pius's excellent negotiating skills, Gasana's very fine translation, or Dr Binaisa's passion for human excrement.

They were still joking, revisiting key moments of the meeting, when they caught up with an armed UN convoy that was travelling in the same direction. Two four-wheel drive vehicles followed an open van that had been fitted with two long benches back to back down its middle. On the benches sat six armed soldiers who could watch for trouble on either side of the road.

'Should we follow or overtake?' asked the driver.

'Let's overtake,' said Dr Binaisa. 'I'm sure there's no danger. We came this way yesterday with no soldiers to guard us, and I think we're still alive. There's no reason for a convoy; the UN likes to pay soldiers just for the sake of spending its budget.'

'And besides,' added Gasana, 'if their staff could travel freely about Rwanda without an armed escort then they couldn't justify their daily danger-pay.'

'But we may as well follow for a while,' suggested Pius. 'Personally I don't like guns, but in this case they're for protection, even if there's nothing to be protected from. If we attach ourselves to this convoy, then it's a way to get protection for free.'

'That's true,' Gasana agreed. 'Let us not say no to something for free out of the UN's budget. And apparently there are sometimes rebels in the Nyungwe Forest. We can overtake after we've passed through there.'

It proved to be a good decision − not because the soldiers were necessary, but because they provided plenty of entertainment. The soldier sitting on the left-hand side closest to the tail end of the van was asleep. The occupants of the KIST vehicle got a good view of him every time the lead vehicle climbed a hill, and every time it did so they held their breath, convinced that, this time, the soldier might slide right off the back of the vehicle. As soon as they had cleared the forest area they overtook the convoy.

'That is a beautiful forest,' declared Angel. 'Why did we not see it when we passed through it yesterday?'

'*Eh!* Yesterday our heads were full of death and violence,' said Dr Binaisa. 'Eyes that are focusing on that kind of past cannot look around and see beauty.'

'That is true,' agreed Angel. 'That lady who showed you around that place yesterday, I don't know how she can bear to look at what she sees every day of her life.'

'I think she looks but she does not see,' offered Gasana. 'Otherwise how can she live her life?' He shrugged his shoulders. 'Maybe we're all like that in some way — even me. For example, I know that many of our Catholic priests helped to kill people — *eh*, even the bishop of that area we went to yesterday, the Gikongoro *préfecture*, he's on trial now as a *génocidaire*. But still I'm a Catholic; still I live according to the teachings of the church that helped to kill us.'

'*Eh*, now you are on a subject for Mama-Grace!' declared Pius. 'We will not hear the end of it before we reach Kigali.'

Angel shot her husband a glance, which he did not turn in his seat to catch, but said nothing.

'Tungaraza has told me that your family attends many churches,' said Dr Binaisa. 'But are you not Catholics?'

'We are Catholics,' explained Angel, 'but in Rwanda we're simply Christians. I'm nervous of attending just one church here, of listening to just one priest. Because how can we know what is truly in that priest's heart after so many showed that love and peace were only words in their mouths? So we attend a different church every second week; in between, we still attend our local Catholic church.'

'Are you not afraid that you might make the mistake of attending the service of a cult?' asked Dr Binaisa. 'All you Tungarazas could end up dead like those

Restoration of the Ten Commandments people in my country. That church killed nearly one thousand people in Kampala alone.'

Angel shook her head and smiled. 'I think I would recognize a dangerous cult, Baba-Zahara. If a priest tells me that I must die or that I must kill others, I'll know that he's not speaking on behalf of God.'

'*Eh*, don't be so sure of that!' warned Gasana.

Angel was silent for a while as she contemplated this warning, which happened to come at the very moment that a familiar warmth began to spread up her throat and across her cheeks. Discussing a serious topic at such a time would only double her discomfort; it was time to lighten up the conversation.

'You know what?' she asked her fellow passengers as she plunged her hand inside her blouse to retrieve a tissue from her brassiere. 'I cannot think right now about those whose job is to guard our souls; I'm too busy thinking about those whose job is to guard our bodies. I'm wondering if that soldier is still asleep on the back of that van.'

That induced much laughter; and they were still in high spirits when they arrived back in Kigali late in the afternoon. As had been agreed before they left, the driver dropped Dr Binaisa at the Tungarazas' compound so that he and Angel could discuss the matter of the birthday cake for his daughter Zahara. After a tumultuous welcome from the children, Pius went down into the yard with them and Titi so that Angel could discuss business with her customer in privacy.

When she emerged from the kitchen with their tea,

Dr Binaisa was on his knees on a sheet of *The New Times* that he had spread out on the lounge floor, his forehead resting on a job advertisement for an administrative assistant at the Russian embassy. Angel seated herself quietly and waited until he had finished his prayers.

'Your church requires you to pray a lot,' she said as he sat down opposite her. 'Even very early in the mornings, around five o'clock. From here I can hear your priest calling you to prayers at the mosque near the post office. That's very far for a man's voice to travel.'

'All the faithful must hear the muezzin's call, Mama-Grace. But now! Let us talk about Zahara's birthday cake.'

Angel reached for her photo album. 'What kind of cake do you have in mind?'

Dr Binaisa shrugged his shoulders. 'Just a cake.'

'Just a cake? *Any* cake?'

'Any cake will be fine. Just write Zahara's name on the top.'

Angel looked at Dr Binaisa as he sipped his tea. She took off her glasses and began to polish them with a tissue retrieved from her brassiere.

'Baba-Zahara, a cake with just a child's name on top is a cake ordered by a parent who doesn't know his child, a parent who is unable to imagine. I know that you are not that parent; it is only that you are tired because you've had a long journey. Perhaps I can guide you, because I'm very familiar with this business of choosing cakes. May I ask you some questions?'

Dr Binaisa shrugged his shoulders again. 'Go ahead.'

'Let us start at the beginning. Does Zahara prefer vanilla or chocolate?'

'Oh, she loves chocolate!'

'You see? Already you're showing me how well you know your child. Okay, so the cake itself will be chocolate. Now, what else does she love? Maybe a kind of animal? A special toy? Something that she's seen and often talks about?'

Dr Binaisa thought for a while. 'You know, since she flew on an aeroplane for the first time she's been excited about planes. Whenever there's one flying overhead she runs outside to look at it. And she loves to visit the airport here at Kanombe. She's even put a picture of an aeroplane on her bedroom wall.'

'Do you think an aeroplane is what she loves most?'

'Definitely. I've even said to my wife that our daughter will grow up to be an air hostess.'

Angel had not yet put her glasses back on. She gave them another polish. 'Perhaps your daughter will grow up to be a pilot,' she suggested.

Dr Binaisa laughed and slapped his thigh. 'You're a very funny somebody, Mama-Grace!'

She persevered. 'Or maybe she'll grow up to be an aircraft engineer. After all, her father is an engineer. A father is always very proud when his child follows in his own footsteps. It's a very big compliment.'

Putting her glasses back on, she watched as Dr Binaisa's smile faded on his lips and his eyes darted from left to right and back again as this new idea struggled to find a place in his mind where it could belong.

'Mama-Grace, what does all this talk of aeroplanes have to do with cakes?'

'Everything, Baba-Zahara!' She gave him a big smile. 'Zahara's birthday cake will look like an aeroplane! She'll be so pleased that her father had that idea!'

Dr Binaisa smiled back at Angel. 'Yes, it is a very good idea.'

'Let me show you some other cakes here in my album so that you can have a sense of how it will look. See, here, this child had a toy tipper-truck and he played with it all day long.'

Dr Binaisa examined the photograph. The entire cake was a yellow truck with blue glass windows and fat black tyres. The back of the truck was beginning to tip up, and its cargo of Smarties had started to slide off the back. '*Eh!* Mama-Grace! This is a very fine cake!'

'Thank you, Baba-Zahara.' Angel smiled and patted her hair. 'But I'll make Zahara's aeroplane even finer. And see this one here. This was for a teenage girl. Her mother said that girl was always talking on her cell-phone.'

'*Eh!*' said Dr Binaisa as he admired the cake. It was in the shape of a big cell-phone, dark blue around the sides with a paler blue panel on the top. A square of light grey was the phone's small screen, bearing the words *Happy Birthday Constance* like a text message. Smaller squares of pink bore numbers and letters, just like a real cell-phone. 'Mama-Grace, this looks real! *Eh!* And look at this one, here. It's a microphone — although I don't know that particular news station. But it looks real!'

Angel beamed. 'But wait till you see Zahara's aeroplane. All the children at the party will love it. And many weeks after the party, the parents of those children will still be talking about the cake that Dr Binaisa ordered for his daughter.'

Dr Binaisa smiled as he imagined that.

'Of course, a cake like that takes much time and much work. It is not a cheap cake, Baba-Zahara. But nobody talks for a long time about a cake that was cheap.'

'You're right, of course, Mama-Grace,' agreed Dr Binaisa. 'So let us plan a cake that Kigali will talk about for many, many weeks.'

In the early hours of the following morning, Angel awoke with a start to find Pius sitting up in their bed, his breath catching in his throat. He had had a dream, he told her, in which he found himself back at the school on the top of the hill. All the classroom doors were shut, but he seemed to know exactly which room he was looking for. He went to it and opened the door. Desperately searching amongst the ghostly bodies that lay across the wooden benches inside, he at last found the one he was looking for: a small child dressed in the remnants of a decaying khaki T-shirt edged with orange. He squatted down on the bench next to the child's body and gently turned it over so that he could see the face.

'Angel, it was Joseph. It was our own son!' Pius struggled to get his breath. 'He looked at me — his face was *white*, Angel! — and he said, "They shot me, Baba." I tried to hold him, but he pulled away from me, and he said, "I can't find Vinas." Those were his words, Angel, and they made me panic. I had to find her! I ran from room to room at that school, calling her name, but she wasn't there...' Pius was breathing like someone who had just run all the way to the top of a very steep hill. 'Vinas wasn't there.'

'Pius, you need to breathe,' said Angel. Taking his right hand, she placed its palm flat against the area between her throat and her breasts, holding it there with her left hand as she flattened her right palm on his chest. 'Breathe with me.'

It was the way they had calmed each other throughout their marriage, the one guiding the other until their breaths were equally deep and slow, in and out in such unison that they lost track of which of them was setting the pace.

At last he was able to speak again. 'She wasn't there,' he repeated, sadly now, exhausted.

They settled back down in the bed, and Angel held him tightly, whispering soothing words into his ear. With Pius's worry of Vinas being lost — of Joseph and Vinas not being in the same place — now running from room to room in her own mind, she had no expectation of sleep. But his breathing took her with him as he slipped into sleep in her arms, and she found him still there when the muezzin's call from the mosque near the post office woke her before dawn.

# 5. An Independence

DESCENDING THE STEPS THAT LED DOWN TO the Chinese shop on Rue Karisimbi in central Kigali, Dr Rejoice Lilimani successfully deflected both a woman intent on selling her some baskets hand-woven from banana-fibre, and a man who was urging her to buy one of his small stone carvings of mountain gorillas. She was on the point of entering the shop's busy and shadowy interior, crammed with shelves of kitchen and household goods, when somebody called her name.

She turned and looked back up towards the road from which the steps descended. Crowds of Saturday-morning shoppers weaved their way past the cars that were parked on the unsurfaced verge, while behind them packed minibus taxis raced along the road in the direction of the post office, on their way to the central minibus station on Rue Mont Kabuye.

Seeing no one who was paying her the slightest bit of

attention – apart from the man with the stone gorillas, who was beginning to descend the steps towards her in the belief that she had changed her mind about making a purchase – the doctor turned and entered the shop.

She heard her name again: 'Dr Rejoice!'

She stepped out of the shop and looked up the steps again, and as she did so the man with the stone gorillas paused in his ascent and looked back down at her hopefully.

'Who is calling Dr Rejoice?' she asked, a look of puzzlement furrowing her brow.

'It's me,' said a voice. 'Here I am.'

The doctor became aware of a movement to her left, where scores of brightly coloured plastic goods – enormous bowls, basins, dustbins and wash-baskets – lined the landing at the bottom of the steps outside the doorway into the shop. Above a purple dustbin a hand waved a piece of white tissue. Dr Rejoice took a step forward and peered around the dustbin into the patch of shade in which Angel sat on a tiny wooden stool.

'My dear! Hello! What are you doing sitting there?'

'Hello, Dr Rejoice.' Angel smiled as she dabbed at her face with the tissue that had attracted the doctor's attention. 'You didn't see me!'

'How was I to guess that you were sitting behind a purple plastic dustbin?' laughed Dr Rejoice. 'Are you okay, my dear?'

'Oh, I'm fine, really. I was inside the shop when I began to feel hot like someone had thrown a blanket over my head, so I had to come outside. They brought me a stool to sit here in the shade till I feel better.'

'Then let me ask them to bring a stool for me, too. I'll sit with you a few minutes.' Dr Rejoice went into the shop, returning moments later with a man carrying a plastic chair. He put it down next to Angel.

'*Murakoze cyane!*' Dr Rejoice thanked him in Kinyarwanda as she sat down. Then she addressed Angel. 'Now tell me, my dear. Are you simply flashing, or are you ill?'

'Oh, I'm fine, really, Dr Rejoice. I'm just flashing. But I'm happy to see you, because I want to thank you. You sent me a new customer.'

'Oh, yes, and you made a delicious cake for her! I was at the party for her brother Emmanuel.'

'Odile is such a nice girl,' said Angel. 'I'm very happy that I met her because she's going to teach my girls about the virus.'

'She'll do an excellent job,' Dr Rejoice assured her.

'She's encouraged me to learn about it too,' said Angel. 'I'll go and spend some time at that place where she works, and I'll speak to the people who go there. My son would have been like them, Dr Rejoice. He was positive, but then he got shot. I never warned him about it when he was a child, I didn't even know about it then. None of us did. It was only later, as others around us began to get sick and die, that we learned what it was and what to call it. So when Joseph brought his children to us in Dar from their home in Mwanza, and he told us that AIDS had come to his house, then I knew that we were going to lose him. It sliced through my heart like a machete, Dr Rejoice. I felt somehow that I had failed him as a mother because I hadn't warned him.'

'*Eh*, my dear!'

'Now my heart will stop beating if I fail my grand-children too. As a grandmother, it's my job to be wise. But how can I be wise if I don't educate myself about this disease that's infecting people in every country on our continent?'

'You are very wise to think that way, my dear. Next time you're at the clinic I'll give you some information to take home to read.'

'Thank you, Dr Rejoice. You know, I'm not even going to wait for next time when one of the children is sick. I'll come to the clinic to fetch that information on Monday.'

'I'll leave it with the nurse at reception in case I'm busy when you come. You know how crazy it is there! I hope we can get another doctor soon; it's too much to expect just one doctor to treat all the students *and* all the staff *and* all their dependants. Now, what did you come here to buy, my dear? I've come for an extra blanket because some members of my family are coming to visit from Nairobi. I don't want you to go inside and feel again like someone has thrown a blanket over your head. Would you like me to shop for you?'

Angel laughed. 'Thank you, Dr Rejoice, but I'm fine now, really. I'll come in with you. I need to buy another mixing bowl for my cakes, because my orders are increasing.' Angel looked at her watch and started to get up from the tiny stool, using the arm of Dr Rejoice's plastic chair for leverage. 'My husband has gone to the market for our weekly groceries. He always manages to get a better price than I do. He says I'm unable to concentrate only on the price of the sweet potatoes that I want because I look at the seller and I think about the work that she has done to clear the land and to plant the seeds and to harvest the sweet potatoes, and I know that she has children to feed. My husband says that as soon as you look at the seller, the seller is going to get more from you. He says that you must ignore the seller and see only what she is selling.'

'He sounds like an economist,' said Dr Rejoice with a smile. 'Are you sure he doesn't work for the World Bank?'

Angel laughed. '*Eh!* If he worked there he wouldn't need to negotiate a fair price; he'd have money to waste. But let's go in now. I must be waiting for him outside the German butchery when he's finished at the market.'

In the afternoon, Angel looked forward to some peace and solitude. Titi had already taken the boys to play with their friends who lived down the road, and the girls were busy dressing up for Zahara's birthday party. Pius had gone to his office to send some emails, but he would be back shortly to take the girls – and Zahara's aeroplane cake – to the party. From there he would go straight to a colleague's house to watch football on TV.

Angel had borrowed a Nigerian video from the wife of one of Pius's colleagues. Such videos were generally unsuitable for children, and she had been warned that this one was particularly full of witchcraft, adultery, betrayal and vengeance. An afternoon alone in the apartment with a good film was exactly what she needed.

'Are you ready, girls?' she called. 'Baba will be here very soon and you know he doesn't like to wait.'

The girls came out of the bedroom looking so pretty in their party dresses that tears began to prick the back of Angel's eyes. Grace was tall with long thin arms and legs that seemed to have little more than bone in them. Her skinny neck seemed barely able to support her head, yet she was fit and strong. Neat cornrows controlled her long hair, ending today in pale blue ribbons that matched her blue and white dress. Angel noticed that there was an even greater distance between the hem of her dress and the lace tops of her white socks than the last time she had worn the outfit. Was this child ever going to stop growing?

Though just a year younger, Faith was a good deal shorter and much rounder. She liked to keep her hair short, and this could make her cheeks appear rather chubby. While Grace looked like a girl on the verge of blossoming into a beautiful young woman, Faith still looked very much like a child. Her lilac and pink party dress stretched tight across her belly.

Physically, the two girls could never be mistaken for sisters. But even though they had barely known each other until they had suddenly found themselves part of the same household a year ago, they had become closer friends than many sisters that Angel knew. In fact, all the children got on well with one another – which was rather a relief, as it would have been very awkward if there had been problems between the two sets of siblings. Benedict was a bit of a worry, though: he was still struggling to find his niche in his new family.

He was closer in age to the girls than he was to the younger two boys, and while he found much of his brothers' play somewhat childish, he did not share his sisters' interests either. This made him a rather lonely child, and Angel suspected that his frequent bouts of illness were at least in part a way of calling some attention to himself. Not that he pretended to be ill (Angel was sure of this, and Dr Rejoice always took his symptoms seriously), but perhaps he was simply more susceptible to germs because he did not feel emotionally strong.

'I wish Safiya could come with us to Zahara's party,' said Faith. 'I wish she could see Zahara's lovely cake.'

'She'll see the photo of the cake in Mama's photo album later on,' said Grace. 'And maybe Mama-Zahara will take photos at the party. Safiya can see those too.'

'And maybe Safiya is right now taking photos of Kibuye to show you,' suggested Angel, who was herself looking forward to seeing photos of the town on the eastern shores of Lake Kivu: perhaps the lake was less beautiful there than it was at Cyangugu. It was a popular place to go for weekends – as Safiya and her family had done this weekend – only about two hours' drive almost directly west from Kigali. On very good roads, Vincenzo had said.

Pius arrived back from his office, bringing with him Dr Binaisa who had escaped from home to the campus, as the busyness and excitement of party preparations had made it difficult for him to concentrate on his students' essays. Pius had found him there a few hours later, and it made sense to bring him to the apartment to collect the cake and then to deliver him to his own home along with the girls.

When he saw the cake waiting on Angel's work table, Dr Binaisa let out a low whistle. Appearing to float above the deep blue sky with white clouds that decorated the cake-board was a magnificent grey aeroplane with wings and tail fins. A pale blue window across the front indicated the cockpit, while both sides of the fuselage were lined with oval passenger-windows in the same pale blue. Across the centre of each wing ran a diagonal band bearing narrow stripes of black, yellow and red — the colours of the Ugandan flag — and on either side of the vertical tail fin, written with the red Gateau Graffito pen, were the words *Air Zahara*. Two rows of candles, five in each row, fanned out from behind the tail within a stream of white icing smoke.

'When you light the candles it will look like the plane's engines are firing,' explained Angel.

For a moment — but only for a moment — Dr Binaisa was lost for words.

'This is a very fine cake, Mama-Grace,' he managed. 'A very fine cake indeed. You know, the day after I placed the order for this cake I began to feel uncomfortable about the price. I told myself it was a lot of money to pay for a cake for a child who is only ten. A girl. I didn't discuss the price with my wife, of course, because financial matters are not a woman's concern. And I didn't want to ask anyone else what they thought about the price, because I didn't want to appear foolish for having agreed to such a high price. But now that I'm looking at the cake, I'm thinking that Mama-Grace has surely charged me too little for all this work.'

'If just one person comes to me to order a cake because they like this one that Dr Binaisa ordered for his child, then I will not think that I charged too little,' replied Angel.

'I'll make sure that many come to you, Mama-Grace,' assured Dr Binaisa.

'I'm glad you're happy, Baba-Zahara. I think this is a cake that will be talked about for many weeks.'

'No, Mama-Grace, you are wrong. It is a cake that will be talked about for many *months*. But I'm worried that Zahara will love it too much. She won't want to cut it and eat it.'

Angel laughed. 'Baba-Zahara must tell her that it's a chocolate cake. Eating it will be the best part.'

A few minutes later, after she had seen the cake safely into the red Microbus and waved goodbye to everyone, Angel put the Nigerian video into the video machine and settled into a chair with her feet up on the coffee table. She was about to press play on the VCR's remote control when somebody knocked on the door.

'*Karibu!*' she called, taking her feet off the table.

But nobody came in. Instead, they knocked again.

'*Karibu!*' she repeated, more loudly this time. But the person on the other side of the door was either deaf or unable to understand plain Swahili. Angel pushed herself up out of the chair and went to open the door. She was hoping that it would be just a passing beggar or someone intent on trying to sell her something — although it would be unusual for such a person to get past Modeste and Gaspard. Perhaps it was one of those

Congolese men who were always trying to sell wooden masks and statues to the *Wazungu* in the compound. The Egyptian bought things from them quite often, so perhaps Modeste had let one of them in to go up to his apartment; but Angel had never encouraged them herself, so there was really no reason for one of them to be knocking on her door, disturbing her quiet Saturday afternoon. In any case, she hoped it was somebody who was going to go away quickly.

She opened the door to find a woman standing there, someone with whom she had exchanged greetings often, but who had never before knocked on her door.

'Hello, Angel,' said Jenna, the CIA's wife. 'I hope I'm not disturbing you. I saw you saying goodbye to your family outside, so I thought you'd be alone and it might be a good time to call.'

'You're not disturbing me,' lied Angel. 'You're welcome, Jenna. Please come in.' She led her guest to the sofa and indicated that she should sit down.

'Thank you,' said Jenna, perching on the edge of the sofa and clasping her hands together in her lap.

Angel looked at her guest. She was an attractive young woman with short dark hair and big green eyes. Her smart, cream-coloured trousers and long-sleeved white blouse indicated that this woman knew how to dress respectfully in a country where women were modest. Her only piece of jewellery was a delicate gold cross that hung from a thin chain around her neck.

'These apartments all look the same,' she said to Angel, her eyes darting around the room. 'We all have the same furniture and the same curtains.'

'Yes,' agreed Angel. 'Sometimes when I'm with Amina, after a while I find myself thinking that it's time for her to leave so that I can go into the kitchen and start baking. But then I realize that it's me who must leave because we're in Amina's apartment, not mine.'

Jenna laughed. 'I've made that same mistake myself. Sitting on the couch at Ken's or Linda's I could just as well be sitting on the couch in my own apartment.'

Angel experienced a sudden feeling of discomfort at the mention of Linda, whom Bosco had seen kissing Jenna's husband. She must change the subject at once. 'I'm happy that you can feel at home in my apartment!' she declared, smiling warmly. 'Let me make some tea for us to drink.'

'Oh, no, Angel, I don't want to disturb you for very long. I only came to order a cake.'

'But ordering a cake is something that takes time and care,' countered Angel. 'It's not a matter to rush. And when you're bringing me business, then you're not disturbing me at all. Here, let me give you my photo album to look at while I make tea. You can see pictures here of other cakes that I've made.'

'Thank you. But do you have coffee instead? We're not big on tea in the States.'

'No problem. My husband prefers coffee sometimes. I'll make you some coffee that comes from my home town of Bukoba, on the western shores of Lake Victoria. It's very good.'

When Angel returned to the lounge with a mug of coffee, another of sweet and spicy tea, and a plate of cupcakes, Jenna pointed to a few of the photos in the album. 'I've seen these cakes,' she said. 'I've eaten them, too. At Ken's place.'

'Ken is one of my best customers,' said Angel. 'I've almost lost count of the number of cakes I've made for his dinner parties. Do you want to order a cake for a dinner party of your own?'

'Oh, no, I'm not a good cook. I couldn't possibly give a dinner party. If Rob wants to invite people, then we take them out for dinner. No, I'm actually here to order a cake on behalf of the American community.'

'*Eh*, that's an important job, to speak on behalf of the American community.'

Jenna laughed. 'Yes, I suppose it is important. I hadn't thought of it like that!'

'And why does the American community want a cake?'

'It's for our Independence Day celebrations. We want a big cake decorated to look like the American flag.'

'*Eh*, that's a good flag!' declared Angel. 'It has red and blue and white, and there are stripes and stars. It's not boring like the Japanese flag. Did you see that photo? I made that cake for Ken.'

Jenna found the right page in Angel's photo album. 'Oh, I was wondering about that cake. It looked different from all the others. Now I see it's the Japanese flag. This one here is nice, though.'

Angel looked at the photo that Jenna was indicating. 'That's the flag of South Africa. It's a very fine flag; it has six colours. *Six!* That cake was for someone who works at King Faycal. There used to be many South Africans working at that hospital, but most of them have left now. They say there was some embezzling or something like that. You know, one thing I enjoy about Kigali is that you can meet people from all over the world here.'

'I guess so,' agreed Jenna. Then she hesitated for a few moments before adding, 'But it's not like that for everyone.'

Angel was confused. 'What do you mean?'

'Well, I'm sure people from everywhere come and order cakes from you, and your husband probably has colleagues from everywhere, and I guess anyone who has a job here is able to meet people from everywhere. But I don't have a job.'

'What kind of job are you looking for?'

Jenna gave a small, strained laugh. 'Oh, I can't take a job. Rob doesn't like me to leave the compound without him. It's not safe.'

Angel had been about to swallow a large sip of tea. She fought the shocked urge to spray the tea out of her mouth and, swallowing it badly, she began to cough. Jenna tutted with concern. Eventually Angel managed to calm the coughing with a few small sips of tea, but by then her face had grown very hot and her glasses needed a polish.

'Are you okay, Angel? Shall I bring you some water?'

'I'm fine, really.' Angel dabbed at her face with a tissue before rubbing her glasses with the edge of her *kanga*. 'It's only that I was surprised when you said it's not safe here. Personally, I've found it very safe.'

'Well, Rob has told me not to go out without him,' shrugged Jenna.

'And when you go out *with* your husband, where is it that you go? How is it that you're not meeting people from everywhere in those places that you go?'

'Oh, we go to the American Club every Friday night. That's when all the people from the States get together. Others are welcome, of course, but usually there are just a handful of people from other places – England or Canada, mostly. And often we go for dinner or parties at the homes of other Americans, or we take them out for a meal. And of course there are Ken's parties here in the compound.'

'And what is it that keeps you busy when you're not out with your husband?' asked Angel.

'Oh, I read a lot,' said Jenna. 'My family sends me books and magazines from home. And I have a laptop, so I spend hours emailing friends and family back home. And I'm on the committee of wives who organize social events for the American community. We meet in my apartment over coffee once a fortnight.'

'You know, Jenna, I've always found that tea and cake make a meeting run more smoothly, and I'm sure that for Americans coffee and cake can work just as well. You can order a plate of cupcakes like these from me any time. I can even make the cupcakes taste of coffee, or I can make the icing taste of coffee.'

Jenna laughed. 'I'll remember that, Angel.'

Angel continued to rub gently at her glasses with the edge of her *kanga*. They were not yet clean. 'Tell me, Jenna, do you like to stay in your apartment so much?

Do you never wish that you could just go out by yourself?'

Jenna breathed in deeply and gave a long sigh. 'Sometimes. Sometimes I feel like I'm going to go mad with boredom. Sometimes I wonder what on earth I'm doing here. But I knew when I married Rob that his work would take him all over the world. We talked about it, and he made it clear that he wanted me to travel with him, he didn't want a wife who was going to insist on staying at home in the States. He told me it wouldn't be easy for me. He was married twice before, you see, he's quite a bit older than me, so he knows about life and about the world, and he knows what to expect. But I'm just a small-town girl. I lived at home with my mom and dad the whole time I went to college, and then I married Rob, and this is the first time I've ever been out of the States. So he did warn me it wouldn't be easy. I can't complain. And he would never let me do anything that would put me in any danger, because he really loves me. So if he says it's not safe for me to go out, then I have to respect that. He... he knows a lot of stuff.'

Angel thought that it was only to be expected that the CIA knew a lot of stuff, because knowing a lot of stuff was the CIA's job. But she also thought that he might be making up a lot of stuff to make his wife believe that it was not safe to leave the compound. That way he could be certain that she was never going to be in the car park of the Umubano Hotel when he was there kissing Linda.

'Okay,' said Angel, 'let's imagine just for a moment that your husband didn't bring you here to Kigali.

Instead, you went with him to another place, any other place, and he said that place was safe and you could get a job there. What job would you look for?'

'Oh, I don't know.' Jenna thought for a while. 'At college I did a degree in modern languages: French and Spanish. But I married Rob as soon as I graduated, so I've never worked — except for teaching kids at Sunday school.'

'So maybe you'd like to teach languages at a school?' suggested Angel.

'Oh, no, I don't think so. I know this'll sound crazy, but to be honest, I don't like kids so much. Before we got married, Rob told me that having kids just wasn't going to work for him... in his line of work... I mean, with all the travelling... and that was a relief to me, because I don't want kids myself. But I think I could be a good teacher to adults. I thought of offering to teach French to some of the American wives here, but Rob said it wasn't a good idea. He said if I became their teacher, then I couldn't be their friend. He said they'd have all kinds of expectations of me as a teacher that I might not be able to meet because I've never taught before, and then they'd feel awkward around me and it would make things difficult for me socially. He said his second wife tried something like that and it ended in disaster for her. He said he doesn't want me to make the same mistake.'

Still not sure that her glasses were properly clean, Angel continued to worry at them with the corner of her *kanga*. 'And what is it that *you* say, Jenna?' she asked with a smile. 'You've told me many things that your husband has said, but he's not the one who's sitting here with me this afternoon. You told me that you're here on behalf of the American community, but you didn't tell me that you're here on behalf of your husband.'

'I'm sorry?'

'Well, imagine that I was sitting here telling you that my husband says what-what-what, my husband thinks what-what-what, my husband knows what-what-what. Then you're sitting there telling me *your* husband's what-what-what. Then our husbands may as well be sitting here talking together instead of us. Really, we would just be mouths to speak our husbands' words.'

Jenna looked surprised and did not speak for a while. Then she said, 'I guess I do spend a lot of time repeating what Rob says. I never noticed that before.'

Angel put her glasses back on. 'That's why I'm asking you about Jenna, because it's Jenna who is visiting me now, not her husband. What is it that *Jenna* says? What is it that is in Jenna's mind? What is it that is in Jenna's heart?'

Jenna opened her mouth to speak but no words came out. Her eyes began to well with tears and to become as red as Prosper's after too much Primus. Angel was alarmed: making a customer cry could surely not be a good thing; she must try to fix her mistake at once.

'*Eh*, Jenna, I didn't mean to upset you, I'm very sorry. Let me make you another cup of coffee and we can talk about other things. You can tell me all about the independence party that the American community will have.'

Jenna dabbed at her eyes with a tissue that she had retrieved from the pocket of her smart cream trousers. 'I'm sorry, Angel. It's not your fault that I'm crying, really it's not. It's... well, it's Rob. You asked me what's in my mind and my heart, and... and I know I talk about him all the time, but... but...' She sniffed loudly and then blew her nose. Then she took a deep breath. 'Angel, I suspect... I suspect that my husband...'

Jenna did not finish her sentence, but Angel could have finished it for her: *I suspect that my husband is having an affair.* This was a suspicion that needed some very sweet tea. 'Jenna, I am going to let you sit here and calm down while I make tea for both of us. I know that you prefer coffee, but really, when someone is upset it is only tea that can help. When someone is unhappy, tea is like a mother's embrace.'

Angel went into the kitchen and set about boiling some milk, leaving Jenna on the sofa to blow her nose and to take deep breaths. She was visibly calmer when Angel returned with their mugs of tea.

Jenna took a sip. 'Hey, this is good. Spicy.'

'It's how we make our tea back home.'

A short silence followed, during which Jenna savoured the tea and prepared herself to speak, and Angel nibbled at a cupcake and prepared herself to register surprise at what Jenna was about to reveal.

'Can I speak to you in confidence, Angel?'

'Jenna, you are my customer and I am a professional somebody. I do not spread my customers' stories. Tell me what is in your heart.'

'Thanks, Angel. It's a real relief to have someone to

talk to about this. I don't even know if what I suspect is true or if I'm just imagining it, and I know that if I voiced my suspicion to anyone in the American community, the news would spread like wildfire. God knows what would happen...'

Angel thought of the gun that Bosco was sure Rob had. 'It's always wise to confide in the right person,' she said.

'Yes.'

'So what is it that you suspect, Jenna?' Angel put down her mug of tea so that she would not spill any when she pretended to be surprised.

Jenna sighed heavily. 'I suspect that my husband has been hiding something from me, Angel. I think he's been lying to me about where he's been and what he's been doing. And you know, he always told me that he left both his previous wives because he caught them having affairs, but now I'm sure *they* were the ones who left *him*. I bet they both found out for sure what I suspect now.'

Angel wanted the surprise to come, and to be over. A pain was beginning to knock quietly on the door of her head, asking to be let in. She wanted her tea. 'And what is it that you suspect?'

'Do you swear not to tell anyone?'

'I swear.'

'Oh God, Angel, I suspect... I suspect that my husband is working for the CIA.'

Angel did not need to pretend. Surprise shot through her body like a bolt of lightning, causing her to jump in her chair and knock the coffee table with her knees so that tea slopped out of both mugs and the cupcakes shook violently on their plate. *'Eh!'* she cried, getting up and rushing into the kitchen for a cloth, and *'Eh!'* again as she mopped up the spilt tea. Then she sat down again and took a big swallow of tea before she could look Jenna squarely in the face. 'The CIA?'

'Yeah. I know it sounds crazy, and I keep trying to convince myself that I must be wrong, but I've overheard bits of phone-calls and I've seen Rob locking documents in his briefcase, and I've often felt one hundred per cent sure that he's lying to me when I've asked him where he's been. His colleagues have let slip at socials that he's been one place when he's told me that he's been another place. Like he's had meetings at night that he told me were with a particular colleague, but then I hear from that colleague's wife that she and her husband were at someone's house for dinner that night. And he won't ever discuss his work with me, he won't ever tell me about his day. He's so secretive.'

Was it really possible that Jenna only suspected what everybody else knew? Was she really so naïve that she did not think that all these signs could be telling her that her husband was having an affair? Angel took her glasses off and looked at them. Did they really need cleaning? She put them back on again. This was a very awkward situation indeed.

*'Eh,* Jenna, I don't know what to say.'

'Yeah, it's a shock, isn't it?'

*'Eh,* I am truly shocked.' Angel reached for another cupcake and slowly peeled away its paper casing. She

thought carefully before she spoke. 'You know, when I was at school in Bukoba, I had a teacher who told us that when you see smoke you can always be sure that it is coming from a fire.'

'You mean there's no smoke without fire?'

'That's what our teacher told us. But, you know, it wasn't the truth. When I grew up, I found that there is something called dry ice. Do you know it?'

'Sure. It keeps ice cream cold out of the fridge.'

'Do you know that when you put water on dry ice it makes smoke?' Jenna nodded. 'So it's possible to see smoke and to think that there is a fire, but really the smoke is from dry ice that has got wet.'

Jenna thought for a moment. 'Are you saying that I might have jumped to the wrong conclusion about Rob?'

Was Angel saying that? No. Rob *did* work for the CIA; everybody knew it. That was not a wrong conclusion. But at the same time, Jenna had not reached the right conclusion, the conclusion that her husband was having an affair.

'Really, Jenna, I'm not sure what I'm saying. What you have said to me has come as a shock, and it has certainly confused me.' Angel took a bite of cupcake and chewed and swallowed it without even tasting it. 'Maybe what I'm saying is simply that you must think very carefully about what you've seen and heard, and what it might mean.'

'I've done nothing *but* think about it for weeks. It's not like I have much else to do with my time.'

'It must be very difficult. But I see from the cross

around your neck that you're a Christian. Perhaps if you pray for guidance at church tomorrow…'

'Oh, I don't go to church here. Rob isn't a church-goer and he says it's not safe for me to go without him. And if it's true that he's with the CIA, he must surely know how unsafe Kigali really is. That's why he doesn't let me do what other husbands let their wives do. The other husbands don't know what he knows.'

Really, this was becoming too complicated. The pain was inside Angel's head now, walking around in heavy boots. It was time to move away from all of this and head back towards the safer business of ordering the cake.

'You know, Jenna, I cannot give you God's guidance, but I can give you my own — and I think that's why you've spoken to me about this. Number one, you need to find out the truth about your husband. Number two, you need to decide what to do with the truth that you find. Those are both things that are between you and your husband. But there is also a number three, and I think I can help you with number three. Number three, you must find a way to keep yourself busy at home to stop this thing eating at your mind like a plague of locusts. You have said that you want to teach adults, and your husband has said that you cannot go out of the compound and you cannot teach the American wives. To me, the answer is clear: you must teach Rwandan women, and you must teach them at home in your apartment.'

Jenna looked at Angel with big eyes. In the silence that followed, Angel finished her tea and swallowed the last bite of her cupcake. When she had finished, Jenna was still looking at her.

'What on earth would I teach them?'

'How to read.'

'I don't know how to teach that.'

'But you know how to read yourself. It's a skill, just like making a cake. I can teach somebody how to make a cake, even though nobody has taught me how to teach somebody how to make a cake. And you can look on the internet for advice on what to do. I've heard that that is a place where you can find any information on any topic.'

'But where would I get my students from?'

'I'll find them for you,' said Angel. 'Leocadie at the shop can read very little, mostly numbers for prices. And Eugenia who works for the Egyptian struggles to read. That's two students already. I won't have to go far to find a small class for you, maybe just four or five. They'll all be women that I know, not strangers. You'll tell me when you're ready to start teaching, and I'll bring the students to you.'

'I... I don't think Rob would like it...'

'How will he even know that there's something for him to like or not? You can teach for maybe an hour or so each day when he's at work. He won't even know.'

'But if I don't tell him what I'm doing, that would be dishonest...'

'Jenna, do you really believe that honesty is so important to your husband?'

Angel watched Jenna as she looked distressed and reached for her tea. She took a sip and swallowed it.

Then she looked at Angel, and a smile began to play on her lips, stretching wider and wider until she was laughing out loud. Angel laughed with her. Even she had to admit that she had had a very good idea indeed.

'Angel, you're a genius!'

'*Eh*, thank you, Jenna. I'm not a genius, but I *am* very, very good at making cakes. So let's discuss the independence cake that brought you to me this afternoon.'

After Jenna had gone and Angel had cleared the tea things off the coffee table, she removed the Nigerian video from the VCR and hid it away on top of the wardrobe in her bedroom where the children could not find it and watch it by mistake; there would be no time for her to watch it now before her family started arriving home. And before they all came in with their clatter and their noise and their stories of the afternoon, she must climb the stairs to the top floor of the building and get a tablet from Sophie to take away the pain that had now moved into her head with its boxes and was beginning to hammer nails into the walls for its pictures.

But Sophie and Catherine were both out and nobody answered her knock. Ken had helped her out with Tylenol before, but on a Saturday afternoon he was sure to be playing tennis at the Umubano Hotel. One flight down from Sophie and Catherine's apartment was Linda's, but Angel was not going to knock on Linda's door because who knew what might be going on behind it? What if she saw Jenna's husband in there with Linda? That would be very awkward. Across the landing from Linda's flat was Jenna's. Well, it was Jenna who had invited the pain into her head, so perhaps Jenna owed her a painkiller. She knocked on the door.

The CIA opened it.

Angel opened her mouth but no sound came out.

'Oh, hi, Angel. You okay?'

She cleared her throat and told herself to behave normally. 'Hello, Rob, I'm sorry to disturb you, I was just wondering if you could give me something for my headache. Sophie usually helps me, but she's out.'

'Sure, come on in. Jenna's just been telling me about visiting you this afternoon. I hope she didn't give you the headache!'

'No, no,' assured Angel, walking into the apartment past Rob and seeing a slightly anxious-looking Jenna. 'Actually, I think it was your flag that gave me the headache. We had to count all the stripes and all the stars in the picture in the children's atlas to be sure that I don't make a mistake with the cake. Do you know how difficult it is to count stripes? Your eyes tell you one number, meanwhile your head tells you a different number.'

Rob laughed. 'Well, I think we owe you a painkiller. Honey, go and see what we've got in the bathroom. Angel, sit down, take a load off.'

'No thank you, Rob, I can't stay. The children will be home very soon.'

'Hey, you know your cakes are really great. We've had them at Ken's.'

'Thank you, I'm glad you like them. Ken is one of my very best customers.'

Angel noticed that Rob's hair was damp and he

smelled of soap. Kigali was not a hot place like Dar es Salaam, where you sweated a lot and had to shower in the afternoon; the altitude here was too high for that. Of course, Angel sweated a lot herself occasionally — but Rob was definitely not having to deal with the same problem. She did not want to think about why he might have needed to shower at the end of a Saturday afternoon that he had not spent with his wife.

Jenna came back from the bathroom rattling a small plastic container of tablets. 'There are only a few left in here, so you may as well take the lot with you. Then you'll have something to take next time you get a headache. We've got plenty more.'

'Oh no, Jenna, thank you, but Pius and I don't keep tablets at home. It's too dangerous... for the children. You know how children can think a tablet is a sweet. Just give me one to take now.'

'You're very wise,' said Jenna. 'Tell you what, I'll keep them here for you and you can come and get one any time you need to. I'm here every day.'

'Thank you very much. I'll remember that. Thank you, Rob, I'm sorry I disturbed you.'

'*Hakuna matata*, as you people say. No problem.' Rob put his arm around Angel's shoulder as he led her to the door. The intimate gesture surprised and shocked her. She barely knew this man; how could he insult his wife by embracing another woman while his wife was standing there watching? Okay, he was an American; Oprah was an American, and she embraced people all the time on her show. But surely in his CIA training he had learned what was acceptable behaviour in other countries and cultures? He was so close to Angel that she could smell the dampness in his hair. The intimacy made her feel as though a fat snake was slithering slowly over her bare feet and she had to remain absolutely still even though her instinct was to scream and run. With nowhere else to go, panic and revulsion gathered in her stomach, mixed like bicarbonate of soda and water, and threatened to bubble all the way up her throat, bringing with them sweet tea and cupcakes. She had to fight this man, even if only in a small way.

Breaking away from his encircling arm she said, 'Oh, I almost forgot. Rob, I know that you're not a church-goer yourself, but my family would very much like to invite Jenna to worship with us one Sunday. Just up the road here at St Michael, near the American embassy. It's a very safe area, and a beautiful service, in English. I was wondering, would it be okay for her to join us one Sunday morning to celebrate our Lord God?'

Rob looked reluctant. Angel persevered.

'Of course, I'm probably asking too much of you. I'm sure that you work very hard during the week, and at weekends you simply want to spend time with your wife. I'm sure you wouldn't like to be without her for some two hours on a Sunday morning, left alone and looking for some way to fill that time.'

Rob's face lit up as if he had just had a very good idea. 'I'm sure I could manage, Angel. Of course Jenna can join you any time she wants. You'd like that, wouldn't you, honey?'

'I'd love it,' said Jenna. 'Thank you, Angel. Thank you.'

As she went down the stairs, Angel carried with her the uncomfortable knowledge that she both deserved and did not deserve Jenna's thanks.

# 6. A Homecoming

EVERYONE AT *LA COIFFURE FORMIDABLE!*, JUST a short walk from the compound where the Tungarazas lived, was deeply impressed by the invitation card. It had been passed around from hairdressers to clients and back again, and was now in the hands of Noëlla, who took care of Angel's hair for a discount in gratitude for the good price that Angel had given her on her wedding cake. Noëlla ran the tips of her long, delicate fingers over the Tanzanian coat of arms, exploring its ridges and dents.

'In English that's called embossed,' said Angel, rather more loudly than was necessary over the hum of the hairdryer under which she sat with her hair in green plastic rollers. 'That picture is the emblem of my country. Do you see there, in the middle of the shield, there's a small picture of our flag? And do you see that the shield is standing on top of our famous mountain, Mount Kilimanjaro? There's a man and a woman holding that shield there on top of the mountain. That's because in my country women are supposed to be equal with men. And do you see there it is written *Uhuru na Umoja*, freedom and unity? That's my country's motto. It means that we're all one people, united and free and equal.'

'*Eh!*' declared Noëlla, 'You have a very fine country.' Giving the invitation back to Angel, she switched off the dryer and lifted it away from her client's head.

'We're trying to be like that here,' said the young woman seated next to Angel who was having long braids woven into her hair by Agathe. 'We're striving to be united and equal. We are all Rwandans now.'

'Exactly,' agreed Noëlla, unwinding the rollers from Angel's hair. 'It doesn't matter if in the past some of us thought we were this and some of us thought we were that. There is no more this or that now. Now we are all *Banyarwanda*. Rwandans.'

'That is a very fine thing to be,' said Angel, who was always heartened by such talk of unity. But she had noticed that this was usually the talk of groups; it was possible for the talk of an individual away from a group to be quite different. She was grateful when the woman seated on the other side of her, whose hair Claudine was relaxing, changed the subject.

'So tell us, Madame, because we are all anxious to hear. What is it that you will wear to this important party at your embassy this evening?'

'Yes, and who has made it for you?' added Noëlla.

Angel laughed. 'I'm sure you're expecting me to complain that Youssou has made a dress that's too tight for me!' Angel had once re-enacted for the three hairdressers an argument that she had had with Youssou about his tape measure being dishonest. Noëlla and Claudine had laughed until tears had rolled down their cheeks, and Agathe — who spoke no Swahili — had joined in when Claudine had translated for her.

'*Eh!*' said the woman being relaxed. 'I've heard about this Youssou, although I've never been to him. But don't think that he's the only tailor in Kigali who makes clothes that are too tight; they all do it. It's because they want to accuse you of gaining weight between when they measure you and when your dress is ready. Then they can charge you extra for the alterations. You know, my neighbour has taught me a very good trick which you must try. You must take a friend with you when you go to your tailor because you cannot do this trick when you're alone. When the time comes for the measuring, you must position yourself so that your friend can stand behind you while the tailor is standing in front of you and you are holding your arms up away from your body like the tailor tells you to do. Without the tailor seeing, your friend must slip two of her fingers between the back of your body and the tape measure wherever he measures. So the tailor will write down a number which is bigger, and then when he makes a dress that is smaller than that number, it is the right size for your body.'

A collective *eh!* echoed around the small salon as the women looked from one to another with wonder on their faces.

'That is a very fine trick,' said Angel. 'I wish I had

known about it before. But let me tell you another trick that I have discovered. I have found a group of women at a centre in Biryogo who are learning how to sew. You can go to them and they'll measure you correctly and they'll sew your dress carefully, and all the time their work is being supervised by their teacher, so it's good. Okay, they're not yet experts like the tailors; they cannot yet make a dress from a picture. But if you take them a dress that you already have, they can copy it and make it in a different colour or a different fabric, and they can even make some small additions or changes like adding some frills or making the sleeves wider than they are on the original dress.'

'How are their prices?' asked Noëlla, who was now styling Angel's hair delicately with a wide-toothed comb so as not to destroy the shape of the curls.

'*Eh*, they're much cheaper than a tailor,' assured Angel. 'They've made my dress for tonight's reception and it fits perfectly. I'm going to look very beautiful amongst all those smart ladies.'

Of course, when Mrs Margaret Wanyika complimented Angel's dress that evening — as a hostess must — Angel was not going to tell her that it had been made by women who not only prostituted themselves, but may or may not be infected. If she were to do so, she was sure that Mrs Wanyika's hair would turn white immediately, and an emergency appointment would have to be made at the expensive salon in the Mille Collines hotel. She did not share this thought with the women in this salon, though; Mrs Wanyika was, after all, her customer.

When Noëlla walked Angel out of the salon and stood

with her in the morning sun for a brief chat before her next client arrived, Angel took the opportunity to ask her about Agathe. Noëlla confirmed that Agathe had never been to school.

'Do you think she'd like to learn to read?' asked Angel.

'Of course she would! She's often said that it's embarrassing for her when her children come home from school and they want to show her what they've written that day. But she cannot go to school herself at her age, and anyway she needs to be at work: she has to feed and educate her children.'

'Do you give her time off for a break every day? Maybe to eat her lunch?'

'Of course I do.'

'Now what if I told you that she could go to school to learn to read during that time every day?'

'What?' Noëlla looked sceptical. 'Where? How would she pay for it?'

'The school is free and the teacher knows French. Agathe would learn to read in French. It would be nearby, in my compound. She would just have to walk two streets along and then two streets down and she would be there.'

'Agathe!' called Noëlla loudly, her voice filled with excitement.

A few moments later, Angel was on her way back two streets along and two streets down. She was just passing a half-built house that had never been completed because the people who had planned to live there had not survived, when Ken Akimoto's vehicle slowed beside her.

'Hello, Auntie!' called Bosco. '*Eh!* What are you doing walking in the street with such a beautiful hairstyle? A lady with such a hairstyle must travel in a car with a driver.'

Angel laughed. 'Hello, Bosco! Are you offering me a lift?'

'Yes, Auntie. I'm on my way to your compound but I can take you anywhere.'

'Thank you, Bosco, I'm on my way home.' Angel opened the door and struggled to climb up into the Pajero without splitting the long skirt that was already straining over her expanding hips. Really, these big vehicles with their high seats were not designed with ladies in mind; it was almost impossible for a lady to remain elegant as she got in. How did the big women in government manage? She must remember to ask Catherine if the minister she worked with had any tips on how to get in and out of a big vehicle with dignity while wearing a skirt. It was an important thing to know how to do, especially if a television camera might be watching you – or a photographer from *Muraho!* magazine. Angel thought she might also use the opportunity of tonight's embassy function to observe ladies' techniques; there were bound to be many big vehicles there. Fortunately the children always thought it a great honour to be the one chosen to sit up in the front of the Tungarazas' red Microbus, and Angel was happy to sit on one of the seats in the back part that could be entered via a more manageable step.

'I've been shopping at the market for Mr Akimoto,' explained Bosco, noticing Angel glancing at the big cardboard box of vegetables in the back as they set off towards the compound. 'He's having guests for dinner again this weekend.'

'I know. I'll be making a cake for him again. But tell me, Bosco, how is Perfect?'

'*Eh*, Auntie, she's a very, very nice baby! She's quiet and still, not like Leocadie's baby. *Eh*, that Beckham can cry! And he's always hungry or else he's wriggling around and moaning about something. When Perfect cries, you can be sure it's not for nothing.'

'That's the difference between boys and girls, Bosco. But remember that Perfect is still very small. Maybe when she's bigger she'll become more like Beckham.'

'No, Auntie, don't tell me that! I used to think I wanted lots of babies, then I met Beckham and I thought uh-uh, babies are not a good idea. But then Perfect came, and she's very, very good, and I can see how much Florence loves to be her mother, so I thought again that babies were a very, very good idea. You're confusing me now, Auntie.'

Angel laughed. 'I think you're confusing yourself, Bosco. You haven't even met the lady yet who will help you to get all these babies.'

Bosco pulled the Pajero to a stop outside the compound and turned to look at Angel with a big, happy smile on his face.

'Bosco?'

Bosco continued to beam.

'*Eh*, Bosco! *Have* you met the girl who is going to become your wife? Tell me!'

Bosco looked shyly down at his left trouser leg, where a speck of dirt needed attention. 'I have met a very, very nice girl, Auntie.'

'Then you must come in and drink tea with me and tell me all about her!'

'I can't come now, Auntie. I still have to unpack Mr Akimoto's vegetables in his apartment and take his crate of empties to Leocadie for sodas for his party, and then I must fetch him from his meeting.'

'Then tell me quickly now, Bosco. Who is this girl that you've met?'

'Do you remember that when I came to fetch the cake for Perfect's christening, I gave a lift to Odile?'

'*Eh!* Odile! You're in love with Odile! I was just telling the ladies in the salon about the place where she works.'

Bosco laughed. 'No, Auntie, it's not Odile that I love. When I took her to her house I met her brother Emmanuel and his very, very beautiful wife.'

Angel felt her heart sinking. 'Bosco, please tell me that you have not fallen in love with Emmanuel's wife.'

'No, Auntie!' Bosco tried to look annoyed but he was too busy smiling. 'Emmanuel's very, very beautiful wife has a young sister who is also very, very beautiful. That sister has a friend called Alice. Alice is the one that I love.'

Angel shook Bosco's hand. '*Eh*, Bosco. I am too happy! You must bring Alice to meet me soon.'

'Yes, Auntie. But I think Modeste is waiting for

you. He is with a man. Perhaps he is a customer.'

The young man with Modeste was indeed a customer. Arriving at the compound, he had asked Modeste in which apartment he might find the Madame of the cakes, and Modeste had reported that Angel was out but would probably be back soon. She had not waited for a *pikipiki*-taxi at this corner, and she had not gone along the unsurfaced road to where she could catch a minibus-taxi; she had gone up the hill on foot, so she had not gone far. The man had decided to wait. Now he sat opposite Angel in her apartment, dressed in a suit and tie and looking extremely handsome and smart. There was something familiar about him, but Angel could not place him.

'Madame, allow me to present myself to you,' he said in English. 'I am Kayibanda Dieudonné.'

The local formality of stating a name backwards with the first name last had initially confused Angel, but she was accustomed to it now. She still found it too uncom-fortable, though, to introduce herself to anyone as Tungaraza Angel.

'And I am Angel Tungaraza, but you must please call me Angel. May I call you Dieudonné?'

'Of course, Madame.'

'Not Madame. Angel.'

'Forgive me.' The young man flashed a smile that made him look even more handsome. 'Angel.'

'Do I know you, Dieudonné? There is something about your face that makes me think that we have spoken before.'

'We have never spoken, Mad... Angel. Not you and I.

But I have spoken to Dr Tungaraza when you have been with him. I'm a teller at BCDR.'

'*Eh!* Of course!' declared Angel, suddenly able to place her guest. Her husband's salary was supposed to be paid into his account at the Banque Commerciale du Rwanda at each month-end, but for one or other reason payment of expatriate salaries – in US dollars – was invariably delayed. It was only Dieudonné who could explain the situation clearly in English to Pius's colleagues from India. Many of the Indians would not deal with any other teller.

'Your English is very good, Dieudonné. I know that your president wants everyone to speak French and English equally now, but that is new; most Rwandans are still learning English, but you've already progressed very far in the language. That tells me that you've spent much time outside your country.'

'You are right, Angel.'

'Then I'll make tea for us and you can tell me your story while we drink it. Here is my photo album of cakes for you to look at.'

Angel made two mugs of sweet, spicy tea and brought them into the lounge on a tray along with two small plates, each holding a slice of pale green cake with chocolate icing. She handed tea and cake to her guest and then settled down opposite him. Dieudonné cut a mouthful from his slice of cake with the side of his tea-spoon and tasted it with obvious enjoyment.

'Mm, delicious!' he declared. 'But this is not my first time to taste your delicious cake. In fact, I've found a picture of the very cake that I've tasted before.' He indicated a photograph on the page at which Angel's album lay open on the coffee table.

'Oh, that one I made for Françoise, for one of the parties that was held at her restaurant.'

'I was at that very party, and in fact I was the one who arranged it. My house is in the same street as Françoise, so I know her place. When I asked if some few of us from the bank could celebrate a colleague's promotion there, she told me that she could get a cake for us. Never before had I heard of eating cake after chicken and tilapia, but Françoise told me it is modern. She said that a cake can say anything that a person wants. This is the very cake that I asked for.' Dieudonné tapped the picture with a slim finger. 'In fact, the colleague who was promoted was too, too happy when Françoise brought the cake to the table. *Eh!*'

As Dieudonné spoke he made large gestures with his hands and arms. This was not the usual Rwandan manner, which was calmer and more controlled; perhaps there was no space for big gestures in a very tiny country that had to accommodate eight million people. No, Dieudonné moved his body more like Vincenzo, Amina's husband who was half Italian. Angel watched him as he took a sip of his tea.

'*Eh!*' he declared, and took another sip. 'I haven't drunk tea like this since I was in Tanzania!'

'You were in my country?'

'I looked for my family there for almost four years.'

'They were lost?' asked Angel. 'Did you find them?'

'They were not there.' Dieudonné took another mouthful of cake.

'You know, Dieudonné, I think you should tell me your story right from where it begins. I'm sure it's interesting and I don't want to become confused by starting to hear the story in the middle.'

Dieudonné smiled. 'In fact, I could have told you my story last week, and I would still be in the middle of my story and I would not yet know the end. *Eh*, last week I didn't even know that the end of my story was going to come this week. But this week I'm able to tell you my story right up to the end.' As he spoke, his bold gestures emphasized his words.

'Okay, Dieudonné, let us leave the end until the end. Start at the beginning, please.'

'Then I must start in Butare, because that is where I was born. My father was a professor there at the National University of Rwanda. I was still a small boy when Tutsis were chased from the university.' He paused, interrupting his story. 'Forgive me, Angel, we do not talk of Tutsis and Hutus any more; we are all *Banyarwanda* now. But I must use those words to talk about the past because in the past we were not yet *Banyarwanda*.'

'I understand,' assured Angel. 'You can speak freely with me, Dieudonné, because you are my customer and I am a professional somebody. We are confidential here.'

'Thank you, Angel.' Dieudonné cleared his throat and swallowed some more tea. 'My father was killed and we fled with our mother into Burundi, but only for a short time because then we fled again, this time to Congo, more specifically the town of Uvira. *Eh!* There were many refugees there, and there was a lot of confusion. I became separated from my family and I found myself being transported south to Lubumbashi with some other small boys. We were schooled there by nuns. I was a good student, so the Sisters arranged for me to go for secondary schooling with some Fathers at a mission school across the border, in the north of Zambia. One of the Fathers there became like a father to me.'

'Let me guess, Dieudonné. Was that Father from Italy?'

Dieudonné looked startled. '*Eh!* How did you know that?'

Angel laughed. 'The way you make gestures with your arms reminds me of someone I know who has Italian blood from his father.'

Dieudonné thought for a while as he chewed and swallowed another mouthful of cake. 'There are ways to father a child even when that child does not have your blood. Father Benedict loved me like the son he—'

'Father *Benedict*?' interrupted Angel.

'What's wrong, Angel? Do you know him?'

'No, no, I don't know him. It's only that you're telling me about a man called Benedict who fathered you and he was not your father; meanwhile, I'm mothering a son called Benedict and I am not his mother.'

'*Eh?*'

'*Eh!*'

'Perhaps God has moved in a mysterious way to bring me to meet you and order a cake.'

Angel contemplated this idea. 'Perhaps. But what can His purpose be?'

Dieudonné laughed. 'God will reveal His purpose only when He is ready!'

'You're right. Please continue with your story, because so far it sounds like a very big international adventure.'

'Okay. So Father Benedict was helping me by making enquiries to try to find my family, although it was difficult. By then many years had already passed since I'd been with them in Uvira. And at the time we became separated I was still small and I didn't know my mother's name. You know we Rwandans don't have a family name; there can be mother, father and six children, and no two of those eight will share a common name. In fact, by the time Father Benedict began to help me, I could no longer remember the name my parents had given me because the nuns in Lubumbashi had given me a new name: Dieudonné. It means God-given.'

He paused in his story to sip more tea and finish the last of his cake. Angel took his plate into the kitchen and cut another thick slice for him.

'So anyway, Father Benedict got news that two girls who might be my sisters were living in Nairobi. By then he had learned that my father had been called Professor Kayibanda at the university, and that my name had been Tharcisse. So he managed to get papers for me with the name Kayibanda Tharcisse Dieudonné, and through the Church I got a scholarship to go and study accounting in Nairobi. I found those two girls, and they were not in fact my sisters. *Eh*, that was a very sad day for me! Anyway, I stayed in Nairobi for three years until I qualified. In that time I got to know other

Rwandans living there, and one of them was convinced that he had met one of my brothers in Dar es Salaam. He said he had even been to my brother's house in Dar and found him living there with my mother.'

'So of course you had to go to Dar yourself.'

'Exactly. I went to the place where the man who was supposed to be my brother was supposed to be working, but they told me there that he had left some months before. They thought he had gone somewhere inland, but nobody knew exactly where. I went to the place where he was supposed to have lived with my mother, but the people there didn't know where they had gone.'

'*Eh!* That was a very difficult time for you.'

'Very.' Dieudonné shook his head. 'Anyway, I took a job in Dar doing the accounts for an Indian gentleman's businesses, and at weekends and in holidays I travelled to almost every town in Tanzania. Babati. Tarime. Mbeya. Tunduru. Iringa.' With each town he named, he gestured in the air as if pointing to its location on a large map suspended from the ceiling between them. 'Everywhere! I did that for nearly four years, but my family was not there.'

Angel tutted sympathetically as Dieudonné ate some cake and swallowed the last of his tea. She wanted to ask him if he had been to her home town of Bukoba on the shores of Lake Victoria, but she knew it would be wrong to direct his story towards herself.

'Anyway, by that time it was 1995. The genocide here was over, and many Rwandans in exile were coming home. I hoped that maybe my family would be among them, so I came home too. I went to the UN High

Commission for Refugees and gave them all the information I knew. I never heard anything from them until Monday morning this week...' Tears welled up in Dieudonné's eyes and he reached for a wad of toilet paper from his inside jacket pocket, tore off a length and dabbed at his eyes.

'Forgive me,' he said.

'There is nothing to forgive you for,' assured Angel. 'There's no shame in a man shedding tears. If a man doesn't cry when he needs to, those tears that have not been cried out can boil in his body until he explodes like one of the volcanoes in the Virunga Mountains. But I'm going to leave you here to cry the tears that you need to cry while I make some more tea for us.'

When Angel came back from the kitchen she saw that her guest had composed himself enough to finish his second slice of cake. Fortunately the cake from which his two slices had come was on the tray that she now carried in from the kitchen, together with their fresh tea. She cut him another thick slice and he held out his plate to receive it without offers needing to be made or accepted.

'Now,' said Angel, settling herself back in her chair and trying to get comfortable despite the restraints of her tight skirt, 'tell me about what happened on Monday morning.'

'A lady from the UNHCR telephoned me at the bank. She told me that they had found my mother and one of my sisters.'

'*Eh!*'

'In fact, they had crossed back into Rwanda from

DRC at Cyangugu and they were looking for me. The lady told me that they were on their way to Kigali that very day, and would be reporting to the UNHCR offices by that evening. Immediately I went to my boss at the bank and requested compassionate leave because my family was alive.'

Again tears welled, and again Dieudonné dabbed. Angel found herself reaching into her brassiere for a tissue and dabbing at her own eyes. Dieudonné calmed himself with a sip of tea before continuing.

'I went home immediately and prepared my house for their homecoming. I went to Françoise and told her my news, and she agreed to cook tilapia for my family's dinner and to send someone with it to my house that night. Then I went to the UNHCR offices and waited for my family to come.'

'That must have been a very difficult wait,' said Angel, now extending the use of her tissue to dabbing at some perspiration that was beginning to form on her brow. 'After all those years of looking, finally you were going to find them.'

Dieudonné blew his nose. 'Yes, it was not easy. They gave me a chair to sit on but I couldn't sit for more than a few seconds. But when I stood, my legs didn't want to hold me, and I had to sit. But I couldn't sit still and I had to stand up. *Eh!* I was up and down like the panty of a prostitute.'

Angel laughed, and Dieudonné laughed with her. 'You must have been very happy and excited.'

'In fact, no,' said Dieudonné. 'What I felt most was fear. I was afraid that they had made a mistake and that the people would not be my mother and my sister. And I was also afraid that I wouldn't recognize my mother. I had been such a small boy when I had last seen her. But in fact, as soon as my mother stepped into the UNHCR compound I knew it was her, and she told me that she had seen my father's face in mine the very minute that she saw me. I was so relieved! Of course my sister and I didn't know each other, but we couldn't stop smiling at each other and crying.'

'*Eh*, Dieudonné, you have told me a very happy story!'

'Yes. And it's only this week that it became a happy story. Last week my story would still have been a sad one.'

They drank tea and ate cake in silence for a few moments, both of them thinking about how suddenly sadness and happiness can change places. It was Angel who broke the silence.

'And what about your other siblings?'

'My one brother is late and the other is still lost; we will continue to look for him. My other sister was violated by some soldiers and she gave birth, but the baby was ill and then my sister became ill and they're both late now.'

Angel heard the word that he was not saying.

He finished his third slice of cake. 'So, Angel, I've come to order a cake because on Sunday afternoon my friends will come to my house to meet my family and help me to welcome them home. One of my father's former colleagues from the university will travel here from Butare to attend the party, and he'll bring his

[137]

daughter who played with my sister when they were small. That will be a good surprise for both of them.'

'For sure it will be a very happy party. I can make the cake on Saturday and deliver it on Sunday morning on the way to church. If you're in the same road as Françoise, I'll find your house easily.'

'You're very kind, Angel.'

Angel laughed. 'You may think that I'm kind; meanwhile, I'm curious! I want to shake the hand of the mother and the sister that you've told me about in your story, so it's not a matter of kindness that I'll bring the cake to your house.'

'Then I must thank you for your curiosity.' Dieudonné reached into a pocket of his jacket and brought out a piece of paper. 'Here, I've drawn a picture of the cake that I'd like you to make. Down the left side here it's red, and down the right side here it's green, and in the middle it's yellow.'

'Like the flag of Rwanda.'

'Yes, but our flag has a black R for Rwanda in the middle of the yellow. On the cake that R is still there, but it's part of the word *KARIBUNI*, which is written going downwards on the yellow.'

'*Eh*, you are a clever somebody, Dieudonné! This will be the perfect cake to say "Welcome home" to your family!'

Just then Titi arrived back from one of her frequent trips to the Lebanese supermarket to buy flour, eggs, sugar and margarine for Angel. She seemed a little agitated and Angel suspected that Titi wanted to speak to her alone, so she declared that Dieudonné had already been away from his family for quite long enough, and that they should complete the formalities of the Cake Order Form as quickly as possible.

As soon as Dieudonné had left the apartment, Angel went into her bedroom to release herself from her tight skirt. When she emerged dressed in a comfortable *kanga* and T-shirt, Titi broke the news that she had just been told by Leocadie: Modeste's other girlfriend had gone into labour. Modeste would go after work at the end of the day to see if she had delivered yet. Very soon the sex of the baby would be known, and that could determine which of the mothers Modeste would choose.

Angel longed to rush upstairs to share the news with Amina at once, but the children would be home from school very soon, and lunch must be prepared for them. Titi put some water to boil in a big pot on the stove and then began to slice some onions. Angel set a smaller pot of water to boil and started chopping some cassava leaves into very small pieces.

'What do you think will happen?' asked Angel.

'*Eh*, Auntie, I don't know,' said Titi. 'But of course Leocadie wants the baby to be a girl, then Modeste will choose her.'

'Yes. Then Modeste's decision will be clear. But if the new baby is also a boy, then he will have two girl-friends, each with a baby boy. He won't know which one to choose.'

'What if the baby is a boy and Modeste chooses his other girlfriend, not Leocadie? Now how will Leocadie feel to see Modeste here guarding this compound every day? Her shop is near.' Titi scooped the chopped onions into some palm oil that she had heated in a frying pan.

'*Eh*, that will be very hard for Leocadie! Tell me, Titi, have you ever seen this other girlfriend?' Angel put the cassava leaves into the smaller pot of water.

'Yes, Auntie. She came once on a *pikipiki* to see Modeste when I was talking to Leocadie outside the shop.' Titi now joined Angel in chopping tomatoes and adding the pieces to the pan where the onions were frying.

'And how did she look? Was she pretty like Leocadie is when she smiles?'

'I didn't see her very well, Auntie, and she wasn't there long. She came on the *pikipiki* and the *pikipiki* driver waited while she spoke to Modeste, then Modeste gave her something.'

'Did you see what it was? *Eh*, the water is going to boil now for the *ugali*; I'll chop these last tomatoes while you see to that.'

Titi measured maize meal into the boiling water and stirred it vigorously.

'We didn't see, but Leocadie thought it was money. She was angry. She pinched Beckham's leg to make him cry, and then he cried and Modeste and his girlfriend had to look at us.'

Angel laughed. She added the last of the tomato to the frying pan and stirred the mixture. Checking on the boiling cassava leaves, she said, 'That was a good trick. It reminded Modeste about his baby and it reminded the other girlfriend about Leocadie.'

'Yes.' Titi smiled. 'And also it showed that other

girlfriend that Leocadie had already given Modeste a son. That girlfriend's baby was in her belly then, but she was still not yet big.'

'And what happened next?'

'That girlfriend saw us watching her with Beckham, then she said something quickly to Modeste and got back on the *pikipiki* and left.'

'And Modeste?' Angel sprinkled ground peanut flour over the tomato and onion mixture and stirred it in.

'Modeste went to sit with Gaspard in the shade. He didn't look at Leocadie again, even though Beckham was still crying.'

'*Eh*, that is bad! You know, I'm worried for Leocadie. I'm worried that Modeste will simply not choose. Because why should he? If he can have two girlfriends and two babies, why should he choose to have one?'

'Ooh, Auntie.'

'That's how it is here, Titi. There are more women than men. Many men are late; many men are in prison. There are not enough men for every woman to have a husband. Some women agree to share a husband, because they've told themselves that a woman who is without a man is nothing. There are even men who've told themselves that, under these circumstances, taking more than one woman is like a service to the community.'

'Ooh, Auntie.'

'But let us not be sad today, Titi. Today I met somebody who told me a very happy story. Come, it's time for you to go and wait outside for the children's transport from school. I'll finish the cooking, then while we're eating our lunch I'll tell everybody the happy story that I've heard today.'

Later that afternoon, it was Amina's turn to hear Dieudonné's story from Angel. By that time the story had become even happier, because Angel was able to add to it Benedict's delight at sharing his name with an important character in the story.

Amina had come to Angel's apartment to help her to dress for the function at the Tanzanian embassy. At the Tungarazas' house in Dar es Salaam there had been a full-length mirror on the bedroom wall and a smaller mirror on the inside of one of the doors of the wardrobe. If Angel had stood in a particular place and angled the wardrobe door carefully, it had been possible to see, in that smaller mirror, a reflection of her back view in the mirror on the wall. But all she had in this apartment was a mirror on the bathroom wall that ended at her waist; she could only judge how she looked full-length and from behind through Amina's eyes.

The fabric of her new dress was royal blue patterned with small butterflies embroidered in gold. The sleeves puffed up and out from the bodice, tapering to a small cuff at the elbow, and a broad row of frills spread out at her middle above a long, straight skirt to create the illusion of a waist. A simple gold chain adorned her neck; small gold hoops hung from her ears; her smart black sandals had kitten heels. She twirled for Amina, who looked at her friend critically before giving her judgement.

'When your husband comes home from work and sees you looking like this, his eyes will jump out of his head and run around the room like they've just scored a goal at football.'

Angel laughed. 'Thank you, Amina. *Eh*, it's nice to wear something smart that isn't tight.'

Amina reverted to their earlier conversation. 'When do you think we'll hear?'

'I don't know. It depends how long the girl is in labour. Titi will go to the shop when Leocadie opens tomorrow. She'll come and tell us the news.'

'We must all support Leocadie tomorrow, because if the girl has not yet delivered it will be a difficult day for her. And of course it will be a difficult day for her if the girl has already delivered a boy.'

'Yes,' agreed Angel. 'I'll speak to Eugenia and some of the others, and we'll form a group and take turns to go and sit with her in the shop. Leocadie has no mother and no sister here to support her; we will be those things for her tomorrow.

# 7. An Inspiration

O N SATURDAY MORNING ANGEL BAKED TWO
cakes: a round one in two layers for Ken
Akimoto's dinner party that night, and a large oblong
one for Dieudonné's homecoming celebration the following day, both in plain vanilla; the remaining batter
made up a batch of cupcakes. In the afternoon, when
the cakes had cooled, she settled down in the peace of
the empty apartment to decorate them. Pius had gone
off in his smart suit to attend the funeral of a colleague
— TB, everybody said, although everybody knew that TB
was not what they meant — and the children were all
upstairs with Safiya, putting together a large jigsaw
puzzle that Safiya's Uncle Kalif had sent her. Titi was
keeping Leocadie company at the shop.

Modeste's other girlfriend had been in labour for
more than two days now, and she had still not delivered.
While some were convinced that the long labour
heralded a baby boy — because boys were difficult even

before they came into the world – others speculated that the mother was deliberately delaying the delivery because she feared that the baby was a girl whose birth would mark the end of her hold on Modeste.

'I don't want to be alone again, Mama-Grace,' Leocadie had said in the small, quiet voice of a child when Angel had been in the shop earlier that morning. 'After... Afterwards... I was alone. Everyone was gone. Then I got Modeste and Beckham. I got a family.'

As the neighbourhood held its breath for the news, people found reason after reason to visit Leocadie's shop for some or other forgotten purchase. For Leocadie – at times tearful, at times brave – business had never been so good.

Angel once again had free rein in decorating Ken's cake, and she decided that she would use the same colours that she would be mixing up for Dieudonné's cake: red, yellow and green. Of course, it was possible for so few colours to be boring, but she was going to create a design that she knew would be meaningful to Ken. When she had delivered a cake to his apartment once before, her eye had been caught by a round design on a big black-and-white poster on the wall of his lounge. She had asked him about it.

'That is yin-yang,' he had explained. 'It's a Chinese symbol meaning balance.'

'It looks like two commas,' Angel had observed. 'Or else two tadpoles: a black tadpole and a *Mzungu* tadpole.'

Ken had laughed. 'Yes, I can see that. A black tadpole with a big white eye and a white tadpole with a big black eye. But it's supposed to remind us that nothing is purely black or purely white; nothing is completely right or completely wrong, totally positive or totally negative. We need to find a balanced way of looking at every situation.'

'But why do you have a Chinese something on your wall?' Angel had asked. 'Are you not a Japanese?'

'Actually I'm Japanese-American. But that symbol has become universal now. I like to sit here and look at it; it can help me to think more clearly.'

So Angel set about re-creating that same symbol now on the top of Ken's round cake. Not in black and white, but in red and green: a green tadpole shape with a big red eye curving around a red tadpole shape with a big green eye. As she did so, she found her thoughts drifting away from Leocadie to Modeste's other girlfriend, who was in the throes of a long and difficult labour. What was going through her mind right now? To deliver a girl would be to lose her boyfriend; yet to deliver a boy would be no guarantee that she would keep him. At the time that she conceived this baby, did she know that Modeste had another girlfriend? Did she know that that other girlfriend was already carrying Modeste's baby? Really, it was a very difficult situation for both of these girls.

Having completed the design on the top of the cake, Angel smoothed yellow icing all the way around the sides of the cake and then, around the bottom of the cake where it sat on Ken's large round plate, she piped alternating red and green scrolls in a similar curved tadpole shape. Standing up, she inspected the cake from the three sides of her work table that were not up against the window. Yes, it was a very fine cake indeed: a universal cake; a cake that spoke about balance.

Sitting down again, she moved Ken's finished cake to the back of her work table and pulled Dieudonné's cake towards her on its board. As she smoothed red icing on to one end of the cake, the quiet of the neighbourhood began to be interrupted by a shout, distant at first, then taken up and brought closer by other voices.

'*Umukobwa!*'

'*Umukobwa!*'

It was a Kinyarwanda word that Angel knew well because she had once had a conversation with Sophie and Catherine about what it meant. The word described someone's function within the family: it said that the purpose of this person's life was to bring in a bride-price to increase the family's wealth.

It was the word for a girl.

The door of the apartment flew open and Titi stood in the doorway, breathless and excited.

'Auntie! The baby is a girl!'

'*Eh!* That is good news for Leocadie!'

Then Titi ran off to share in the happiness of the news with the rest of the neighbourhood, returning briefly later on to report that Modeste and Leocadie were indeed to marry. By then, Angel had already finished decorating Dieudonné's cake, creating the black letters down the central yellow part of the flag with strips of liquorice from the shop at the petrol station on the corner opposite the American embassy because there had not been enough of her black Gateau Graffito pen left to do the job. She had used up the last of the red, green and yellow icing on the batch of cupcakes.

No sooner had Titi hurtled off again to spread the news of the betrothal, than Dr Binaisa and his daughter Zahara came to visit, bringing with them the photographs of Zahara's birthday party. The children were still upstairs in Amina's apartment, so Zahara ran up to call everyone down.

Angel and Amina chatted in the kitchen as they boiled up a big pot of milk, and Dr Binaisa and Vincenzo made sure that the children did not mess cupcake or icing on to the photographs as they looked at them. Safiya was particularly excited to see the pictures, as she had missed the party by being away in Kibuye.

'Mama-Grace, this cake is so beautiful!' she declared as Angel and Amina carried trays of tea in from the kitchen. 'Look, Mama!'

Amina looked over Safiya's shoulder at the aeroplane flying above the clouds with the candles burning behind it. '*Eh*, Angel! That is a very fine cake! I think it's the finest you have ever made so far.'

'Everyone at my party said they had never seen such a beautiful cake,' said Zahara. 'All the mothers and fathers were asking Baba about it.'

'It's true,' Baba-Zahara confirmed. 'I felt very proud of myself that it was my idea to order such a cake.'

Angel put down the tray and gave her glasses a quick wipe on her T-shirt. 'Yes, a parent has to think very carefully about what cake to order for a child's birthday. You cannot order just any cake.'

'You're right, Mama-Grace,' declared Dr Binaisa. 'Everybody wanted to know who had made the cake and where they could find you. But do you know my colleague Professor Pillay? He teaches entrepreneurship.'

'Yes, I know him, his children school with ours.'

'Well, he brought his daughter to the party and he wanted to know about the cake and he asked if I had one of your business cards!'

Angel laughed. 'My business cards? That is not something that a person needs here. Okay, big people have them. But why? Everybody already knows who they are.'

'Exactly. Here you simply ask where to find the person you want, and somebody tells you where to go. A good name shines in the dark. But Professor Pillay said no, somebody without a business card is not a professional somebody.'

Amina cut in. 'That professor is wrong! Angel doesn't have a business card but she's a very professional somebody. Perhaps the problem lies with that professor, because he doesn't know how to ask somebody a simple question about where to find the best cake-maker.'

All the adults laughed, and Dr Binaisa said, 'When Professor Pillay's daughter's birthday comes and she wants a cake as nice as Zahara's, then he'll come to me and ask where to find you. Then I'll ask him if he's sure he wants to order a cake from somebody who is not professional!'

'He'll come to Angel because she's the best,' said Amina.

'And the day that Professor Pillay comes to me, I'll ask him for *his* business card!' said Angel.

*

It had been a happy day, thought Angel that night, sitting propped up with pillows, hot and unable to sleep, as Pius snored quietly beside her under a blanket. Even though watching Dr Binaisa with his daughter and Amina with hers had made her long for Vinas to be there; and even though Pius had come home from his colleague's funeral too drained for her to tell him how sharply she had been feeling their daughter's absence, still it had been a happy day.

She fanned her face with the copy of Oprah's new *O* magazine that she had borrowed from Jenna, listening to snatches of song from Ken Akimoto's party at the other end of the building. Tonight some wine-fuelled voices were singing their own version of 'Massachusetts' — *and the lights all went out in Kisangani* — shouting the name of the town in DRC where war was imminent, and then laughing loudly at their own cleverness.

Ken had been very excited by the cake and had declared it Angel's most beautiful yet. That had been very gratifying indeed. Now she thought about the meaning of the symbol on the cake and worked at applying it to the major event of the day. She would think of the good parts of the situation as belonging in the green half of the symbol, and the bad parts as belonging in the red half.

Modeste was going to marry Leocadie, and they were going to be a family with their baby, Beckham. That was green. But there was a circle of red inside the green, and that was that Leocadie already knew that Modeste was the kind of man who would have other girlfriends, and that he must give some of his small salary to help with his other baby. The other girlfriend's situation was red: she had lost her boyfriend to another woman and would be raising her baby daughter alone. What could be in that girlfriend's green circle? Perhaps that her situation was now clear — which it would not yet be if she had delivered a boy — and that Modeste had promised to help her financially with the child. There were not many men who could be relied on for that. If Modeste had power and satellite TV at home, programmes like *The Bold and the Beautiful* and *Days of Our Lives* would tell him about a test that could be done by a doctor to see if a man was really the father of a baby, and then if he wasn't he could decide not to pay. But that test had not yet come to Rwanda; here a man could decide not to pay without even knowing about such a test.

Then Angel tried to think about the marriage of Modeste and Leocadie that would happen soon. That was definitely on the green part of the cake. Modeste was alone because everybody else in his family had been killed. Leocadie was also alone. Her father had been late for a number of years; her mother was in prison, and her two brothers had fled into DRC with others who were also thought to be *génocidaires*. Perhaps it was even possible that members of Leocadie's family had person- ally killed members of Modeste's family; there was still so much confusion, and there were still so many accused whose cases had not yet even been scheduled for trial, that it was not yet possible to piece together the story of every individual death. So for two such people to find love together was definitely green: they were true *Banyarwanda*. But was the red circle inside that green the history of their families? Or was that so big that it was the entire red half of the cake? *Eh!* She must not think about it too much because it might give her a headache and she could not go to anyone so late at night to ask for a tablet. Perhaps Ken Akimoto's symbol was only useful for thinking about things that were small and simple. Perhaps there were some things that were just too big and too complicated. Politics, for example. And history. Perhaps those were things that were not about balance.

She thought instead about how pleased she was that so many people had praised the aeroplane cake that she had made for Zahara. When people praised her cakes she felt very happy indeed — and very professional. She put down the magazine and eased herself down to a horizontal position, careful not to wake Pius, and tried to discern the words of the song from Ken's party: ... *did you think I'd crumble; did you think I'd lay down and die?*

A short while later she recognized more words, in a man's voice this time: ... *knock, knock, knocking on Heaven's door...*

Eventually she heard the sounds of Ken's party spilling out into the street and dissolving into shouted goodbyes and the slamming of car doors.

Finally she slipped into sleep.

But not for long.

In the early hours of Sunday morning, she was dragged from her sleep by sounds of screaming and shouting in the street outside the compound. She sat up and reached for her glasses from their usual night-time spot, on the floor under the bed where she would not tread on them by mistake. Pius was already at the window, looking out from between the curtains.

The screaming outside began to be echoed from inside as the children in the next bedroom awoke in fear. Angel rushed into their room, switching on the overhead light and speaking as calmly as she could.

'It's alright, children. That noise is all outside; there's nothing bad in here.'

Daniel and Moses were crying; Benedict was torn between being a child and joining in, and being brave as the oldest boy. Faith was still too sleepy to react, and Grace was peeping between the curtains to see what was happening in the street. Titi sat bolt upright in her bed and stared at Angel with very big eyes.

'Auntie, has the war come again?'

'No, Titi, everything's fine. Come, children, come away from the window. Let's all move into the lounge. Come, bring your blankets. Let's not catch cold.'

Angel switched on the neon overhead light in the lounge and ushered everyone in. Grace soothed Moses, and Titi rallied sufficiently to comfort Daniel. When Angel was sure that all of them were going to be okay, she went back into her bedroom and joined Pius at the window.

'What's going on?'

'It's all Kinyarwanda and French, so I can't follow exactly,' said Pius. 'It seems there's a problem between Jeanne d'Arc and that *Mzungu*.'

Angel peered into the darkness. While there were some streetlights on the tarred road that went past the side of their compound, the dirt road on to which the building fronted was not lit. Angel saw that Patrice and Kalisa, the night security guards, were trying to interpose themselves between Jeanne d'Arc and a young man whose shirtless torso glowed palely in the darkness as he gesticulated wildly. Angel recognized him.

'That's the Canadian from the top floor.'

'Who is he? Have I met him?'

'No, he's new. I don't know his name. He's come for just a short time, as a consultant.'

'It looks like he wants to hit Jeanne d'Arc. His words sound very angry.'

Angel thought about all the times that she had watched *Oprah* in Amina's flat without sound. Now she read the situation outside her window in the same way.

'Look, Jeanne d'Arc is very upset. I'm sure it's about money. Perhaps the Canadian is refusing to pay her and she's demanding the amount that was agreed. But how will anybody hear anything if she cries like that?'

Pius opened the wardrobe and took his cell-phone out of his jacket pocket. 'Should I phone the police?'

'The police? But they'll arrest Jeanne d'Arc because she's a prostitute!'

'No, they'll arrest the Canadian because he's a *Mzungu*! They won't believe a foreigner over a Rwandan.'

'But they'll have to take both of them to the police station because everybody is looking now. That *Mzungu* can easily pay them dollars to go free, but Jeanne d'Arc will have to pay them in another way. That will be very unfair. It's best if Kalisa and Patrice can sort out the problem without the police.'

'You're right.'

'I'm going to make hot milk for the children. Shall I make some for you, too?'

'Yes, thank you. Call me when it's ready; I'll keep an eye on things until then.'

Angel went back into the lounge, where six pairs of sleepy eyes looked at her in fright and confusion.

'It's nothing,' she assured them all. 'It's only two people having an argument and forgetting that others are trying to sleep. They'll grow tired soon and then we can sleep again. Titi, come and help me in the kitchen. We'll all drink some hot milk and honey and then we'll feel much better.'

In the kitchen, Titi whispered, 'It's not the war, Auntie?'

'No, Titi, it's not the war. We're safe.'

Relieved, Titi filled the kettle with water and set it to boil on the oven top while Angel spooned Nido milk powder into each mug. Then Angel opened a large plastic jar that had once held Toss washing powder, and from it scooped a teaspoon of thick, sweet honey into each mug. The honey came from the honey cooperative in the road behind La Baguette, the Belgian bakery where many *Wazungu* liked to sit and have tea and pastries, and where the cakes — many people had assured her — were very expensive and not nearly as nice as Angel's. She liked going to the honey cooperative, where you could take your own container and fill it from a tap at the base of an enormous bucket of honey. Daniel and Moses particularly enjoyed working the tap and watching the thick, shiny liquid folding into the bottle. Buying from there was a way of supporting the women who farmed bees as a way of earning a living. Okay, the bees could sting those women. But still, it was safer than Jeanne d'Arc's way of earning a living.

By the time the water had boiled and the sweet milk had been made, Pius had joined the children in the lounge.

'It's all over now,' he said, 'and the police didn't need to be called. Everyone's gone home. Let's drink our milk and go back to sleep.'

But the broken night of sleep left everyone drowsy, and later that morning — much to her embarrassment — Angel found herself sitting in a pew at St Kizito's suddenly aware that she had slept through most of the sermon. In the afternoon, Pius, Titi and the children all took a nap, and Angel settled herself on the sofa, with her feet up on the coffee table, to read Jenna's *O* magazine. She had not got very far when Sophie came to visit. Angel made tea for them and they took it down to a shady corner of the compound's yard where they sat on *kangas* spread out on the ground.

'Did you hear all the noise in the night?' asked Angel.

'No,' said Sophie. 'Catherine and I slept in Byumba last night; the volunteers there were having a party. We just got back a while ago. But Linda told us about it. We met her on the stairs.'

'*Eh*, you're lucky you weren't here; you wouldn't have slept well last night.'

Sophie laughed. 'Do you think I slept well in a sleeping-bag on the floor with nine other people in the same room?'

Angel shook her head. 'What did Linda say? Does she know what it was about?'

'Mm, she spoke to Dave this morning, so she got the inside story.'

'Dave is the Canadian?'

'Mm. Apparently he agreed a price with Jeanne d'Arc, and afterwards he took the money out of a box in his cupboard and counted out the money that they had agreed, and he paid her.'

'Oh, I was thinking that maybe he didn't pay her.'

'No, he did pay her. But wait, that's not the end of the story. Then Dave goes to the loo, and when he comes out again his cupboard is open, the box is open and all his money's gone – and so is Jeanne d'Arc.'

'*Eh?* She took his money?'

'All of it – nearly two thousand dollars. So he runs to the window and sees Jeanne d'Arc coming out of the building and he shouts for Kalisa and Patrice to stop her. Then he pulls on his trousers and runs down to the street to get his money back.'

'*Eh!*'

'Apparently Jeanne d'Arc denied taking his money. She told the guards that the only money she had was the money he'd given her for sex. Dave threatened to call the police, but of course he would never have done that; he wouldn't exactly have been seen in a good light himself. But anyway, she believed the threat and it frightened her, so eventually he managed to get all of his money back.'

'All of it? Including the money for the sex?'

'*And* some other money that was hers! And apparently

he's feeling very full of himself today, bragging about getting free sex and how a sex-worker tried to... well, excuse my language, Angel, but he's bragging that she tried to screw him and he screwed her instead. Apparently he thinks that's hilarious.'

'*Eh*, this Canadian is not a nice man. How can he cheat Jeanne d'Arc like that?'

'He was stupid. He opened that box of money in front of her and she saw him putting it back in the cupboard. That was throwing temptation in her face.'

'Exactly. Okay, he doesn't know Jeanne d'Arc. But surely he knows that somebody who is doing that job is not a rich somebody. Stealing is wrong. But if he was showing her a box of dollars it's like he was asking her to take it. Now he hasn't even paid her for her work.'

'And it's not like she can take him to court to get her money.'

Angel shook her head and said, 'Uh-uh.' Then she took a sip of tea, swallowed it, and said, 'Uh-uh-uh,' shaking her head again.

'And he thinks it's a big laugh,' said Sophie.

'But, *eh!* What is he doing with two thousand dollars in his apartment? Who is he consulting for?'

'The IMF – the International Monetary Fund.'

'The IMF? He's working for the IMF and he doesn't want to give a poor somebody the money that he promised to give? Even after that poor somebody did what was agreed? Uh-uh-uh. He can afford to pay Jeanne d'Arc a hundred times that money and instead he's made her an even poorer somebody while he puts all the money in his own pocket and laughs at her with his friends.'

At that point the sound of a door opening on to a balcony made them both look up at the building. The Egyptian appeared in the small space next to the enormous satellite dish that occupied most of his balcony, yawned and stretched.

Sophie spun round on the *kanga* so that her back was to the building and whispered, 'Oh, please, please don't let him see me!'

Taken by surprise, Angel instinctively cast her eyes downwards to avoid any interaction with the man. 'What's wrong?' she whispered to Sophie.

'Is he still there? Can you see?'

Angel made a show of glancing towards the side entrance to the yard, swinging her eyes in a casual upward arc along the way. In the split second that her eyes took in the Egyptian's balcony, she saw that only the satellite dish remained there.

'He's gone back in,' she whispered, 'but the door's still open. What's going on?'

Keeping her voice low, Sophie said, 'I'm just too embarrassed to greet him. God knows how I'll behave if I meet him on the stairs or end up at a dinner party with him.'

Angel was very confused. 'Why? What has he done to you?'

'Oh, it's an embarrassing story, Angel. Actually, I don't know whether to laugh or be angry.'

'Then you must tell me the story,' insisted Angel. 'Maybe I can help you to decide.'

Sophie smiled. 'Well, yesterday morning, around noon, I was getting ready for our trip up to Byumba in the afternoon, and waiting for Catherine to come back from the Ministry, when his maid came knocking on my door.'

'Eugenia.'

'Eugenia? Oh, I didn't know her name, but I recognized her as Omar's maid.'

'Omar? That's his name?'

'Mm. Anyway, she said that her boss had sent her to me... to ask for some condoms!'

'*Eh?* Condoms?'

'Can you believe it?'

'*Eh!*'

'I mean, I hardly know Omar! We've just greeted each other on the stairs and that's all. If we were friends then maybe he could ask me that, or even if maybe we'd had a discussion once and I'd told him I was teaching the girls at school about HIV and AIDS and using condoms. *Maybe.*'

'*Eh!* For a man to ask a girl for condoms is not a polite thing. Uh-uh. More especially when you're not even his friend.'

'Mm! So I was really shocked and all sorts of things went through my head. I thought maybe he fancied me and was trying to see if I was available. Because you know, there are men who think that if a woman has condoms it means she's available for sex with anyone.'

'Yes, I've heard that. One of my customers told me of a case in South Africa where a man was going to rape somebody and she was afraid of getting AIDS from him so she told him that *she* had AIDS and she made him wear a condom. She gave him that condom herself.

Then the judge decided that that man had not raped her because she had given him that condom; it meant that she had consented.'

Sophie shook her head. 'That judge could *only* have been a man!'

'*Eh*, but I've interrupted your story now. So what did you do?'

'Well, then I thought that maybe Omar wanted to have sex with this woman, with Eugenia, because we've seen him coming and going with one girlfriend after the other. So I thought he was maybe insisting on sex and she was insisting on a condom and she came to me as another woman to ask for one. So if that was the case, then I couldn't refuse.'

'You're right, Sophie. Under those circumstances you cannot refuse. Uh-uh.'

'Mm, and all of this happened in my head within about a second, and as soon as I'd decided that I couldn't refuse, then I was stuck with another decision. She said Omar had sent her to ask for *some* condoms. Not *a* condom: *some* condoms. So how many was I expected to give?'

'*Eh!*'

'Everybody knows that when a neighbour comes and asks you for some sugar, you give a *cup* of sugar. That's the etiquette. But what's the etiquette for condoms? How many do you give? There are no etiquette books where you can look up something like that.'

'I can see that that is a very difficult thing to decide.'

'Especially with someone like Omar. Catherine's bedroom is directly above his and she can hear how...

well, how active he is, especially at weekends. His bedroom window is always open, and I'm sure nobody does it more loudly than him. So he might have been expecting or needing a huge number. But then, he has his Land Rover sitting outside in the street and it's nothing for him to go and buy some condoms any time. That pharmacy opposite the bank is open twenty-four/ seven. But, anyway, this was Saturday morning and loads of places were open. So I could have given him just a small number to tide him over and then he could have gone to buy more.'

'So what did you decide?'

'Well, eventually I decided to give him one of those packs of Prudence that Catherine gives out at her work-shops. There's a strip of three or four in there.'

'I'm sure that was a good decision,' assured Angel, casually glancing up at the Egyptian's balcony again to satisfy herself that he was not standing there listening to their conversation. 'But I can understand why you don't want to greet him now.'

'Mm, what's he going to say to me: *Hello, Sophie, thanks for the condoms, I really enjoyed them*?'

Angel started laughing and Sophie joined her, and soon their laughter was echoing around the com-pound's yard. But it stopped suddenly when they heard the noise of a balcony door. Angel's eyes shot upwards and, despite herself, Sophie swung her head round to look.

Titi stepped sleepily out on to the balcony of the Tungarazas' apartment and waved and smiled.

'There you are, Auntie!'

'Hello, Titi,' called Angel. 'Is everybody okay?'

'Yes, Auntie, they're still sleeping.'

'*Sawa*, Titi. Please make more tea and bring it for us. Thank you.'

As Titi went back into the apartment, Angel turned to Sophie and said, '*Eh*, I'm glad that Titi was not the Egyptian! Even I won't know how to greet him now.'

'At least you'll just have to try not to laugh. I'll be so embarrassed and I'm sure I'll turn scarlet, then he'll think I'm blushing because I fancy him and he'll be convinced I'm ready for sex with him because I have condoms ready and waiting.'

Angel laughed. 'I'm sorry, Sophie, I know I shouldn't laugh, because this could be a serious something, but I can't help it.'

'It's okay, Angel, you've made me laugh about it too.'

'Then you've found the answer to your question!'

'What question?'

'The question about whether you should laugh or be angry about this story.'

Sophie smiled. 'What would I do without you to talk to?'

'*Eh*, you have many friends to talk to,' said Angel, 'and I'm happy to be one of them. But I'm sorry to be giving you tea without cake today. I made many cupcakes yesterday but there were many visitors.'

'That's okay, Angel. Actually, that's what I came to talk to you about. You've fed me so much of your delicious cake this year, and now at last I'd like to place an order.'

'*Eh*, Sophie, is your birthday coming?'

'No, no. Actually, the cake I'd like to order is only

part of what I'd like to ask of you. Perhaps I should tell you everything before I presume to place my order. You might not agree, and then I won't need the cake.'

Angel looked confused. 'Sophie?'

'Okay, let me explain. All this year I've been trying to encourage the girls at my school to think about their futures. They don't know how lucky they are to be attending secondary school – most girls in Rwanda never go beyond primary level.'

'Yes, and not just in Rwanda. Ask anyone you meet from any African country and they'll tell you it can be like that at home too.'

'Mm, a girl's only a temporary member of the family; she's going to grow up and marry into some-body else's family, so educating her is seen as a waste of money. So these girls are very lucky to be getting a secondary education – especially in a school for girls only, where they aren't going to be harassed by boys. But there are very few jobs available in Rwanda, espec-ially for the girls who aren't academic enough to go on to university, so I want them to think about *creating* jobs for themselves.'

'You mean they must become entrepreneurs?'

'Mm!'

'Do you know that professor who teaches entrepre-neurship at KIST, Professor Pillay?'

'Mm, he's coming to speak to the girls this week.'

'Oh, here's Titi with our tea.'

Titi was edging sideways down the steps into the yard, trying simultaneously to watch where she was putting her feet and to keep an eye on the mugs of tea that she was balancing on a tray. Sophie jumped up from the ground and went to meet her at the bottom of the stairs. Taking the tray from her, she said, '*Asante*, Titi. Thank you.' It was one of the few things Sophie knew how to say in Swahili.

Titi beamed at her and then went back up the stairs as Sophie carried the tray over to Angel.

'So, anyway, some of the girls have at last understood what I'm on about, and they've formed their own club, and to flatter me as their English teacher they've given it an English name. It's called Girls Who Mean Business.'

Angel clapped her hands together. '*Eh*, that's a very good name for that club! And that club is a very good idea.'

'Mm, and once a fortnight they're going to invite someone to come and talk to them after school. Professor Pillay will be the first, and he'll give them some background on the whole idea of entrepreneurship. Then after him they want to ask women who run their own businesses to come and tell them their own stories.'

'To give them some steps that they can follow themselves?'

'Mm, and to inspire them generally.'

'That's a very good idea.'

'So, Angel, will you come and inspire them a fortnight after the professor?'

Angel had been about to take a sip of tea. She put her mug back down on the tray and looked at Sophie. 'Me?' Then she clapped her right hand over her chest and asked again. '*Me?*'

'Of course you, Angel! You're a woman! You run your own successful business! You're ideal!'

'But what would I say to them?'

'Just tell them how you started your business; maybe tell them about any mistakes you made or any important lessons you learned along the way.'

'*Eh!* I remember at first I didn't know how to calculate how much I must charge for a cake. I only thought about what the customer would think was a good price to pay. I didn't know about counting the number of eggs in a cake and calculating how much I had paid for each egg and what-what-what. It was a while before I learned how to make a profit!'

'You see? That's *exactly* what the girls need to hear! And you can tell them about your successes as well, and show them your photo album of all the beautiful cakes that you've made.'

Angel was warming to the idea. 'And I can speak to them about what it means to be a professional somebody.'

'That will be wonderful, Angel.'

Then suddenly Angel stopped smiling and looked at Sophie with a disappointed expression. 'But Sophie, how will I be able to tell them anything? I don't know Kinyarwanda! I don't know French!'

'No problem,' assured Sophie. 'Their English is okay; not great, but okay. I speak enough French to help out if there's anything they can't follow, and I'm sure some of them will understand if you want to use a few words of Swahili. We'll all translate for one another and everyone will understand.'

'Are you sure it'll work?'

'Listen, if people want to understand something, they find a way to understand it. I know those girls. I'm sure they'll all be very interested in what you have to say.'

'Okay. And I can show them my Cake Order Form, the one you typed for me. That speaks many languages.'

'Good idea. Practical stuff is what they need, not just theory. I suspect Professor Pillay is going to be a bit too theoretical, so they'll need loads of practical stuff after that. And that's why I want to order a cake from you; I want them to experience your product!'

'That's a very good idea! Of course they must taste my cake! And of course I'll give you a very good price because you're a volunteer.'

'Thank you, Angel. And thank you for agreeing to come and inspire the girls.'

'I'm happy that you invited me, Sophie. And I'll be happy to meet your Girls Who Mean Business. Now, what is their cake going to look like?'

'Oh, I'll leave that to you, Angel, I'm sure you'll have much better ideas than me. There's still a fortnight to go, so there's plenty of time for you to think about it. When you've made a decision and calculated a price, just let me know and we can fill in a Cake Order Form and I'll give you the deposit.' Movement on the stairs into the yard caught Sophie's attention. 'Grace! Faith! Hello!'

'Hello, Auntie Sophie,' said the girls as they took turns to bend down and give her a hug.

'Grace,' said Angel, 'before you sit, please run up to

the apartment and bring Mama's diary and a pen.' As Grace turned and dashed towards the stairs Angel said to Sophie, 'I must write this in my diary now. *Eh*, imagine if I forgot to come and talk to your girls! That would not be a good example of a professional somebody!'

Sophie laughed. 'Don't worry, I won't let you forget. Now, Faith, would you and Grace like to come and play on my laptop upstairs for a while?'

'Ooh, Auntie, yes please!'

'Are you sure, Sophie? They won't be in your way?'

'Of course not. You know I love them; they remind me of my nieces back home. And Catherine's out with her boyfriend, so they won't be disturbing her.'

'Okay, let's all go upstairs then. There's no need for Grace to come down here with my diary. Go and tell her, Faith.'

Faith shot off up the stairs as Angel and Sophie gathered their four empty mugs on to the tray, shook the red soil from the *kangas* that they had been sitting on, and headed back up towards Angel's apartment.

'*Eh*, Sophie, by the way!' said Angel, stopping a quarter of the way up the flight of stairs. 'I know another woman who runs her own business. Perhaps you can invite her to come and inspire your girls as well.'

'Great! Who is she?'

Angel paused for a moment, then looked at Sophie and said, 'Jeanne d'Arc.'

The two women laughed all the way up the stairs.

# 8. An Engagement

ANGEL FELT THE PERSPIRATION COLLECT INTO a droplet and begin to trickle slowly downwards from her temple, but she was unable to move either of her arms to extract a tissue from her brassiere. Her left arm was pinned to her side by a very old man who was sitting half on her lap and half beside her, while her right arm was immobilized by the thigh and left buttock of the young man who stood next to her, bending right over her. Her eldest grandson pressed himself on to her lap, snivelling miserably. Really, this was not a convenient time for the Change to be asserting itself.

Unable to see ahead clearly, she hoped that it was safe to assume that she would not be the only passenger wanting to alight from the minibus-taxi at her stop, which should be coming up very soon. She was right: two or three other passengers began to hand their fares forward to the conductor who stood over her, signalling their intention to disembark at the next stop. She clutched the money for their fares in her right hand, but recognized that she would be unable to give it to the conductor without either squeezing her fist up between the metal of the minibus's door and the man's buttocks or pulling it up in front of him between Benedict's back and the man's private parts. She decided to risk neither.

As the driver brought the taxi to a halt, the conductor skilfully slid the door open with his right hand behind his back and stepped out backwards. Angel handed him her money and he assisted her by lifting the child from her lap and placing him on the ground so that she could step out herself, clearing a space through which others could disembark and new passengers could board. The taxi drove off, and Angel led Benedict to the shade of a flamboyant tree, where she delved into her brassiere for a tissue with which to dab at her face and another for Benedict to use to wipe his eyes and blow his nose.

It was still early; they had had the first appointment of the day, and they would be home before half-past nine. She took the boy by the hand and they set off together towards their compound that lay at the far end of the dirt road. As they walked, she did her best to comfort him.

'You were very brave, Benedict. Nobody likes to go to the dentist, but you were strong like a big boy, a teenager. Mama was very proud of you.'

Benedict attempted a smile.

'Now, I know that when we get home you won't be able to eat because your mouth is still hurting, but you can drink. Would you like Mama to make you some tea, or shall we stop at Leocadie's shop and buy you a soda?'

'Fanta please, Mama!' Benedict declared emphatically.

Of course, the dentist had just lectured Angel on the advisability of cutting down on the amount of sugar in her children's diet. He had even specifically mentioned sodas and cakes as being very bad for a child's teeth. But this dentist came from an island somewhere far away in the Pacific Ocean, and he had the strange idea of being a Christian but worshipping on a Saturday instead of a Sunday — just like Prosper. Angel knew that it was very unfair to judge an entire congregation by the regrettable behaviour of one of its members, but Prosper was the only Adventist she knew personally, so it was difficult for her to be objective. If she could become acquainted with some others who were more sensible than Prosper, she might be able to convince herself that this dentist's advice should be taken seriously; but until somebody could persuade her that his advice was indeed good, it was better simply to ignore it. She would try to remember to ask Dr Rejoice about it.

They walked past a high yellow wall over which deep red bougainvillea blossoms spilled. Behind the wall, invisible from the road, sprawled the big white house that was shared by the families of two of Pius's Indian colleagues, where the boys went to play with their school friends Rajesh and Kamal. Miremba, the Indian boys' young Ugandan-Rwandan nanny, had become a close friend of Titi's, and the two girls had gone into town together that morning.

As Angel and Benedict neared Leocadie's shop, its owner stepped out, and saw them approaching.

'Mama-Grace!' she called, giving a wave and a big smile. Really, she was so much happier now that the business with Modeste's other girlfriend had been settled. Apparently the girl had decided to go with her baby and stay with her aunt near Gisenyi, right up in the north of the country.

'Benedict, why are you not at school today?' she asked, when Angel and the boy reached her shop. 'Are you sick?'

'I went to the dentist,' said Benedict, opening his mouth wide to show Leocadie the hole where a tooth had been extracted.

'*Eh!*' said Leocadie. 'You're a brave boy. Was he brave, Mama-Grace?'

'Very,' assured Angel. 'He had to miss a day of school because those dentists don't work on Saturdays. He'd like a Fanta *citron* now to help him to feel better, but all our empties are in the apartment.'

'No problem, Mama-Grace, you can take a Fanta now and I'll remember that you owe me one empty.'

'Thank you, Leocadie. Now tell me, have you and Modeste started to make plans for your wedding?'

'Not yet,' said Leocadie, stepping into the shop and reaching into the fridge for a Fanta. As she opened its door, the fridge cast just enough light into the dim interior of the container for Angel to make out the still form of Beckham, lying asleep on the lowest shelf between the bags of sugar and the rolls of pink toilet paper. 'But what plans will we make, Mama-Grace? We have no family, so there'll be no negotiations about bride-price. And we can't have a wedding party because we don't have money.'

Angel suddenly felt very sad for this girl, whose only happiness was that her fiancé had chosen her above another girl who had had his baby too. And, Angel noticed, Leocadie had now reached the stage of disowning her relatives — incarcerated and in exile — as family. Perhaps Angel was partly to blame for that, because she had given Leocadie an honest account of her meeting with the girl's mother in jail in Cyangugu: her mother was simply no longer there. Then Angel thought about her own daughter, and about the silence, the distance, that had grown between them.

Had Vinas ever felt that her mother, like Leocadie's, was simply no longer there?

Suppressing the startling urge to sob, Angel heard herself speaking before she even knew what it was that she was going to say.

'Leocadie, it is not true that you have no family, because I'm going to be your mother for this wedding.'

'Mama-Grace?'

'I'll help you to plan everything, and of course I'll make your wedding cake for the reception.'

'*Eh*, Mama-Grace!' Leocadie's eyes began to fill with tears. 'But we cannot afford…'

'Nonsense! God will help us to find a way. You leave everything to me. Now, take my hundred francs for Benedict's Fanta so that I can take him home and put him to bed. He needs to rest after all his fright and pain.'

Leocadie reached for the note that Angel handed her. 'Thank you, Mama-Grace. You're a very good mother.' Then she began to weep. 'I'm very happy that you'll be my mother for my wedding.'

'Don't cry, Leocadie, you'll wake up Beckham, and then *he'll* cry.' Angel did not add that she might join them.

After saying their goodbyes, Angel and Benedict walked the last few metres along the road, past the big green skip that had at last been emptied of the neighbourhood's rubbish, towards the corner where their compound lay. They could see Gaspard and Modeste standing there with two men who had apparently paused for a chat on their way up the hill. Each of the men carried a wire cage, the larger of which held a large grey parrot and the smaller of which held a small monkey. There must be a market for such creatures — many could be seen for sale on street corners — but Angel found it hard to understand why anyone would want to share their home with an animal that needed to be fed but contributed nothing in return. A chicken or a cow was a useful animal; but a parrot? A monkey? Uh-uh.

Benedict, on the other hand, was fascinated by the small grey monkey whose button eyes gazed absently from the black of its face through the bars constraining it. He squatted down beside the cage, which the man had now put down on the ground, and said hello to the creature. Something in the boy's voice — perhaps the kindness of his tone — awoke the monkey from its stillness, and with its eyes never leaving Benedict's, it took hold of the bars with both hands and flung its body around violently within its prison, all the while screeching like a terrified child. Letting go of the bars, it flung itself against the side of the cage and toppled it over sideways, screeching all the more loudly and appallingly. This unleashed an echoing wail in Benedict, clearly distressed at having triggered such wretchedness in the creature, and as the man bent to right the cage, Angel scooped the boy up in her arms and carried him inside.

A while later, after Benedict had been calmed and had finally drifted off to sleep tucked up in his bed, and after Angel had changed out of her smart, tight clothes and settled down to review what she was going to say that afternoon to the Girls Who Mean Business, a soft, continuous knocking began at the door. Recognizing it as Modeste's knock, and knowing that it was futile to call for him to come in because he did not feel it was his place to do so, Angel went to the door and opened it.

'Madame,' said Modeste, 'here is a customer for your cakes.'

Next to him stood a soldier, an earnest-looking young man dressed in camouflage uniform and khaki wellington boots with a semi-automatic rifle slung over his shoulder. The thick welt of an ugly scar snaked its way down from below his left ear and across to somewhere under the right lapel of his uniform.

Angel thanked Modeste as he left, and then turned her attention to the soldier. '*Unasema Kiswahili?*'

'*Ndiyo, Bibi.* Yes, I speak Swahili.'

'Good. I'm sorry that I cannot yet speak Kinyarwanda to you.'

'*Hakuna matata, Bibi.* No problem.' He flashed a smile of chocolate-coloured teeth at Angel.

'*Bwana*, you are very welcome in my house, but I'm afraid that your gun is not welcome here. My husband and I do not allow guns to come inside.'

'*Hakuna matata, Bibi.*' The young man removed his weapon from his shoulder and leaned it up against the wall outside the door to Angel's apartment, clearly intending to leave it there. Angel felt a stab of panic.

'That is not a safe place for a gun to rest, *Bwana*. There are children who live in this compound. One of them could pick it up and then there could be a terrible accident.'

The soldier glanced at the gun. 'You're right, *Bibi*. Let me leave it with your security guard outside.' He ran out with the gun to give it to Modeste and then came back and sat down opposite Angel in her lounge.

'Allow me to introduce myself, *Bibi*. I am Munyaneza Calixte, a captain in the army.'

'I'm happy to meet you, Captain Calixte. Please call me Angel; I'm not comfortable with *Bibi* or Madame.'

'*Sawa*, Angel. I've come to you because they tell me that you're somebody who makes cakes for special occasions.'

'That is true, Captain Calixte. Do you have a special occasion coming up?'

The soldier nodded. 'I'm taking a fiancée.'

Angel clapped her hands together and beamed. 'An engagement! That is indeed a special occasion! I'll make tea for us and you can tell me all about it. Meanwhile, you can look at my photos of some other cakes that I've made.'

Angel prepared two mugs of sweet, spicy tea and put a few cupcakes — iced in red and dark shades of green and grey — on to a plate. She carried them on a tray into the lounge where she found the soldier examining her photo album studiously.

'Do you see any cakes that you like?' she asked, placing the tray on the coffee table.

Captain Calixte looked uncertain. 'I think that you'll need to advise me on the kind of cake to order, Angel. I'm not certain what my fiancée will like best.'

'I'm always happy to advise my customers,' assured Angel. 'But before we settle with our tea, come and look here on my work table. I'd like to show you my most recent cake. There's no picture of it in my album yet.'

On the table sat an extended oblong cake decorated in a way that made it immediately recognizable — though its design had been simplified and modified — as an enormous version of the Rwandan 5,000 franc note. Against a pale pink background, the words *Banque Nationale du Rwanda* ran across the top edge of the cake in capital letters that were dark green at the top and red at the bottom; to the right of these words was the large figure 5000, also green at the top and red at the bottom. Running across the bottom edge of the surface of the cake was a red stripe with a green stripe immediately above it, and outlined in pale pink above the two stripes, with the colours showing through, were the words *cinq mille francs*, and again the number 5000. Those letters and numbers had been very difficult for Angel to write with her icing syringe; next time Ken Akimoto went home to Washington, she would send a note to June requesting a white Gateau Graffito pen.

Captain Calixte looked at the cake in wonder. He reached into a pocket and removed a 5,000 franc note so that he could compare it to the cake.

Angel pointed at his note. Going up the left hand side of the original banknote were three dark grey triangles decorated with leaves over which the figure 5000 appeared in pale pink, and a drawing of a black-and-white bird sitting on a branch. 'This part was too difficult and there were too many details,' she explained. 'I made it simpler: just one grey triangle with 5000 written over it in pink.'

'That is very good. I can see that you've taken away some of the details, but still when we look at it we know that it is this banknote.'

'And these dancers here,' said Angel, pointing to the picture in the central area of the soldier's banknote. 'That was going to be much too complicated. I couldn't copy that.' In the picture on the note, seven male dancers performed in traditional costume: leopard-skin skirts, straps of beads worn crossed over the chest and long, flowing straw-coloured headdresses that looked like blond *Mzungu* hair. In front of them were four female dancers in sleeveless T-shirts and knee-length wrapper skirts, a string of beads around each forehead and strings of bells or seed-pods around their ankles.

The captain shook his head. 'No, this picture is too complicated for your cake, I can see that. But what is this that you've written instead?'

'Well, I've taken these words from the note here,

*Payables à vue*, and I've added *aux Girls Who Mean Business*. That is the name of a club that I will address this afternoon. They're all girls who plan to run their own businesses when they've finished their schooling. Now, if you look down the sides of the cake here, all the way around I've put thin red stripes to indicate that this is actually a large pile of money.'

'*Eh*, that is clever. So this cake is saying that those girls will make a lot of money from their businesses.'

'Exactly.'

Angel had initially thought of making an American dollar cake rather than a franc cake, but when she had looked carefully at a $100 note from Pius's wallet, she had seen that it was very boring: cream with grey and only a little bit of green, and a big picture of an ugly old *Mzungu* man. That was not something that was going to inspire these girls; and in any case it was very possible that none of them had ever seen a $100 note, and so they might not be able to recognize immediately what the dollar cake was saying. No, the Rwandan money was a much better choice; it would speak to them in a language that they knew.

The two sat down and sipped their tea. Angel watched as her guest's chocolate-coloured teeth bit into a chocolate cupcake; she could almost hear the Adventist dentist's gasp.

'Captain Calixte,' she said, 'this is my first time to talk to a soldier in the Rwandan army, and if I am to advise you on your engagement cake it will help me to know something about you. Would you tell me about your fiancée and something about your life as a soldier?'

Calixte swallowed his mouthful of cake and then washed it down with a large sip of tea. 'My life as a soldier,' he said slowly, turning his head and gazing towards the window. He was quiet for so long that Angel wondered if she should not perhaps say something to summon his mind back from wherever it had wandered. At last he turned back to her, and, leaning forward, looked her squarely in the eye. 'Can I speak freely with you, Angel?'

'Of course you can,' she assured him. 'You are my customer. I'll never repeat what you say to me because I know how a professional somebody is supposed to behave.'

'That is good. And also you are *umunyamahanga*, a foreigner, so it's safe for me to talk to you. It's only that I was taken by surprise to think about *my life as a soldier*. Of course, I've often thought about *being* a soldier, but I've never thought of that as my life. It was not the life that I wanted.' Again his gaze shifted towards the light of the window.

Angel waited a few moments before she prompted him. 'So, is it better that I ask you about *being* a soldier?'

Angel's guest turned back to her and — to her relief — laughed. 'You can ask it either way, because whether I like it or not, being a soldier and my life as a soldier are in fact one and the same thing. Until so far, anyway.'

'Tell me about it, then.'

'*Sawa*. Before my life as a soldier, there was my life as a schoolboy. I lived near Ruhengeri with my father; we were alone because my mother and my sisters did not survive the genocide. I was not a very good student, but

I dreamed of becoming a teacher one day in a vocational school. I was very good with my hands: woodwork and carpentry. My father taught me. One day I was walking home from school with three other boys, and some soldiers stopped next to us in a truck. They asked if we could direct them to some or other place that was some distance away, and they said they'd pay us if we went with them to show them exactly where it was. Of course my friends and I agreed to go with them, and we climbed into the back of the truck. There were many soldiers there. But it soon became clear that they were not interested in finding the place that they had asked us about, and they drove with us for many, many kilometres, refusing to let us out. It began to get dark and one of my friends began to panic, and he started to insist that we be let go; but still they refused. Then at last when the night was completely black, they pulled off the road. My friend who was panicking pushed at some of them and climbed down from the truck, cursing them. They laughed at him, and then they shot him dead.'

'*Eh!*' Angel spilled some of her tea on to her *kanga* but did not notice. '*Dead?*' She thought of Joseph, dead in his house from a robber's bullet.

'Dead. Then they laughed some more and told us they would shoot us too if we gave them any trouble. Late that night we arrived at a place and we were taken to some tents to sleep. There were other boys there, and they told us they had also been taken. We were going to be trained as soldiers, they said. And so that was the end of my life as a schoolboy and the beginning of my life as a soldier.'

'That is a very bad story,' said Angel, shaking her head. 'Was it not possible to run away?'

'We knew that if we tried to run we would be shot. We saw it happen to others. We were dependent on the soldiers for food and we had no idea where we were or what would become of anybody who actually managed to escape. So eventually we stopped thinking about escaping and we concentrated on becoming good soldiers. We thought that once they trusted us with guns then we could get away. But somehow, by the time they gave us guns, we had lost the will to get away. We had become soldiers.' Calixte shrugged, unable to explain.

'It's not my first time to hear a story like that,' said Angel. 'I know it's not an impossible thing to happen; it has happened in other countries.'

'They took me to fight in Congo, close to Kisangani. I was there for a very long time. *Eh!* The things we did and saw there!' He shook his head. 'I cannot speak of those things. My heart had already been empty for a long time, and the only way for me to continue day after day was to make my mind empty, too. There are months, years even, that I could not remember now, even if I wanted to.' He drank some tea and finished his cupcake. 'So that is my life as a soldier.'

Angel was silent for a while before she asked, 'And what about your father?'

'I never saw him again. Some time ago I had the opportunity to go to Ruhengeri, but I found that he was already late. I don't know if he ever searched for me. I don't know what he thought that day when I didn't come home from school.'

'*Eh*, that is very sad,' said Angel.

Calixte shook his head. 'Things are sad only when you allow yourself to feel them.'

'And you don't allow yourself to feel them?'

'I told you: my heart is empty.'

Angel tried to lighten the mood, which had become uncomfortably heavy. She smiled hopefully. 'But you are in love, Captain Calixte! You're getting engaged! How can your heart be empty?'

He shook his head again, laughing in a hollow way. 'I'm not in love, Angel. There is no love in my heart. I told you: it is empty.'

'But if your heart is empty, then why are you marrying?'

'That is simple: because my *mind* is no longer empty.'

'Captain Calixte, you are confusing me now,' said Angel, removing her glasses and holding them in her lap. 'What is it that is now in your mind?'

He took a sip of tea. 'A plan.'

'A plan?'

'Yes, a plan. A way out. I don't want to be a soldier, Angel; it was never what I wanted. I want to be demobilized, but that is not what I want; many soldiers have been demobilized, and there is nothing for them to do. I never completed my schooling, so what would I do outside the army? There is nothing. So I'm going to marry a *Mzungu*, and she will take me with her to her home country. That will be my escape.'

Angel thought about this for a moment. 'And in your plan, what is it that you will do when you are with your *Mzungu* in her home country?'

Again he laughed. 'Why will I need to do anything? I won't need a job.'

'So your fiancée is rich?'

'All *Wazungu* are rich.'

Angel began to rub gently at her glasses with the edge of her *kanga*. Captain Calixte was right: the *Wazungu* in Kigali were certainly paid extremely well by their international organizations. In addition to their pay, some even received an extra hundred dollars a day to compensate them for having to live in a country that they said was dangerous; most Rwandans did not earn that much in a month. But did the girl who was going to marry this soldier know that it was only her money and her passport that he wanted? That she was only useful to him for his plan?

'Have you proposed yet, Captain Calixte? Has she in fact agreed to be your fiancée?'

'Not yet. But of course she'll agree. It will be impossible for her to say no to me.'

Angel's mind leaped to the soldier's semi-automatic rifle. Surely he would not force the girl at gunpoint? The rubbing of her glasses became somewhat frantic as a disturbing thought entered her mind: the soldier sitting in her lounge might be quite mad. It was not impossible for war to push a man over the edge. But if he planned to force this girl to marry him, then why was he ordering a cake to celebrate their engagement? The idea of the cake made Angel feel a little easier.

'Why will it be impossible for her to say no to you, Captain?'

'Because I've studied *Wazungu* women carefully,' he

replied. 'I've noticed three things about them: number one, they like beautiful things; number two, they like events to be well planned; and number three, they're concerned about their safety.'

Angel thought for a moment, pausing in her rubbing. 'Actually, I cannot disagree with any of those things.'

'So when I ask her to marry me, first I'll give her this beautiful thing.' He reached inside his collar at the back and removed a long string that had been hanging around his neck, concealed inside his uniform. Suspended from the string by a knot was a small bundle of dirty brown fabric. He undid the knot and extracted from the piece of fabric a small, glittering diamond.

'*Eh!*' Replacing her glasses, Angel took the diamond and examined it carefully. 'This is indeed a beautiful thing, Captain Calixte. And *Wazungu* women do like to get a diamond when they get engaged; it's their tradition.' She handed the diamond back. 'But are you a rich somebody yourself that you can afford this diamond?'

Calixte laughed as he wrapped the diamond in the fabric again, knotted it back on to the string and repositioned it around his neck. 'You don't need money to get a diamond in the Congo, Angel. All you need is quick fingers – or a gun. Do you think the soldiers are there only to fight?'

Calixte sat back and drained his tea. Angel did not offer him more.

'Okay, so you have this beautiful diamond. Now how will you show her that you are good at planning?'

'That's where the cake comes in. We'll be able to have

an engagement party the minute she says yes.'

Angel cleared her throat before speaking. 'But do you not think that maybe she would like to plan the party ahead of time and invite her friends?'

'She can phone them.'

'I see. But then... will the party not be... unplanned?'

'No, it will be planned, because I've planned the cake. *Wazungu* cannot have a party without a cake.'

Angel did not try to press the point; to do so could be to persuade him not to order the cake that he had come to order. 'And so how will you deal with the third matter, the matter of her security? Will she feel that she's safe simply because you are a soldier?'

'Not at all. I'll show her my certificate.' He reached into his trouser pocket and brought out a piece of paper, which he unfolded and handed to Angel. It was a photocopy of some kind of official document in Kinyarwanda and French, with an official-looking stamp in the lower right-hand corner.

'What is this certificate?' she asked. 'What does it say?'

'It says that I have tested negative for HIV.'

Angel looked for any words that she might recognize. Sure enough, there were the letters VIH — the French for HIV — and a French word that looked very like the English word *negative*. On a dotted line across the middle of the document, the name Munyaneza Ntagahera Calixte had been typed. It was definitely Calixte's certificate. But was this man she was talking to definitely Calixte? A person had to be so careful in such matters, because it was very easy for somebody to pretend to be negative with a borrowed certificate. That was one of the dangers that Angel had learned from Odile. Then she noticed the date on the official stamp.

'Captain Calixte, this test was done almost two years ago.'

'So?'

'So is it not possible that this result is... well... *old*? Will your girlfriend not want to see a certificate that is new?'

'Why would she want that?'

Angel felt exasperated. Was this man ignorant as well as mad? 'How long has your girlfriend known you, Captain Calixte? Does she trust you?'

'She doesn't know me yet, Angel, but I'm sure that she'll trust me when I present myself to her with my diamond and my certificate and my cake.'

Angel looked at him and blinked a few times, saying nothing. Then she cleared her throat and said, 'I'm confused, Captain Calixte. Are you telling me that you and your fiancée-to-be have not actually met?'

'No.'

'No, that is not what you are saying, or no, you have not actually met?'

'We have not met. But I'm planning to introduce myself to her as soon as my cake is ready.'

Angel took off her glasses and closed her eyes. She took a deep breath. 'So you're planning to introduce yourself to her, show her your certificate, ask her to marry you, give her the diamond and have her phone her friends immediately to come and eat the cake that you've brought to celebrate your engagement.'

'Yes. We can marry here or in her country; that is of no importance to me. But what is essential is that she will take me with her when her time here is finished. That is how I will escape. That is my plan.'

Angel had still not opened her eyes. She desperately wanted a cup of milky, spicy tea with a large amount of sugar in it, but if she made one for herself she would be obliged to make one for her guest as well — and her guest was in all probability somebody who belonged in the psychiatric hospital at Ndera. She did not want him to stay in her apartment any longer than necessary.

'Right,' she said, opening her eyes and putting her glasses back on. 'So let us make sure that your cake is a very fine one. Now, you don't know this girl, so you don't know what kind of cake she would like. We'll have to choose something—'

Calixte interrupted. 'But *you* know the girl, Angel. I've seen you talking to her on the street, outside the church of St Michael. You can advise me on what she would like.'

Angel was not sure that she could take any more, but she had to ask the question.

'Who is she?'

When Calixte gave her the name, she sighed deeply and dropped her head into her hands.

For her talk to the Girls Who Mean Business, Angel wore the same dress that she had worn to the function at the Tanzanian embassy; it made her look smart and professional, and it had the added advantage of being sufficiently loose to ease her ascent to, and descent from, the front seat of Ken Akimoto's Pajero, which had been reserved in advance for the trip to Sophie's school.

Carefully balancing the board bearing the money-cake on her lap, Angel told Bosco about the man who had visited her earlier that day.

'*Eh*, Auntie! I think you did not feel safe with that soldier in your house. Did you think he was going to shoot you when you refused to make his cake?'

'No, of course not; his gun was outside with Modeste. But he made me feel very uncomfortable. I think he's not right in his head.'

'Why, Auntie?'

'Why? Bosco, have you not listened to my story? How can you ask me why I think he's mad? *Eh*, Bosco! Please go more slowly on these corners, otherwise my cake will be spoiled.'

'Sorry, Auntie, it's only that I want you to arrive at the school on time. I promise that I won't let your cake be spoiled. It's very, very beautiful.'

'Thank you, Bosco.'

'Of course I listened to your story, Auntie. It was the story of a boy who was forced to become a soldier and to do terrible things. Now he wants to escape from that into a better life. What is mad about that, Auntie?'

Angel thought about it. Bosco's summary made Captain Calixte sound perfectly sane. 'But he really expected her to agree to marry him!'

'Auntie, do you think he's the only man here who would like to marry that girl? Even Mr Akimoto likes her; it's only that he already has a wife in America. I would ask her to marry me myself; it's only that I don't love her.'

'Of course I'm not saying anything bad about her; I'm sure there are many men who would like to propose marriage to her. But this soldier had gone as far as planning everything.'

'So when a man plans to do something that other men only dream of doing, then that man is mad?'

The conversation was not going well for Angel. 'You're confusing me, Bosco,' she said, and then was quiet for a while.

Eventually Bosco said, 'Auntie knows that there are many girls here who want to marry *Wazungu* so that they can have a better life somewhere else. And girls like that are not just here; they're in Uganda too.'

'You're right, Bosco. In Tanzania, too.'

'Are those girls mad, Auntie?'

'*Eh*, Bosco! I can see that you want me to say no, those girls are not mad. And then you're going to ask why do I say a man is mad when he wants the same thing.'

Bosco laughed. 'Exactly, Auntie.'

Angel found herself smiling. 'You know, Bosco, I think that maybe you've been giving too many lifts to Sophie and Catherine. I can see that they've taught you not to accept one idea for girls and another for boys.'

'It isn't Sophie and Catherine who have taught me that, Auntie.' Bosco grinned broadly.

'Ah,' said Angel. 'Alice.'

'Yes, Auntie.'

'When am I going to meet this Alice, Bosco? You keep telling me I'll meet her soon.'

'Very, very soon, Auntie.' Bosco drew to a halt where another dirt road crossed the one they were on, and checked directions to the school with a man who was pushing a bicycle with a heavy basket of potatoes strapped behind its seat. They turned left.

'Anyway,' said Angel, 'I'm glad that the soldier came to see me today, because his visit gave me another idea for my talk this afternoon. You know, Bosco, I've never before refused to make a cake. Okay, once or twice I've had to say no because somebody has asked me too late, like they ask me at lunchtime and they want the cake that afternoon. But I've never before refused. And I've never before even thought that one day I might get an order that I would refuse. So it's good that it happened today, because now I can talk to the girls about my personal experience of ethics.'

Pius spoke often about ethics, and would occasionally try to stimulate discussions on the subject with the children.

'Let us say,' he would declare over supper, 'that the Tanzanian national football team needs a sponsor because they cannot afford to travel to play in the Africa Cup. Now, let us say that the makers of Safari beer offer to sponsor our national team. Is it right for the national team to accept that sponsorship?'

The boys would say yes, and then Faith, seeing her grandfather's reaction to the answer yes, would say no.

Grace would have a reason. 'No. Because if the players drink the Safari, they won't be able to play well and they'll lose.'

Titi would have a more general answer. 'Beer is not a good thing, Uncle.'

'They should not accept,' Pius would explain, 'because those of our players who are Muslim will not agree to play for a team that is paid for by alcohol. It would not be ethical for them to be part of that team. And so to accept that sponsorship would be to exclude players of a certain religion. And that in itself would not be ethical.'

The children and Titi would look at Pius with big eyes.

Angel would change the subject.

But today Angel was grateful for those discussions because they had helped her to know what to do this morning. Obviously she must warn her friend about Captain Calixte; it would be wrong not to. But Captain Calixte was her customer, so she was obliged to be professional and to keep her conversation with him confidential; therefore it would not be right to tell her friend. Clearly, she could not have the girl as a friend *and* the soldier as a customer. But if she did not accept the soldier as a customer — if she refused to make a cake for him — it was possible that he could persuade other people not to do business with her. And if she *did* accept him as a customer, he might send a lot of business her way from his friends in the army. So which was more important: friendship or business? That was going to be a good question to discuss with the Girls Who Mean Business.

At the school gates, two girls in smart school uniform were waiting to welcome Angel and to lead her to the classroom where the club was meeting and where Sophie was waiting for her. Angel tried to insist that Bosco should go home because without the cake to carry it would be fine for her to travel home in a minibus-taxi, but Bosco was vehement about waiting there for her.

The talk went very well indeed: the girls were excited and interested, and there was not a single problem with language that could not be overcome. Some were grateful to discover that Angel had a business *and* a family, as they had imagined that they were going to have to choose one over the other. And Angel's story about ethics — she made sure that they recognized that she was not *naming* the soldier or anyone he spoke about as that would not be ethical even though he had not become her customer — sparked a lively debate. The cake, of course, was a tremendous success.

At the end of the talk, the president of the club stood up and gave a short speech, thanking Angel in particular for her practical tips which were so welcome after Professor Pillay's theoretical analysis, and Angel was presented with a gift: a small picture-frame woven from strips of banana-fibre. The applause warmed Angel's heart, more than making up for her difficult morning.

Leaving Sophie to gather up her books and lock the classroom, Angel walked to the Pajero carrying the now empty cake-board at her side, with her photo album tucked under her arm, and holding in her other hand the slice of cake that she had saved for Bosco. He was not in the vehicle. She looked around and saw him sitting in the shade of a tree, talking to a girl in school uniform. Leaving the cake-board leaning against the

Pajero and the photo album on the vehicle's roof, she made her way towards the tree.

Seeing her heading towards him, Bosco scrambled to his feet, brushing down his trousers to rid them of any leaves or dirt that they may have picked up.

'Hello, Auntie. Did it go well?'

'Very! *Eh*, I've enjoyed myself this afternoon!'

Bosco indicated the girl, who had picked herself up and dusted herself down much more delicately than he had. 'Auntie, please meet my friend Alice.'

'*Eh!* Alice!' said Angel, shaking the girl by the hand. 'I'm happy to meet you.'

'I'm happy to meet you, too, Auntie.' The girl spoke to her in English. 'I'm sorry that my Swahili is not good, but I have a good English teacher.'

'Miss Sophie is your teacher?'

'Yes, Auntie. We are very lucky to have an English teacher who has come to us from far away in England.'

'Very lucky,' agreed Angel. 'Bosco has been telling me for a long time that he will introduce you to me soon.'

Bosco grinned. 'This afternoon I told you it would be very, very soon, Auntie.'

'That is true, Bosco. So, Alice, I believe you are the friend of Odile's brother's wife's sister?'

'Yes, Auntie. My friend is here at this school with me, and it is her older sister who is married to Odile's brother Emmanuel.' The girl's pretty smile transformed her rather plain face.

'And are you not a Girl Who Means Business?'

Alice laughed. 'No, Auntie, I am a girl who will study at university.'

'That is very good. *Eh*, Bosco, I saved a piece of cake for you, but now I see that I should have saved two pieces.'

'No problem, Auntie,' said Bosco, taking the piece of cake that was wrapped in a paper serviette and giving it to Alice. 'I've tasted Auntie's cakes before, but now it is Alice's turn.'

'Oh, thank you, Bosco. Thank you, Auntie. I will not share this with my friend because she has already had a piece; she is a Girl Who Means Business. I will hear from her everything that you said, Auntie.'

'That is good.' From the corner of her eye, Angel saw Sophie walking towards the Pajero to get a lift back to the compound with her and Bosco. She shook Alice by the hand again and told Bosco to take his time saying goodbye to Alice as she wanted to hear Sophie's opinion of her talk. Bosco gave her the keys to the vehicle.

As soon as the two women were settled inside the Pajero, Angel turned around to face Sophie and said, 'That friend that I did not name when we were talking about the ethical question of that soldier that I did not name?'

'Mm?'

'Sophie, that friend is you.'

# 9. A Farewell

THE SEASON OF SMALL RAINS HAD COME TO Kigali, settling the dust and bringing short and sudden showers that the dry red soil drank thirstily. But the rain had done little to improve the water shortage in the city, and for the past hour or so the taps in Angel's apartment had failed to yield as much as a drop. Fortunately the Tungarazas kept a yellow plastic jerry-can in the kitchen which was always full of water so that tea could still be made under such circumstances.

Angel and Thérèse now sat sipping their tea in the shade of the compound's yard as they waited for the results of the baking lesson to cool. Thérèse examined the notes that she had been making on a sheet of paper.

'So, if a four-egg cake needs two cups of flour and a cup each of sugar and Blue Band, can we say that for each and every egg there must be half a cup of flour and a quarter of a cup each of sugar and Blue Band?'

'Exactly, Thérèse. And half a teaspoon of baking powder. You mustn't forget the baking powder, because without it the cake will not rise. When I came to your house to test your oven, that mixture that I brought with me had only two eggs and one cup of flour. That was a very small cake, but it's wasteful to make a big cake in an oven that might not work.'

'I was so happy that it worked!' declared Thérèse. 'I remember as we waited for that cake to bake, I was afraid that it would come out in one of the ways that you had warned me, that it would burn on one side or rise higher on one side than the other. But it came out just perfect and *eh*, I was relieved.'

Angel had met Thérèse during one of her visits to the centre in Biryogo where Odile worked. Thérèse had sought her out as she sat chatting to a woman who lay on a mat on the floor of the small hospice area at the back of the centre.

'Madame,' Thérèse had said, 'I believe you are the lady of the cakes.'

'Yes, I am. My name is Angel.'

'I am Thérèse.' They shook hands. 'Nurse Odile told me that you were here.'

Angel glanced at the woman lying on the mat; she was now drifting towards sleep. 'Please sit with us, Thérèse. I don't want to leave this lady alone.'

Thérèse lowered herself to the ground, sitting opposite Angel with her legs stretched out in front of her. Unwittingly, she blocked from Angel's view the mother and baby who had unsettled her like a hundred startled frogs leaping into a still pond. For a moment – just a brief moment – the mother and her desperately ill little one had looked like Vinas and her third baby, the one who was late after only a few months.

Angel smiled with relief at the woman who now offered those hundred frogs the opportunity to climb back on to dry land and to settle there, allowing the water in the pond to be still again. 'Tell me about yourself, Thérèse, and tell me why you have come to talk to the lady of the cakes.'

Thérèse smiled back. Something about her reminded Angel of Grace: she was tall and slight, but with an air of strength.

'I am sick, Angel, but I am well. I'm lucky that the centre has chosen me to receive the medication. I have two young daughters and I must remain well to look after them until they grow big.' Angel found herself having to concentrate: Thérèse spoke with the rapid fire of an AK-47. 'My husband is late and also my youngest child, a boy, but my girls are well; they are not sick. It's my responsibility to earn money to feed us all and to send my girls to school. If they can complete their schooling, then one day they'll be able to live in a better part of Kigali than Biryogo.'

Angel took advantage of a brief silence as Thérèse paused to reload. 'That is a good dream for your girls. How are you earning money, Thérèse?'

'That has been a problem because I don't have a job. But Angel, I have an oven! It belonged to my husband's mother and it came to me after she was late and I never used it because it needed a tank of gas and that is too expensive. We were using the oven as a cupboard, but then I heard about you and I got the idea that maybe I can use it to bake some cakes and sell them.'

'That is a very good idea!'

'Yes. I've been buying boxes of tomatoes at the market and then selling them in small bags on the street, and from that I've managed to save money. Now I have enough to buy a tank of gas, and I've cleaned the oven and it's ready to use for baking cakes.'

'*Eh*, you've worked hard.'

'Yes. But I don't know how to bake cakes.'

'*Eh?*'

'No. So I'm asking you, Angel, will you teach me how?'

Angel had explained to Thérèse that it was not every oven that could bake a cake: some were too slow, some became too hot and some became hotter on one side than the other. First they would have to test Thérèse's oven, and if it was a good oven for cakes, then Angel would be very happy to teach her. The following week Angel had visited Thérèse, taking with her a small baking tin — already greased and floured — and a plastic container that had once held Blue Band margarine, in which the mixed ingredients for a two-egg cake were sealed.

The gas oven had stood gleaming in the corner of the cramped one-roomed home, with the tank of gas standing next to it. Angel could see at once that the oven was tilting slightly backwards on the uneven surface of the bare soil on which it stood. She had sent Thérèse's daughters to ask around amongst the neighbours for the loan of a bottle of Fanta, and when the girls had returned, she had laid the bottle on its side on the top of the oven. Together with Thérèse, she had pushed bits of cardboard under the two back feet of the oven until the girls, standing on a crate to see, had declared that the bubble of air was now in the middle of the bright orange liquid in the bottle. The oven was now level.

Anxiously, they had waited for the oven to heat up to number three on the dial, and then they had put the cake inside and waited anxiously again while it baked. Angel had found herself regretting that she had brought the batter from home already mixed: perhaps Thérèse's girls would have enjoyed — as Vinas always had — scraping their small fingers around the sides of the mixing bowl and licking them clean. Neighbours had joined them in their vigil. When Angel had at last declared the cake done and withdrawn it from the oven to reveal an evenly browned, level surface, the neighbours had erupted in applause and Thérèse had shed a few tears. Somehow, that two-egg cake had stretched far enough to allow every onlooker a taste.

Now the time had arrived for Thérèse to learn how to bake her own cakes, and her first efforts were cooling in Angel's apartment as the two women sat in the yard drinking their tea.

Angel was about to speak when Prosper came down the stairs into the yard, stamping his feet down hard on each step and muttering to himself angrily. Ignoring Angel's greeting, he marched to the door of his office, unlocked it and went inside, slamming it shut behind him.

'*Eh!* Why is that man angry?' asked Thérèse.

'I don't know,' replied Angel. 'Maybe he went to drink Primus at the bar nearby and he found it closed.'

'*Eh*, my husband was like that,' said Thérèse. 'When there was no beer in his belly, it was like two armies were fighting each other inside his head.'

'*Eh*, and with others it's the beer itself that invites those armies into their heads and then lines them up against each other.'

Both women shook their heads and tutted for a while, then Angel said, 'When we've finished our tea, I'll teach you how to make two kinds of icing, one with Blue Band and one with water.' She shifted slightly on her *kanga* to move her bare feet out of the encroaching sunlight. 'It's enough to know how to make those two kinds. There are other kinds, but they're expensive because they need chocolate or eggs.'

'No, I don't want to know about expensive icing. I'm not going to be a person who makes expensive cakes, and I don't think that I'll take orders for beautiful colours and shapes like in your photo album. I think I'll mostly make cupcakes, because those will be easy to sell on the street, and then I can make a big cake when there's a big event like football or basketball, and I can sell slices there.'

'That's a good plan.'

'I think I'll make more money from cakes than from tomatoes.'

'That is true,' agreed Angel. 'There are many tomatoes in Kigali, and anybody can sell a tomato. A tomato is not a special thing. But a cake is a very special thing.'

'Very special,' agreed Thérèse. 'It is only a person who has an oven who can bake a cake.'

Smiling, they drank their tea quietly for a few moments as Angel prepared herself to raise a subject that, when she allowed herself to focus on it, troubled her deeply.

'Tell me, Thérèse, may I ask you a personal question?'

'Of course, Angel.'

'Is your mother still alive?'

'My mother? No, unfortunately she's late.'

'And did you... Did you ever tell her that you were sick?'

Thérèse took a sip of her tea before answering. 'Yes, I did. It was only when my baby boy died that they advised me to have the test. I was shocked when they told me I was positive—'

Angel interrupted. 'Odile told me that that is the way, the time, that many mothers discover that they're positive. When a baby is late.'

'It's true, Angel.'

'And, Thérèse, how was it when you told your mother?'

'*Eh*, it's a very hard thing to tell a mother! And I regret so much that I told mine. It upset her too much. Truly, Angel, I think it was my news that made her late so soon.'

'*Eh?*'

'It shocked her too much, and I think she preferred to die before she had to watch me die. We didn't know then about the medication. If I could go back in time and untell her, she could be alive today and not worrying about me being sick — because I'm well.'

'That is not an easy thought for you to have, Thérèse. I'm sorry.' Angel swallowed a sip of tea. 'Now… say you met a girl who was sick. Would you advise her not to tell her mother?'

'*Eh!* That is a very difficult question to answer. Each and every case is different, and only the girl herself will know what to do.' She drained her mug. 'Although, in my case I thought I knew what to do but I did the wrong thing. I wish I hadn't told the truth, Angel. A lie would have been so much kinder to my mother. Sometimes a lie can hold more love in its heart than the truth.'

Angel was contemplating this when a shout began in the street, distant at first and then brought nearer by voices closer to the compound: '*Amazi!* Water.'

'*Eh*, the water has come back,' said Angel, scrambling to her feet. 'Let us wash the mixing bowls so that we can make the icing.'

Later, as they had arranged, Angel and Thérèse knocked on the door of Jenna's apartment. It was exactly eleven-thirty.

'Perfect timing, Angel,' said Jenna, opening the door. 'We've just finished today's lesson.'

'That's good,' said Angel. 'Jenna, this is Thérèse, my student.'

'Delighted to meet you, Thérèse,' said Jenna in French, shaking Thérèse's hand. 'Let me introduce you to *my* students. That's Leocadie, and next to her is Agathe, and on the other side of the table there's Eugenia and Inès.'

Thérèse worked her way around the table, greeting the women in Kinyarwanda and shaking each of them by the hand.

'Good morning, ladies,' said Angel in English. 'I'm sorry that I don't know French, and if I speak Swahili then Jenna and Agathe will not understand me, and if I speak the small bit of Kinyarwanda that I know, Jenna won't understand me. So I'm going to speak in English and Jenna will repeat after me in French.'

As Jenna translated, Angel put down the plate that she had been holding.

'Ladies, you are honoured to be the first people in Kigali to taste cakes baked by our sister, Thérèse.' As Jenna translated, everyone looked at Thérèse, who beamed and dipped her head. 'It's a new business for her; a new way of supporting her two girls. Our job today is to taste these cakes and to help Thérèse with our opinions and advice.'

Nestled together on the plate were a number of cupcakes: half of them decorated with pale yellow butter icing — made with margarine — and half with white glacé icing. Not wanting to spoil her first cakes in any way, Thérèse had been too nervous to add colour to her own icing, but she had observed and taken notes as Angel had coloured the icing for her own batch of cupcakes. She had been amazed by the number of colours it was possible to make from just three: red, blue and yellow.

Jenna and her students applied themselves earnestly to their task. The cakes were unanimously declared to be extremely delicious, and there was discussion about which type of icing would be more popular. Finally, agreement was reached that, while some adults might prefer the glacé icing, children would probably prefer the butter icing — and that Thérèse could probably charge more for a cake with butter icing on it because it made the cake look a bit bigger.

'*Eh*, that is very good advice,' said Thérèse. 'Thank you. Now I'm going to ask my teacher to try one of my cakes, and then I'm going to eat one myself.'

Silently, six pairs of eyes watched Angel as she peeled away the paper case and took a bite. She chewed slowly, savouring her mouthful, then swallowed.

'Thérèse,' she said, with a serious and solemn expression befitting a teacher, 'this is a very fine cake indeed.'

Five pairs of eyes swung towards Jenna, who mimicked Angel's expression as she translated. The women erupted into laughter and applause, and finally Thérèse felt that she could relax and eat a cake herself. As she took her first mouthful, a broad grin spread across her face.

'Okay, ladies,' said Jenna, clapping her hands together with an air of authority, 'time to go. You all need to get back to your jobs, and I need to make this place look like you were never here before my husband even thinks about coming home for lunch.'

'*Eh*, Inès,' said Angel as the women walked down the stairs, 'I think you should fetch Prosper from his office before you go and open up the bar. I think he wanted to have a beer there earlier when you were closed for your lesson.'

'*Eh*, that Prosper!' said Inès, shaking her head. 'I've

told him many times that the bar is shut from half-past ten to half-past eleven on weekdays now.'

'I'm sure that he doesn't want to accept that,' said Eugenia. 'When there's something that a man wants, it is *now* that he wants that something. Waiting is something that is very difficult for a man to do.'

Angel thought of Eugenia being sent to get condoms for the Egyptian.

'*Eh*, men?' said Leocadie, shaking her head. 'Uh-uh.'

'Men? Uh-uh-uh,' agreed Inès.

'And my shop was shut, too,' said Leocadie. 'Prosper couldn't buy beer there, either.'

'Exactly,' said Angel. 'Now he's sitting inside his office with the door shut, and you know there's no window there, and no light. He's sitting in the dark.'

The women laughed. They had reached ground level now.

'Okay,' said Inès with a sigh. 'I'll go and get him.' She headed towards the stairs leading down into the yard.

'*Eh*, and make sure he takes his Bible with him,' Angel called after her, still laughing. 'Ask him to show you the verses that talk about the virtue of patience.'

Early that afternoon, just after Titi had finished washing up after lunch and had settled for her afternoon nap, Angel received a surprise visitor.

'Gasana! Welcome!' she said, ushering the translator into the apartment. 'Children, you remember Mr Gasana, who works with Baba? We went to Cyangugu with him.'

Gasana stretched across the coffee table around which the children sat on the floor, and on which their homework books vied for space, shaking each of the children by the hand.

'I can't stay long, Mrs T; the driver has just dropped me here while he goes for fuel, and then he's taking me to a meeting. But I need to discuss some business with you very quickly.'

'Then let us sit at my work table,' said Angel, indicating an upright wooden chair next to the table and sitting on another herself. 'Do you want to make changes to your order?'

'In a way, Mrs T. I know from your Cake Order Form that I signed that it's not possible for my deposit to be refunded, so I'm not actually *cancelling* my order. But I was wondering, Mrs T, could I *postpone* it?'

Angel considered this. 'So you want to change the delivery date?'

'Yes. But I'm not sure yet what date I'll need the cake.'

'But is it not for the first meeting of your new book club? Are the people not able to come?'

'*Eh*, Mrs T, it's me who is unable to come! The others are still very excited. Everybody has managed to read *Things Fall Apart*, even though we have only one copy, and we're all ready to discuss it. But I've just received news that my brother in Byumba is late.'

'*Eh*, Gasana! I'm very sorry for your loss.'

'Thank you, Mrs T. So now I'll have to go and arrange for burial, and of course I can't be here for the book club this weekend. I've spoken to some of the others, and they say they don't want to have the meeting without me because the club was my idea, and it's my book.'

'Of course.'

'And I don't know yet when everybody will be free again, so I can't set the date yet.'

'No, I understand. You can just tell me when you're going to be ready for the cake. I'm sure it will be soon.'

'I hope so,' said Gasana, but he shook his head. '*Eh*, Mrs T, I'm obliged to inherit my brother's wife and his four children. Obviously we cannot all fit in my small house. I don't know how I'm going to afford to have a wife and children. Marriage was not in my immediate three-year plan.'

'That is very difficult,' Angel sympathized. 'It was not in our immediate three-year plan to raise five more children, but circumstances arose that made us have to change our plan.'

Gasana glanced at the children. 'I understand your situation, because Dr T has told me, more specifically about your son. And to tell the truth, Mrs T, I think my brother was sick, and that is why he's late. Now I don't know about his wife and the children. I don't know if they're well.'

'Let us pray, Gasana,' said Angel. 'I hope you won't think that I'm being too direct if I suggest to you that you should... be careful?' This advice surprised Angel herself: before getting to know Odile and spending time at the centre, she would have considered such a subject too delicate even to think about, let alone to mention openly.

Gasana laughed. 'No, you're not too direct, Mrs T!

In fact, nobody is direct like Dr Rejoice, and she's already given me a lecture and a big handful of Prudence! She's one of the people who'll be in the book club. *Eh*, Mrs T, are you sure I can't persuade you to change your mind and join the club? All the books we'll read will be in English.'

'Thank you, Gasana, but I told you before that I'm not an educated somebody; I'm not somebody to read books. But you know, I'm going to make an exception in your case and return your deposit to you, because I haven't used it yet to buy ingredients.' Angel reached into her brassiere and removed some banknotes. 'I'm sure you'll need this money for the funeral.'

'Mrs T, I'm very grateful to you.' Gasana accepted the money that Angel counted out and handed to him. 'Thank you for understanding my situation.' He glanced at his watch. 'Where is that driver now? I must be at the Ministry of Justice by half-past two!'

'The Ministry of Justice! That sounds important. What are you doing there?'

'Earning money for KIST as usual!' Gasana replied. '*Eh*, your husband is very good at hiring out my services! There's a big report there that needs translating from French to English. I don't know many details yet; this is the first meeting about it.'

'Actually, I needed a translator myself, today,' said Angel. 'I'm picking up bits of Kinyarwanda okay, but French is very hard for me. I wish I had my late daughter's language skills. *Eh!* Already as a child she knew Swahili and English on top of Haya, our home language in Bukoba, and then she learned some German from

[209]

her father. Pius had to know it for his studies. I know if she was here she'd be picking up French like *that*.' Angel clicked her thumb and middle finger together rapidly several times.

'French is a difficult language just to pick up, Mrs T. You should take some lessons. We teach it at KIST in the evenings, you know? And we also teach English. Our president has said that everybody should become bilingual.'

'Yes, I know. But Gasana, is everybody here not already bilingual?'

'Mrs T?'

'Well, I've looked in the children's dictionary, and it says there that bilingual means you can speak two languages. People here can already speak two languages at least: Kinyarwanda and French, or Kinyarwanda and Swahili, or some other two. But when your president talks about bilingual, he means only English and French — *Wazungu* languages. Does he mean to say that our own African languages are not languages?'

'*Eh*, Mrs T! Now you're speaking like somebody who reads books! Really, you should join our book club! Or at least come to our university to learn French.'

Angel smiled. 'I can't attend evening classes, Gasana. Evenings are a time for me to be with my family; and I can't spend our money on private lessons during the day.'

A loud and insistent hooting started up outside the compound.

'*Eh!* That's the driver!' declared Gasana, and he jumped up from his chair, shook Angel by the hand, thanked her again, and shouted goodbyes to the children as he hurtled out of the apartment.

Angel looked at her watch. It was almost half past two; she had half an hour to supervise the children's homework before Mrs Mukherjee would arrive with her sons Rajesh and Kamal, and their nanny Miremba.

At five to three, she sent Grace and Faith up to Safiya's apartment to continue with their homework, and woke Titi from her afternoon nap. At exactly three o'clock the Mukherjees arrived, and Angel suggested that Titi and Miremba should take all the boys down to the yard with their football so that she and Mama-Rajesh could talk business.

'Yard is safe, no?' asked Mrs Mukherjee, a thin, nervous woman who was constantly wringing her bony hands together.

'Completely safe,' assured Angel. 'The children play there every day.'

'Not too much of germs?'

This was difficult. Angel knew from Dr Rejoice that there were germs everywhere, so of course there must be germs in the yard. But Dr Rejoice had also told her that it was wrong to protect children from all germs. That was the fashion in Europe now, and many *Wazungu* were becoming sick because they had never learned how to fight germs when they were small. But Angel did not think it would be useful to try to explain that to Mrs Mukherjee.

'No germs,' she assured her.

The boys and their carers were dispatched to the yard and Mrs Mukherjee stationed herself at the window to watch them while Angel made tea. She was barely able to coax her guest away from the window when she brought the tea and cupcakes to the coffee table, and it was with a great show of reluctance that the woman sat down opposite her. Angel tried to distract her from the imminent deaths of her boys in the yard.

'These cakes look beautiful with your outfit,' she said. She had deliberately picked out the cakes from the morning's colour-mixing lesson that would compliment the deep purple of her guest's *salwar kameez*. She eyed the design of the outfit now: surely the long dress over the trousers – with slits where it passed over both thighs – would enable a woman to get into and out of a big vehicle elegantly? It looked very fashionable on Mrs Mukherjee's thin body: would it work over her own expanding hips?

Mrs Mukherjee gave the plate of cakes a cursory glance. 'Mrs Tungaraza, did you read *New Vision*?'

'Call me Angel, please, Mrs Mukherjee. I do read it sometimes.' Once or twice a week Pius would bring a copy of the Ugandan newspaper home.

'Ebola!' declared Mrs Mukherjee, leaning forward across the coffee table with an air of conspiracy. Then she sat back in her chair and said again, this time almost defiantly, 'Ebola!'

Angel was not quite sure what to make of this. 'Has Ebola come to Kigali?'

'No!' Mrs Mukherjee's bony hands flew to the sides of her head for a moment. 'No! If Ebola is coming to Kigali then we are booking tickets to Delhi. Immediately!' Her right hand added emphasis to this final word by executing a chopping motion into the palm of her left. She shook her head vehemently.

'Where exactly is this Ebola, Mrs Mukherjee?'

'Uganda!' Mrs Mukherjee raised both her arms in an exaggerated gesture. 'Right next door to Rwanda! Ebola is killing in two weeks. *Two weeks*, Mrs Tungaraza!'

'Angel, please. Let us not be formal.'

'Two weeks. Blood is coming from the eyes, the ears, the nose. *Finished!*' The chopping motion came again.

'But I think we're safe here in Kigali.' Angel removed her glasses and began to clean them with the corner of her *kanga*.

Mrs Mukherjee shook her head. 'Ugandans are here! In Kigali! Working with our husbands! Dr Binaisa. Mr Luwandi...'

'But Ebola is not a disease specifically of Ugandans, Mrs Mukherjee.' Angel's rubbing of her lenses became more insistent.

'Ugandan children are at school with our children. My boys will stay home until the Ebola is finished. I told my husband. I told that it is a Himalayan blunder to send our boys to school when the Ebola is next door. He agrees to my decision.'

Angel had met Mr Mukherjee, who lectured in Information Technology. He was the exact opposite of his wife: big and broad with a quick sense of humour and sensible ideas. He would definitely have disagreed with his wife on this issue, but he probably understood that there was nothing to be gained from saying so. Angel saw the wisdom in this.

'You are very wise, Mrs Mukherjee,' she conceded.

'I'll discuss it with my husband tonight, and perhaps we'll keep our children at home, too.'

The lie was rewarding: for the first time since her arrival, Angel suddenly had her guest's full attention. The two women smiled at each other as Angel replaced her glasses.

'Do try your tea, Mrs Mukherjee. I've heard that it's similar to a tea that is made in India.'

Mrs Mukherjee took a sip. 'Oh, yes, cardamom. In India we are putting cardamom and lemon in green tea.'

'I've always wanted to visit your country,' Angel lied.

'It is a very beautiful country,' beamed Mrs Mukherjee.

'And your country has delicious food, very spicy. In my country, especially along the coast, the cooking is still influenced by the people who came from India to build the railway many years ago.'

Mrs Mukherjee slapped both her hands on her thighs and declared, 'I cook for you one day.'

'That will be wonderful. Thank you. But I've cooked for you today. Please have a cake.'

Mrs Mukherjee chose a cupcake with lilac icing, peeled away its paper cup and took a bite. Angel savoured the secret that — that very morning — a woman with HIV had stirred that cake mixture to get a feel for the correct consistency. To reveal that secret to Mrs Mukherjee would surely be to send her into a frenzy of panic and ticket-booking.

'Very tasty. Obviously you will bake the cake for my husband's cousin-brother, no?'

'Oh, is he visiting here?'

'Yes. He was in Butare, at the National University. Two-years contract is finishing in three months, but he was deciding to prepone and return back early.'

'So he's on his way back home?'

'For the short visit. Now is time for me and my husband to go home, too. I told my husband no more contract.'

'How long have you been here, Mrs Mukherjee?'

'Almost three years. *Three years!* I told my husband if he is renewing contract I am taking the boys home to Delhi. Too much of germs are here.' Mrs Mukherjee finished her cupcake.

'Are there no germs in Delhi?'

'The Ebola is not there.' Mrs Mukherjee shook her head vehemently. 'And no AIDS.'

Angel resisted the urge to polish her glasses again. Without saying a word, she picked up the plate of cupcakes and held them out to her guest, who took one iced in crimson and peeled away its paper case before continuing.

'And the servants in Delhi are better.'

'Are you not happy with Miremba?'

'She isn't knowing good English. Now the boys are speaking bad English. But what to do?' Mrs Mukherjee raised both her arms into the air again. 'Rwandans are not speaking much of English.'

Mrs Mukherjee was clearly unaware that the reason why Miremba spoke English at all was that she had been raised in Uganda, the country where Ebola was even now killing people in two weeks. Angel must remember to warn Miremba never to reveal this fact to her employers. It was time to move the conversation on.

'So, Mrs Mukherjee, tell me about the cake that you want to order for your husband's... er... cousin-brother, is it? Will you be having a party to say farewell to him?'

'Yes. Most of the Indian community here will come.'

'And this cousin-brother's family? Have they been here with him in Butare?'

'No, no. The family is at home in India. He married after already coming here. His parents found a nice girl for him. He went home for marriage and immediately he impregnated his wife. Very successful honeymoon. Very successful. Now he's going to meet his son at home.'

'*Eh*, that is something nice for him to look forward to!'

'Yes. Obviously he will try to impregnate again before going for his new job in England.'

'So his family will not go with him to England?'

'No.'

'Does his wife not mind being left alone to raise his children?'

'No, no. His wife is with the parents. She married well, an educated man. No complaints.'

'And you also married an educated man, Mrs Mukherjee. But you came here with him.'

'The boys are older. If they are babies, no. The wife cannot accompany the husband with babies. Better to stay home with the parents.'

Better for the husband, certainly, thought Angel. It was very convenient for him simply to be away for that whole period of sleepless nights and soiling. Angel had herself not accompanied her husband when he went to Germany for his studies, though the children were no longer babies then. When Pius had first gone to do his Master's degree, Joseph had been eight and Vinas six. After his Master's, Pius had been awarded another scholarship to do a PhD, so when he finally came home, his children were already fourteen and twelve. Of course, he had come home once a year during that time, and once a year Angel had been able to visit him there, leaving Joseph and Vinas in the care of her parents.

Angel had often wondered about the effect on the children of their father's long absence. It had certainly made it easier, she felt, for both of them to choose to live far away from their parents: Joseph in Mwanza, where he had an important job as the manager of a factory that manufactured packaging for Lake Victoria's fishing industry; and Vinas in Arusha, where she taught English. It had probably also influenced Vinas's love for Winston: it was not unknown for girls who missed their fathers to marry men who were older. And perhaps, Angel acknowledged, her own absences during her annual visits to Pius in Germany had helped to prepare the ground for the distance that had come between her and Vinas.

'And what was your husband's cousin-brother doing at the National University, Mrs Mukherjee?'

'Also computer, just like my husband. All men in my husband's family are doing computer.'

'I believe India is an expert country for that.'

'Yes. Now Rwanda is wanting to become the expert

country too. The government of Britain is helping for that – but the power here is on-off, on-off, not like in India. No power outages in India.'

'I have an idea, Mrs Mukherjee. Because most of the Indian community will attend this farewell party, and because India is an expert country in computers and your husband's cousin-brother is himself an expert in computers, perhaps the cake should look like a computer keyboard?'

Mrs Mukherjee thought about this idea while Angel looked for a page in her photo album.

'I have never made a keyboard cake before, so it will be unique for your husband's cousin-brother. But here are some other cakes that I've made to look like things. This one here is a tipper truck, and this one's a cell-phone, and here's a microphone, and an aeroplane. I've also made one that looks like a pile of 5,000 franc notes, but that photo is not yet printed.'

Mrs Mukherjee examined the photos carefully. 'Computer keyboard,' she said. Then she looked at Angel and said, 'Good idea, Mrs Tungaraza. The cake will be computer keyboard.'

'Good!' declared Angel, and for the next few minutes they busied themselves with the Cake Order Form. Angel began by quoting an exorbitant price, knowing that Mrs Mukherjee would insist on negotiating it down. The final price was only slightly lower than what she had hoped to get away with, and since it was substantially lower than the price she had originally quoted to Mrs Mukherjee, both women were happy with the deal. They sat back to finish their tea.

'Tell me, Mrs Mukherjee,' began Angel. 'I'm busy organizing bride-price for Leocadie who works in the shop in our street. By the way, I'll be coming to each and every family in the street about that soon. But for now I'm very interested to ask about bride-price in your country. I've heard that in India it's the girl's parents who must pay bride-price to the boy's parents.'

'Yes. Dowry. My parents were giving to my husband's parents the fridge, the freezer, the motor-car. All new; nothing second-hand. Also jewels; many, many jewels. My husband is an educated man, so there were many gifts.'

'*Eh!* Here it is different. The boy's parents must give bride-price to the girl's parents. Pius's parents gave my parents eight cows. *Eight!* But they would have taken six. Pius was already close to getting his degree when we married, and he was going to become a teacher. In those days there were not very many boys from Bukoba who were getting degrees at Makerere University in Uganda.' Angel stopped speaking suddenly and looked anxiously at her guest. 'Of course, there was no Ebola in Uganda then, Mrs Mukherjee. My parents knew that it was a good marriage for me.'

'Good marriage,' agreed Mrs Mukherjee. 'The girl in the shop is not yet married?'

'Leocadie? No. But she'll marry soon.'

'What about the baby?'

'It's the father of the baby that she'll marry.'

Mrs Mukherjee shook her head and raised both her arms in the air. 'Baby before marriage is bringing shame to the family!' she declared. 'In India, there is no marriage for girls with babies. Those girls are no good.'

'But sometimes a man wants to be sure that a girl is fertile and can deliver a healthy baby. He doesn't want to find out after he's already paid bride-price and married a girl that she cannot deliver. And if a girl has already delivered a healthy baby to a man, then her family can negotiate for more cows.'

Mrs Mukherjee shook her head. 'No. No good.'

Angel recognized that it was going to be difficult to persuade Mrs Mukherjee to contribute any money to the wedding of Leocadie and Modeste. She would have to try her luck with Mr Mukherjee.

Getting up and walking towards the window, she said, 'Shall we call the boys up for some cake?'

As the Tungarazas ate their supper that night, Angel surprised everyone by declaring that she had decided that she wanted to learn some French.

'Why?' asked Pius. 'We can manage fine here with Swahili and English.'

'But when I'm with somebody who doesn't know Swahili or English, then we can't talk. Like Agathe from the hairdresser's. All we can do is smile and nod at each other and then somebody else must be there for us to talk to each other through that person. And today at Jenna's, everybody there knew French except me.'

The passage of a forkful of steamed *matoke* from Pius's plate to his mouth was interrupted for long enough for him to say, 'But Jenna could translate for you.'

'Yes. But there won't always be someone there to translate for me. I can't take such a person with me wherever I go.'

'I hope you don't want to go for evening classes,' said Pius.

'No, of course not.'

'And a private teacher during the day would be expensive.'

'Yes, I know.'

'We can teach you, Mama,' said Faith. 'We're learning French at school. You can look at our books and we can explain everything to you.'

'*Eh*, that is a very good idea, Faith, thank you.'

It was exactly what Faith's mother would have said, and although Angel would have preferred Vinas herself to have been there saying it, it was exactly what she had hoped to hear.

# 10. An Escape

As Angel sat in the unfamiliar lounge sipping at a cup of tea made the bland, English way, she prayed silently for forgiveness. There were a number of things for which she hoped to be forgiven. Above all, it was a Sunday morning, and on a Sunday morning she should, of course, be in church with her family. Today her family had gone to a Pentecostal service in the big blue-and-white striped tent that was home to the Christian Life Assembly church. Right now they would be singing hymns and praising the Lord, while Angel was sitting here, in this house that she did not know, aiding and abetting a deception. Well, three deceptions, really — one of which might possibly cancel out the sin of the second, though she was not entirely sure about that. First, while not actually *lying* to Jenna's husband, she had participated in allowing him to believe that, this morning, his wife would be safely at St Michael's Catholic Church — near the American embassy — with the Tungaraza family; and yet, here was Jenna in this unfamiliar lounge with Angel and two strangers instead. But perhaps it was not wrong to lie to the CIA about his wife being at church, because he himself was lying to his wife and was — in all probability — lying in bed with his neighbour Linda at this very moment. Of course, by providing somewhere else for his wife to be, Angel was aiding that deception; and that was the second reason why she needed forgiving — although deceiving a deceiver was perhaps not so much of a sin. Thirdly, there was the extremely troubling matter for which Angel asked forgiveness every Sunday: the matter of not telling Jenna about her husband's infidelity — although Angel felt sure that if she *were* to tell Jenna, that would also be something for which she would need to ask forgiveness. It was a very complicated situation indeed.

So Angel prayed for forgiveness; but prayer was also a time to give thanks, and she gave silent thanks now for a number of things as she took another sip of the rather insipid tea. As always, she was grateful for a new customer — in this case Kwame, the man in whose lounge she now sat. A few days earlier, Pius's Ghanaian colleague, Dr Sembene, had come to see Angel to order a cake on behalf of Kwame, who would be hosting a small gathering that Sunday afternoon. Kwame's wife, Akosua, would be visiting from Accra, and a number of Ghanaians would be coming to greet her and to hear news from home. Of course, Angel had tried to get as much information as possible about Akosua from Dr Sembene in order to design the perfect cake for her —

but, never having actually met Akosua, Dr Sembene was able to tell Angel only one fact about her. That had meant three things: that the cake that Angel had brought with her this morning, while both colourful and much-admired, was rather non-specific; that Angel and Jenna would have to pretend to be going to church while spending time with Kwame and Akosua instead; and that Angel had another reason to give thanks. Yes, the one piece of information that Dr Sembene had been able to give Angel was very important indeed: Akosua was a trainer of literacy teachers.

Jenna and Akosua were so caught up in their conversation that they had not noticed when Kwame's cell-phone had rung and he had stepped out into the garden — filled with colourful frangipanis and canna lilies — to take the call, apologizing to Angel for interrupting their conversation. Kwame had been telling her about his work as an investigator for the trials that were taking place in Arusha, in Angel's country. The suspects awaiting trial there were accused of planning and leading the killings in Rwanda, and Kwame was part of the international team that was gathering evidence and witnesses against them.

Angel put down her cup of tea and reached down to the ground for the plastic bag at her feet. It contained two more reasons to give thanks. Akosua had brought with her from Accra a large number of lengths of beautiful cloth to sell, produced by a group of women who supported themselves by buying cheap cotton fabric, dying it, then printing special designs and patterns on it before selling it for a healthy profit.

Akosua had told her that each of the patterns had a special meaning, and that in the past only men had been allowed to use those patterns, always printing them in black on a limited range of colours. What the group of women was doing was both traditional and modern.

Angel fingered and admired the two lengths that she had bought. The fabric of one was a light orange colour, printed in bright yellow and gold with a design that was about people cooperating with one another and depending on one another. Akosua had told her what that pattern said: *Help me and let me help you.* This was the cloth that would become her dress for Leocadie's wedding to Modeste.

'You have chosen two beautiful pieces,' said Kwame, who had come in from the garden and was easing himself back into the chair across from Angel.

'*Eh*, but it was difficult to choose! They're all so beautiful. At first I wanted to choose that green one, because Akosua told me that the pattern on there said: *What I hear, I keep.* I like that, because I'm a professional somebody and I know about confidentiality. But I'm sure you know about that in your work, too.'

'Absolutely. No witness wants to come forward without some kind of guarantee of confidentiality. But it's very difficult here, because if somebody sees somebody talking to me, then automatically they assume that person has revealed something to me about somebody else, and then there can be threats of reprisals. Although, of course, many people feel more comfortable talking to an investigator who belongs to neither this group nor that. Still, confidentiality remains a very big problem. By the way, if you *had* taken that green piece with the confidentiality pattern, it would have given you two very different outfits. Those pieces you have chosen are quite similar.'

'Yes. But as soon as Akosua explained this other one to me, I knew I had to have it.' Angel indicated the second of her two pieces, a pale lemon yellow printed with gold and bright orange. 'This pattern talks about reconciling and making peace. As soon as I heard that, I knew that I must buy it for a special wedding dress, and then I must have this other one that is like it, rather than the green one, because I'm going to be the bride's mother at that wedding.'

'Oh, your daughter is getting married? Congratulations.'

'Thank you, Kwame. She's not my daughter, my daughter is unfortunately late. But I'm the bride's mother for the wedding. It will be a special wedding, an example of this reconciliation that everybody is talking about here.'

Kwame shook his head sadly. 'Oh, Angel, that is a wedding that I need to witness! My job makes it very difficult for me to believe in reconciliation, even though I fully want to believe in it. I *need* to believe in it.' Kwame glanced towards his wife, who was talking animatedly with Jenna, and lowered his voice a little. 'I was here before, you know.'

'Before?'

'In 1994. I was one of the UN blue berets. Our job was to keep the peace, but of course there was no peace to keep. And we had no mandate to *create* peace by preventing or stopping the killing because we could not use force. In effect, we were here simply as witnesses. That's why I've come back here now to do this job. I want to find a way to put things right, to contribute, to make up for my powerlessness, my uselessness before. I feel for these witnesses. I know that their silence might protect them from harm by others, but it can also destroy them from the inside. The counsellor who helped me afterwards told me that sometimes you need to dig deep into a wound to remove all the poison before it can heal. These people need to tell what happened; they need to get it all out. Of course it wasn't my own people's slaughter, my own family's slaughter, that I witnessed — so there's no way I can claim that I was a witness in the same way that these people were.' Again Kwame glanced towards Akosua to make sure that she was not listening. 'Actually, I've never told my wife about the things I witnessed here.'

Angel spoke in a low voice, too. 'Not even when you first got back home?'

'No. I didn't know her then. We've only been married a short while. If she had known me then, she would never have married me. I was a mess. And if she knew what I'd seen she'd never have let me come back here. Absolutely not. She would have worried too much about me.'

Angel was quiet for a moment. She wanted to say that it was important to tell the truth, but then she remembered her own lies, the ones for which she had been asking forgiveness just moments earlier. Then she thought of her daughter, who had concealed from her the truth that her marriage was over, leaving Angel to discover by accident from the household help over the phone that Baba-Faith had not lived there for months, and she thought about what other truths Vinas may have concealed, and about what Thérèse had said about a lie holding love in its heart. Then she thought about the testimony that witnesses might give about Leocadie's mother in the prison in Cyangugu, and about Odile, and what she might have witnessed and experienced. And then she did not want to think any more.

'Sometimes,' she said with a sigh, 'life can be too complicated. But Kwame, you must come to this special wedding that I'm organizing. I'll be sure to give you an invitation. Perhaps what you'll witness there will help your own wound to heal.'

'I hope so, Angel. Thank you.'

A loud hoot sounded on the other side of the gate. Pius was on his way back from church with the red Microbus full of happy and excited children, and it was time to go home. On the way, Jenna was more animated than Angel had ever seen her.

'Oh, Angel, thank you so much!' she kept declaring. 'Akosua's helped me to see where I've been going wrong with my literacy class, and how to put it right. And it's great to know that I've been doing at least *some* things right!'

'Jenna, you need to calm down,' Angel warned. 'Remember that when you get home, you need to look like somebody who has been talking to God. You need to look like you have peace in your heart.'

*

After a satisfying lunch of spicy beans cooked with coconut and served with sweet potato and cabbage, Pius retired to the bedroom for an afternoon nap, and Angel settled with Titi, the children and Safiya in front of the television. Ken Akimoto had recently returned from one of his trips home to America, bringing with him a new collection of films that his family had taped for him. Angel had chosen one of them that Sophie had said would be fine for the children to watch.

Less than half an hour into the film, someone knocked on the door. Not welcoming the interruption, Angel went to the door instead of simply calling for the visitor to come in. It was Linda, saying that she wanted to order a cake.

'I can see that you're busy, though, Angel, so maybe I should come back another time.'

'No, no, Linda, I'm never too busy for business. But we can't talk in here. Would you like to go out into the yard?'

'Not a good idea with these sudden rainstorms – and it's probably still muddy out there from the last one. Come upstairs to mine.'

'Okay, let me just get what I need and tell my family where I'll be, and I'll see you up there in a minute.'

Angel gathered a Cake Order Form, her photo album, her diary and a pen, and set off up the stairs to Linda's apartment, trying very hard not to think about what Linda might have been doing in her apartment that morning while Jenna had been out. As she ascended the final flight of stairs, she decided that it would be easier to focus instead on Bosco, and the desperate love that he had once felt for Linda; there was nothing awkward or unethical in that story to make her feel uncomfortable. In fact it was a happy story now, because Bosco had decided to love Alice instead.

She found the door open and Linda inside opening a bottle of Amstel. A sleeveless black T-shirt stretched tightly across her full breasts, ending about ten centimetres above where her short denim skirt began, and exposing a silver stud in her navel. Her long dark hair was tied back loosely in a ponytail.

'Come in, Angel, have a seat. Would you like a beer? Not that local Primus or Mützig rubbish. They say Amstel's illegally imported from Burundi so they're cracking down on it. It's really hard to get now, but somehow Leocadie still manages to find it.'

'No thank you, Linda. I don't drink.'

'You're not a Muslim, are you?'

'No, I'm not a Muslim, I'm just somebody who doesn't drink.' Angel settled herself into a familiar-looking chair.

'You don't know what you're missing, Angel. This place is so much easier to take when you're not stone-cold sober all the time, believe you me! Can I make you some tea instead?'

'That would be very nice, thank you.'

Linda moved across to the far end of the lounge which served as the kitchen area and switched on an electric kettle. Her apartment had only one bedroom, and Angel was relieved that the door to it was shut. She did not want to be faced with the sight of an unmade bed or any other evidence of the morning's activities —

sinful activities that Angel herself had made possible.

'I've just come from having lunch with friends at Flamingo. Have you eaten there?'

'The Chinese? No, it's too expensive for us to eat out. We're a family of eight. *Eight!*'

'Oh, but you should go out sometime just with your husband. Leave the kids with your Titi and get him to take you to the Turtle Café one Friday night. Great live music, sexy Congolese dancing.' Linda swivelled her hips provocatively.

'*Eh*, Linda, I'm a *grandmother!*' Angel laughed. 'That is not a place for people as old as Pius and me.'

Linda smiled as she poured boiling water on to a tea-bag. 'Maybe not. But I'd go mad if I had to eat at home all the time. Milk? Sugar?'

'Yes, please. Just three sugars. But I've been with Pius to functions at a few places here: Jali Club is very nice, and Baobab. And a colleague of his had a small birthday dinner at Carwash. A friend of mine has a restaurant in Remera called Chez Françoise. Do you know it?'

'No, I don't. What kind of food do they serve?'

'Barbecued fish and chicken, brochettes, chips, that kind of thing. And if you want to hold a party there, Françoise can order one of my cakes for dessert.'

'Oh,' said Linda, handing Angel the mug of tea and sitting down opposite her with her bottle of beer. 'Now that sounds interesting. What kind of place is it?'

'It's like a garden, with tables and chairs under shelters made of grass. And the cooking is done there outside as well, over a fire.'

'That sounds like just the sort of place I'm looking

for. I want to throw a small party next weekend, but this flat's too small and I don't want to cook. I thought of asking Ken if I could use his place, but it'd be nice to go somewhere different.' Linda lit a cigarette and inhaled deeply.

'Go and have a look at Chez Françoise and see if you like it. Bosco knows the place; he can take you there.'

'Bosco? Who's Bosco?'

'*Eh!*' thought Angel, and she knew at once that she could never, ever tell Bosco that Linda did not know who he was. Aloud she said, 'Bosco is Ken's driver.'

'Oh, right. But I've got my own car, I'll just get some directions from you.'

'Okay.' Angel took a sip of her tea, the second time she had had to drink English tea that day. At least she had had a good cup of properly made tea when her family had got home that morning. 'Is it a party for your birthday, Linda?'

'God no, it's a much more important celebration than that. I just heard yesterday that my divorce is now final.' Linda raised her bottle in the gesture of a toast and took a large gulp of beer.

Angel did not know what to say. *Wazungu* these days did not take their marriages seriously. Divorce meant that you had failed in your marriage, and to fail was never a good thing. How could failure be a reason for celebration? Really, it should be a reason for shame.

'Oh, don't look at me like that, Angel. My marriage was a bloody disaster. Mum and Dad bullied me into it. They wanted their daughter to marry a nice conservative career diplomat, the son of their nice conservative friends. Trouble was, he was as boring as hell, so I rebelled and got involved in human rights work, which of course was an embarrassment to his precious career.'

Angel wondered if Linda's human rights work could not also be an embarrassment to the CIA. But perhaps it did not matter if they were not actually married. Certainly Jenna's work as a literacy teacher could not embarrass him – although of course it would embarrass him if his bosses ever discovered that one of their agents was not able even to detect a covert operation that was under way in his own home.

'So, do you think that your husband is also going to celebrate this divorce?'

'God yes. He certainly won't be crying into his sherry, that's for sure. Now he can find himself a wife who'll keep her mouth shut and be totally uncontroversial, a sweet hostess for embassy functions.'

Angel thought of Mrs Margaret Wanyika, who was exactly the kind of wife that an ambassador needed: well-groomed, unfailingly polite and always in agreement with her husband and her government's policies. She tried to imagine Mrs Wanyika wearing a tight, short vest and a mini-skirt that showed off a pierced navel, sitting opposite a guest at the ambassador's home, smoking a cigarette and drinking beer from a bottle in the middle of the afternoon, speaking her own mind after a morning in bed with her neighbour's husband. No, nobody would recognize her as an ambassador's wife if she behaved like that – and Ambassador Wanyika would certainly chase her away before anybody confused her with a prostitute.

'I can see that you two were not a good match.'

'We were a bloody disaster. Thank God we recognized that before we brought kids into the world.' Linda lit another cigarette. 'So this party, Angel. It's to celebrate my escape, so I want a cake that suggests escape or freedom in some way.'

'Do you want to look through this to get some ideas?' Angel offered her photo album, but Linda waved it away.

'I've seen loads of your cakes at Ken's. I'll leave the design up to you. I'm sure you're much more creative than I am.'

'Okay, I'll think about it very carefully so that I don't disappoint you. But I'll need to know how many people will be at the party so that I know how big to make the cake, and then we can work out the cost.'

'Fine. Whatever.'

Linda opened another bottle of Amstel as they filled out a Cake Order Form, and then she opened her purse and counted out the total price. Angel saw that her purse was extremely full of banknotes.

'I couldn't be bothered with deposits, Angel. Now I know I've paid you and I don't owe you anything.'

'Thank you, Linda.' Angel folded the proffered banknotes and tucked them into her brassiere. 'You know, it's interesting that you've told me about a divorce today, because I was planning to come and tell you about a wedding.'

'Oh? Whose wedding?'

'A wedding of two people that everybody in this compound knows.'

'Oh God, don't tell me. Let me guess. Omar's going to marry Eugenia? Prosper's going to marry your Titi? Dave the Canadian is going to forgive Jeanne d'Arc and marry her?'

Linda collapsed into laughter and Angel joined her, laughing harder than she had in a long time. Her laughter forced tears from her eyes, and she had to delve into her brassiere for a tissue. It was quite a while before she was able to speak.

'No, none of those, Linda. No, Modeste is going to marry Leocadie.'

'Oh, great. Doesn't she already have his baby?'

'Yes. Beckham. But they're not people with family; they're alone. So I'm going to be the mother of the wedding and I'm asking everyone in this compound and this street to help out with a contribution, because all of us are their family.'

'Of course I'll contribute.' Linda stubbed out her cigarette and reached for her purse again. 'Do we get an invitation to the wedding if we make a donation?'

'Yes, of course.' Angel could see that Linda was deciding how much to give. 'You *Wazungu* who are earning dollars are able to contribute very well. It's nothing to you, but it's everything to people who have nothing.'

Linda reconsidered and fingered an additional note.

'And let us not forget that even now, on a Sunday afternoon, it is Modeste who is outside guarding your vehicle from thieves.'

Linda took another note from her purse.

'And Leocadie is the one who is able to find Amstel for you when it is very difficult.'

Linda took two more notes from her purse and handed the money to Angel, who tucked it into her diary to keep it separate from the cake money that was in her brassiere.

'Thank you, Linda. You're a very generous somebody.'


Later that evening, Angel found herself seated in another of the compound's one-bedroom apartments, this time on the top floor of Ken Akimoto's side of the building. So far she had visited all of the people in the compound whom she already knew well, and she had collected a sizeable amount of money from them for the wedding. Sophie had given her a big brown envelope in which to keep it all so that she did not have to walk around with banknotes bulging out of her diary. But Sophie and Catherine had surprised her with their reluctance to contribute money – and their reason was not that they were volunteers with little money to give.

'How can you ask us to contribute to *bride-price*, Angel?' Catherine had asked, looking appalled. 'Why should we contribute to the purchase of a woman by a man?'

'Or at least, the purchase of her womb and her labour,' Sophie had clarified.

'No, no, that's not how it is,' Angel had hastily explained. She had forgotten about the sensitivities of *Wazungu*, especially *Wazungu* who were feminists. 'I'm just saying bride-price because that's what people here understand. But Modeste has no family who want to buy Leocadie for their son, and Leocadie has no family

[236]

who want to sell her. This money that I'm collecting is for Leocadie and Modeste and Beckham, to pay for a nice wedding and to give them a good start as a family.'

Satisfied, Catherine and Sophie had contributed generously.

'Leocadie *did* bring me a Coke when she heard that I was in bed feeling nauseous the other day,' Catherine had conceded.

'And Modeste *does* keep Captain Calixte away from the apartment,' Sophie had added.

Then Angel had called upon several of the families she knew who lived in the houses lining the dirt road on which the compound — and Leocadie's shop — stood. Starting at the far end and working her way back towards the compound, she had avoided the homes where she did not know the people; those she would tackle during the day rather than in the gathering darkness of evening when people might be suspicious of somebody they did not know asking for money. She would also wait a few days before approaching them so that news of her collection for the wedding could have time to reach them from the neighbours who knew Angel and had already contributed. Of course, some of the people she knew had been out that evening, and she would have to remember who they were so that she could call on them another time. But her memory was not very reliable these days; she would make a note of their names in her diary as soon as she got home.

As she went from house to house in the street, she thought about what Catherine and Sophie had said about bride-price. She had never felt that Pius had *bought* her — or her womb, or her labour — in any way. He had simply approached her parents in the traditional, respectful way to ask for her hand in marriage; and he had compensated them for the expenses that they had incurred in raising her. But she did have a cousin in Bukoba who had not been able to conceive, and the girl's husband had returned her to Angel's uncle and demanded the return of the cows that he had paid. Angel could see that that had been no different from buying a radio that does not work and then taking it back to the shop for a refund.

The Tungarazas' own children had been both traditional and modern when it came to bride-price. Pius had handed over the cash equivalent of a reasonably sized herd to the parents of their daughter-in-law, Evelina. Vinas, on the other hand, had said she could not be bothered with anything like that; she was happy enough to be marrying a man she loved, whose family had already invested everything they had in helping him to qualify as a teacher-trainer, and whose father was in any case already late. Angel and Pius had been satisfied enough with both of these arrangements — and although they had never discussed it, Angel felt that they would be glad if their three grandsons grew up to be more modern; they could certainly not afford high sums to be negotiated for the wives of three more boys.

As she had emerged from the yard next door to the Mukherjees with yet another contribution tucked into her envelope, she had met two men ambling towards her in what would now be total darkness were it not for a small sliver of moon. They wore long white Indian shirts over trousers and sandals, and their smiles glowed whitely as they greeted her.

'Mrs Tungaraza, hello!'

'Hello Mr Mukherjee, Dr Manavendra. Have you been for your evening walk?'

'Yes indeed,' said Mr Mukherjee. 'But we do not normally see you out walking in the evenings. Are you alone? Is Tungaraza not with you?'

'I'm alone, Mr Mukherjee, but I'm on my way home to my husband. I usually see you walking in the evenings with your wives. Where are they this evening?'

'Ebola!' declared Dr Manavendra. 'Our wives won't leave the house until the scare is over.'

'But that's in Uganda,' said Angel, 'far from here. And yesterday in *New Vision* it said that nobody had died from it there for twelve days now.'

'Yes, it's nearly over in Uganda,' said Mr Mukherjee with a laugh. 'Soon the hysteria in our house will be over, too. At least I managed to insist that the boys should go back to school. By the way, Mrs Tungaraza, the cake you made for my cousin-brother was excellent.'

'Excellent,' agreed Dr Manavendra.

'I'm so happy that you liked it.' Angel's own smile gleamed in the moonlight. 'I'm happy, too, that I met you here on the road this evening so that I don't need to disturb you at home. I'm collecting dowry contributions for Leocadie, who works here in the shop. She wants to get married but she has no family to help her. I'm acting as her mother for the negotiations and the wedding.'

'Oh, very good,' said Mr Mukherjee, reaching for his wallet in the back pocket of his trousers.

'Yes, yes,' said Dr Manavendra, mirroring his colleague.

Angel held out the envelope with the mouth of it open so that the two men could place their contributions directly inside it.

'Thank you very much. It's very difficult for people who have nothing and no family, especially when those around them are earning dollars.'

'Very difficult,' agreed Mr Mukherjee, closing his wallet and replacing it firmly in his back pocket. 'But, Mrs Tungaraza, you must go home now. It's not safe for a lady to be out on her own at night; there's always a possibility that eve-teasing can occur.'

'Always a possibility,' agreed Dr Manavendra. 'Let us escort you home.'

'Oh, I'll be fine, really.'

'No, we insist. Come along.'

The two men walked with Angel past Leocadie's shop and past the big green skip that was already filled to overflowing again with the neighbourhood's rubbish.

'*Oof*, this is smelling very badly,' said Mr Mukherjee.

'Very badly,' agreed Dr Manavendra.

'On Thursday or Friday last week I saw them removing that skip up the hill, that one just near the kiosk for international phone calls,' said Angel. 'So maybe they'll get to this one this week.'

'We hope,' said Dr Manavendra.

'Yes, we hope,' echoed Mr Mukherjee. 'There's nowhere for us to put our rubbish without making mess.'

They left Angel within a few feet of the entrance to her building, when Patrice and Kalisa had greeted her and it was clear that she was safe, and turned back towards the home that their families shared.

Despite the cool night air, Angel's head was feeling very hot, so instead of going inside immediately, she sat herself down on one of the large rocks that lined the walkway to the entrance and fanned her face with the envelope of money, careful to hold it closed so that she did not shower banknotes out into the night as she did so.

The compound's owner had recently made an attempt at beautifying the front of the building with a few shrubs and some plants in enormous clay containers. Just next to the entrance was a large bush of a plant that flowered only at night, small white blossoms with a very strong perfume. The plant exhaled its perfume as Angel sat on the rock beside it, and her fanning brought its scent right to her nostrils.

Immediately — almost violently — the smell brought back a flood of memories: Vinas phoning to say she was too busy to come to Dar with the children for the school holidays, she would send them alone on the plane; Vinas phoning to check that they had arrived safely, to hear Pius's and Angel's assurances that no, her two were not too much for them on top of Joseph's three who already lived with them; Vinas's friend phoning in a panic to tell them about the headache that no number of painkillers would take away, about using her key because Vinas had not answered her knock, about rushing her to Mount Meru Hospital where the doctors had shaken their heads and told her to summon the family urgently; finding Vinas already cold in the morgue when they arrived; gathering the children's things to take back with them to Dar; sitting on the edge of Vinas's bed, trying to imagine the intensity of the pain that had pushed so many tablets out of the empty bubble-packs on her bedside table; needing fresh air, going out into Vinas's night-time garden, sitting under just such a night-blooming bush, gulping in the same perfume, sobbing because God had not felt it enough to take only their son.

'*Madame? Vous êtes malade?*' Patrice stood before her, peering into her face with concern.

'*Non, non, Patrice, ça va. Merci.*' Angel reached into her brassiere for a tissue and dabbed at her eyes and her hot face. Then she added, '*Hakuna matata. Asante.*'

She gave a reassuring smile and Patrice retreated. Really, she must pull herself together. All of that was well over a year ago now, and dwelling on it was not going to bring her daughter back. It was not helpful to be sad when she needed to be strong. There were five children − *five!* − in her care now, and that was where her attention should be.

And she had a wedding to organize. Leocadie and Modeste were going to have a perfect day: nobody was going to weep because their cake was unprofessional. There was so much to do! It was time to make a start on the residents of the compound whom she did not know well, and that was going to be a challenge.

And so it was that she found herself sitting in the Canadian's one-bedroom apartment, watching him enjoy one of the cupcakes that she had brought with her to sweeten her request. He was a tall man, somewhere in his late thirties, with very short brown hair and rimless spectacles. Angel noticed a gold band on his wedding finger.

'I'm not even going to be here for this wedding,' he said, his mouth still full, 'so it's hardly my responsibility to help pay for it. I'm only here on a short-term consultancy.'

'What exactly is it that you are consulting about, Dave?'

'I'm helping the government to prepare its interim poverty-reduction strategy paper for the IMF.'

'*Eh*, that is very interesting. Do you have some good ideas for reducing poverty here?'

He laughed and shook his head. 'That's not my job. I just have to make sure these guys write the paper the way they're supposed to write it. *Their* job is content, *my* job is form — although I'm finding myself having to assist with the sections on frontloading priority actions and mechanisms for channelling donor resources to priority programmes.'

Angel thought for a moment. 'Is that a way of talking about how to give money where it's most needed?'

His smile was condescending. 'In a way.'

'And tell me, does it ever happen that a donor gives money for one thing only to find that the money is used for something else instead?'

'All the time. It's expected — or, at least, it's not unexpected.'

'It's expected? Then why does the IMF give the

money if it expects that it will not be used for the right thing?'

'Ah, but the IMF doesn't *give* money. It *lends* money. Ultimately all that matters is that it gets the money back, with interest. If the country doesn't use it the way it said it would, or if it uses it the right way but the project turns out to be a failure, that's not our concern; it's not our responsibility.'

'I see.'

'So anyway, Angel, I'm meeting some people for dinner tonight at Aux Caprices du Palais, and I need to get showered and dressed. This wedding you're organizing doesn't concern me, so I don't think it's right to expect me to contribute. Rwandans are always holding their hands out asking for money.' He stood up.

Angel remained seated. She spoke without looking up at him. 'Yes, there are many beggars here. It's unfortunate that their poverty has not yet been reduced so that they can stop doing that. Those beggars are very inconvenient for visitors, especially for visitors who can afford to eat their dinner at the most expensive restaurant in the city. But those who have jobs are not begging, and this is a marriage of two people with jobs. The job of a security guard for this compound is very important. If something bad happens here, it's the security guards who will protect us. For example, if somebody steals money from us, it's the security guards who will stop that thief in the street outside and prevent that thief from running away with our money. They are the ones who will make sure that we will get our money back. They are the ones who will solve our problem for us before the police become involved and before there is any embarrassment to our families.'

The Canadian stared hard at Angel. Then he threw his head back and laughed out loud, clapping his hands together.

'Bravo, Angel! You really are good! You know, I don't give a damn about all this reconciliation crap you spouted about this wedding, and I don't feel I owe anybody anything, certainly not the money that I work damn hard for. But I do admire your tactics, I really do.' He turned and went into his bedroom. Angel watched him go to the wardrobe and take out a box. He removed a banknote and then replaced the box in the wardrobe and came back into the lounge. Angel stood up.

'I don't suppose you've got change for a hundred-dollar bill?'

'Of course not,' said Angel, taking the note and tucking it into her brassiere.

'Of course not,' echoed the Canadian.

'Thank you, Dave. I hope you enjoy your dinner at Caprices.' Angel put her hand out. Reluctantly, the Canadian shook it.

As she walked down the stairs Angel put that same hand over her breast and felt the shape of the money in her brassiere. She had not put it with the rest of the money in her envelope because it was not going to go towards the wedding. She was going to give it to Jeanne d'Arc, one Rwandan to whom the Canadian most certainly *did* owe his money.

Of course, she had asked for the money for one thing

and was going to use it for something else. But that was not unexpected.

Still, it was undoubtedly a lie. Silently, she offered up another prayer for forgiveness.

# 11. A Welcome

THE DRIVER OF THE *TAXI-VOITURE* OPENED THE back door and carefully took the cake-board that his passenger handed to him to hold while she got out of the car. He looked at the cake admiringly. It seemed to have been built up out of red-earth bricks sealed together with grey cement. On the upper surface of the cake was a large window giving a view into a dark grey interior. Thick vertical bars in light grey blocked the window, but the central bar had been broken and the bars on either side of it had been bent. Tied to the lower edge of one of the bars was a thick plait of powder-pink marzipan that looked like fabric; it hung out of the window and down over the edge of the cake, settling into a pool of plaited fabric on the cake-board.

'What does this cake say to you?' Angel asked the driver, paying him the agreed fare and relieving him of the board.

The driver pocketed Angel's fare as he spoke. '*Bibi*, it

says to me that somebody has escaped from prison. He has broken the bars on the window, and climbed out on a rope that he has made from his prison uniform.'

'*Eh*, that is exactly what I want this cake to say! Thank you.'

The taxi driver furrowed his brow. '*Bibi*, is this a cake for somebody who has escaped from prison?'

'No, no. It's a cake for a *Mzungu* who has divorced her husband. She's having a party tonight here at Chez Françoise because her marriage was like a prison and now she's celebrating because she feels like she has escaped.'

'Eh, *Wazungu*!' said the taxi driver, shaking his head.

'Uh-uh,' agreed Angel, shaking her head too.

'Angel! Are you going to stand there all morning talking to the taxi driver or are you going to come inside and drink a soda with me?' Françoise had appeared at the gate leading into her garden, with blue plastic rollers in her hair and a green and yellow *kanga* tied around her short, stocky frame. She led Angel through the garden that constituted Chez Françoise, shouting instructions along the way to a woman who was wiping down the white plastic tables and chairs with a cloth.

'*Eh*, that cake is beautiful!' declared Françoise, as Angel placed it carefully on the counter of the small bar just inside the entrance to the house. 'This Linda is a very strange *Mzungu*, but thank you for sending her to me. It's not often that *Wazungu* come here, and tonight there'll be a party of sixteen. Tell me, Angel, is that girl always only half-way dressed?'

Angel laughed as she endeavoured to balance her buttocks — tightly encased in a smart long skirt — on a high wooden bar stool that rocked slightly on the uneven floor surface. She held on to the edge of the bar-top to prevent herself from toppling over.

'*Eh*, Françoise, I hope she dresses more modestly when she talks with big men about human rights being violated. How is a minister going to listen to what she is saying about rape, meanwhile she is showing him her breasts and her stomach and her thighs?'

'At least he'll be *thinking* about rape!' said Françoise, laughing and shaking her head. 'Fanta *citron*?'

'Thank you.'

Françoise retrieved two bottles of lemon Fanta from one of the two large fridges that stood against the wall behind the bar, and levered off their tops. She placed two glasses on the counter before climbing on to a bar stool on the other side of the counter, opposite Angel.

'But seriously, Angel, even if she covers up her body, she's still too young. Big people cannot take a young person seriously.'

'Exactly. It's only with age that a person becomes wise.'

'Yes.' Françoise drank some of the soda that she had poured into her glass. 'Whoever is paying her big *Mzungu* salary, they are wasting their money. Because what can she achieve here? Nobody will listen to her.'

'But still, they're *spending* their money; sometimes that's all that matters to some organizations. They can say to everybody: look how many dollars we are spending in Rwanda; look how much we care about that country.' Angel sipped her soda before continuing. 'But let us not complain too much, Françoise. Tonight

[249]

her *Wazungu* friends will be spending their *Wazungu* salaries here at Chez Françoise.'

'Yes.' Françoise smiled. 'I'm going to make everything perfect for them so that all of them will want to come back again.'

'A good way to impress them tonight will be to serve Amstel.'

'Yes, thank you for giving me that tip earlier. I phoned a friend in Bujumbura and she was able to get two cases to me. Well, there *were* four cases, but the customs officials on both sides of the border had to be taken care of. But I think that will be enough to please these *Wazungu*. I do need more customers.'

'Is business still not good?'

'It can always be better. A lot of customers come just to drink, and then they go home to eat. Or they come here with their stomachs already full. It's only when they eat here that I can make a good profit.' Françoise sighed and shook her head. 'It's not easy to raise a child alone.'

'*Eh*, it must be very difficult,' said Angel. 'I'm lucky that I still have Pius; I don't know what I would do without him. I'm not an educated somebody who can get a good job with a good salary.'

'Me neither,' said Françoise. 'I thank God that my husband built this business in our garden many years ago. After they killed him and our firstborn, all I had to do was keep it going.'

'*Eh*, Françoise! I knew that your husband was late, but I didn't know that they had killed your firstborn too!'

'You didn't know?' Françoise looked surprised.

Angel shook her head. 'You never told me, Françoise. How can I know something that I'm not told?'

'I'm sorry, Angel. I thought you knew because everybody knows. Everybody round here.' The circular gesture that she made with her right arm to indicate everybody in the vicinity — perhaps even everybody in Kigali — triggered a serious wobble of her stool. Steadying herself by clutching at the counter, she went on. 'But really, when I think about it, how can somebody from outside this place know without being told? So let me tell you now, Angel.' She took a sip of soda, and when she spoke again there was no sadness in her voice, there was no emotion at all. 'They killed my firstborn as well as my husband.' Her words seemed to come from a barren hardness deep inside her, a place of cold volcanic rock where no life could take root and thrive.

'I'm very sorry, Françoise,' said Angel, sorry for Françoise's loss but also sorry for having made her friend tell her that she had lost a child. Perhaps she should simply have pretended that she knew already. Perhaps she should simply have kept quiet so that Françoise could, too.

But Françoise showed no signs of wanting to keep quiet. 'It happened right there,' she said, pointing towards the gate that opened on to the street from the garden. 'I watched it.'

'*Eh!* You watched it?' Angel clapped her hand over her mouth — carefully maintaining her balance on the stool by keeping hold of the counter-top with her other hand — and looked at Françoise with wide eyes.

'Yes. I'd gone to check on my mother-in-law because she wasn't well, and the stress of what was happening was making her even more ill. Gérard was still a small baby, so I strapped him to my back and took him with me. I was still breast-feeding. When I came back in the evening the darkness was already coming. I saw from the end of the road that there were many people near our gate, and I thought that they were customers. But as I got closer I saw that they were young men with machetes and soldiers with guns. I knew at once that they had found out.'

Françoise's hand was steady as she drank from her glass.

'Found out what?'

'We'd been hiding people here, protecting them from the killers. There's a space in this house between the ceiling and the roof; I don't know how many we put in there. And round the back there's a lean-to where we keep the wood for the cooking fire. Some hid in there, behind the wood.'

'*Eh!* Were these people your friends?'

'Some were friends; some were neighbours. Some we didn't know.'

'But you risked your lives for them?'

'Angel, you have to understand what was happening. Every day the radio told us that it was our duty to kill these people; they said that they were *inyenzi*, cock-roaches, not human beings. But if we had killed them, we would not have felt like human beings ourselves. How could we live with the blood of our friends and our neighbours on our hands? How could we look people in the eye, as one human being recognizing another, and then take their lives? There were thousands who did what they were told to do, thousands who had no choice because it was kill or be killed. But we felt that we had a choice because we had this bar.'

Angel was confused. 'I don't understand. What does this bar have to do with it?'

'We'd heard about what was happening at Mille Collines. Thousands were hiding there from the killers. Whenever the soldiers went to that hotel looking for *inyenzi*, the manager gave them beer to drink and they went away.'

'So you thought you could do the same?'

'Yes — but of course on a much smaller scale. And it worked for a while. Until that evening when I hid behind the wall of a garden across the road with my baby on my back and I watched them hacking his brother and his father to death, along with the people from in the ceiling and from behind the wood.' Françoise took another sip of her soda. She seemed unmoved by her own story, as if she had just spoken about buying potatoes at the market.

'*Eh!*' Angel found the horror too difficult to imagine. Yes, she had lost her own children, unexpectedly, and her son's death had been violent. But she had not watched either of them die. She and Pius had begun to prepare themselves to lose Joseph from the moment he had told them that he was positive, even though he was still fit and well. Even so, when the police had come to their door in Dar es Salaam to tell them what they had learned from their colleagues in Mwanza, the shock of his loss had been devastating, and it had taken them a long time to learn to cope with it. Then they had lost Vinas, too, and they had still not even begun to cope with that. They had not even spoken – really spoken – to each other about it yet. When they did, would Angel be able to do it in the way that Françoise did, without showing any emotion? Perhaps Françoise simply had no emotion left to show.

'What did you do after that, Françoise?'

'I sat behind that wall for a long time, praying to God to keep my baby quiet until the killers had moved on. Then I spent the whole night making my way slowly by slowly back to my mother-in-law's house – because where else did I have to go? But when I got there at dawn, I found that the killers had already been there before us.'

'*Eh!*'

'Yes. So I fled up north to where a relative worked on a pyrethrum farm. I was safe there; nobody was going to try to kill me, because nobody there knew that I was guilty of trying to save lives. It wasn't long before Kagame's forces came and put an end to the killings. When it was safe enough to come back, I expected to find the bodies still here, but they had all been taken and buried in a mass grave somewhere. All I could do was clean up this place and begin again.'

'*Eh*, Françoise, you have told me a very sad story,' said Angel, shaking her head. 'But at least you survived.'

Françoise rolled her eyes up in her head, slid down from her bar stool, and drained her glass. Then she took a deep breath, and with one hand on her hip and the other on the bar counter, she said, 'Let me tell you something about surviving, Angel. People talk about survival as if it's always a good thing; like it's some kind of a blessing. But ask around amongst survivors, and you'll find that many will admit that survival is not always the better choice. There are many of us who wish every day that we had *not* survived. Do you think I feel blessed to live in this house with the ghosts of everyone who was killed here? Do you think I feel blessed to go in and out through that gate where my husband and my child were killed? Do you think I feel blessed to see what I saw that night every time I close my eyes and try to sleep? Do you think I feel blessed not knowing where the bodies of my husband and my firstborn lie? Do you think I feel blessed in any way at all, Angel?'

Angel looked at her friend. For the first time ever, Françoise had shown emotion – and that emotion was anger. 'No, I'm sure you don't feel blessed. Survival must be a very difficult thing, Françoise.'

'I tell you, Angel, if I'd been alone that night, if I hadn't had Gérard on my back, I would have come out from behind that wall and said to the soldiers, I am that man's wife, I too am guilty of protecting *inyenzi*, I too must die. I did not do that. But there are many, many times when I wish I had. If I had known then what survival was going to be like, I would not have chosen it.'

'*Eh!* It's a very sad thing that you're telling me, Françoise.' Angel reached into her brassiere for a tissue, removed her glasses, and dabbed at her eyes.

'I'm telling you because you're my friend, Angel – and because you're not from here, so I can be honest with you. It's difficult for us to say these things amongst ourselves. But what I'm telling you is not something unusual. There are many survivors who feel like I feel. There are many who regret surviving, who would like to make the other choice now.'

Angel thought about what Françoise meant. 'Are you talking about... suicide?'

'Yes.'

'That is not a good idea, Françoise.'

'I know. As Catholics we know that we will go to Hell if we suicide ourselves.'

Angel looked away, unable to speak. She closed her eyes and pressed her tissue to them. Françoise went on.

'And what's the point of going to Hell after we die? Because we already live there now. It wouldn't make things any better for us – and in fact it would make things worse because we'd be stuck there for eternity. At least if I stay alive I can hope for Heaven. I will certainly not miss the opportunity to die if it comes my way again.'

Angel shook her head and was silent for a while before she spoke. She put her glasses back on. 'Françoise, my friend, you have educated me today. These things have not been easy for me to hear, but now I understand better. Thank you for telling me.'

'No, Angel, I am the one who must thank you. Thank you for being someone who has ears that want to hear my story and a heart that wants to understand it. And thank you for sending a big group of *Wazungu* to Chez Françoise.' Françoise flashed her teeth in a wide smile, and Angel found herself smiling back. What they had spoken about had already been put away, like potatoes that have been brought home from the market and placed inside a cupboard in the kitchen.

'I'm sure it will be a very good party, Françoise. Those *Wazungu* will enjoy themselves, and they'll tell others to come here.'

'*Eh*, and when they see your beautiful cake they'll tell others to come to you.'

'Let us hope.'

'Yes. Let us hope.'

It was shortly before noon when Angel eased herself out of a packed minibus-taxi at Kigali's central station. The sun was extremely hot now, but Angel did not have to meet Odile until 12.45, so there was no need to make herself any hotter by hurrying. She walked slowly up to the traffic circle at Place de la Constitution and headed in the direction of the post office, looking for a place where the road was safe to cross. She passed the row of men who sat on chairs placed on the unsurfaced roadside, each behind a small desk and typewriter, preparing documents for the clients who stood over them dictating or issuing instructions. Beyond them she was approached by a few money-changers, the overflow of the large crowd who operated outside the post office.

'*Change, Madame?*'

'*Non, merci.*' Actually, she did want to change some money — the hundred-dollar note that the Canadian had given her — but she wanted to do that at the bank, even though she would get a much better rate from the money-changers on the street.

She crossed the road and made her way back around another section of the outer perimeter of the traffic circle, turning right into Boulevard de la Révolution. On the corner was the Office Rwandais du Tourisme et des Parcs Nationaux, where people went for permits to visit the gorillas in the rainforest in the north. She was not sure why anybody would want to do that, but it was popular enough amongst *Wazungu*.

The boulevard was wide and shady, lined with tall eucalyptus trees, and Angel appreciated its coolness as she approached another, smaller traffic circle, the Place de l'Indépendance. Here she found a young man sitting at the roadside selling second-hand shoes. She greeted him in Swahili and he returned her greeting, jumping to his feet. The shoes were laid out neatly in pairs on the ground. Angel scanned them keenly, searching for the perfect shoe to complement her dress for Leocadie's wedding. Alas, there was nothing here that would do.

'Are you looking for something special, Auntie?'

'Yes, but I don't see it here. It must be yellow or orange, or at least white. Smart-smart.'

'Wait here, Auntie,' instructed the young man. Shouting instructions in Kinyarwanda to a boy who stood on the other side of the road, he raced up the road on his bare feet, whistling, shouting and gesturing frantically.

The boy on the other side of the road eyed Angel and then, bending to pick up what lay at his feet, he crossed to where she stood. He bent again, and placed his bath-room scale at her feet.

'*Deux cents francs, Madame,*' he said.

'*Non, merci,*' said Angel.

'*Cent francs, Madame.*'

Angel shook her head. '*Non, merci. Non.*' The degree to which her skirt strained across her buttocks and thighs already told her as much as she wanted to know. Why should she pay a hundred francs to stand on that scale and find out a number that would only add to the weight that she carried? The boy moved his scale away and squatted down sulkily next to it, eyeing Angel to make sure that she did not try to make off with any of his friend's shoes.

Within minutes, the shoe-seller was back, panting towards her with two other men in pursuit, each carrying a large sack over one shoulder. They rushed towards her, each desperate to be the first to reach her, and spilled the contents of their sacks at her feet, talking non-stop in Kinyarwanda. Scrabbling amongst his wares, one retrieved a white shoe with a high heel and a strap across the top secured at the side with a gold buckle. Angel could see at once that it would be too small for her. She shook her head.

The other man produced a bright yellow sandal that would fit Angel well enough. She took it from him and examined it thoughtfully. The colour was good, but the heel was very flat, making it too casual for the wedding. She handed it back, shaking her head.

As both men continued to scrabble about for the perfect shoe for her, Angel became aware of a child's high-pitched shouting, rapidly gaining in volume. Looking to her right, she saw a very small boy hurtling towards her, clutching something gold and shiny to his chest. Reaching her, the boy drew to a halt and, gasping for breath, held up what he had been carrying. It was a pair of gold court shoes, clearly second-hand but still smart, with a heel that was not too high and not too flat, in a size that would fit Angel and look beautiful with her wedding outfit. Having regained his breath, the small boy was now babbling ceaselessly up at her in Kinyarwanda.

'What is he saying?' she asked the original shoe-seller in Swahili.

'He says his mother is selling that shoe for a very good price, Auntie. He wants you to go with him to pay his mother. She is selling on the street just before the pharmacy.'

'Thank you. Please thank these other gentlemen for me and tell them that this boy has brought me exactly what I'm looking for. I'm sorry that I cannot buy from all of you.'

The young man smiled. 'No problem, Auntie. Maybe next time.'

Angel took the small boy's hand and allowed herself to be led to where a woman sat at the side of the road with a few pairs of shoes laid out before her. They negotiated a reasonable price, and Angel handed over some money from her brassiere while the woman placed the shoes in an old plastic bag. Seeing somebody with money to make a purchase, several sellers of pirated music cassettes approached Angel, but she waved them off with a smile and crossed the road to the entrance of the Banque Commerciale du Rwanda, where a bored security guard checked that her plastic bag did not contain a gun before allowing her to enter.

Once inside the plush, modern building, she made her way around to the foreign currency section of the bank. As usual, there was a large queue of people waiting at the Western Union money transfer section, but the other cashiers were not too busy. She stood behind the stripe on the floor where people were supposed to wait until the cashier was free. There was just one customer busy at the window ahead of her, a large man in West African attire who was waiting patiently for paperwork to be completed. At last he signed, took his own copy, and, thanking the cashier, walked away.

Angel approached the window, removing the hundred-dollar note from its place of safety inside her brassiere. The cashier was still busy putting the previous client's paperwork together with a paper-clip and had not yet looked up at her. When he did, his eyes lit up above his reading glasses and a large smile spread across his face.

'Angel!'

'Hello, Dieudonné. How are you?'

'*Eh*, I'm very well, Angel. And how are you?'

'Fine, fine. How are your mother and your sister?'

'Oh, everybody is very well, thank you. And how are your children and your husband?'

'Everybody is well, thank you, Dieudonné.'

'*Eh*, I'm happy to see you. You're lucky that you came just at this time, because in a few minutes I'll be on lunch.'

'Yes, I thought so. I've just brought some dollars to

change into francs, and then I'm meeting a very good friend for lunch, a lovely Rwandan girl.'

'That is very nice.' Dieudonné took Angel's single banknote and began counting out a large pile of Rwandan francs.

'Dieudonné, it would make me very happy if you would join us for lunch. I like my friends to know one another, and I'm sure that you two will like each other.'

Dieudonné laughed as he handed the money over to Angel. 'Then I would like to meet her! But I have only one hour for lunch.'

'No problem. I'm meeting her nearby, at Terra Nova, opposite the post office. They have a buffet, so we can get our lunch quickly.'

'In fact I go there quite often. Shall I meet you there in ten minutes?'

'Perfect.'

Angel tucked the wad of francs into her brassiere and headed out of the bank with her gold shoes in their plastic bag. She made her way back down the shady boulevard, greeting the shoe-seller with a smile as she passed him, and then round into Avenue de la Paix before crossing the road at the post office, where the crowd of money-changers assailed her.

'*Change, Madame?*'

'*Madame! Madame! Change?*'

'*Non, merci.*'

She entered the yard of the outdoor restaurant where a waiter was settling Odile at a white plastic table in the shade. She smiled when she saw Angel, standing up to kiss her left cheek, then her right, then her left again.

'How are you, my dear?'

'I'm well, Angel. Thank you for suggesting that we meet here for lunch. Usually I just eat at the restaurant at work, but it's nice to take a break like this, especially at the end of the week.'

'It's nice for me, too. Usually I eat at home with the children, but I thought it would be good to spend some time with my friend away from her work — and away from my work, too. The children are safe without me because Titi is there.'

A waiter brought a cold Coke for Odile, levered open the bottle, and poured it into a glass. Angel asked him for a cold Fanta *citron*.

'Odile, I hope you don't mind. I've just bumped into another friend of mine, and I invited him to join us for lunch. He's a very nice young man. Very nice indeed.'

Odile smiled nervously. 'Angel! What are you trying to do?'

Angel smiled back. 'I'm trying to introduce two of my friends to each other. I want them to know each other; that's all. They are under no obligation to like each other.'

In the event, though, Odile and Dieudonné *had* liked each other, and Angel found that extremely satisfying as she sat in her cool lounge later that afternoon, fanning her face with a Cake Order Form and appreciating the looseness of her *kanga* and T-shirt. Her bare feet were up on the coffee table, her ankles swollen from the heat and the busyness of her day. The girls were working on their homework with Safiya upstairs while the boys were out in the yard with Titi, kicking their ball around half-heartedly in the heat.

Half dozing, Angel assessed that, overall, it had been a successful day: people had admired her prison-escape cake; she had gained a new perspective on the matter of survival; she had found exactly the right pair of shoes for Leocadie's wedding; and, best of all, Odile and Dieudonné had found plenty to talk about over their plates of delicious *matoke*, rice, fried potatoes, cassava leaves, carrots, beef and chicken.

There were two troubling aspects of the day, however, and it was these that now prevented her from succumbing fully to sleep. The first was the unsettling comment that Françoise had made about living life in Hell and then being stuck there again after death. That was an idea that would not simply lie down and sleep. The second troubling thing was what had happened when Angel had returned to the compound after lunch. As she had slid down from the back of the *pikipiki* where she had sat sideways with one arm around the rider's waist and the other clutching her gold shoes in their plastic bag to her breast, she had noticed immediately that Modeste was holding a semi-automatic rifle.

'Modeste,' she had said, paying the driver of the *pikipiki*, 'what are you doing with that gun?'

'It is not mine, Madame. It belongs to Captain Calixte.'

'*Eh!* Captain Calixte?'

'Yes, Madame.'

'Where is he?' Panic had begun to pound at the walls of Angel's heart.

'Inside, Madame.'

'But did I not tell you that if he came here looking for Sophie, you must tell him that she is out?'

'Yes, Madame.'

'So why is he inside now?'

'He is not visiting Mademoiselle Sophie, Madame. Mademoiselle Sophie is out. He is visiting Mademoiselle Linda.'

'*Eh?* Linda?'

'Yes, Madame.'

'Is Linda at home?'

'Yes, Madame.'

'I see. It's good that you didn't let Captain Calixte into the building with his gun, Modeste.'

'Yes, Madame. Madame said that I must not if he came again.'

'I'm glad that you remembered. But now I'm worried about Linda. How long has Captain Calixte been inside?'

Modeste shrugged his shoulders. 'Not long, I think.'

Angel was debating with herself whether she should ask Modeste to leave the gun with Gaspard and come upstairs with her to knock on Linda's door, when Captain Calixte himself emerged from the building's entrance. When he saw Angel, he pointed at her angrily.

'You!' he shouted. 'This is your fault!'

Modeste moved closer to Angel in a protective gesture, and out of the corner of her eye she saw Gaspard detach himself from the shadows of the trees on the other side of the road and cross towards them.

'Hello, Captain Calixte.' Angel kept her voice calm. 'What is it that is my fault?'

'That *Mzungu* upstairs refused me!' The soldier spat the words out between his chocolate-coloured teeth. 'If I had taken a cake, she would have accepted my proposal, I'm sure of it. It's your fault that she refused me.'

Very quietly, seemingly unnoticed by the soldier, Gaspard had now taken up position immediately behind him, ready to seize him if necessary.

'Sophie is out this afternoon, Captain Calixte. How can a *Mzungu* who is out refuse you?'

'Not *Sophie*!' He stamped one of his wellington boots on the ground. 'That other *Mzungu*! The one who is just divorced.'

'Do you mean Linda?'

'Yes. Linda.'

'But, Captain, you didn't ask me to make a cake for your proposal to *Linda*! Now how can it be *my* fault that she refused you when you didn't take a cake?' Angel's tone was soft, reasonable.

The captain looked confused, and then − quite visibly − his anger left him in the way that breath leaves a party balloon when the hold on its stem is released. In a sulky tone, he said, 'She wouldn't even look at my certificate.'

'That is very sad, Captain Calixte. But you know, Linda is very happy that her marriage is over. She is even celebrating her divorce with a party tonight. A girl like that is not going to accept a marriage proposal at this time. Not from anybody.'

The captain thought for a while. 'You're right, Angel. It is only that I've proposed marriage to her at the wrong time.' He shook his head. 'I'm sorry that I said it was your fault.'

'No problem, Captain Calixte.'

The soldier had taken his weapon and left, and Angel had come inside, her mind troubled. Okay, nothing bad had actually happened. But really, Captain Calixte was not a stable man. It was not right that he should be walking around with a gun. And yet he was. This – and Françoise's troubling comment about Hell in this life *and* eternally – made Angel anxious, preventing her from dropping off to sleep now with her feet up on the coffee table.

But had she fallen asleep, she would very soon have been woken by a heavy knock on the open door of her apartment.

'Hello?' called a deep male voice. 'Angel?'

Angel took her feet off the coffee table and stood up, calling as she did so for the visitor to come in. The head that looked around the open door was bald on top with a band of black hair from ear to ear at the back and a neatly trimmed black beard from ear to ear at the front.

'Hello, Angel,' said the Egyptian, talking through his alarmingly big, hooked nose.

'Mr Omar!' said Angel.

'Just Omar,' he said, shaking Angel's hand. 'I hope I'm not disturbing you?'

'Not at all, Omar. Please come and sit. You know, I've called at your apartment a few times this week, but you've always been out.'

'Yes, Eugenia told me.' Omar sat down heavily opposite Angel. 'I believe you're collecting money for a special wedding?'

'Yes. One of our security guards is going to marry the girl who runs the shop in our street. I'm organizing the wedding for them because they have no family except for us in this compound.'

'Of course I'll contribute.' Omar stood to retrieve his wallet from the back pocket of his trousers and then sat down heavily again. He took a few notes from his wallet and handed them to Angel, then left his wallet on the coffee table. 'And I'd like you to make a cake for me, Angel.'

Angel smiled as she stood up. 'Then I'll give you my album of cakes to look through while I make tea for us to drink. We cannot discuss business without tea!'

Angel gave Omar her photo album and went into her bedroom to put his contribution with the rest of the wedding money in the envelope that she was keeping on the top of the wardrobe for safety. Then she went into the kitchen to make tea.

When she came back into the lounge carrying two steaming mugs, Omar was admiring her photos.

'You're very clever, Angel. Something of an artist, in fact.'

'Thank you, Omar.' Angel put the mugs on the coffee table and sat down, patting her hair with her hand. 'I'm sorry I can't offer you cake to eat with your tea. I wasn't here at lunchtime, and the children ate all the cake instead of eating their rice and beans.'

Omar suddenly made an alarming sound through

his enormous nose, rather like the sound of hippos mating in the shallows of Lake Victoria. But he was smiling and his belly was moving up and down. Angel smiled nervously.

'That's children for you,' he said. 'Mine would do just the same.'

'Oh, you have children?'

'Yes, yes. A son of sixteen and a daughter of thirteen. They're both in Paris with their mother. My daughter, Efra, she's coming to visit me here next week. That's why I want a cake. She's been angry with me, but I think we've negotiated a kind of peace.' Omar took a sip of tea. 'Oh, this is very good, Angel. What's the spice?'

'Cardamom. It's how we make tea in my home country.'

'Cardamom?'

'Yes.'

Omar put down his tea and sank his head into his hands.

'Omar?'

When he looked up, his pale brown complexion had turned slightly red. He shook his head. 'This will not do,' he said. 'I've been trying to forget an unfortunate incident, but it seems I cannot.'

'Omar, you're not making sense to me. Please tell me what's bothering you. It may be that I can help you.'

Omar made the alarming sound of mating hippos again, but this time it was much quieter, as if the hippos were in the distance — perhaps as far from Mwanza on the shore of the lake to Saa Nane Island — and he looked embarrassed. 'Perhaps you can, Angel. Some time back I was preparing *fattah*...'

'What is *fattah*?'

'It's a dish that we cook in Egypt, very well known. I'll cook it for you one day. Anyway, I had just started when I realized that I had no cardamoms left. So I sent Eugenia to my upstairs neighbours to ask for some.' Omar stopped talking and took a sip of tea. He put the mug down on the coffee table. 'But she came back with *condoms* instead.'

Angel could not stop herself from laughing. Omar looked at her and began to laugh as well, great blasts of mating grunts exploding from his nose. The more he made his hippo noise, the more Angel laughed, and the more she laughed the more he did, too.

Several minutes passed before either was capable of speech.

'I suppose it *is* quite funny,' said Omar, wiping tears from his eyes with the handkerchief that he had retrieved from the pocket of his trousers. 'But I've been so very embarrassed about it.'

Angel was dabbing at her eyes with a tissue. '*Eh*, Omar, your story is very funny to me – more so because I've already heard part of it from Sophie.'

'Oh, no! Please tell me, Angel, what does she think of me that I send my servant to get condoms from her?'

'She's very embarrassed, Omar. In fact, she's been trying to avoid meeting you on the stairs.'

'I've been doing the same! I don't understand why Eugenia got it so wrong! Alright, her English *is* limited, but we were in the kitchen, I was busy cooking, I needed cardamoms. How could she think I wanted condoms?'

Angel was still battling to control her laughter. 'I

suppose to be sent for condoms is not a new thing for her. And perhaps a condom is a more familiar thing to her than a cardamom,' she suggested. 'But tell me, Omar, how did this *fattah* of yours taste when you added the condoms?'

Again the mating bellow blasted from Omar's nose, and Angel doubled up with laughter. Having heard the noise from the yard, Titi came up to check that everything was okay. She left again when Angel waved her away.

'No,' said Omar, struggling to get his breath, 'I had to go out to buy some cardamoms. I didn't want to risk sending Eugenia to any other neighbours. I wish I'd known that you had some here.'

'Always,' said Angel, dabbing her eyes again. 'You can always get them from me. But I think that is one spice that you will not run out of again.'

'True, true. But, Angel, what should I do about Sophie? How should I explain the mistake to her?'

'I can explain it to her if you like,' Angel offered. 'Then perhaps you can talk about it together afterwards. I think she'll be nervous if you go and knock on her door before she understands what happened.'

Omar looked as though a weight had been lifted from his shoulders. 'I'd be very grateful if you'd do that for me, Angel. Thank you.'

'No problem. I'll tell you as soon as I've explained what happened, and then you can go and talk to her.' Angel sipped her tea. 'Now. You said that you want a cake for your daughter.'

'Yes. She'll be here for just over a week and I want to

make her feel welcome, because things have been difficult between us since her mother and I split up.'

'And do you have an idea of how you want the cake to look or what you want it to say?'

'Yes. I saw one in your album shaped like a heart. I think it should be like that.'

'That's a very good shape for a situation like this,' agreed Angel. 'What colour do you think it should be?'

'Oh, red, definitely. It's her favourite colour. And perhaps it can have her name on the top. Efra. I'll show you how it's written in Arabic and you can copy it.'

'That would be good,' said Angel.

They spent a few minutes completing the formalities of the Cake Order Form and making arrangements for delivery before sitting back to finish their tea.

'You know, Omar, I've heard that some of the first *Wazungu* that came here thought that the Tutsi people had originally come from Egypt.'

'Oh, that's a misconception that's driving us mad! I think you know I'm a lawyer for the genocide trials here?' Angel nodded. 'Many of the accused try to use that as an excuse. Some half-brained colonial explorer thought the Tutsis looked more Arab than African, so he speculated that they must have come from down the Nile. That gave the *génocidaires* a perfect excuse to get rid of them.' Omar hooked the index and middle fingers of each hand and waved them in the air to indicate quotation marks. '*They don't belong here so let's send them back down the Nile to where they came from!*'

'Yes, they put all those bodies into the Kagera River and the river carried them to Lake Victoria.'

'The source of the Nile.'

'But they look nothing like somebody from Egypt!'

Omar pointed to himself with both hands. 'How many Tutsis have you seen who look like me?' A loud snort of derision blasted from his nose. 'Whoever the half-blind colonial was who made that observation should be charged with genocide, even though he's long dead. His words lit the fire in which the genocide would be cooked up – and the Belgian administration added fuel to the flames by exaggerating the differences.' Again Omar made quotation marks in the air. '*Tutsis are superior, so let's privilege them. And let's make everyone carry a card saying if they're Hutu or Tutsi – just so that we can tell the difference.* But of course the very perpetrators who are using what the colonials said as an excuse for their killing, they are the ones who are quick to reject everything else that the colonials ever said.'

Angel thought for a minute. 'I wonder if those colonials had any idea back then what the consequences of their actions would be today.'

'Oh, I'm sure they couldn't have known. I doubt if they would have cared, either.' Omar drained his mug and cradled it in his large hands. 'It's the same today. Government leaders don't think twice about borrowing money from the big financial institutions because they'll only have to pay it back in forty years' time – and in forty years' time it'll no longer be *their* responsibility because a different government will be in power. And who cares about polluting the atmosphere and destroying the planet? *We're* not the ones who'll have to live with the long-term consequences. And how many of us ever stop to think about the consequences of our own actions on a daily basis? Look at me. I fooled around. It was fun. So I fooled around some more. Now my marriage is over and my son refuses to speak to me, and my daughter and I are struggling to be friends.'

Angel tried not to think about struggling to be friends with her own daughter. 'I suppose you're right, Omar. Perhaps it isn't human nature to think very far ahead.'

The two said nothing for a while as they contemplated this. It was Angel who broke the silence.

'But now you have an opportunity to make things better with your daughter, Omar. What do you plan to do while she's here?'

'Oh, I've deliberately not made any plans. I don't want her to accuse me of making decisions without consulting her; whenever I do something like that she shouts: *Objection!*' Omar's quotation marks shot up into the air around this word. 'I'll put a few options to her and then she can make up her own mind.'

'That'll be good. You know, Efra is not much older than my girls. Perhaps they can spend some time together while she's here.'

'Good idea. Thank you, Angel.' Omar put his empty mug down on the coffee table and stood up, tucking his wallet back into his back pocket. 'And thank you in advance for speaking to Sophie for me.'

'No problem,' said Angel, beginning to laugh again.

Omar smiled broadly and said goodbye, trying hard to suppress his laughter. He managed until he had made it up one flight of stairs, and then the sound of

hippos mating in the shallows of Lake Victoria reverberated throughout the stairwell and blasted out of the
building.

Gaspard and Modeste looked up from the bananas
that they were eating outside and exchanged a knowing
glance: the sun was not yet down and the Egyptian had
already started having sex.

# 12. A Confirmation

BOSCO SIGHED HEAVILY AND BANGED THE PALM of his right hand down hard on the steering-wheel of Ken Akimoto's Pajero. Angel was right: it *was* good for Alice that her father was trying hard to secure a scholarship for her to study in America. But it was certainly not good for Bosco.

'Now, Auntie, what am I supposed to do while she's in America for her degree? For three years, Auntie. Three years is a very, very long time!'

'I'm sure she'll come home for holidays during that time, Bosco. *Eh*, Bosco! Be careful of these potholes! I don't want my teapot to break.'

In her lap, Angel cradled a beautiful blue-grey teapot, hand-made by Batwa potters at the workshop outside Kigali that she had just visited with Bosco. She had thought long and hard about what to give Leocadie and Modeste as a wedding present, and at last she had decided that the most appropriate gift would be some of this pottery. The Batwa were a tiny minority in Rwanda, small not just in number but also in stature, and Angel had not heard about them before she came to live in Kigali. Of course she had heard about Hutus and Tutsis – in 1994 the whole world had heard about them – but she had not heard about this third group of tiny people who, long ago, used to live in the forests. They, too, had suffered terrible violence and discrimination, but Angel could not remember hearing about them in any of the news reports. It was only right, she thought, to commemorate the union of two of the three groups with a gift made by the third.

She had gone to the pottery workshop with no clear idea of exactly what she was looking for. It was Bosco who had pointed the teapot out to her. He had said that it was a good gift for Angel to give because she was always giving people tea to drink; it was something that would always remind Leocadie of her wedding-mother. And he was right.

'Sorry, Auntie,' he said now, slowing down the Pajero. 'Auntie, it's not just that Alice will be away for three years. You know that since I got Perfect as my niece, I've wanted a baby of my own. Now, how can I wait three years for that?'

'But Bosco, you knew when you met Alice that she intended to study at university. She was not one of the Girls Who Mean Business.'

'Yes, Auntie. But I thought she would attend classes here, at KIST.'

'And how was she going to attend classes *and* have a baby?'

'There are classes in the evenings, Auntie. She could look after the baby in the day while I'm at work, and then in the evening I could look after the baby while she attends classes.'

'That's a good plan, Bosco. But is it a plan that you and Alice made together?'

'No, Auntie,' said Bosco, slowing down further as he navigated his way around two cyclists.

'These days a man cannot make decisions on his own, Bosco. It was different before — when I was your age — but these days a man cannot just tell a girl what to do. There has to be consultation, negotiation. I'm sure Alice knows about these things, because Sophie is her teacher.'

Bosco was quiet for a while before he said, 'Then, Auntie, is it okay for me to ask her not to go to America?'

Angel looked at him. 'What do you think my answer to that question is going to be?'

He made a tutting sound with his tongue against the roof of his mouth and sighed heavily. 'It's not okay, Auntie.'

'Yes. If she gets the opportunity to go, then of course she must. She's still young, Bosco.'

'I know that, Auntie. If she goes, then I think I must love somebody else instead. Somebody who is not so young.'

'*Eh*, Bosco, the way you say that makes me nervous. It makes me think that you already know this somebody else that you're going to love.'

'No, Auntie.'

'Are you sure, Bosco?'

'I'm sure, Auntie.'

Angel was not convinced. 'Are you very, very sure, Bosco?'

'*Eh*, Auntie!' Bosco gave an embarrassed smile. 'Okay, I thought for a while of loving Odile. But Odile cannot bear children.'

'*Eh?* She cannot?' This was something that Angel had suspected, because it explained why Odile had never married. The purpose of marrying was to have children, and a woman who could not bear children was of little use to a man.

'Uh-uh. In the genocide they cut her with a machete in her parts, her woman's parts. I like Odile very, very much, she is very, very nice. But I want to have babies, so I'm not going to love her. No, Auntie, there is nobody else that I'm going to love. Not yet.'

'That's good. Because Alice has not gone to America yet, and maybe she won't go at all. It's not easy to get a scholarship.'

'I know, Auntie. I'm just trying to plan ahead.'

'*Eh*, Bosco!' Angel spoke so loudly that Bosco almost swerved the Pajero off the road. She clutched her teapot protectively. 'Sorry, Bosco. I forgot to tell you! It's only now that you're talking about planning ahead that I remember.'

'What, Auntie?'

'*Eh!* Captain Calixte proposed marriage to Linda!'

'To *Linda*?' Bosco stared at Angel with his mouth open. 'Is Auntie serious?'

'Watch the road, Bosco! Of course I'm serious! It was

less than one week after Linda heard that she was divorced. *Eh*, news travels very fast here!'

'Very, very fast, Auntie. Please tell me that Linda refused him.'

'Of course she refused him.'

'That is good, Auntie.'

'She's still sleeping with the CIA.'

'That's bad, Auntie. Does the CIA's wife suspect?'

This was a difficult question. As far as Angel knew, Jenna suspected only that her husband worked for the CIA. But Jenna was her customer, so Angel was not at liberty to disclose this to Bosco. Okay, Linda was also Angel's customer. But Linda had never confided in her about sleeping with Jenna's husband, so it was fine to talk about that. But Jenna's suspicions were a different matter.

'I think she might suspect something. But she's very busy with her literacy class now.'

'Does the CIA suspect?'

'No. He still has no idea of what's happening in his own apartment every morning.' Angel laughed, and Bosco joined in.

'He's not a good CIA,' he said, shaking his head.

They drove in silence for a few moments. Angel ran her hands over the shiny roundness of the teapot in her lap, feeling very happy with her purchase. She was happy, too, that Ken had agreed to let Bosco drive her to the Batwa pottery workshop. And of course she was happy that Bosco was her friend.

'*Eh*, Auntie!' said Bosco suddenly. 'I forgot to tell you! Alice told me that her friend, the one who is the sister of Odile's brother's wife, that friend told Alice that Odile has a boyfriend now!'

'A boyfriend? Odile? Are you sure?'

'Very, very sure, Auntie.'

'*Eh!* Do you know this boyfriend's name, Bosco?'

'No, Auntie. But Odile's brother's wife told her sister, and then her sister told Alice, that he works in a bank.'

A wide smile lit up Angel's face. She was very happy indeed.

Later that afternoon, as she finished decorating a cake that had been ordered for a retirement party the following day, Angel received a visit from Jeanne d'Arc. The children had just settled down to do their homework in the lounge, so Angel made tea and took her guest down to the compound's yard, where they sat on *kangas* spread out in the shade.

Jeanne d'Arc was an extremely beautiful young girl, and it was easy to see why men were attracted to her — even though she dressed much more modestly than many of the other girls in her profession. Today she wore a long maroon skirt over low-heeled black sandals that revealed toenails painted in a dark red colour. The same colour adorned the nails on her long, slim fingers. Draped around her shoulders and secured with a small gold brooch at one shoulder was a thin, black shawl that hung in soft folds to her knees. Long, thin extensions fell down her back from neat rows radiating back from her forehead.

'I'm happy that you came to see me, Jeanne d'Arc,' began Angel. 'I have something for you.'

'For me, Auntie?' Jeanne d'Arc looked confused.

'Yes.' Angel reached into her brassiere where she had slipped the money when she had left Jeanne d'Arc in the kitchen to watch that the milk did not boil over. She held the roll of Rwandan francs out to her guest. Jeanne d'Arc looked at the money but did not take it.

With a furrowed brow she said, 'What is it that you want me to do, Auntie?'

Angel gave her what she hoped was a reassuring smile. 'This is your money, Jeanne d'Arc. I got it for you from the Canadian.'

'*Eh?*' Jeanne d'Arc still did not take the money.

'Yes. I know that he took back from you the money that he owed you, and also some other money that was already yours. I don't know how much that was, but this is what I got from him.' Angel took Jeanne d'Arc's right hand and placed the money in it, closing her fingers around it.

'Oh, Auntie,' said Jeanne d'Arc, 'I am so ashamed! I tried to steal from that man. I should not have done that.' She tried to hand the money back to Angel, but Angel raised both her hands with the palms facing forward and would not take it. 'Please, Auntie, I cannot have this.'

'Jeanne d'Arc, did you not do sex with the Canadian?'

'Yes, Auntie, I did, but...'

Angel gave her no time to continue. 'So did you not earn that money?'

'Yes, Auntie, but...'

'And did he not take from you money that you had already earned?'

'Yes, Auntie, but...'

'But nothing, Jeanne d'Arc! Okay, you tried to steal some money from him. But he took that money back, so that matter is finished. And in fact *he* stole that money from *you*. That money is rightfully yours and you must have it. Do you not want the money that you earned? Do you not need it?'

'*Eh*, I need it, Auntie.'

'Then you must have it. I insist. I will not take it back, Jeanne d'Arc.'

Angel sipped at her tea for a while to give the girl time to think, and watched her taking deep breaths and turning the roll of banknotes over and over in her hand. At last she looked up at Angel.

'Thank you, Auntie, I will take it. Thank you for getting it for me.'

'No problem.'

Then Jeanne d'Arc peeled off one of the notes and handed it to Angel. 'Auntie, I would like to contribute to the bride-price for Modeste and Leocadie. I was going to contribute only a small amount, but now I can give more.'

Angel accepted the note and tucked it into her brassiere, watching as the girl placed the rest of the notes inside a small black handbag.

'Thank you, Jeanne d'Arc. The herd of cows is becoming big now.'

'I'm glad, Auntie. *Eh*, I'm happy to have my money; thank you again.' Her beautiful face broke into a smile. 'It has saved me from having to pay for our room with sex.'

'Good. You said *our* room, Jeanne d'Arc. Do you share a room with another girl?'

'No, Auntie, I have my two young sisters and a small boy. I've been their mother since '94.'

'But you look like you still need a mother yourself! How old are you now?'

'I think I'm seventeen, Auntie.'

'Seventeen?'

'Yes, Auntie.'

'So you were eleven when you became their mother?'

'Yes, Auntie.' She shrugged. 'I was the oldest one left. Our parents were late, and also our brothers.' She shrugged again.

'And the small boy?'

'After we fled into the forest, we found him there by himself. We couldn't just leave him, he was very small then.' Another shrug.

'And how have you been taking care of these children, Jeanne d'Arc?'

'At first — afterwards — we went back to our family's farm. We grew potatoes and cassava there, and some bananas. But it was very difficult for us because the men that we had seen kill our family, they were still there, they were our neighbours on the other hills. Some people came from an organization, some *Wazungu*, and they tried to help us, but they could not find anybody from the boy's family who was still alive. Really, we could not stay there. Then we all came to Kigali.'

'And have you been prostituting yourself since then?'

'Yes, Auntie. Those men had already violated me. I

was already spoiled, so it didn't matter. But my sisters were not spoiled, so I wouldn't let them work. My work pays for their schooling and our clothes and food, and also our rent.' She flashed a beautiful, shy smile at Angel.

'*Eh*, I'm proud of you, Jeanne d'Arc.'

'Thank you, Auntie. Now my first sister, Solange, she's going for her confirmation in the church, and I want her to have a party with her friends to celebrate. I've come to ask Auntie to make a cake for her party.'

'*Eh!* I will be honoured to make that cake!'

'Thank you, Auntie. Just something small and simple, please.'

'It will be a beautiful confirmation cake, Jeanne d'Arc. I'll give you a very good price. Tell me, how old is Solange?'

'At her school they say she's eleven. I think she's twelve or thirteen, but she's very small. I think the reason she's small isn't because she's young; I think it's because she didn't get enough food for a long time.'

'Is she about the same size as Grace, or as Faith?'

Jeanne d'Arc thought for a while. 'Maybe she's like Faith, but I'm not sure. Maybe she's smaller.' She shrugged.

'Okay. Both of my girls have already been confirmed. Grace had her own confirmation dress, and then it was altered for Faith. Why don't you bring Solange to visit us, then we can see if the dress fits her. If it needs altering in any way, you can take it to a place in Biryogo where there are some ladies who are learning to sew. They do good work and they're very cheap. I'll tell you where the place is. Solange will have a nice dress for her confirmation. She'll feel very proud.'

Tears began to well in Jeanne d'Arc's eyes. 'Auntie, you are very kind. It hasn't been easy for me to be a mother to children who are not my children, and now you are being a mother to me when I'm not your child. You are Leocadie's mother for the wedding, too. And I know that your children here are not your children but your grandchildren. I'm sorry that your own children are late. They were very lucky to have you as their mother.'

'*Eh*, Jeanne d'Arc. *Eh!*' Tears welled in Angel's eyes, too, now.

'Auntie?'

Angel delved into her brassiere for a tissue. '*Eh*, I'm sorry, Jeanne d'Arc.' She took off her glasses, put them in her lap and dabbed at her eyes. 'It's only that I wasn't a good mother to my own daughter.'

Jeanne d'Arc took Angel's hand that was not busy with the tissue and held it tight. 'No, Auntie, I don't believe that. You were a good mother to her.'

Angel's sigh was deep as she shook her head. 'No, Jeanne d'Arc. A good mother does not let her daughter marry a man who is going to disappoint her, to hurt her.'

Still holding Angel's hand, Jeanne d'Arc sipped at her tea. 'Was she in love with him, Auntie?'

'*Eh!* Very much!'

'Girls have told me that to be in love is a very nice thing, a happy thing. Did you not want her to be happy, Auntie?'

[286]

'Well, yes, of course I did.'

'Then I think you were a good mother, because you let her be happy, even if you were not. Now, say you didn't let her marry him, then you would be happy but she would be unhappy. Does a good mother not put her daughter's happiness before her own?'

Angel managed a smile despite her tears. 'That is true, Jeanne d'Arc. But somehow things were never the same between us after her wedding. She was far from us in Arusha, meanwhile we were in Dar es Salaam. But there was another kind of distance between us, too. We spoke often on the phone, and always she told me that everything was okay, but later I found out that it wasn't. She had another baby some time after Faith and Daniel, but he was weak, Jeanne d'Arc. Late within some few months.'

'I'm sorry, Auntie.'

'*Eh!* That was a bad year for all of us, because my son was shot by robbers at his house.'

'*Eh!* I'm sorry, Auntie.'

'And then my daughter's husband left her, and she didn't tell me. It was only by mistake that I heard it from her helper.' Angel clicked the tip of her tongue against the back of her teeth.

'You're confusing me now, Auntie. First you told me that you were a bad mother. Now I think you're telling me that she was a bad daughter. Now I'm not sure who it is that Auntie feels she needs to forgive.'

'Now *you're* confusing *me*, Jeanne d'Arc!'

The girl placed her mug of tea on the ground so that the hand that was not holding Angel's could help her to make her point. 'What you have told me is this, Auntie. You think you made a mistake because you let her marry a man who was not good. But that man made her happy for some time. And Auntie, what we know here, in this country, is that our lives can be short. If we have the chance to be happy, we must take it. Even if it is a short happiness, we are glad to have it. Now your daughter, when she was no longer happy, she kept it secret. Why, Auntie? Because she loved you. She didn't want you to be more unhappy, you were already unhappy because of your son.'

'*Eh*, Jeanne d'Arc!' Angel squeezed the girl's hand, remembering Thérèse's words about a lie holding love in its heart. 'Part of my head is telling me that you're right, meanwhile the other part is still confused. That is something that I will think about later. But there's also another secret that she didn't tell me, a secret that I haven't yet told myself...' The same hundred frogs that had leaped, startled, into a still pond at the centre in Biryogo were now in a panic in her stomach, thrashing about desperately. Perhaps the sweetness of her tea would calm them. She put down her wet tissue, picked up her mug and drained it.

'Auntie, in Kinyarwanda we say that a hoe cannot be damaged by a stone that is exposed. I think it means that the truth will hurt us only if it remains hidden.'

'That is a good saying, Jeanne d'Arc, and I'm going to tell you the truth now, because I feel it is time for me to tell it. I will be hearing it for the first time myself as I tell it to you. It is what I've come to suspect, and now, right now at this minute, I'm accepting that it's true.'

Feeling one of the frogs trying to scramble up from her stomach into her mouth where it would prevent her from speaking, she swallowed hard. Then she took a deep breath, and spoke rapidly as she exhaled, anxious to say it, to hear it. 'My daughter was sick, Jeanne d'Arc. She found out that she was positive when her baby was sick. That's why their marriage broke up, because AIDS came to their house.' She had no more breath to exhale.

Jeanne d'Arc finished her tea, waiting quietly as Angel gulped in air and swallowed hard.

'But that is just a small secret. It's not something that I'll be ashamed to tell others, now that I've told myself, even though many of us are still not comfortable to talk about that disease. To catch such a disease does not make a person a sinner. A foolish somebody, yes. A careless somebody, yes. An unfortunate somebody, yes. But a sinner? No.'

Jeanne d'Arc nodded her head to every yes, and shook it to the no.

'That disease is just a small pebble, Jeanne d'Arc, it is not the stone that will break the hoe. You know, I'm going to stop being angry at Vinas for lying to me, because I've been lying to myself. I've told myself stories about stress, about blood pressure, about headaches. But the hoe has sliced straight through those stories now. I have another story, I have it ready to tell, but I know now that the hoe will not even notice it. That story is that it was an accident that Vinas took so many painkillers, that she was confused by her headache, that she failed to count.' The frogs stopped moving, stunned. Nothing could stop Angel now. 'Jeanne d'Arc, the stone that I need to dig up, the truth that I need to expose is this. My daughter wanted to die. She took those pills to suicide herself.'

When Angel stopped speaking, she was surprised to notice that she was no longer crying; she realized that she had in fact stopped crying as soon as she had decided to tell the truth. She felt empty of emotion, the way that Françoise had seemed when she had told her own story. Telling it had shifted something in her. Putting her glasses back on, she looked at Jeanne d'Arc and saw that there were tears in the girl's eyes.

'*Eh*, Jeanne d'Arc! I didn't mean to upset you. How can you weep for my story when your own is so much worse than mine?'

Jeanne d'Arc let go of Angel's hand, removed a length of pink toilet paper from her handbag and blew her nose delicately. Then she breathed in deeply before saying, 'Auntie, I'm weeping for *you*, not for your story, because the pain of loss is heavy in your heart.'

'There is a heavier weight than loss in my heart, Jeanne d'Arc. Everybody knows that suicide is a sin, that it sends a soul to Hell. *Eh*, it's very hard for me to know that Vinas is there.'

'Yes.' Jeanne d'Arc was silent for a few moments before she continued. 'But I think that Vinas chose to do what she did in order to save others, Auntie. When she suicided herself, did she not save her parents from the pain of watching her suffer? Did she not save her children from the pain of watching her die? I think that when a person dies to save others, Hell is not the place for her soul. I think the Bible tells us that such a soul belongs in Heaven.'

Angel looked at Jeanne d'Arc. How could someone so young be so wise? 'That is true, Jeanne d'Arc. After all, Jesus died to save others. Do you think that God—'

Angel's question was interrupted by a thumping sound and a loud *eh!* echoing in the stairwell, and then Prosper came tumbling out into the yard, landing spreadeagled in the dust.

'*Merde!*' he shouted, standing up and dusting himself down.

'Prosper?' said Angel. 'Are you okay?'

Prosper observed Angel and Jeanne d'Arc through eyes that were very red. 'I'm fine, Madame. I just fell over something on the stairs on my way down. Modeste and Gaspard must take better care with the cleaning.' He swayed slightly on his feet. 'Madame, I could not help overhearing before I fell that you were talking to this girl about God and Jesus. That is very good. The Bible tells us much about the sin of prostitution.'

'Yes,' said Angel. 'It tells us that Jesus forgave prostitutes and allowed them to enter the Kingdom of Heaven.'

'*Eh*, Madame! I hope that you have not been forgiving this sinner!'

'Actually, Prosper,' said Angel, smiling now, 'she is the one who has been forgiving a sinner.'

'*Eh!*' Prosper shook his head and moved unsteadily towards the door of his office. 'You ladies are very confused. I myself will find some verses in the Bible for you to read.'

They watched him struggle with the key and then enter his office, and they waited for him to emerge with his Bible. But he did not come. Then, softly at first but growing louder, came the sound of snoring.

Angel and Jeanne d'Arc looked at each other and began to giggle.

That evening, as Titi and Angel were busy preparing the family's supper in the kitchen, Pius settled down in the lounge to read the copy of *New Vision* that Dr Binaisa had passed on to him. The Ebola scare was well over now, and the boys were with the Mukherjee boys down the road, playing under the watchful eye of Miremba. In their bedroom, the girls and Safiya were styling one another's hair.

Pius was half-way through reading about new allegations concerning the smuggling of diamonds and coltan out of DRC, when his concentration was broken by a knock at the door.

'*Karibu!*' he called, but nobody came in. Putting his newspaper down on the coffee table and grumbling to himself, he got up and went to open the door. Standing there were two young men who were clearly not from this part of Africa.

'Good evening, sir,' said the one who was wearing smart grey suit-trousers, a white shirt and a tie. 'I hope we're not disturbing you. We're looking for a Mrs Angel.'

'Oh, Angel is my wife,' said Pius, assuming that these must be customers for Angel's cakes. 'Please come in. Angel!' he called. 'You have visitors.'

Angel came out of the kitchen, wiping her hands on a cloth. 'Hello,' she said with a smile.

'Hello, Angel,' answered the young man in the tie. 'Omar upstairs sent us to talk to you. I hope this isn't an inconvenient time?'

'Not at all,' Angel lied. Emotionally drained after her talk with Jeanne d'Arc, she was in no mood at all for business, but as a businesswoman she was obliged to remain professional at all times.

'I'm Welcome Mabizela, and this is my friend Elvis Khumalo.'

Angel shook hands with them and introduced them to Pius, who shook hands with them, too.

'Please come and sit,' said Angel, and the four of them sat down around the coffee table. 'I think that Mabizela and Khumalo are South African names?'

'*Ja*,' said Welcome with a smile, 'we're from Johannesburg. I've come up here to facilitate workshops on reconciliation, based on my experience working with the Truth and Reconciliation Commission in South Africa.'

'*Eh!*' said Pius, sitting forward with interest. 'I'm sure you have many interesting stories to tell.'

'Don't say that to him, Pius, he'll never shut up. *Eish*, he'll be telling his stories all night!' Elvis shook his head and laughed.

Angel looked at Elvis, who was dressed far less conservatively than his friend in a smart red T-shirt and tight black denim jeans. Short extensions hung loosely around his head.

'And what is it that *you* do, Elvis?' she asked.

'I'm a journalist, mostly freelance, always looking for a story I can sell.' The smile that he flashed was brilliant white. 'In fact that's why Omar suggested we come and see you. He said you're organizing a wedding, and I want to find out more about it. Maybe it's worth a story.'

'Angel,' said Pius, 'I want Welcome to tell me his stories about South Africa, and Elvis wants to talk to you about the wedding. Why don't we invite our visitors to join us for supper?'

'Of course,' said Angel, clapping her hands together. 'Please say you'll eat with us.'

'Oh, we can't impose on you like that...' began Welcome.

'Nonsense!' declared Angel. 'There's plenty of food for everyone. Really, we insist that you stay.'

Elvis glanced at Welcome before saying, 'In that case, we can't refuse. Thank you, Angel, we'd love to.'

Angel went into the kitchen to redirect the dinner preparations to satisfy two more mouths. Both of their guests were thin — but healthy young men usually had big appetites whatever size they were. The chicken pieces that were roasting in the oven would have to be removed from the bone when they were cooked, and chopped into smaller pieces. She would make a stew of peas and carrots in peanut sauce, and add the chicken to that. The rice that was already cooking was not going to be enough, and it was too late to add to it — but it could finish cooking and the family would eat it tomorrow. Instead, she would make a big pot of *ugali* to have with the chicken stew.

As she and Titi busied themselves in the kitchen,

Angel listened to snatches of conversation from the lounge. Pius was questioning Welcome on the significance of the distinction between what South Africa called '*truth* and reconciliation' and what Rwanda called '*unity* and reconciliation'. Could truth not make reconciliation impossible, he was asking. Was unity a possibility in the absence of truth? Angel was glad that there was someone else in their house tonight who could field her husband's questions; it was not a debate in which she herself felt confident of any answers.

When the *ugali* was just a few minutes from being ready, Angel and Titi emerged from the kitchen, and Titi was introduced to the guests before being sent to fetch the boys from the Mukherjees.

'Take the torch, Titi,' said Pius. 'There's no moon tonight and the street is dark.'

Angel accompanied Safiya upstairs so that she could have a quick word with the girl's mother.

'Amina, we have unexpected guests for supper, and you know that we have very little space. Can I send the girls up here with their plates of food?'

'Of course, Angel,' said Amina, wiping her hands on a tea towel. 'We'll be ready to eat our own meal as soon as Vincenzo has finished washing.'

'Thank you, Amina. They'll come in a few minutes.'

Back downstairs, Angel had Grace and Faith wash their hands, then sent them upstairs with a plate each of *ugali* with the sauce of chicken stew. The boys arrived home with Titi, washed their hands, and were dispatched to their bedroom with their plates of food, where Titi would join them soon.

Then Titi brought a big plastic bowl into the lounge, and as each of the guests and Pius in turn held their hands over it, Angel poured warm water from a jug over their hands while they washed them. Titi dished up for herself in the kitchen and retired to the bedroom with her plate.

Angel, Pius and their guests sat around the coffee table, forming balls of *ugali* in their fingers and dipping them into the large bowl of chicken stew. As they ate, Pius and Welcome discussed the theoretical and philosophical aspects of reconciliation, while Angel and Elvis concentrated on one practical example: the wedding of Leocadie and Modeste.

'I think this is a story for a magazine rather than a newspaper,' suggested Angel. 'There must be photographs of the wedding so that readers can see that these are real people, and that reconciliation is not just an idea.'

'I agree one hundred per cent,' said Elvis. 'It'll need to be much longer than the average newspaper story anyway. Both parties will need to tell their story.'

'That's true,' said Angel, reaching for the bowl of *ugali* and beginning to shape another ball with a dip in it to hold the sauce. 'But, Elvis, I must tell you that this is a story that will interest many journalists. Very many. From all over Africa, and even from Europe and America. Magazines like *Hello!* and Oprah's new *O* magazine will be interested. You know that a magazine in South Africa will not want to buy the story from you if every other magazine in the world is already telling the same story.'

'Absolutely,' agreed Elvis. 'Of course I would want exclusive rights to the story, and exclusive access to everyone involved.'

'Yes, and I am the one who will decide who gets exclusive access, because I am the wedding mother and I am the one who can advise the two parties whether to talk to a journalist or not.'

'I understand,' said Elvis, smiling. 'So let's cut to the chase, Angel. What is it that will persuade you to grant a particular journalist exclusive rights to the story?'

She was ready with her answer: 'The magazine that is going to tell this story must sponsor a small piece of the wedding.'

'I see. And what small piece of the wedding are we talking about?'

'The cake.'

'The cake?' Elvis looked at Angel with a mixture of relief and surprise. 'Just the cake?'

'Yes. It's going to be a very beautiful cake that I'm going to make myself. When we've finished eating I'll show you photographs of other cakes that I've made.'

'Okay. Let me make a few calls tomorrow and I'll let you know in the next day or two if that's going to be possible.'

'Okay, Elvis. I won't give anybody else exclusive rights until I've heard from you.'

The meal progressed with a mix of political debate, story-telling and happy laughter, and afterwards Elvis made appreciative noises as he looked through Angel's photo album – particularly when he saw the cake of the South African flag.

The guests expressed reluctance at having to go, but felt that they must because there were young children in the house who needed to get to sleep.

'Where are you staying?' asked Pius. 'Can I give you a lift?'

'Oh, thank you, no, we're close by,' said Welcome. 'At the Presbyterian Guesthouse. It's less than ten minutes' walk from here.'

'*Eh*, but you cannot walk tonight,' declared Pius. 'There's no moon, and there are no streetlights along this road. You won't find your way, I guarantee. No, I'll take you there in the Microbus. I insist.'

As soon as Pius had left with the South Africans, Angel and Titi began cleaning up in the kitchen and Benedict was sent upstairs to fetch the girls. Titi took the chicken bones, carrot peelings and other rubbish out to the skip in the street so that they would not attract cockroaches or make the kitchen smell in the night, leaving Angel to transfer the uneaten rice from the pot in which it had cooked to a plastic bowl to store in the fridge. As she occupied herself with this task, Angel thought about the two young men who had just shared dinner with them. Unless she was very much mistaken — which she was sure she was not — they were more than just friends. South Africa was truly a very modern country indeed.

Suddenly the door of the apartment flew open and Titi came rushing into the lounge, trembling and whimpering, with tears running down her face.

'*Eh*, Titi!' said Angel, coming out of the kitchen. 'What's happened?' She went over to Titi, put her arm around her shoulders and led her to the sofa, where she sat down beside her. The children gathered round and looked at Titi with big eyes as she struggled to control her breathing.

'Grace, bring Titi a glass of water,' commanded Angel. 'Faith, bring tissues. *Eh*, Titi, whatever has happened you are safe now. There's no need to cry. Nothing bad will happen to you in here.'

Titi wiped away her tears with the tissue that Faith had brought and took a sip from the glass of water that Grace had handed to her.

'*Eh*, Auntie!' she said, shaking her head. '*Eh!* I was not thinking when I took the rubbish to the skip. I forgot that it had been emptied.' She took another sip of water. 'When I opened the lid to put the rubbish inside, a voice in there spoke to me and hands grabbed the rubbish from me.'

'*Eh*, the *mayibobo* are back,' said Angel. A group of street children sometimes slept in the skip at night when there was enough space inside. It provided warmth and shelter and — perhaps most importantly — instant access to anything that the neighbourhood was discarding, some of which might pass for food.

'It was very dark, Auntie,' said Titi. 'I saw nothing. Then I heard a voice, and hands started grabbing. *Eh*, it frightened me!'

'Of course it did, Titi. You've had a very bad fright. But you're fine now. Why don't you go and wash and prepare yourself for bed, and I'll make some hot milk and honey for you.'

'Thank you, Auntie.'

While she waited for the kettle to boil, Angel checked that all the children had washed their feet and brushed their teeth, and settled them into their beds with the promise that Baba would come to say goodnight in a few minutes. After taking Titi her warm milk in bed, she went back into the kitchen and filled the rice-pot with water to soak overnight, thinking as she did so that the few grains of rice that clung obstinately to the bottom and sides of the pot would probably seem like a big meal to one of the *mayibobo* outside in the skip. Then she thought about the small boy who was living with Jeanne d'Arc, and about Jeanne d'Arc's younger sisters. If Jeanne d'Arc was not willing to do what she was probably doing at that very moment – perhaps even in this very compound – to keep them off the street, those children could well be in that very skip.

When Pius came back from delivering their visitors to their guesthouse, he found Angel frying onions in a big pot.

'*Eh*, why are you cooking at this time of night?'

'There are *mayibobo* in the skip. I just want to take them something to eat.'

'I see. And have you forgotten the reason why I uprooted us all and left my comfortable job in Dar to come and work here in Kigali as a Special Consultant?'

'No, Pius, I haven't forgotten.'

'It was because I need to earn more money so that we can give our grandchildren a good life.'

'I know that.'

'But now it looks to me like you intend to use my salary to feed the entire world.'

Angel emptied the rice from the plastic bowl into the pot with the onions and gave it a good stir. 'No, Pius, I just intend to use a bit of my money from my cake business to put a bit of food into those homeless children's bellies before they fall asleep on everybody's stinking rubbish.' She silenced her husband with a look. 'Our children are waiting in their warm beds for their Baba to come and say goodnight.'

Angel added a small amount of *pilipili* to the rice and onions to give the dish some flavour and warmth, and stirred until the rice had heated through. Then she spooned the food back into the plastic bowl.

Pius was coming out of the children's room as she carried the bowl towards the door of the apartment. She hesitated for a brief moment before speaking.

'Pius, when I come back, I want us to talk.'

'What about?'

'About something that I told myself today.'

'*Eh?*'

'Oh, Pius, is it not time for truth and unity and reconciliation to stop being just theories in our house?'

'What do you mean, Angel?'

'I mean...' She lowered her voice to a whisper, conscious that the children were not yet fully asleep. 'It wasn't an accident, was it?'

Pius's eyes widened, and he stared at his wife for almost a full minute without blinking. It was the way that a small animal on a bush road might stare at a car coming towards it at night.

'I mean, Vinas,' she whispered. 'The pills...'

He shook his head, exhaling strongly as if he had

been holding his breath for a very, very long time. 'No. It was no accident.' His eyes were damp as he reached out a hand and squeezed Angel's shoulder gently. 'Come back quickly, Angel. It really is time we faced the truth together.'

Outside, Angel found Kalisa sitting on one of the big rocks that lined the path to the building's entrance. She asked him to take the food to the *mayibobo* in the skip.

'When they've finished, the bowl must come back to me. I'll wait here.'

'Yes, Madame.'

Angel took Kalisa's place on the rock and stared up at the stars in the very black sky. There were people who knew about stars, who could tell you the name of every star in the sky. She knew that one of the stars was called Venus, like the name of her daughter. Okay, it was actually a planet, not a star — she knew that from the children's atlas — but it shone in the sky just like the stars. But she did not understand how it could be important to learn the name of every single star in the sky; surely it was better to know the name of every person in your street?

She thought of the cake that she was going to make for Solange's confirmation. She and Jeanne d'Arc had agreed on a vanilla cake in the shape of a Christian cross, white on top to convey purity and with a turquoise and white basket-weave design piped around the sides to match the confirmation dress, which was white with turquoise ribbons threaded through it. Solange's name would be piped in turquoise across the top.

Suddenly Angel was blinded by lights shining in her eyes as a large vehicle came down the hill and turned off the tarred road into the dirt road. The Pajero drew to a halt next to her.

'Everything okay, Angel?' asked Ken Akimoto.

'Everything's okay,' she said, feeling that yes, it was going to be. 'Thanks, Ken. I'm just enjoying the night air.'

'Okay.' He drove to the other end of the building and parked outside his own apartment. Bosco was his driver only during office hours; after that, Ken was perfectly capable of driving himself. Of course, Bosco was much more than Ken's driver, and was happy to be sent on any number of errands.

Angel smiled as she thought about what Bosco had told her that morning: Odile had a boyfriend! Dieudonné would be a good partner for a woman who was not able to bear children; having grown up without his parents, in the care of other people, he might easily be persuaded to think of adopting one or two of the thousands of children who filled the country's orphanages. Which was a lot better for them, she considered, than filling the country's rubbish skips.

Then she became aware that something very important had happened. She had been sitting out here next to the same night-blooming plant that grew in Vinas's garden in Arusha, and she had not been thinking about her daughter. She had not felt overwhelmed by her death. She sniffed the air. Yes, the plant had indeed been exhaling its perfume as she sat there. But the scent had not undone her.

'*Eh!*' she said to herself, unsure if it was right or wrong to have let go of some of her grief. She took off her glasses to give them a clean, but saw that they did not need it, and put them back on again. She closed her eyes to get a better sense of what she was feeling. Yes, she was still very sad. But somehow, in a small way, part of her despair had changed. It had turned to hope.

When she opened her eyes, Kalisa was emerging from the total darkness and approaching her with a small child dressed in reeking rags. The little girl was running her small fingers around the inside of the bowl before licking them clean. She handed the bowl to Angel with a big smile.

'*Murakoze cyane*. Thank you very much,' she said.

# 13. A Rising Up

THERE WERE TWO THINGS THAT PLEASED ANGEL the following Sunday morning, and one thing that jumped around anxiously in her mind like a monkey in a wire cage.

The first thing that pleased her was that, on the way home from church that morning, the family had seen a man at the side of the road selling bags of *senene*. They knew the *senene* had finally arrived in Kigali for their second visit of the year because, for the past two nights, they had seen them swarming around the streetlights on the tarred road next to their compound. Last night they had taken the paraffin lamp that they kept for use during power failures, and they had put it outside in the dark yard to attract the bright green grasshoppers. Daniel and Moses had had a great deal of fun – though very little success – trying to catch them in their hands and put them into the empty Toss jar that Faith held for them with a piece of cardboard covering the top. Faith did not mind holding a jar full of insects, and she did not mind sliding the cardboard aside for another to be put inside — but whenever one of them flew into her or actually landed on her, she would scream and drop the plastic jar, allowing all of them to escape. At last Angel and Pius had called a halt to the children's fun by summoning them in, concerned that the lamp might be attracting mosquitoes as well as grasshoppers. At that stage there were only eight *senene* in the bottle: one for each member of the household.

But now they had bought a whole bagful of them, and their lunch was going to be delicious! Pius had pulled off all the wings and legs for Angel, and she had already simmered them in salted water for half an hour. The final step in preparing them would be to fry them, but Titi would do that just before the meal so that they would be crispy and piping hot.

Alone in the apartment now, Angel looked at her watch. What was she going to do for the next half hour or so? Jenna had gone to church with them that morning, and when they had found the *senene*-seller on the way home, Angel had offered to cook some grasshoppers for her — but Jenna would not hear of it. If she had accepted, Angel could have been busying herself with their preparation right now. But unfortunately she would have to find something else to occupy her time.

Without wanting to be there, she found herself standing at her work table, looking down at the cake that she was to deliver that afternoon. No cake had ever disturbed her quite as much as this one. Okay, it was not the cake itself that disturbed her. In fact, it was a very beautiful cake indeed: a round vanilla sponge in two layers, iced in pure white with a sprinkling of tiny red roses with green leaves across the top. What disturbed her was the occasion for which the cake had been ordered: the cutting of a girl.

Of course, she had heard of this practice, although it was not part of her own culture. Catherine had told her — in response to Angel's discreet enquiry — that it was not something that happened in Rwanda; yet it seemed that some groups of people who practised it at home in their own countries were also practising it here. It was not an idea that Angel liked at all, and she would certainly not choose it for Grace or Faith. To cut out and stitch up a girl's private parts to make them look more attractive to a man was surely not a reasonable thing to do. And people said that it made sex painful for the girl when she grew up, so that she would not be tempted to do it with anyone other than her husband. But what kind of husband would be able to achieve pleasure for himself, knowing that what he was doing was causing his wife physical pain? There were many complications from the practice — even from the less severe form, where less of the girl was cut — and if the girl did not die from an infection, her baby could easily die during delivery if there was nobody there to cut her parts open again to let it out.

So why had Angel agreed to make this cake? She was still not entirely sure, although she knew that her reasons were complicated. Okay, she could have refused. She had refused to bake a cake for Captain Calixte, because if he became her customer, professional ethics would not have allowed her to warn Sophie about his intentions. But in this case, who was she going to warn that the girl was going to be cut? The girl herself? She had no right to do that. The Rwandan authorities? She could not do that to the girl's family. And in any case, she had been sworn to secrecy even before she had agreed to make the cake, so she would not have been able to tell anyone, even if she had refused the order. *Eh*, this would be a very difficult ethical dilemma for the Girls Who Mean Business to discuss!

But something else gnawed at Angel like a monkey chewing away at the bars that restrained it: had she accepted the order because she was... curious? She had been invited not just as a cake-maker but also as a witness. Was her curiosity about the idea of cutting more important to her than the girl's pain? *Eh!* That was a question she might not want to know the answer to. She must stop thinking about it immediately, otherwise she was going to give herself a headache.

She went and sat on the sofa with her feet up on the coffee table and gave her glasses a good polish with the edge of her *kanga*. As she did so, she felt heat rising up her throat to her face. She closed her eyes and examined the sensation: it was not because she felt ashamed about what she was going to do that afternoon, and it was not because she was bothered by her unclear motives. No, she was simply flashing again. Really, this was becoming very tedious indeed – although, in truth, it had been happening less and less. She must remember to ask Dr Rejoice exactly how long it was going to go on. Surely a woman could not be stuck in the Change for ever? Surely she would eventually arrive at a point where she had... well... *Changed*? Angel mopped the perspiration from her hot face with a tissue and decided to think about something happier.

Her other reason to be delighted that day — apart from the *senene* — was that very soon Grace and Benedict would be home after spending two nights away. She focused now on how it had come about that they had gone away for the weekend.

She had just come back into the building after going out to buy sugar at Leocadie's shop, where Leocadie had shown her the beautiful wedding veil that the sewing class in Biryogo had made for her. The cloth that they had used was the bed-net that Sophie and Catherine had given her when Beckham was born, and that Leocadie had never used.

'They told me my baby must sleep under that net every night,' Leocadie had said, shaking her head. '*Eh*, these *Wazungu*! Do they think that mosquitoes live only in our bedrooms and bite us only when we're sleeping?'

'*Wazungu* are very afraid of malaria,' Angel had said.

In truth, one or two *Wazungu* had succeeded in persuading her at least to consider putting nets above the children's bunk-beds; and when she had discussed the idea with Dr Rejoice during Benedict's last bout of malaria, the doctor had told her something that had convinced her that it was a very good idea indeed. Dr Rejoice had explained that, if a mosquito that was not carrying malaria bit Benedict while he had malaria, that mosquito now carried malaria because of Benedict.

Then that mosquito could take Benedict's malaria and give it to somebody who was too sick to fight the disease — somebody who already had AIDS, for example. That had made Angel see malaria in a new light — and she did not want anybody in her family to be responsible for somebody dying because their body was weak with AIDS. It was not just a matter of protecting her family from malaria; it was a matter of protecting the health of others in the community as well. She had gone the very next day to the pharmacy to ask about the bed-nets that Dr Rejoice had told her to ask for — the ones that had the special mosquitocide on them — but they were much too expensive. The pharmacist had told her that they were priced high for *Wazungu*, because only *Wazungu* bought them. She had resolved to buy some in Bukoba when they went home for their holidays at the end of the year, because they would be cheaper there.

But she had not told Leocadie any of this, because she had not wanted her to feel badly about using the bed-net to make her wedding veil — which was, after all, very beautiful.

As Angel had come back into the building with her bag of sugar, Omar and his daughter had been coming down the stairs. She had already met Efra, who had spent some time in the Tungarazas' apartment watching a video with Grace and Faith. She was a slight girl who could have been gorgeous had it not been for the replica of her father's enormous nose dominating her face. Unfortunately, it was not possible to forget about her nose by not looking at her face, because her voice seemed to come out of it when she spoke, in the same way that her father's did. But at least her laugh came out of her mouth — and did not make people think about animals that were mating.

'Angel!' Omar had trumpeted. 'I'm so glad that we saw you. Efra has decided that she would like to go and see the gorillas this weekend, and we wondered if a couple of your children would like to join us?'

'*Eh*, Omar, that is a very nice idea, thank you. But it's very expensive to see those gorillas...'

'Oh, it'll be my treat! It won't cost you anything; I'll cover the cost of the permits, the hotel, everything. It'll be my pleasure. And Efra would love to experience it with other children. Please say yes!'

'How can I say no to that, Omar? Thank you very much. Let me speak to them tonight and see who would like to go.'

'Just two of them, Angel, if that's not going to cause too many arguments. There won't be room for more in the Land Rover. Sophie will be joining us, too.'

'Sophie?' Angel's surprise had been obvious.

Omar's laugh had reverberated around the entrance hall and hurtled out of the door, where it had stopped a boy who was walking down the road with boiled eggs to sell. He had looked towards the entrance of the building with both surprise and fear, as though a fully grown hippopotamus might lumber out of the doorway and attack him at any moment. Angel had noticed Efra's embarrassed, downcast eyes.

'Sophie has forgiven me since we spoke about our little misunderstanding concerning a certain spice. Thank you so much for explaining things to her, Angel.

I know a volunteer can't afford a trip to the gorillas, so I offered to take her with us at my expense to compensate for any embarrassment that I caused her.'

'*Eh*, you are a very generous somebody, Omar!'

'Not at all. No need to let me know which two of your children are coming. I've booked two suites at the Hotel Muhabura in Ruhengeri; boys will share with me, girls with Efra and Sophie. We'll leave after school on Friday afternoon and come back Sunday morning. I'll have them back before lunch, guaranteed.'

That evening, Angel had discussed Omar's offer with Pius before saying anything to the children. They had agreed that it would be best for them to choose which two would go, rather than to let the children decide amongst themselves. It would be best, they had reasoned, for Grace and Faith to go; they were the eldest, and they had already made friends with Efra. They had told the girls about Omar's generous offer just before putting them to bed.

Later that night, when Angel and Pius had turned off the television after the nine o'clock news in English and were about to retire to their room, Faith and Benedict had slipped quietly into the lounge.

'Mama,' Faith had appealed to Angel, 'I don't want to see gorillas.' She had been on the verge of tears. 'They are very big, Mama, and I'm still small.'

'Baba,' Benedict had appealed to Pius, '*please* let me go instead of Faith! I want to see the gorillas. Please, Baba. Please let me go!'

And so Grace and Benedict had gone – which was good, Angel and Pius had reasoned after the children had gone back to bed: the eldest two children of their son Joseph would have a small holiday together, and perhaps it would help to create a closer bond between the two.

Now, sitting on the sofa in her empty apartment and fanning her hot face with a Cake Order Form, Angel waited for them to return. A quick jolt of excitement shot through her as she heard a vehicle drawing to a halt outside the building, but then she recognized the sound of the engine: it was Pius in the red Microbus, back from sending emails from his office computer. Upstairs with Safiya, Faith heard the vehicle, too, and ran down the stairs, only to be disappointed when it was not her brother and sister who walked in through the building's entrance. Both Pius and Faith joined Angel in the lounge. No sooner had they sat down than the sound of children's voices came in from the street. Faith ran to the building's entrance and was disappointed again: it was Daniel and Moses coming back from the Mukherjees' with Titi.

At last, when Faith was nearly out of patience with waiting, and Pius was nearly out of patience with Faith's restlessness, Grace and Benedict arrived home in a flurry of excitement. Omar, Efra and Sophie came into the Tungarazas' apartment with them.

'How was the trip?' asked Pius, shaking Omar's hand.

'Excellent!' declared Omar. 'Great fun! I think your two enjoyed it, especially Benedict.'

'He was like a different person,' said Sophie. 'I couldn't believe it, Angel! Normally he's so quiet, but he hardly stopped talking all day yesterday. He talked to our guide all the way up the mountain, and to one of the trackers all the way down he mountain. Then at the park headquarters we met a vet who treats the gorillas and we could hardly tear Benedict away from him.'

Angel was surprised. 'What was he talking about?'

'You'll have to ask him,' said Sophie. 'They were speaking Swahili.'

'And did you see any gorillas?' asked Pius.

'Oh, many,' answered Omar. 'How many did we count, Efra?'

'Eleven,' Efra said through her nose. 'But we're not sure, because we might have counted the same one twice. It's hard to tell them apart, but the guide knows all their names.'

'*Eh!* They have names?'

'And Mama, there was a baby!' said Benedict. 'The guide said it was born in July. The mother was sitting on the ground with her back against a tree, and she was holding it just like Leocadie holds Beckham.' Benedict mimed a mother cradling and rocking her baby.

'*Eh!*'

'We stayed in Gisenyi last night,' said Omar. 'Your children said they'd never been to Lake Kivu before, so we decided to drive there yesterday after we'd finished with the gorillas, rather than spending another night in Ruhengeri.'

'*Eh*, Omar, you've been too kind to them!'

'Not at all. I was happy to treat them, and it was good for Efra to have their company. But let us leave you now and they can tell you all about it themselves. Come, Efra.'

'Yes, I must go, too,' said Sophie, 'if my legs can get me up those stairs. Honestly, Angel, I thought I was fit, but trying to walk on all that slippery vegetation at high altitude really took it out of me. My legs felt like jelly for hours afterwards!'

A few minutes later, Angel went into the kitchen where Titi was stirring a large pot of *ugali* to accompany the *senene*. She carried in her arms the clothes that the children had worn when they had climbed up the mountain to see the gorillas.

'Just look at these, Titi!'

'*Eh!*' Titi stopped stirring and covered her mouth with both hands, staring with big eyes at the filthy garments. Caked in mud that had hardened, they were stiff like cardboard.

'Now how are we going to get these clean?' asked Angel.

Titi thought for a minute, tentatively touching one of the garments. 'After lunch I'll take them outside, Auntie. I think if I hang them on the washing line and hit them, a lot of this mud will fall off.'

'That's a good idea.'

'Then we can rinse them in water to get more of it out, and soak them in Toss until tomorrow morning.'

'That sounds like a good plan. *Eh!* But you must see their trainers! Those I've put outside on the balcony. I don't want to think what those children looked like when they came down from the mountain dressed in these clothes!'

'Ooh, uh-uh,' said Titi, shaking her head and

picking up the wooden spoon again. 'I think they looked like the *mayibobo* in our skip.'

'Uh-uh!' Angel shook her head. 'I hope not.'

Lunch was indeed delicious, and the family happily tucked in to the *ugali* and *senene* as Grace and Benedict told them all about their adventure.

'We had satellite TV in the hotel,' said Grace. 'And we telephoned the kitchen from our room and they brought us tea!'

'*Eh!*' said Titi.

'The big gorilla,' explained Benedict, 'the one who's the boss of the group that we saw, his name is Guhonda. He's called a silverback because he's old and the hair on his back is grey.'

'Like Baba's?' asked Moses.

Benedict looked at Pius. 'Yes, but on his back. *Eh!* He was very big, even bigger than Baba.'

'Were you not afraid?' asked Angel.

'They didn't want to hurt us, Mama; they're gentle and peaceful.'

'There was a swimming pool at the hotel in Ruhengeri *and* at the hotel in Gisenyi,' said Grace. 'Efra knows how to swim. Can I learn, Baba?'

'We'll see,' said Pius.

'The vet had a monkey sitting on his shoulder, not like the monkeys they sell here. It was black and white with a long tail. He said it came from Nyungwe Forest.'

'There was a disco at the hotel in Gisenyi. Efra and I watched all the people that were coming to dance. One man was dressed like Michael Jackson!'

'The vet let his monkey sit on my shoulder. *Eh!*'

'Efra's going to get a new nose in Paris. She showed me a photo that a computer made of her face with a smaller nose.'

'Every gorilla has a different nose-print, just like every person has different fingerprints.'

'We had steak and chips in the hotel, and for breakfast we had eggs on toast.'

'Gorillas eat *senene* too, but of course not cooked. And ants. But mostly they eat leaves.'

'Omar's Land Rover has air-conditioning.'

'Can I get a monkey, Baba?'

'Can I get a new nose, Baba?'

After lunch, Pius — who would hear of neither a pet monkey nor a new nose — settled down for a nap, and Titi took the children down to play in the yard while she tried to beat the dried mud out of their clothes.

Angel kept an eye on her watch, not wanting to be early or late for the cutting. She was still not sure that she wanted to go — or, if she *did* want to go, why. Quietly, so as not to disturb Pius as he dozed on their bed, she stood in front of her open wardrobe and examined its contents. What was a person supposed to wear to a cutting? The black dress that she wore to funerals? No, nobody had died — and the family obviously saw it as a happy occasion, because they had ordered a cake. Cakes were for celebrations. She must wear something smart, but not too smart: she did not want her outfit to suggest in any way that she approved of what was happening. Finally she settled on the comfortable *boubou* in emerald green with tie-dyed swirls of lime green that she had bought from one of the clothing stores in Avenue de Commerce, and her smart black sandals with kitten heels.

After a final cleaning of her glasses, it was time to leave. She picked up the small, square board on which the round cake stood, and left the apartment, closing the door behind her so that no one would wander in and disturb Pius as he slept. Then she walked up one flight of stairs and knocked at Amina's door.

'Angel, *karibu!*' Vincenzo smiled broadly as he opened the door and made an exaggerated gesture to usher her in.

Angel almost dropped the cake when she saw the other guests who were sitting in Amina's lounge. Fortunately Amina had rushed forward to take the board from her.

'*Eh*, Angel, this is a very beautiful cake,' declared Amina. 'Look, everybody.'

Safiya, Dr Rejoice and Odile got up from their chairs and came to look at the cake, declaring it to be one of the most beautiful they had ever seen. Angel tried hard to concentrate on making sense as she answered their questions about how she had made the tiny red roses, but her mind was in turmoil with questions of her own. Dr Rejoice and Odile? Why were *they* here? How could they be comfortable with the cutting of a girl? It was not part of the culture that either of them belonged to. Angel stopped talking in mid-sentence when it struck her that they might be asking themselves the very same questions about her. Perhaps their answers were as complicated as her own.

'Angel?'

'Hm?'

'You were about to tell us what we would find inside the cake, between the two layers,' said Dr Rejoice.

Angel recovered quickly. 'That,' she said, forcing a smile, 'is a surprise. You will know that only when you cut it.'

'And speaking of cutting,' said Vincenzo, 'shall we begin?' He gestured for everyone to sit around the coffee table.

*Eh*, thought Angel, were they going to cut Safiya right here? Right here on the coffee table? But Safiya sat on one of the chairs.

Vincenzo placed his Qur'an in the centre of the table. 'Now, I'm sure you know that what will happen here today is not understood everywhere, and in some places it is even illegal. But it is part of our culture, and that is something that people have no right to question. No right at all. But still there are those who might want to persecute us – or even prosecute us – for this practice. So I'm going to ask you all to swear that you will never tell anybody about what happened in this apartment this afternoon. Nobody: not husbands, boyfriends, friends, parents, children. Nobody at all. Never.'

'Safiya, that includes you,' warned Amina. 'Remember that we spoke about this? You are not to tell *anyone*.'

'I swear, Mama.'

'Right, let us swear on the Holy Qur'an,' said Vincenzo, placing his hand on the book on the table. Everyone followed his lead. 'Now, swear that you will never tell.'

Each of the women swore aloud, in her own way, that she would never tell.

'Now,' continued Vincenzo, removing his Qur'an and placing it beside him on the sofa, 'your Holy Bible please, Odile.'

Odile produced her Bible from her bag and placed it in the centre of the table where the Qur'an had been. Each of them placed a hand on the book and swore again never to tell.

'Right,' said Vincenzo, 'now that you've sworn on both our holy books, you may continue. Safiya, come and give Baba a hug. I'll wait for you all in the kitchen; I'll have our coffee ready when you've finished.'

Angel followed the girl and the other women into Safiya's bedroom, Dr Rejoice carrying her doctor's bag with her. When they were all in the room, Amina closed and locked the door. Angel felt her heart beginning to beat a little faster. She was nervous now about the un-familiarity of the practice, and it unsettled her that people were involved whom she knew. Okay, she would probably have been even more anxious if the people who were involved were strangers. But she would never have expected *these* people to be involved.

'Where shall I sit?' she asked.

Amina surprised Angel by speaking in a whisper. 'Anywhere is fine, Angel.'

Then, instead of lying down on her bed as Angel had expected, Safiya kneeled down on the floor and reached under her bed. She slid out a tray on which several bottles of soda lay, alongside a bottle-opener. This was very confusing indeed.

Amina gave a quiet laugh, stifling it in the palm of her hand. Then she spoke in a whisper again. '*Eh*, Angel! You should see your face!'

Dr Rejoice and Odile began to giggle too.

'Angel, did you think that we were really going to cut Safiya?' whispered Odile.

'I'm sorry, Angel,' Amina said softly, taking her hand. 'Come and sit here with me.' Angel sat next to Amina on the bed, while Safiya began to open bottles of soda. Still holding Angel's hand, Amina whispered, 'I couldn't tell you the truth until you had sworn on your holy book that you would never tell. I'm sorry, my friend. I know that you're a professional somebody and you know how to keep a secret, but this is a very big secret, one that could break our family apart. Safiya understands that, don't you, my dear. You know that Baba must never know that we didn't cut you?'

'I understand, Mama. I'm happy that you're not going to cut me. Will you have Fanta or Coke, Mama-Grace?'

'Thank you, Safiya, a Fanta please.'

'I'm sorry we have to drink out of the bottles,' Amina said to her guests. 'But Vincenzo would have been suspicious if he'd found glasses missing from the kitchen.'

'I want to be sure that I understand,' said Angel, as Dr Rejoice sat down on a chair next to the bed, and Odile and Safiya settled on a small rug on the floor. 'You are not going to cut your daughter, but you are going to let your husband believe that your daughter has been cut?'

'Yes,' said Amina.

Angel shook her head, still confused. She took off her glasses and reached into her brassiere for a tissue to clean them with. Lies — or at least deceptions — between a husband and a wife were not a good thing. She knew that now from what had been happening in her own marriage. Okay, she had not been lying to Pius, she had simply been lying to herself. But the two of them had been avoiding the truth — and, really, it was such a relief for them to be communicating honestly again now. Surely it would be better for Amina to be honest with Vincenzo? 'But why did you not just refuse, Amina? Why did you not say to your husband that you would not let your daughter be cut?'

'*Eh!* If I had refused, Vincenzo would have taken Safiya to somebody behind my back, and she *would* have been cut!'

'But could you not have persuaded him that cutting was not a good idea?'

'Angel, he has been talking about cutting Safiya since she was very small, and I kept telling him that, as her mother, I would know the right time for it. I could not delay any longer, because very soon Safiya will become a woman. If I had even once argued with him or told him that I didn't agree, then he would have taken her to be cut. Or he would have been suspicious of me. But I've never once told him that I won't do it, so he will not think of suspecting anything.'

'She's right, Angel,' said Dr Rejoice. 'You know how men are. If they tell us, say, that we must never drink alcohol — *eh*, forgive me for this example in a Muslim household, Amina — but if they tell us we must not drink alcohol and we say, *Who are you to tell me that?* or *I will drink alcohol whenever I want to*, or even *What is your reason for saying that?*, then they will always be smelling our breath and looking in our cupboards for bottles. They won't trust us if we question what they say. But if they tell us we must never drink alcohol and we say, *Of course, my husband, I will do as you say, I will never drink alcohol*, then we can drink alcohol right in front of them and they will not see it.'

Odile stifled a laugh. 'You are right, Dr Rejoice. I remember that I used to have an uncle who didn't want his wife to grow cassava because he didn't like it. He wanted her to grow only potatoes. Every planting season she would tell him that she was not going to plant cassava, and every season she planted it. He would walk in his fields without noticing it; he never saw it because he believed it was not there.'

Angel put her glasses back on. 'You're right,' she whispered, knowing now how blind she had chosen to be herself. Then she looked at Safiya. '*Eh*, Safiya, you're learning some very good lessons while you're still young!'

The girl smiled shyly. 'Yes, Mama-Grace. I'm happy that I'm not going to be cut like Mama was.'

'That was a very bad day for me,' said Amina. 'I was young, a few years younger than Safiya is now. Nobody told me what was going to happen. Nobody prepared me. Suddenly I was called in from playing outside and my mother held me down on the ground and a woman I didn't know cut me with a razor-blade. *Eh*, I cannot describe that pain to you! And the shock!' Amina covered her face with both hands for a few seconds before continuing. 'When my daughter was born, I told myself that I would never, never let that happen to her.'

'I understand,' said Angel. 'But how is it that Dr Rejoice and Odile are here? I didn't know that you knew one another.'

'Don't think for one minute that Amina is the only woman who has ever done this,' said Dr Rejoice. 'In Kenya there are many women who are refusing. I helped a few of them there, including a few from Sudan.'

'Yes,' said Amina, 'and by chance I met one of those women in the market some months back. I could see that she was Sudanese and we talked and became friends. She's the one who told me about Dr Rejoice, and then the doctor introduced me to Odile. Okay, they're not from our culture, but I knew that Vincenzo could never object to a doctor and a nurse performing the cutting. I decided we must do it this weekend, because Ramadan will start sometime next week, and when it's over, who knows where new contracts will take us in the new year? It wouldn't be easy for me to find such friends to help me in a new place.'

'Yes, it wouldn't have been easy,' agreed Dr Rejoice, 'but you would have found them, my dear. We're supporting one another more and more. It's like we understand now that we're much stronger when we stand together, especially in places where we're being beaten down.'

'Yes, like bread,' offered Odile, and everyone looked at her, not understanding what she meant. 'I mean like the ingredients for bread,' she whispered. 'I've watched the women making bread at the centre. The ingredients do nothing on their own, but when they're all together, they stick together and rise. They get beaten down and they rise again.'

'Exactly,' whispered Dr Rejoice. 'But Angel, you're not looking happy.'

'Well, I'm just trying to think if anything bad can come from this in the future — because it's always wise to think ahead to the consequences of our actions. Of course, none of us will ever tell...' everyone murmured agreement, '...but there is one person who is sure to find out.'

'Are you thinking about the husband I'll marry, Mama-Grace?'

'Yes, Safiya, I am.'

'I'm not going to marry a man who wants a wife who has been cut. I'm going to marry a man who is modern.'

'Yes,' agreed Amina. 'If we were living in Kismaayo where I was born, or even in Mogadishu, where I grew up and was cut, then it would be difficult. But we spend a lot of time in Italy, and we live wherever Vincenzo works. There'll be many opportunities for Safiya to meet a man who is modern.'

'And maybe,' suggested Dr Rejoice, 'by the time Safiya is ready to marry, all men will be modern, and we'll no longer need to pretend to obey them.'

They all laughed at that idea, covering their mouths with their hands so as not to make a noise.

'But, my dears, it is time for us to begin,' said Dr Rejoice. 'Let us be serious now.'

'Have you all finished your sodas? Okay, Safiya, lay

the empty bottles back on the tray and slide it back under the bed. I'll take them from there tomorrow when Baba's at work.'

Remaining in her chair, Dr Rejoice reached into her bag and removed a rolled-up white doctor's coat. As she slid her arms through the sleeves, Odile reached into the bag for two pairs of surgical gloves. She and the doctor put them on. Then Odile handed Dr Rejoice a swab and a syringe needle in sterile packaging.

'Come and sit here on my knee, my dear,' Dr Rejoice said to Safiya. 'Good girl. Now, I'm going to prick your finger, because Baba must see your blood. It will hurt a little bit, but I want you to cry out as if it's hurting a lot. Do you understand?'

Safiya nodded.

'Scream nicely for Baba,' instructed Amina.

As Dr Rejoice jabbed the needle into the girl's finger and immediately withdrew it, Safiya let out a wail so convincing that Angel had to stifle a maternal urge to hold her and comfort her.

'Good girl,' Dr Rejoice encouraged, squeezing a few drops of blood from Safiya's finger on to the swab. 'Okay, now the other hand. Odile, see to that finger, please.'

With another swab, Odile wiped Safiya's pricked finger with surgical spirit and then pressed hard on the tiny wound with the swab to stem the bleeding. Dr Rejoice was ready to prick a finger on Safiya's other hand.

'Scream nicely for Baba again,' coached Amina. 'He'll be so happy when he hears it.'

Safiya's second scream was louder and more sustained than the first.

'Now some crying please, my dear,' instructed Dr Rejoice as she squeezed more blood on to her swab. 'Okay, Odile, over to you.'

Odile took care of the second finger exactly as she had done the first.

'Right, it's done,' said Dr Rejoice with a smile. 'Now you can tell people that your daughter has been *circumcised*,' Dr Rejoice made quotation marks in the air with her fingers, in the same way that Omar had done. 'When you do that with your fingers, they'll think that you mean that *circumcised* is not the right word for what happened to your daughter because female genital mutilation is nothing like the circumcision of a boy. But really your fingers will mean that it did not happen. But they won't know that.'

'*Eh*, that is a very clever trick!' said Angel, grateful to have an honest way to tell Pius about this — should he ask — without breaking the vow that she had sworn on the Holy Bible. 'I must remember that in the future.' She stood up as the others did the same. 'But Amina, are you sure that you and Safiya will be able to hide the truth from Vincenzo?'

'Vincenzo has asked us not to tell him the truth,' explained Amina, doing her best to look innocent. 'Vincenzo himself made us swear that we will tell *nobody* what happened here. If we tell him, then we'll be breaking the oath that we swore on the Holy Qur'an.'

The women giggled softly, and Safiya, who had been wailing plaintively, found it difficult to continue.

'Right,' said Dr Rejoice. 'Odile and I will go out first. Safiya, when we sit to drink our coffee, you need to pretend that it's a bit painful. Okay, everyone?'

Everyone nodded and Dr Rejoice unlocked the door. She left Safiya's bedroom and headed towards the kitchen, where Vincenzo was sitting on the counter.

'Vincenzo, my dear, do you have a spare plastic bag?' she asked, making sure that he noticed the bloodied swab and the syringe needle that she carried. 'I forgot to bring one.'

Vincenzo produced a used plastic bag that had been folded away in the cupboard for use as a bin-liner later on. He held the bag as Dr Rejoice dropped in the swab and needle then peeled off her surgical gloves and put them in, too. Then Odile placed her own bloodied swab in the bag, making sure that Vincenzo saw it, and peeled off her gloves.

'Everything went smoothly,' Dr Rejoice assured him with a smile. 'Your daughter is very brave. Thank you, Vincenzo, I'll take this bag and dispose of it properly at the clinic.'

Vincenzo went into the lounge and hugged his daughter and then his wife. 'I'm so very happy today,' he beamed. 'Come, sit,' he said to everyone. 'Coffee is ready.'

'May the doctor and I use your bathroom to wash our hands?' asked Odile.

'Of course, of course, it is there, next to the kitchen.'

He rushed back into the kitchen while Amina carried the cake over to the coffee table. Dr Rejoice and Odile came back from the bathroom and sat down just as

Vincenzo came back with a tray filled with steaming cups of coffee, some small plates and a knife.

'This cake looks so beautiful,' he said. 'It's almost a pity to cut it.'

'But it *must* be cut, Baba,' said Safiya, smiling sweetly at her father as she perched right on the edge of her chair trying to look uncomfortable. 'That is what a cake is for.'

The women did not dare to look at one other.

'You're right,' declared Vincenzo, leaning over and kissing Safiya on her forehead. 'Amina, would you like to cut it?'

'No, no, Vincenzo.' Amina busied herself with the coffee so that she did not have to look at her husband. 'You cut it. I think the rest of us have already finished with cutting.'

Throwing back his head, Vincenzo let out a loud laugh. With relief, the women joined in. 'That's very good, Amina,' he said. 'Okay, I'll cut for everyone.'

'Yes, let's see this special surprise that Angel has put in the cake for us, between the layers,' said Dr Rejoice.

With a dramatic gesture, Vincenzo plunged the knife into the cake and pushed it down all the way through to the board. Then he moved the knife a few centimetres and did the same again. As he slid the blade of the knife under the slice, everybody watched in silent anticipation. He drew the slice sideways out from the cake. Between the two layers was a thick layer of bright green icing. Then it was deep red. Then green again. Then red.

Vincenzo placed the slice on a plate and tipped it on to its side so that everyone could see the squares of red alternating with green that filled the space between the layers.

'*Eh*, Angel,' said Amina, 'that is very clever. How did you do it?'

'Do you think I'm going to tell anybody my secrets?' demanded Angel.

'It's beautiful,' said Odile. 'Everybody has heard of decorating the outside of a cake, but I've never seen something like this inside a cake.'

'No,' said Dr Rejoice, 'when you look at the outside, this is not what you expect to find inside. It's a nice surprise, isn't it, ladies?'

'It's really nothing,' said Angel, although she was very happy to be complimented.

In truth, she had been so confused about her feelings about what the cake was for that she had felt the need to apply the principle of Ken Akimoto's yin-yang symbol to the idea. Recalling the red and green yin-yang cake that she had made for Ken, she had mixed up some red and green icing — which were in any case the colours that she was going to use to make the roses and leaves for the top of the cake. But she had recognized two things: first, that she could not put a yin-yang symbol inside Amina's cake, because some people would get slices with green in the middle and others would get slices with red in the middle, which would have been difficult for her to explain; and second, that her feelings about the issue were too complicated to separate into yin and yang. So, starting with a red dot in the middle of the lower layer, she had piped concentric circles of green alternating with red. As she piped each green circle she had tried to think of positive things, such as the loyalty that she felt towards her friend Amina, and the importance of preserving cultural traditions. And with each red circle she had allowed herself to fret about things such as the oppression of women and the pain that Safiya was going to suffer. She had found the concentric design more interesting than the yin-yang symbol – and also more confusing, because each new red circle was bigger than any of the circles that it enclosed and could therefore outweigh all the green circles inside it. She had been relieved – though not totally comforted – that the last circle to fit on the cake had been a green one.

'This coffee is from Italy,' Vincenzo boasted as he handed a cup to Angel. 'The finest coffee in the world.'

Angel added some milk and a large amount of sugar. 'I'm sure it's very fine coffee,' she said, 'but I know without tasting it that it's not the finest in the world. That is the coffee that comes from my home town of Bukoba, on the shores of Lake Victoria.'

As they drank their coffee and ate their cake, the conversation flowed freely and the mood was light. Every now and then a sharp look from Amina reminded Safiya to look uncomfortable on her chair. When Safiya and Amina started to talk about the coming Ramadan and Dr Rejoice got trapped in a conversation with Vincenzo about road-building, Angel took the opportunity to speak to Odile.

'I want to thank you, Odile,' she said quietly. 'You've been very kind and slow with me, helping me to be ready to see what was already clear to you about my daughter.' Odile acknowledged her words with a quick nod of her head and a sympathetic smile. Angel continued, keeping her voice low. 'But this is not the time for that particular conversation. People are saying that you have a boyfriend, Odile.'

'*Eh!*' Odile looked down, embarrassed. 'Are people really talking about me?'

'You know this country better than I do, Odile. Pius says that gossip is the national sport.'

Odile smiled and shrugged. 'He's right, Angel, and I think we could probably win a gold medal at the Olympics. But, yes, I've been seeing your friend Dieudonné.'

'I'm very happy to hear that. I knew that you two would like each other.'

'*Eh*, I was a bit angry when you planned for us to meet at Terra Nova. But now I forgive you!'

'Good.'

'Oh, I meant to tell you. Your friend Jeanne d'Arc came last week to have the confirmation dress altered. I did as you asked, Angel. I explained to her that the sewing classes were for sex workers, to help them to earn a living in a safer way.'

'Was she interested?'

'She seemed to be. She had her two sisters and a little boy with her, but she said she would come back again another time. *Eh*, that little boy is a darling! Have you met him?'

'No.'

'He's very small; he looks only about six years old. But he must be older, because he was already walking when Jeanne d'Arc found him.'

'What's his name?'

'They call him Muto; it means small. When they found him, he didn't know his given name.'

'Is he okay? I mean, I think he's small from not getting enough food.'

'Physically he's fine, and there seems to be no damage mentally. In fact, Dieudonné thinks he's a bright child.'

'Dieudonné has met him?'

'Yes, he came to eat lunch with me at our restaurant when Jeanne d'Arc was there. We looked after Muto while Jeanne d'Arc and her sisters were sorting out the alterations.'

Hope shot through Angel's body like the pain of treading on a sharp stone with bare feet: it was sudden and intense, but it faded rapidly.

She must not allow herself to hope for too much.

# 14. A Wedding

O N THE MORNING OF THE DAY BEFORE THE wedding, Angel stood at her work table decorating the wedding cake. There were six pieces: one very large and five smaller, all of them round. Thérèse had come the day before to help her with all the mixing and beating, and that had given her the time that she had needed to finish making the scores of sugar-paste flowers – bright yellow petals with orange centres – that she had been working on all week. Now she concentrated on positioning those flowers perfectly on the white tops of the five smaller cakes. The sides were iced in the same bright orange colour as the flowers' centres, and pale lemon-yellow piped stars surrounded the rim of each cake where the white tops met the orange sides.

She had already finished decorating the larger cake. The top was the same bright orange as the sides of the smaller cakes, and its sides were decorated in a basket-weave design of white and the same bright yellow as the petals of the flowers. To match the smaller cakes, the rim where the top met the sides was studded with pale lemon-yellow stars. Towards the outer edges of the orange surface circled a pattern that Angel had created by repeating the knot-of-reconciliation design from the fabric of Leocadie's dress, in lemon yellow outlined with bright yellow. And right in the centre of the cake stood the plastic figures of a bride and groom, the pink of their skin coloured dark brown with one of the children's watercolour paints.

The next day, Angel would assemble the six pieces on the special metal stand that had been manufactured to her specifications by one of Pius's colleagues, a professor of Appropriate Technology. From the heavy base rose a central rod about half a metre high, on top of which was a round metal platform with a small spike in the middle. This would hold the board on which the large cake would stand. Fanning out around the central rod, angled down at about forty-five degrees, were five more rods of the same length, each ending in a horizontal platform with a small spike in the middle. The five smaller cakes would go on those.

Angel glanced out towards the balcony where the cake-stand stood. As soon as she had finished positioning the flowers on the smaller cakes, she would go out there and check if it was dry yet. Bosco had managed to find some tiny tins of gold paint at an Indian shop on Avenue de la Paix, and he had spent an hour or so the previous afternoon transforming the dull grey aluminium of the stand into glistening gold.

Angel smiled to herself as she worked, sure that this wedding cake was going to look spectacular — and that she was going to look equally spectacular standing next to it — in the photographs that Elvis would take for *True Love* magazine in South Africa. Noëlla had done her hair for her earlier in the week: black extensions braided back from her forehead to the crown of her head, from where black and gold extensions hung loosely to her shoulders. The style was glamorous, without being inappropriate for a grandmother, and was similar to the looser, longer, more youthful style that Agathe had braided for Leocadie. Angel had been reluctant to spend any money on having her hair styled, because she had been planning to wear an elaborate headdress, but Leocadie had persuaded her to opt for a smaller head-covering beneath which braids could hang that would echo her own.

'I want people to see that we are mother and daughter,' Leocadie had said — and of course it had been impossible for Angel to object to that.

In Angel's wardrobe hung the dress that Youssou had created for her from the soft Ghanaian fabric with the pattern that said, *Help me and let me help you*. Titi had gone with her for the taking of the measurements, and had stood behind her, secretly inserting two fingers between Angel's body and the tape measure at every point where Youssou had measured. The result was a dress that fitted perfectly: a well-tailored, fitted bodice with cap sleeves tapered out over her hips and continued to flare out to create a wide, flowing skirt that fell softly to her feet. A strip of the same fabric tied ornately around her head, plus the gold court shoes that she had bought on the street, would complete the ensemble.

It had been a hectic week for Angel: a week of organizing caterers and florists and what seemed like a hundred other people, each of whom would be required to perform a particular function to ensure that the wedding and the reception went smoothly. The florist and the people who hired out tables, chairs and marquees had tried to charge her inflated prices – until she had returned to their premises with Françoise.

'Does this woman look like a *Mzungu* to you?' Françoise had demanded of them in Kinyarwanda, her left hand firmly on her hip as she gestured with her right. 'Of course not! Our sister here is from Bukoba, just the other side of the border, a border that is only there because, long ago, *Wazungu* drew a line and said here is Rwanda and here is Tanzania. Now, if you want to say that people from that side of the line must pay more, then you are saying that you are happy that those *Wazungu* drew those lines all over Africa long ago, that they were right to take our land and cut it up however they wanted. Is that what you want to say? *Is it?* Of course not! No, our sister will pay what *Banyarwanda* pay.'

And every night, at the end of each hectic day, Angel and Pius had talked in the way they always used to talk before the circumstances of their daughter's death had given them something not to talk about. AIDS had been a difficult word to speak about their son, but the bullet that had taken him had taken away their need to speak it. Now they spoke it about their daughter, together with another word: suicide. During the past week, both of those words had passed between them so often that they had lost their power, in the way that an old coin that has lost its shine seems to have less value. They were just words now, words that they were able to speak with understanding rather than dread.

It had hurt them both that Vinas had not felt able to tell them that she was ill – although, in truth, they did understand her motives. After all, Joseph had waited to tell them until his wife was very ill and he needed their help with the children. He had done that to spare them the worry, just as Vinas had. And both Pius and Angel had to admit that, should either of them – God forbid – find themselves with frightening or devastating news about their own health, love might well persuade them to put it away at the back of the top shelf of the highest cupboard for some time before fetching it down and showing it to each other. Really, it was not too hard to understand.

'But I still wish that Vinas had let me be closer to her after her marriage, Pius.'

'And *I* still wish that Joseph had chosen to follow an academic career. But each bird must fly on its own wings, Angel.'

Pius was still not fully convinced that Vinas had not condemned herself to an eternity in Hell. It was a complicated muddle of doctrine and ethics, he felt, a muddle that he needed to work through and clarify in his own mind even though he longed to be able to accept the more straightforward conviction at which Jeanne d'Arc had helped Angel to arrive.

'*Eh*, Angel, if I could re-dream my dream about looking for Joseph amongst the dead on that hilltop at Gikongoro, I want to believe that he would say to me, "Vinas is here, Baba," And he'd lead me to her, and they'd both be there together, in the same place.'

Last night, Pius had come home from work looking more at peace than he had in a long while. Instead of eating lunch in the staff canteen, he had joined Dr Binaisa in his fast and told him the full story of what had happened to Vinas.

'One of my brothers did the same thing,' Dr Binaisa had said matter-of-factly. 'Soon after he was diagnosed, he drove his car into the back of a truck full of *matoke*. People said it was a tragic accident, but of course we knew it wasn't. And another brother simply disappeared when he began to get sick. *Eh*, we suspect the fish in Lake Victoria have eaten well off him!'

Pius had been shocked by this attitude. 'But what does Islam say about suicide?'

'*Eh*, it's a terrible sin! If you suicide yourself, you'll be roasted in the fires of Hell.'

'Then do you not worry yourself about those brothers of yours who are roasting in Hell?'

'Tungaraza, there are more important things on this earth to worry myself about. My worry will not change what anybody else has already done. I'm alive and I have children to raise, and that is where I need to focus my attention.'

On the afternoon of the day before the wedding, Angel kept the boys and their friends the Mukherjee boys occupied with the video of *Gorillas in the Mist* that she had borrowed from Ken Akimoto. No longer the quiet one, Benedict was the star of the afternoon: the one who had seen gorillas; the one who recognized Ruhengeri on the screen because he had been there; the one to whom the other boys deferred.

The girls and Titi were dispatched to their bedroom to style one another's hair for the wedding. They wanted Safiya to come down and help them, but she needed her rest because she was fasting for Ramadan for the first time.

As the video played, Angel sat at her work table and went through her list of things to do, checking and re-checking for anything that might not have been confirmed and re-confirmed. The ceremony itself had been arranged: a short and simple Catholic service in the Sainte Famille church. Angel would walk down the aisle with Leocadie and present her to Modeste, who would be waiting at the altar in his brown suit that had been made for him by a tailor in Remera, and his tie that the women at the centre in Biryogo had sewn for him from the same fabric as Leocadie's dress. Next to Modeste would be his best friend and fellow security guard, Gaspard. Their guard duties at the compound would be performed tomorrow by two KIST security guards who were happy to make some extra money on their day off. Angel checked that she had re-confirmed with them, and that she had explained to them the situation regarding Captain Calixte, who was on no account to be allowed into the building with his gun.

Ken Akimoto had offered his Pajero as the wedding car; Bosco would take it to the florist tomorrow morning to have it adorned with flowers and ribbons, and in the afternoon he would drive Leocadie and Angel to the church. After the ceremony he would drive them, together with Modeste and Gaspard, to the reception in the compound's yard.

Early tomorrow morning, people would come and protect the yard from any possible rain showers by securing an enormous tarpaulin to the railings of the first-floor balconies at one side, and to the top of the boundary wall at the other. Patrice and Kalisa had already removed the last of the builder's rubble from the corner of the yard by taking a small wheelbarrow-load each night to a building-site a few streets away where they had come to an arrangement with the night security guard. The Tungarazas' trailer had been taken away and left for safe-keeping in Dr Binaisa's yard. Tomorrow, people would deliver round plastic tables and chairs for the guests, as well as a long high table to go under the washing lines for the bride and groom; the lines themselves would be draped with loose folds of white muslin, and the posts supporting them would be adorned with flowers and ribbons. Angel had re-confirmed all of those arrangements.

She had also re-confirmed with the students from KIST who would be helping out: Idi-Amini, an earnest young returnee from Uganda who owned a PA system, would be in charge of sound and music; Pacifique, who was using his camera to pay for his studies, would be the official photographer at the service and the reception; and the institution's troupe of traditional dancers would perform for the guests' entertainment.

Goats had already been slaughtered, and their meat would be cooked over open fires by the women from the restaurant at the centre in Biryogo, who would also cook huge pots of rice and vegetables. Beer and sodas would be supplied by Françoise, who would keep them cool in large aluminium tubs filled with iced water that would be kept out of the way in the section under the building that was still waiting to house a generator. Several of the Girls Who Mean Business would be on hand to serve the drinks and food, and Thérèse, Miremba, Eugenia, Titi and Jeanne d'Arc would wash guests' hands and help with serving. The food would not be served until the sun had set, so that Muslims and non-Muslims could eat together.

Assured that there was nothing more that she could do at this stage, Angel looked up from her list and watched the boys watching the video. Moses had drifted off to sleep, and Kamal, the younger of the Mukherjees, was struggling not to do the same. Rajesh was watching with interest, while Daniel kept glancing at Benedict to get a sense of how he should react. As he watched Dian Fossey discover the dead body of one of her beloved gorillas, tears filled Benedict's eyes. *That boy has found something to love in place of his late father*, thought Angel: *surely he is going to work with animals when he grows up.*

In the evening of the day before the wedding, Pius came home from work exhausted. Over dinner he explained that he and a small team of colleagues had just finished putting together an important application for a prestigious – and generous – new award for innovations in renewable energy technologies. Their entry was a bread oven that the university had developed and manufactured, capable of baking 320 bread-rolls every twenty minutes using only a quarter of the wood that a conventional oven used.

'So it will save the forests here, Baba?' Benedict asked.

'It will help, certainly.'

'Then I'm sure it will win the prize.' Benedict was confident.

Pius laughed. 'How can you be so sure?'

'Because the oven will make bread to feed people so that they don't die, and it will also save the forest so that the gorillas don't die. That is a very important oven, Baba.'

'*Eh!* You are too clever, Benedict,' said Angel, proud of the boy.

'I hope you're right,' said Pius. 'You know that my job here is to help the university to generate income, to make its own money so that it can keep itself running. Publicity from the award would help a great deal. But the winner will only be announced next year. What's more important is that we'll know soon if they want me to stay here for another year.'

'How soon will we know?' asked Angel.

'They've promised to let us know by the end of next week. You know that expatriates are only here until Rwandans have qualified to fill the positions that we're filling now. Apparently, every year at this time the expatriate staff become very nervous and start to whisper about who will have their contracts renewed and who will go home.'

'Are you nervous, Baba?' asked Grace.

Pius laughed. 'No, Grace, I'm not nervous. But I'd like to know soon so that I can start to make arrangements. If we're going back to Dar es Salaam, then we must contact your school there; and if we are going somewhere else, then I need to start researching that somewhere else on the internet.'

'We can go somewhere else, Uncle?'

'Possibly, Titi. The University of Dar es Salaam gave me extended leave, so I can still be away for another couple of years after this one. If they don't renew my contract here, I'm not obliged to go back there immediately. I'm sure there'll be other options.'

'What about us, Baba?' asked Daniel. 'Where will we go?'

'You'll come with me wherever I go,' assured Pius. 'We're a family. And Titi, that includes you.'

Titi beamed. Grace and Faith had styled the section of her hair from her forehead to the crown of her head in neat cornrows, leaving her hair behind that to stand tall and natural in a halo-effect around her head. Grace's long hair had been cornrowed all over, and Faith's shorter hair had been parted into neat, small squares and tied into little bunches with elastic bands.

'Rajesh and Kamal are going to live in India next year with Mama-Rajesh,' said Daniel, 'even if Baba-Rajesh lives here.'

'That's not going to happen to this family, Daniel,' said Angel. 'We're going to be together, wherever we are.'

*

Angel cried at the wedding. The entire service was in Kinyarwanda, so she did not understand all of it — although she did understand a lot more of it than she would have at the beginning of the year. But her tears had nothing to do with her frustration at not following the language; they were caused in part by memories of the wedding of her own daughter, Vinas, with its unprofessional cake, and in part by the obligations of her role at this wedding. The mother of the bride was fully expected to shed tears of joy, especially when her daughter looked as beautiful as Leocadie did. Youssou had stitched the pale lemon-yellow fabric with its gold and orange pattern into a separate blouse and skirt. The skirt fitted snugly over Leocadie's hips then flared out and flowed softly around her gold sandals, and the sleeveless blouse had been tailored to her shape with a scoop neck and with small gold buttons running down the front. The white net veil that had been made by the women at the centre in Biryogo flowed down from a gold Alice band around her shoulders and as far as her waist.

Throughout the ceremony, Beckham sat on Titi's lap in the front pew, kicking his legs and sucking at a corner of the shirt that the Biryogo women had stitched for him from the remnants of Leocadie's pale lemon-yellow fabric.

Afterwards, after Pacifique had made them pose at the entrance of the church for photographs, an alarming number of the guests crowded into the red Microbus with Pius, Titi and the children, and the wedding party got into Ken Akimoto's Pajero with

Bosco at the wheel and Angel sitting next to him in the front. Angel noticed again — as she had done on the way to the church — that it was very easy to climb up into a big vehicle in a skirt that was voluminous rather than straight and tight. Perhaps this was the answer that she had been searching for. She also noticed that Bosco was rather quiet.

'Is everything okay, Bosco?'

'*Eh*, Auntie!'

Angel could not tell from the side view of his face, as he concentrated on driving, exactly what emotion he was feeling.

'What is it Bosco?'

'*Eh*, Auntie, Alice's father has found a scholarship for her in America.'

'*Eh!*'

'He spent a very, very long time on the internet looking at American universities. He owns an internet café in town, so he was able to search every day at work. Now he's found a university that will accept Alice and pay her fees and books and everything. That university is very excited about Alice, because they've never had a student from Rwanda before.'

'*Eh*, that is exciting news for Alice, Bosco!'

'Yes, Auntie, for Alice. But now I must find some-body else to love.'

'I'm sorry, Bosco. That is very sad.'

'Very, very sad, Auntie,' said Bosco as he pressed his hand down on the Pajero's horn to tell the neighbour-hood the happy news that he was driving a new bride and groom.

The wedding reception in the yard of the compound was a joyous occasion. Prosper fulfilled the role of Master of Ceremonies with the zeal of a man proclaiming from the pulpit, peppering his speech with quotations from the Bible and even managing – every now and then – to say something light-hearted enough to raise a laugh and a smattering of applause. There was thunderous applause for Angel, though, when Prosper announced how much money was in the bride-price envelope. Of course, in the absence of Leocadie's parents, that money belonged to the bride and groom – and it was enough to buy them a small two-roomed house. The house would have no electricity or water, but it would be their own. There were not many young couples who could start their married life so blessed, and throughout the party people continued to approach Angel to congratulate her.

'That is a very fine herd of cows, Mama-Leocadie!'

'*Eh*, Angel! Those cows have very big horns.'

'Mrs Tungaraza, when our daughters are ready to marry, you are the one who will negotiate bride-price for us!'

'So many cows, Auntie!'

It was only much later, after all the speeches had been made and the tables and chairs had been pushed back so that the dancing could begin, that Prosper succumbed to an overindulgence in Primus and slid quietly from his chair on to the ground beneath the high table. Angel considered simply leaving him there, but in the end she fetched Gaspard, who fetched Kalisa, and together they carried Prosper to the seclusion of his office, where it would be safe for him to remain until morning.

Long before that, just after the sun had set and the guests who were fasting had arrived and the food could be served, Angel's heart was warmed by the sight of Odile entering the yard with Dieudonné, who was carrying a small boy on his shoulders. She rushed to greet them.

'Hello, Angel,' said Odile. 'Don't worry, we're not bringing extra hungry mouths to your party! We've just come to speak to Jeanne d'Arc.'

'There's food here for many hungry mouths,' assured Angel. 'You're very welcome. But tell me, Dieudonné, who is this handsome young boy on your shoulders?'

'This is Muto, the boy Jeanne d'Arc has raised. Muto, greet Auntie.'

Clinging on to Dieudonné's head with his left hand, Muto leaned down and shook Angel's hand with his right.

'Good boy,' said Dieudonné. 'We took him swimming with us at Cercle Sportif this afternoon. Now we want to check with Jeanne d'Arc if it would be okay for him to sleep over at Odile's tonight.'

Odile smiled at Angel. 'He's made friends with Emmanuel's children. They taught him how to swim.'

Angel's heart was ready to burst. Would the next wedding cake she made be for this couple? Would they adopt Muto? She pointed to the far end of the yard where Jeanne d'Arc was pouring water from a jug on to Omar's hands as he rinsed them over the plastic bowl held by Titi. 'There she is. I'm sure she'll be very happy for you to have Muto.'

As she watched them weaving their way towards Jeanne d'Arc, stopping to greet guests whom they knew and to introduce Muto to them, Angel was approached by Grace and Benedict, both of them looking agitated.

'Mama, please tell him the meat is *goat*,' begged Grace. 'He's saying it might be *gorilla*!'

'Benedict? Where did you get that idea?'

'They told me in the Virunga Mountains, Mama,' said Benedict. 'Our guide said people kill gorillas and sell the meat. They call it bush-meat. Sometimes bush-meat is a deer or another kind of animal, but sometimes it's a gorilla or a monkey.'

'*Eh!*' declared Angel. 'Do you think that I'm the kind of person to kill a gorilla and serve it to my guests?'

'I *told* you, Benedict,' said Grace.

'But are you *sure* it's goat, Mama? Did you see the goats being slaughtered with your own eyes?'

Like his grandfather, this boy was somebody who needed evidence rather than mere assurance. 'No, Benedict, I did not see it with my own eyes, but I know somebody who did. Come with me and we'll ask her.'

Angel led Benedict out through the compound's driveway, where the gate had been left open for the guests to come and go, to the roadside where the women from the restaurant at Odile's centre in Biryogo were loading plates with meat from their roadside fires and vegetables from their enormous pots. The Girls Who Mean Business were balancing the platefuls on trays and then carrying them down the driveway to the guests.

'Immaculée,' said Angel to one of the women, 'this is my son, Benedict.'

'I'm happy to meet you, Benedict,' said Immaculée, not pausing in her work for a second. 'I've already met your sisters, Grace and Faith.'

'Immaculée, Benedict is anxious to know what the meat is that you've cooked. He's seen gorillas in the forests of the Virunga Mountains, and he's afraid that it is a gorilla that has been slaughtered for this wedding.'

'*Eh*, Benedict!' Immaculée stopped what she was doing and squatted down on her haunches to talk to the boy. 'You're right to worry about gorillas being killed, because it is gorillas who bring tourists to our country with their dollars. But you're wrong to worry that this is gorilla meat that we are serving. I slaughtered these goats with my own hands.'

Benedict smiled at her, relieved, and went back to join the other children at their table.

'Thank you, Immaculée,' said Angel. 'That boy has some strange ideas. *Eh*, you ladies are doing a good job here. Don't forget to save some food for the *mayibobo* in the skip.'

Immaculée laughed. 'They were the first to eat, Angel! Do you think we can cook food just down the road from them and make them smell it for hours before we give them some to eat?'

After the empty plates had been cleared away, the traditional dancers performed again to get the guests in the mood for dancing, and encouraged Leocadie and Modeste to join them. Beckham remained strapped to Leocadie's back all the time, safely protected from mosquito bites by the mosquitocide in the veil that covered him. Amina slipped into Leocadie's empty seat next to Angel.

'Our girls are growing up,' she said, indicating with a nod of her head for Angel to look at Grace and Safiya. Ignoring the dancers, the two girls were focusing all their attention on the young man who was beating the drum. Tall and bare-chested, he stood apart from the dancers, beating out a rhythm for them on a large drum that hung from a strap around his neck to the level of his groin. Without taking their eyes off him for a second, Grace and Safiya exchanged comments and giggled.

'*Eh!*' said Angel, shaking her head. 'Trouble is going to come knocking on our doors very, very soon!'

Later, when the guests had begun to dance to the music that Idi-Amini was selecting carefully and playing through his PA system, Angel observed two other girls looking at another young man in exactly the same way. She went over to join them.

'Thank you for performing here today,' she began, speaking to them in Swahili. 'Your traditional dancing is very, very beautiful.'

The girls surprised her by answering in English. 'Oh, thank you, Mrs Tungaraza. Thank you for the work. It's just a pity that not much of our fee comes to us after we've paid to hire our costumes and drums.'

'*Eh?* You don't have your own costumes?' The girls shook their heads. 'That is not good,' said Angel, shaking her head with them. 'But I have an idea. You must speak to my husband, because he is the one who is helping KIST to raise money. Perhaps you can persuade him that KIST should buy costumes for you, because you are the university's official dance troupe. Then when you perform at occasions like this, KIST can keep some of the money and the rest can come to you.'

'That is a very good idea, Mrs Tungaraza. KIST will soon recover the cost of the costumes and start to earn a profit; and without having to pay for costume hire, we'll be in a win-win situation.'

'*Eh*, you're speaking like a business student!' observed Angel.

The girl laughed. 'Yes, I'm doing management. But I'm sorry, Mrs Tungaraza, we have not introduced ourselves. I am Véronique, and my friend is Marie.'

Angel shook hands with both of them. 'Are you also studying management, Marie?'

'No, I'm doing civil engineering. We'll both graduate next year, then I'm hoping to go to Johannesburg for Masters.'

'Well, your English is very good. I'm sure you'll be able to study there very easily.'

'Thank you, Mrs Tungaraza. At KIST we follow the government's policy of bilingualism.'

'Don't underestimate yourselves, girls,' said Angel. 'Actually, you're multilingual, because you know Kinyarwanda and Swahili as well as French and English. Please, girls, let us not think as Africans that it is only European things that are important. When you two become ministers of what-what-what in your government, you must set an example to others by saying that you are multilingual.'

'*Eh*, Mrs Tungaraza!' said Véronique, laughing. 'We are not going to become ministers of what-what-what!'

'Somebody is going to become those ministers,' assured Angel. 'Somebody who has studied at KIST or the National University in Butare. Why not you?'

Véronique and Marie exchanged glances.

'Mrs Tungaraza, you have given us a new idea,' said Véronique. 'I have only thought as far as graduating and getting a job in Kigali as an accountant. Now I will think about the possibility of bigger things.'

'That is good,' said Angel. 'But the reason I came to talk to you was not to turn you into government ministers. I came to talk to you because I saw you looking at that young man.' Angel nodded her head in the direction of Elvis Khumalo, who was deep in conversation with Kwame.

Once again, Véronique and Marie exchanged glances, this time looking embarrassed.

'He looks nice,' said Marie, shyly.

'Oh, he is a very, very nice young man,' assured Angel, 'and I will introduce you to him in a moment. But first I must tell you that he is not a man who likes girls.'

'Mrs Tungaraza?'

'He's from South Africa,' explained Angel. 'I have even met his boyfriend.'

'*Eh!* He has a boyfriend?' asked Véronique. She looked at Angel with big eyes.

'That is a fashion in America,' said Marie, disappointed. 'I didn't know it had come to South Africa too.'

'South Africa is very modern,' said Angel. 'But let me introduce you to him, Marie. He lives in Johannesburg and he can tell you all about studying there.'

Angel took the girls over to Elvis and introduced them, leaving them to talk. Earlier, Elvis had photographed the wedding cake from many different angles, including from a first-floor balcony, where he had lain on the ground and angled the camera through the railings, under the ropes of the massive tarpaulin that covered the yard. From above, the cake had looked like a giant sunflower. Elvis had taken other photographs during the wedding, of course: photos of the bride and groom, the dancers, the women cooking in the street outside the compound, Angel and Leocadie in their beautiful dresses – but he had concentrated particularly on the cake because that was the part of the wedding that *True Love* had sponsored. Angel could not wait to receive a copy of the magazine with her cake featured in it. She would be sure to show it to Mrs Margaret Wanyika so that the Tanzanian ambassador to Rwanda would know that a Tanzanian living in Kigali was famous in South Africa – and also, if the truth be told, so that Mrs Wanyika could see how beautiful a wedding cake could be when it was not white. Of course, Angel would not mention to Mrs Wanyika that the man who had taken the photographs and written the article had a boyfriend.

'Thank you for inviting me, Angel,' said Kwame, whose conversation with Elvis had been interrupted by the introduction of the girls.

'It's my pleasure, Kwame. I hope this wedding has helped you to believe in reconciliation.'

'Oh, it will take a lot to make me believe in that, Angel.' He smiled broadly. 'But I'm pretending to believe in it, just for tonight.'

Angel smiled back at him. 'And how does it feel to pretend to believe?'

Kwame considered his answer before he spoke. 'It feels good,' he said. 'Peaceful. Perhaps that's how people here get through each day.'

'*Eh*, Kwame! You just concentrate on feeling good and peaceful. Don't worry yourself tonight about whether people believe in reconciliation in their hearts or just pretend in their heads to believe in it. Tonight you're going to be happy! By the way, have you seen what Leocadie and I did with Akosua's fabric?' Angel gestured at her dress.

'It's beautiful. Elvis has promised to send me copies of his photos so that I can send them to Akosua. She'll show them to the ladies who printed the fabric and I'm sure they'll be very excited.'

'Make sure that Elvis writes down in his notebook the name of that group of ladies. That must be in his article for the magazine. *Eh*, this is a truly pan-African cele-bration today! A wedding in Central Africa, organized by somebody from East Africa, cloth from West Africa, a magazine from South Africa. *Eh!*'

'Ah, pan-Africanism!' said the CIA, who had appeared silently at Angel's elbow. 'That sounds like an interesting conversation.'

Angel introduced Kwame and the CIA, and left them to talk while she steered Véronique away from Elvis and Marie, who were discussing Johannesburg's nightlife.

'I'd like to introduce you to a very nice young man, Véronique. He is like a son to me.'

'Does he like girls?' asked Véronique.

Angel laughed. 'Very much! Now, where is he? I saw him dancing just a moment ago.' Angel scanned the dancers. There was Modeste, dancing with Leocadie, and Catherine's boyfriend with Sophie. Gaspard was with one of the Girls Who Mean Business, and Ken Akimoto was with another. The drummer from the dancing troupe had attached himself to Linda, who was wearing something very small and very tight. Omar was dancing with Jenna, and Pius was doing his best with Grace. At last Angel spotted the young man she was looking for, and as the song faded, she grabbed him away from Catherine.

'Bosco, I want you to meet Véronique. Véronique, this is my dear friend Bosco.'

The two shook hands, assessing each other shyly with fleeting glances from downcast eyes.

'Véronique will graduate from KIST next year,' said Angel. 'She is not one of those girls who want to study overseas. She is going to work in Kigali as an accountant.'

'That is very, very good,' said Bosco.

'Bosco works for the United Nations,' continued Angel. 'He has a very good job there as a driver.'

'*Eh*, the United Nations?' Véronique sounded impressed: it was well known that a driver for the UN earned more than she could hope to earn as an accountant for any Rwandan business.

Angel left the two alone and moved off to where she

recognized two men standing at the edge of the party, sipping sodas.

'Mr Mukherjee! Dr Manavendra! Welcome! Are your wives not with you?'

'Hello, Mrs Tungaraza,' said Mr Mukherjee. 'No, my wife is at home with Rajesh and Kamal. There is no one to look after them.'

'Ah, yes,' said Angel. 'Miremba is working here tonight. And where is Mrs Manavendra?'

'At home, too,' said Dr Manavendra. 'She is fearing germs.'

'Too many germs from shaking hands,' explained Mr Mukherjee. 'Very dangerous habit in Rwanda.'

'Very dangerous habit,' agreed Dr Manavendra. 'But we came to greet the couple. They look very happy.'

'Very happy,' agreed Mr Mukherjee. 'It's a lovely party, Mrs Tungaraza.'

'Lovely,' agreed Dr Manavendra.

As Angel listened to the two men echoing each other, a voice behind her caught her attention. The words poured a bucket of iced water down her spine.

'I think it's time you and I had a talk. We've been sharing the attentions of the same man, and everybody knows it.'

The voice was Linda's.

Angel wanted to turn around, but she knew that she could not bear to see the pain on Jenna's face as she learned about her husband's infidelity with Linda. Yet she had to turn around, because she had to support her friend. *Eh!* Why did this have to happen now? It was going to spoil Leocadie's wedding!

She turned around. Facing Linda was not Jenna, but Sophie.

'Ah, yes,' Sophie said. 'But everybody knows that Captain Calixte only came to you because I didn't want him. I was the one he really wanted.'

'That's a lie,' declared Linda. 'He only asked you to marry him because I was already married! The minute my divorce came through he was knocking on my door.'

Linda and Sophie collapsed into fits of laughter.

Relieved, Angel excused herself from the two Indians and went to look for Jenna. She found her chatting to Ken, who was rather full of Primus.

'When this party's finished, you must come to my apartment for karaoke,' he said to Angel, rather more loudly than was necessary.

'Thank you, Ken, but I think I'll be too tired. It's been a very long day for me!'

'Everything's been beautiful, Angel,' assured Jenna. 'Ken, I hope you're going to invite that young man who's been doing the music to come for karaoke. He's been singing along, and his voice is great.'

'Good idea,' declared Ken. 'Maybe we can use his mikes so that more people can sing.' He moved off rather unsteadily towards Idi-Amini.

'I'm glad I have a moment alone with you, Angel,' said Jenna. 'I want to tell you that I've made a very big decision.' She looked around her before leaning closer to Angel. 'I'm going to leave my husband.'

Angel was surprised — and she was also confused by her own reaction: the end of a marriage was sad, but this news made her feel happy.

'When we go home for the holidays at the end of the year, I'm not going to come back.'

'*Eh*, Jenna, I'll miss you! And what about your students?'

'They can read now—enough to carry on without me, anyway. I've kept in touch with Akosua by email, and she's been encouraging me to go back to college and train in adult literacy. When I'm qualified, I'll definitely come back to Africa — but I'll come back alone. Don't tell a soul, Angel. I'm not going to say anything to Rob until we're back in the States.'

'Of course I won't tell.'

'Oh, look,' said Jenna, pointing towards the high table. 'It looks like Leocadie and Modeste are preparing to leave.'

Angel made her way towards them.

'Thank you so much, Mama-Grace,' said Leocadie, tears beginning to well in her eyes. 'I never believed that somebody like me could have such a beautiful wedding.'

Modeste pumped Angel's hand vigorously. '*Eh*, Madame!' he said, '*Muracoze cyane! Asante sana! Merci beaucoup!*'

Angel fetched Bosco — who was no longer talking to Véronique, but assured Angel that he had got her cellphone number — and organized the guests into a line for the couple to greet them all on their way to the Pajero, where Bosco waited to drive them to the house in Remera where Modeste rented a room.

Most of the guests left soon after that, and the stragglers took up Ken Akimoto's invitation to end the party in his apartment with the karaoke machine. Angel did not even think about clearing up the yard; there was the whole of Sunday to do that, and several women had volunteered to come and help. With the gate at the end of the compound's driveway firmly shut, and with Patrice and Kalisa on duty in the street — and Prosper still asleep in his office — everything would still be there in the morning.

She checked on the children and Titi in their bedroom and then slipped out of her smart wedding clothes, wrapping a *kanga* around her waist and pulling a T-shirt over her head. She made two mugs of sweet, milky tea in the kitchen. Covering one with a plate, she carried both of them out through the entrance to the building and sat down on one of the large rocks next to the bush that bloomed in the dark, filling the night with its perfume. She placed the mug with the plate on the ground and took a few sips from the other.

A group of women's voices blared from Ken's windows. Angel caught some of the words: *for sure... that's what friends are for...*

Next week she would go with Pius and a group of students on an outing to the Akagera National Park, a game reserve in the eastern part of Rwanda where it bordered with Tanzania. At the end of the following week the entire family would go in the red Microbus to Bukoba, where they would spend Christmas with various members of Angel's and Pius's families. From there, Titi would go by ferry across Lake Victoria to Mwanza, to visit a cousin and some friends. After that, in the new year, who knew where they would go? Angel thought that she could feel at home wherever they went.

A few minutes later, the lights of a vehicle shone into Angel's eyes, and the red Microbus pulled up outside the building. Pius was back from giving some of the wedding guests a ride home. As the sound of the engine died, she heard a new song in the air: *ah, ah, ah, ah, staying alive, staying alive...*

She shifted to the edge of the large rock and patted at the space beside her. 'Sit with me here,' she said to her husband. 'I made you some tea.'

'Oh, that is exactly what I need,' said Pius, settling down on the rock next to Angel and picking up the mug of tea that had been kept warm by the plate.

Sitting in the cool Rwandan night, the quiet of the city interrupted by song and laughter, they sipped their tea together.